D1443960

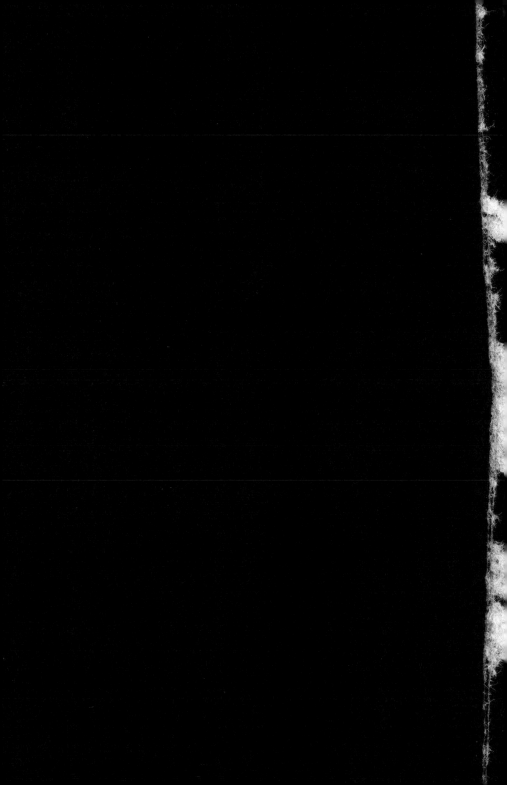

ONE GIRL
IN ALL THE WORLD

ONE GIRL
IN ALL THE WORLD

KENDARE BLAKE

HYPERION
Los Angeles   New York

First Edition, January 2023
10 9 8 7 6 5 4 3 2 1
FAC-004510-22350
Printed in the United States of America

This book is set in Minion Pro, Bourbon/Fontspring; Aurelia Pro/Monotype
Designed by Tyler Nevins

Library of Congress Cataloging-in-Publication Data
Names: Blake, Kendare, author.
Title: One girl in all the world / by Kendare Blake.
Description: First edition. • Los Angeles ; New York : Hyperion, 2023. •
   Series: Buffy: the next generation ; book 2 • Audience: Ages 12–18. •
   Audience: Grades 10–12. • Summary: Frankie Rosenberg, the world's
   first slayer-witch, has hordes of demons—both of the real and the
   metaphorical variety—to contend with when a rebooted Hellmouth
   begins luring evil back to Sunnydale.
Identifiers: LCCN 2022021453 • ISBN 9781368075077 (hardcover) •
   ISBN 9781368075169 (ebook)
Subjects: CYAC: Witches—Fiction. • Vampires—Fiction. • Demonology—
   Fiction. • LCGFT: Paranormal fiction. • Novels.
Classification: LCC PZ7.B5866 Onk 2023 • DDC [Fic]—dc23
LC record available at https://lccn.loc.gov/20

Reinforced binding
Visit www.HyperionTeens.com

ONE GIRL
IN ALL THE WORLD

PROLOGUE

The woman cut a slim silhouette against the sunset as she walked along the deserted highway. It was a long walk on the way to nowhere: This particular road had been bypassed and blocked off—she'd slipped past two very broken-down road closed *signs—and ended on the edge of what was briefly the great Sunnydale sinkhole. Of course that sinkhole didn't last; it was quickly shored up with dirt to become the shiny New Sunnydale, with a much lower elevation.*

It was a long walk. She wasn't tired; she was a slayer after all—it took a lot more than cooling desert and flat asphalt to wear her out—but she was weary. Weary in her bones, weary in her soul. She adjusted the bag on her shoulders and kept going until she reached the spot where their bus had stopped after they'd defeated the First. Where Buffy had gotten out and looked over the destruction. Where she had started making plans for all of their futures.

The woman kicked pebbles and watched them roll down the hill, now a nice, sloping decline rather than a sheer drop-off into hell, and frowned at New Sunnydale glittering below. All of those people, living like nothing had happened. Sinkhole? What sinkhole? I'm sure that collapse was just a one-time thing. No reason to waste all this prime California real estate.

She scowled down from beneath her hood. They were idiots, all of them. Optimistic idiots. The entire place was cursed; she felt it the moment she portaled in. The wrongness. The wicked current pulsing through the soil. The . . . Hellmouth residue, getting all over everything. She knew she had a slayer's senses, but there was no way that regular people didn't feel it. That much seeping evil left a mark. It weaved through a person. It became a part of them, so much so that the whole damn citizenry had evacuated before it all went down, without having to be told. They just knew.

But people were people, and they'd rebuilt it anyway. Like the people who had rebuilt the Overlook Hotel. Or the ones who kept on building houses on top of old cemeteries without moving the bodies first. Those were just movies, sure, but the rebuilding was realistic. When it came to their own destruction, humans were predictably industrious. So New Sunnydale had risen from the ashes. And then the red witch had returned to watch over it and to raise her little abomination.

The woman swallowed. It felt foolish to even set one foot on that unstable ground, but she did it, one foot after the other, down and down and down, through shrubs and young trees, past silent bulldozers and construction equipment—because even after eighteen years, the city was still a work in progress—until she reached the street. From there she let her slayer sense guide her, but even if she hadn't had it, she would have known the way to the Hellmouth by following the school signs. In grand Sunnydale tradition, the idiots had built the high school right on top. Again.

When she reached it, she stood outside, staring at the brick and the stark white walls, the flowering vines with their blossoms closed for the night. New Sunnydale High School was clean and crisp, lit by so many streetlights that it was a challenge to find shadows to slip into. I am not evil at all, it declared. But it was lying.

She broke in through a back door near the sports field—and by "broke in" she meant opened an unlocked door without permission—and made her way to the basement.

And to the Hellmouth.

Being so close to it sent goose bumps up and down the backs of her arms. It made her want to run away. It made her want to scream. And even though there was no definitive marking, no X-marks-the-Hellmouth, she knew just where it was. And it felt like it knew just where she was, too.

She walked to it and took off her pack, then reached inside to pull out a large, glowing orb. It was bright and almost pretty; the green swirled through with flecks of blue like bits of glitter on a sea of thick paint. It looked a little like a bowling ball, if bowling balls could throb, and it cast the entire space in a strange, ethereal green. After a moment of deliberation, she grabbed a fire blanket off a shelf and used it to cover the orb before setting it down on top of the Hellmouth.

She let go of it gently, expecting it to roll. But it stuck. So firmly and so fast she wondered if she'd have been able to pick it up again. Not that she bothered to try. It was where it belonged. A nice welcome-back present for the Hellmouth. Something to draw its favorite demons, like a demon magnet, or a demon beacon.

It would give the new slayer something to do.

The woman stood.

"Phase one commenced," she said before tugging her hood down lower and slipping out of the school the same way she came in.

PART ONE

SUNNYDALE:
THE DEMON DESTINATION

CHAPTER ONE

THE VAMPIRE-WELCOMING COMMITTEE

Sunnydale Cemetery was a pretty nice place. Green. Spacious. Bordered and dotted with leafy trees that whispered in the dark. White stone pavilions had been erected here and there to serve as a housing for flowering vines, and the hedges were full and well groomed, planted in rows and groves so as to create corners and private spaces. For mourning, or picnics—concealing crouching demons or what have you. The point is, some landscape designer had an absolute field day, and the end result was more akin to a park than a resting place for the dead.

It didn't suit the vampire at all. He sniffed and caught the faint perfume of roses. He narrowed his yellow eyes, but the white marble benches only stood out brighter beneath the light of the waxing crescent moon. He was new in town, having caught the number 29 bus up from Phoenix. It had been a long trip. Long hours spent being a sun-fearing lump underneath a blanket, of bored kids running up and down the aisles, of bathroom stops and the sound of plastic wrappers being torn off gas station snack foods. His poor stomach had rumbled—gas station snack foods made the blood nice and greasy, and once the sun went down, he'd considered popping up and eating the whole bus. But then he'd have had to drive the rest of the way, and he was still better on a horse than a stick shift. Besides, he wanted to save his appetite for Sunnydale.

Sunnydale, California. Mother of the Hellmouth. Cradle of monsters. A town that had seen more carnage than a stack of scary movies. It had been dormant for decades, languishing under the protection of the slayers, and the red-haired witch who broke the world. But lately Sunnydale—or more accurately, the Hellmouth that dwelled beneath it—had started to pulse, and the ears and snouts of demons everywhere turned again toward the heartbeat. The Hellmouth was calling. Begging its children to tear away the facade of the city—the palm trees and street fairs, the coffee shops on every corner—and let it show its true, wicked face.

As for the slayers, they were gone, whisked away, right off the earth; killed in an explosion said some, or by a massive spell said others. No fewer than five demon doomsday cults had tried to take credit, but the vampire didn't care one way or another who had done it. He only cared that they were dead, and Sunnydale was his for the taking.

He paused at a fresh grave and placed his hand against the loosely packed soil, listening for another vampire waking below. He could use a local to show him the ins and outs. In all his hundred years of afterlife, he'd never been to Sunnydale. He preferred to spend his time in the southwest, where he'd been turned. He liked to lure tour groups out to the ghost towns. Then he would set the corpses up in the ruins of an old saloon, like mannequins, to confuse whatever poor sap eventually found them. By his count, he'd killed 4,219 people. More than that, actually, because it had taken him a few years to start counting, marking each with a notch in the holster of his six-shooter, which gradually became notches in a belt:

first brown leather, then black, now some clever new leather made from the skins of cactuses. He'd buried belts filled with notches all over the territories of Nevada, and Arizona, down into western Texas. But the cactus belt was new. Notch-free. And he planned to fill it with notches for Sunnydale townsfolk.

But so far the legendary city of the Hellmouth was falling short of the stories. The streets he'd walked through on the way from the bus station were clean, marked by engraved paving stones and made bright by solar lights. And now the cemetery—with its new, straight headstones and demure marble grave markers. From somewhere not far off, he heard the soft gurgling of a fountain.

Where were the rowdy demon bars? The demon gambling that went on until dawn, bloodthirsty creatures around a card table racking up huge debts of kittens? Where were the cracked, spider-filled crypts? Where were the foolish teenagers, making out in cars, begging for their throats to be ripped out?

And then, as if she'd heard his wish, there came a voice through the darkness. A girl's voice, from several rows of graves over. A soft glow emanated from that direction, too, as if from candles, and he licked his fangs. The little idiot was in the graveyard holding a séance. Humans were a useless lot—useless in his time, and in the century since it seemed they'd only gotten worse—but he did appreciate their constant fascination with the great beyond.

He crept through the graves, savoring the increasing nearness of the kill, the glimpses of the girl in the space between the headstones. Oh, but she was a pretty thing. Long black hair, straight as a horse's tail. Tan skin and big brown eyes made warm by the candlelight. Dark red lips. She wore a collar, too, the kind a mean dog might wear, with silver studs and a buckle. That struck him as odd, but he didn't waste much time considering the fashion choices of his dinner. And she wasn't alone! His mouth watered as his second course came into view: a fine-looking Black lad sitting across from her in the grass, holding a candle and trying not to get burned by the wax. They didn't look like they belonged much together; his buttoned shirt was pressed like a good mama would have done it, and his eyes behind the lenses of his glasses were focused and calm while the girl's were restless and narrowed.

He would eat the girl first. He saw her first after all, and it would be kind of fun watching the calm leave the boy's carefully composed expression. He wondered if the boy would run. Or if he would try to fight back. He would probably freeze like a frightened deer and simply wait for his turn.

The vampire crouched, ready to spring. He was so focused on his meal that he failed to notice the other girl running swiftly toward him through the cemetery, her hair in a messy red bun and her legs clad in loose, comfortable organic-cotton pants. She leapt up onto the headstone beside him, and caught him totally by surprise with a flying back kick.

"Hi!" Frankie said, trying to keep her voice perky and semiwelcoming as the vamp rolled upright in the grass. "Where ya from?"

The vampire growled and got to his feet in one smooth motion, a twist as graceful as a gymnast getting off a mat. So graceful that Frankie made a mental note to practice it later with Spike. The vampire brushed imagined dirt off his finely cut black suit, and the moonlight caught on the silver of his rather large and intricately designed belt buckle. It looked like a snake, intertwined with a . . . What did they call those western ropes? A lariat. It looked like a snake entwined with a lariat.

"That is a really nice belt buckle," Frankie said, and pointed with the tip of her stake.

"Thank you, darlin'," the vampire said, and she wrinkled her nose at his accent. "You'll be adorning the belt it's attached to momentarily. The first notch, right about here." He tapped the space just left of the buckle.

"Seems like a waste of good leather, marking it up like that," she said, and to her surprise, he straightened and looked down at it with a shrug.

"You know, I actually don't know whether it'll suit for notching. It's some newfangled kind of leather, made from cactus skins."

Frankie lowered her stake. "Really?" Her eyes widened. It looked just like high-quality leather. "That is such a cool eco-alternative!"

"Frankie."

The vampire looked over the headstones at the other two—Frankie's friends Hailey and Sigmund—who had stood, still holding their candles.

"Get that stake back up," Hailey said. "Eco-friendly or not, the vamp must be dusted."

"I know," said Frankie. "But it seems like such a waste, to let the belt go poof with the rest of him. Think I can wrestle it off him first? Or maybe I can steal it with magic."

"I don't think your telekinesis is fine-tuned enough to unbuckle a belt and tug it through several belt loops," said Sigmund. "And it's an unnecessary risk."

"I agree," said Hailey. "But if you can, I wouldn't mind having that belt buckle. It's kind of badass."

"What is happening here?" the vampire asked. The girl with the messy red bun on the top of her head carried a stake. And she kicked harder than his old pistol.

"I'm sorry," said Frankie. "You're right. This is supposed to be about you. So, as I was saying, where ya from?"

"Did you come by bus or by car?" Sigmund asked, setting down his candle and picking up his cloth-bound journal. "By train? By cargo plane perhaps?"

The vampire looked from Frankie to Sigmund and back again. Then he reached out and grabbed Frankie by the shoulders and threw her over three rows of graves. She landed in the grass, but not before bouncing off the headstone of one Michael Truman, 1958–2021.

"Ow," she groaned. "Why don't they make headstones softer?"

"Padded headstones," said Hailey. "Definitely something to consider. Watch out on your right!"

The vampire pulled Frankie up by the arm, and she tried to smile as she looked into his fangy face, buying herself a moment to remember their next survey question. But before it came to her, he backhanded her across the jaw and sent her sailing. At least this time she missed the graves when she landed. The vamp leapt on her again, and she thought she heard him mutter something about a little lady with no manners before she rolled backward and drove her heels into his chin, throwing him into a backflip. He got up with a snarl— much less gracefully this time—and just as she was about to jump in with a fast kick-punch-spinning-kick combination that Spike had demonstrated on her the previous week, the vampire was tackled by a blur of muscle and New Sunnydale Razorbacks letter jacket.

"Dammit, Jake!"

"I got him!" Jake cried as the vampire twisted free. "Er, I don't got him. But I'll get him!" He threw a punch. The vampire ducked it and sniffed.

"You smell like a werewolf," he said. "What are you doing, fighting with these people?"

"Werewolves are people, too, bro," Jake replied, and landed his punch this time, sending the vampire reeling.

"Jake," Sigmund called. "The census!"

"Oh, right." Jake turned back to the vamp. "So, where's that accent from? El Paso?" The vampire sprang, and Jake went down

14

underneath the weight. "He's surprisingly strong," Jake groaned. "So he must be old . . . I'd say at least fifty, maybe over a hundred!"

Sigmund jotted it down in his notebook as Frankie drove her stake through the vampire's back and into the heart.

He reared up in surprise, and Frankie had just enough time to gaze at the cactus-leather belt longingly before he, and it, exploded in a cloud of dust.

"Sorry," she said as Jake coughed through the cloud. "I saw my opening."

"He didn't seem the talkative type anyway," said Hailey. "I doubt you would have gotten much info even if you'd parried for an hour." She prodded Sigmund fondly in the chest. "So much for tonight's entry in the Sunnydale Vampire Census."

"Perhaps this is a waste of time." Sigmund adjusted his glasses on his nose, and even though he insisted that he had no combat-aggressive demon powers from the Sage demon side of his family tree, Frankie thought she heard a snarl behind his sigh.

"No way, babe, this is a really good idea." Hailey slipped her arm around his shoulder. "Gathering data on where the demons are coming from will be totally useful in determining the reach of the Hellmouth." They'd started tracking demons at the first of the year, and so far, the farthest one had come from was western Montana. Most were arriving from LA and Las Vegas. Nothing really from the Midwest, which had made Sigmund postulate that perhaps the hellmouth in Sunnydale was respecting the territory of the hellmouth in Ohio, though Frankie couldn't imagine that hellmouths had a code of ethics.

Frankie wiped the point of her stake clean against the leg of her pants and tucked it into the pocket of her hooded sweatshirt.

"Well, he definitely had an accent. And I think I heard him call me 'little lady.'"

"What a condescending pig," Hailey joked. "But no, seriously, what a condescending pig."

"I really wish I could've gotten that cactus belt. I mean, how cool is that? Plant belts." She eyed Hailey's studded black choker. Maybe she could get her a cactus-leather choker for her birthday! If Hailey ever told her when her birthday was. Getting personal details from Hailey was like pulling teeth.

"I was trying to hold him up so you could steal it," said Jake. "Sorry."

"It's okay." Frankie clapped a bit of vampire dust off the chest of his jacket, and he smiled. She could tell he was tired; he'd met up with them in the cemetery after lacrosse practice. And he was rusty: More lacrosse practice meant fewer patrols and less training. They hadn't seen much of him since the start of February, when the season started. He might be scarce until at least May, longer if they made the playoffs, but that was unlikely. Frankie had never been so grateful for the New Sunnydale Razorbacks' lack of sports ability. She missed Jake. She needed him around.

"Can we go home now?" Jake asked, yawning. "I have an early captain's meeting before school."

"And you have an early Scooby meeting after that," said Frankie.

Jake groaned. "Can we move it to our free period? Isn't that why your mom mojo'ed our schedules to match?"

"Fine, whiner, I'll text Spike." Hailey slipped her arm through Sigmund's and kissed him on the cheek. "I'm so glad you decided not to go out for lacrosse. At least one of our demons has his priorities straight."

Sigmund smiled happily. "Jake has to have a sports-slay balance. He did warn us."

"I did." Jake gave Sigmund a nod, like he was touched that Sigmund remembered.

"Well, what should we mark this vampire down as?" Sigmund asked. He reopened his journal. "If we had to guess. Even a region might be helpful."

"Arizona," Hailey said after a moment of contemplation. "Tombstone, Arizona."

"That's a pretty specific guess," said Sigmund, writing it down.

"Well, he just seemed like such a cowboy. And in that black suit? Like a gentleman cowboy. Like Doc Holliday." Her eyes widened. "You don't think he WAS Doc Holliday?"

"I hope not," Frankie said as she led them out of the cemetery. "If he was, he was too easy to take down."

Sigmund chuckled, and she tugged down the edge of his notepad to read what he had written:

February 9—the night Frankie the vampire slayer slayed Doc Holliday.

"Sigmund," Frankie mock-scolded. "You know that's how rumors get started."

But Hailey only laughed. "You mean that's how *legends* get started."

CHAPTER TWO
HOT UNDEAD LIBRARIANS

The next day during their free period, Frankie waited for the rest of the Scoobies on one of the long cement benches in the quad, her books spread out to save the seats. Not that anyone would have tried to sit there. The quad was almost empty, and though Frankie was rarely alone anymore—Hailey, Jake, Sigmund, or a combination thereof always seemed to be with her—when she was on her own, nobody tried to join in. She should have been used to that. She'd spent her entire high school career making sure that's how it was. But she'd sort of thought her new-found slayer confidence would change things somehow. Like being a slayer gave off some kind of magnetism.

But magnetism wasn't what being a slayer was about. The slayer wasn't the most popular girl at the party. She wasn't the class president. She was a secret, and she worked in the dark. Frankie was perfect for that. Day or night, she was still mostly invisible, despite Hailey's fashion and makeup tips. Of course maybe she wouldn't be if she actually used them—but wearing makeup and fashionable clothing while being a slayer was impractical. Eyeliner got into her eyes when a vamp punched her and made them water. And cute dresses were only cute until they got demon guts smeared all over them. She'd already had to toss two into the rag bin, which was a complete waste. And Frankie hated waste.

She and everyone else would just to deal with it: Her face was simply her face, and her clothes were simply her clothes.

Well, unless Grimloch came back to town and offered to take her someplace really nice.

She pulled a spellbook onto her lap and hid the contents with her notebook as she flipped through the pages. She jumped when Hailey grabbed her shoulders from behind.

"Easy," Hailey said. She waited for Frankie to move some books out of the way and sat down hard on the bench. "Shouldn't your slayer sense have told you I was right behind you?"

"My slayer sense almost threw you across the quad," Frankie said, arching her brow.

Hailey grinned. "You look like your mom when you do that."

"Do what?"

"That thing. With your eyebrow."

Frankie touched her face. "Speaking of my mom, where were you last night? I thought you were only stopping by Sigmund's for a minute, but I didn't even hear you come in."

"We were watching a movie."

"What movie?" Frankie pressed, and she didn't miss the faint flush that rose to Hailey's tan cheeks.

"A movie." Hailey shrugged. "It was a musical, I think. What's the big deal?"

"The big deal is my mom has started to mumble about having to put her foot down. With you and Sigmund, and the unsupervised alone time." Frankie watched Hailey carefully. She expected she would scoff or cross her arms. Maybe get mad. Instead she just smiled. "You like my mom's curfew?"

"No." Hailey stretched her legs out and crossed them at the ankles. Her black boots were of the delicate sort today (Victorian-style, with low heels and laces), and she'd paired them with a short black skirt. Goth pretty is how Frankie thought of it, instead of Goth tough. "But I don't *un*like it. I never had a mom to tell me not to do things, you know? I was ten when my parents died; too young to do anything wrong. And Vi was very . . . not a mom. So let Willow put her foot down. Maybe she'll even ground me. What's that like?" She laughed when Frankie made a face. "Besides it might be kind of fun if I had to sneak around to see Sig. He's so . . . good, you know? It would totally freak him out. All those buttons and ironed clothes. I just love to wrinkle him up."

"You're twisted." Frankie studied Hailey from the corner of her eye. She ought to ask about Vi and if Hailey had heard from her—they'd been searching since they defeated the Countess that fall, but all they'd found was a hastily-cleared-out space in a vacant ware-house, where Vi had clearly been squatting—but then she shook her head. Lately, any mention of Vi and Hailey's face would slam shut like a book Frankie wasn't supposed to be reading.

"Ladies." Jake jumped over the bench and swept Frankie's books into a messy pile before plopping down beside her. "And Frankie."

Frankie pursed her lips and reordered her things, straightening pages in her notebooks. "Jeez, Jake, you look terrible." He wore sunglasses, his expression tired and slack, and his reddish-gold hair was able to move in the breeze. "You didn't even bother to over-gel your hair."

"I'm going to over-gel *your* hair," he said.

"Huh?"

"Sorry. I'm tired. Too tired to tort, let alone retort." He stretched, and it looked like it hurt. "Start of the season. I am not in shape."

"But you're constantly running," said Hailey. "And you're a werewolf. Don't you have, like, superhuman strength?"

"Playing is different," Jake said. "Uses different muscles. And I didn't say I wasn't still the best on the team. By far." He reached across Frankie to slap Hailey on the knee. "Get your boyfriend to try out. Give me a little demon backup."

As if on cue, Sigmund's shadow fell across them. He was looking particularly put-together, in a navy blazer from his old school layered over the top of a sweater vest of all things. No matter what Hailey said, it must have been really hard to wrinkle him.

"How many times do I have to tell you, Thriller? No. Demon. Powers."

"That's a lie," said Jake. "You can charm people."

Beguile people, was more like. When Sigmund turned on the charm, or when he did accidentally when he was nervous, he became so enchanting that it was almost like being blinded. The rest of the world fell away, and all that remained was Sigmund DeWitt.

"That's not much use on a lacrosse field," the half demon said.

"Depends on how much you use," said Jake.

"Isn't that cheating?" Hailey asked.

"Have you seen our team? We need to cheat." He yawned.

"Maybe you should take a few more nights off," Frankie suggested. "Catch up on sleep. Things have been quiet anyway."

"Local neck-wound deaths have been staying nice and low since we turned the Countess into skewerable meat cubes." Hailey grinned.

"And there's still been no word from missing sisters or really old demon underwear models." With his head back and eyes closed,

Jake didn't see the ripple that passed through them as he spoke. No, there had been no word from Vi. She had appeared to save Spike and help them defeat the Countess, and then disappeared again without even a hint of an explanation. Not even for Hailey, the sister who'd thought she was dead—killed in the Slayerfest explosion. And there had been no messages from Grimloch either. Since he'd left town to search for his slayer, the demon–hunter god of Thrace had seemingly turned back into a myth.

And how rude was that? Hadn't he said he would keep one ear on Sunnydale in case she needed him? Hadn't he said that he cared, and that Frankie would see him again soon? Frankie's face scrunched sourly. Sunnydale was quiet, so she didn't need him. And if she really thought about it, he hadn't said "soon." He hadn't even said he cared. But he had implied it, pretty strongly. At least in her opinion.

He has more important things to do, Frankie thought. *Like finding his slayer. The one he loves. The one we all hope is still alive.* She frowned. That sounded like she was trying to convince herself, and that made her feel guilty. It also made her feel like an idiot for thinking Grimloch might feel something more for her than what he did.

"Where is Spike?" Jake threw his head back and cried, "Why is he always late?"

"No need to howl so dramatically," said Sigmund. "He's right there. With the coffee clutch."

The vampire-slash-Watcher lingered near the doors, surrounded by what looked to be nearly every unattached adult woman in the school.

"Isn't that our lunch lady from the cafeteria?" Hailey asked.

"Yeah," said Jake. "She's still wearing the plastic gloves for food handling."

"Looks like she'd rather be Spike handling. Is he getting a tan?"

"I don't think he can," said Frankie as her Watcher extricated himself and made his way toward them. "The spell my mom cast to keep him safe from the sun on school grounds—I'm pretty sure it blocks ALL the rays. SPF a million."

"Wow, look at you," Hailey said when Spike reached them. "You're like a boy band without the band. Or the pulse. Can you technically be a heartthrob if your heart's not beating?"

"And can you be a boy band with that old-glamoured face?" Jake added. "Or would it be an old-man band? Like the Eagles."

"Leave him alone." Frankie swatted Jake lightly. "It would be an age-appropriate librarian band."

"What an awful band," said Sigmund, and Hailey laughed into his shirt.

"Good morning to you, too, Scoobies," said Spike, brow arched. He sipped his coffee, which Frankie knew was spiked with blood. Or sometimes it was just plain blood.

"How do you explain the red in the cup?" Hailey asked, pointing to the rim.

"Red-velvet creamer. Now let's get cracking, shall we? I have to run an update on the periodicals database."

"You're getting really into the librarian . . . ining," Frankie said. Spike didn't respond, so she shrugged and recounted the events of the patrol as her Watcher ineffectively pretended to care. She talked, watching as he dipped a finger into his blood and licked it clean. As he shifted his weight. Any moment, she expected him to start giving her the *wrap it up* sign, so she took a breath and loudly declared, "And that's when I became a legend by dusting Doc Holliday."

Spike blinked. "You dusted who?"

"See? You weren't even paying attention. Are all Watchers like this? Did Giles used to get bored and drift off listening to Aunt Buffy?"

"I didn't drift off. It's just . . . fairly routine." He pursed his lips. "No word from Vi Larsson, no word from the Hunter of bloody Thrace, and no new leads on what happened to the slayers. No need for . . . any of this." He gestured vaguely to them with his coffee cup and sighed. "You lot use the rest of the period to study."

"Study what?" Hailey asked. "Like, demons?"

"Like school things. You know, the things you need to know to graduate and keep from working the night shift at Doublemeat Palace," the vampire said as he walked away.

Frankie's brow knit. She loved Doublemeat Palace. She had ever since she was little and Buffy had told her the "meat" was secretly vegetarian. She got up and started to load her things into her backpack.

"Where you going?" Hailey asked.

"Extra time with the Watcher. Training stuff. You and Sig don't need to come. Just hang here, and I'll see you later."

"What about me?" asked Jake, already stretching out to lie across the bench.

"You curl up and dream of chasing lacrosse balls."

She followed Spike inside and found him in his office, paging through the thick volume of the *Watchers Codex* without actually reading it.

"Thought I told you to study."

"Yeah, but I thought I should tell you more about the fight. The vampire had this really cool way of regaining his feet. I thought we could practice flips and roll-backs and coming out of tucks—we wouldn't need weapons, so it wouldn't seem suspicious if someone came in. . . ."

"A student and the librarian tumbling around on the floor? That wouldn't look suspicious at all." He gave her a puzzled look. "That's something you can practice at home, Mini Red. What do you really want?"

She wasn't sure. He'd just seemed bothered. And she didn't like to see her Watcher bothered. "Was it too much teasing out there? About the coffee ladies? We were only joking. I mean, they are age-appropriate—or as age-appropriate as you can get, since you're two hundred. As long as you aren't dating married Mrs. Merriman, we'd be totally thrilled—"

"I'm not dating any of them," Spike said. "I'm not going to be dating anyone."

Frankie took off her backpack and hopped up to sit on the edge of his desk, her feet resting on his empty chair.

"Because of Buffy," she said.

Spike snorted. "How do you figure?"

"Well . . . you were a couple a long time ago. And you never really stopped caring about her. And now that we don't know what happened in the explosion—if she's gone, or if she survived—maybe you feel like you're in limbo? Frozen in time?"

"I'm an undead high school librarian. I AM frozen in time." He looked at her fondly. "You're a fairly perceptive thing, aren't you, Mini Red? When it comes to other people's feelings."

"Does that mean I'm right?"

Spike shook his head.

"Buffy and I were never a couple. Or not what mentally well people would call one, anyway. I made too many mistakes. Big ones. Un-bloody-forgivable ones. But after the fight with the First, and after I came back . . . in those years afterward, we came close. Coupla times. But we never . . ." He gazed past her, out through his office door, and Frankie knew he wasn't seeing the library. He was seeing Buffy and all those moments. All those near misses. "We never got it right. And yeah, now she's gone again, or missing, and if I wasn't on hold before—" He raised his eyebrows. "I guess I'm on hold now. Feels like I should be. Until we know."

"But, Spike, she wouldn't . . . I mean I don't think she would—"

"Don't you lecture me on bleeding hearts." He pointed his finger. "It's been more than three months since Broody McUnderwearModel left town, and I don't see you making googly eyes at any of these lads. Valentine's is coming up, you know. Do you have one?"

"A valentine?" Frankie scoffed. "Valentine's Day is nothing more than a good excuse to stock up on discounted day-after boxes of chocolate."

"That's true," said Spike. "We should pick up some of those. But back to the point: *I'm immortal.* I can afford to be frozen awhile. You're not, and you need to forget about Grimloch the Hunter of Hotpants and get out there and . . . cavort."

Frankie hopped down from the desk. "Easier said than done. What about Ms. Ames from the English department? You two would make a great couple."

"Look, that coffee thing is a poetry club if you must know," Spike snapped. "We meet tonight, and it's my turn to bring the cookies." He sighed. "I'm sorry about what I said out there. About it not being necessary. It's just all this waiting is not my style. I should be out there, looking for her. I should be doing . . . what that bleeding underwear model is doing."

"But we need you here," Frankie said.

"I know." The vampire's jaw tightened, his eyes drifting again. "And I do get the sense that something is coming."

"What's coming?"

"Nothing." He snapped back to attention and waved her off, putting on his tweed jacket to go do librarian things. "You run along now, Mini Red." She nodded and went. As she pushed through the doors, she heard him grumble, "Doc Holliday wasn't even a vampire. The blood on his lips was from tuberculosis. Don't they teach any worthwhile history these days?"

CHAPTER THREE

WHEN YOU GO LOOKING FOR TROUBLE IN SUNNYDALE . . .

All through her afternoon classes, Frankie fought daydreams. Most of them, she was embarrassed to admit, were about Grim. But now they were also about Spike. Not about Spike in *that* way, gross, but about ways to cheer him up. She imagined finding a spell to return the missing slayers. She imagined Buffy returning to all of them, and the look on Spike's face. He would weep, probably, and then he would hug Buffy, and hug Frankie, and tell her that she'd done it, that he couldn't believe it but she'd done it, she'd brought them back, and then he wouldn't be sad, or restless in a Sunnydale that seemed determined to be safer and less demon-infested when it should have been the opposite. The slayers were gone, and they were all holding their breaths, waiting for the other shoe to drop, for the next clue to start them on the path that led to the slayers' eventual rescue. Vi Larsson, showing up during the battle with the Countess like a white knight, had seemed like that clue. But then she disappeared, and everywhere they chased her they met with a dead end.

It had been months now. And Frankie had begun to fear that

they were wrong. There was no great mission ahead with a reward of shiny slayers. The explosion had been it. Not the start of something but the end, and they were just pointlessly hoping, dragging their feet as New Sunnydale marched on around them.

"Frankie. Frankie!"

"Huh?" She looked up into her history teacher's confused expression. "I'm sorry, Mrs. Matthews, I didn't hear the question."

"The question was the bell," Mrs. Matthews replied. She gestured to the rows of empty desks. "It rang. A while ago."

"Oh." Frankie smiled and sheepishly gathered her pens and notebook. "I guess I missed it. I was thinking about tonight's homework."

"There is no homework. And don't turn in extra—I don't have time to grade it." She touched Frankie on the shoulder when she got up to leave. "Wait. As long as you're lingering, linger a minute longer. What's going on with you, Frankie? You used to be a very good student. An ace, really. And now you're all over the place."

"My grades have only dropped half a letter," Frankie said quickly.

"Half a letter. And you're willing to accept that?"

"No! Well, yes, kind of. I knew something was going to give with all the late nights, and really it almost doesn't matter anymore because chances are I'll be pursuing a career in law enforcement or private security, I thought about UFC or that pro-wrestling stuff, but isn't that cheating?" She stopped and blinked up at Mrs. Matthews perplexed face. "Sorry, what was the question?"

"Frankie . . . are you okay?"

"I'm great." Frankie grabbed her things. "I am having trouble focusing and I'm going to work on that, and there's not a lot of time at night to do homework and I have added what feels like about a million shall we say 'extracurriculars' to my schedule, but I'm still only willing to accept half a letter drop in my grades because I've worked hard at them my whole life and who needs sleep?" Her voice rose as she stalked away. The reminder about her flagging academics had done nothing to improve her already-troubled mood, but that wasn't Mrs. Matthews's fault, so she turned around and popped her head back into the classroom. "Mrs. Matthews?" she called. "Thanks for worrying."

In the halls, she plowed through students like the prow of a ship: head down, books hugged tightly to her chest, her red bun pointed slightly forward like a bull's horns. New Sunnydale was too damned quiet. Where were the demons, coming to challenge her? Where were the Big Bads, looking to kill a slayer and make a name for themselves?

"It's like we don't even have a hellmouth anymore," she muttered as she burst through the doors and into the crisp sweater-weather sunshine. So nice and safe, a pretty day, perfect for traipsing through fields of daisies and singing. It was no wonder that Spike was feeling stagnant, and that Sigmund had the time to come up with a project like the demon census. They'd done so much training, so many patrols, and for what? "Where is the evil?" Frankie hissed, and stormed out past the sports field into the border of trees, where she could kick shrubs and rant in peace.

Maybe the Hellmouth only conjures as much evil as the current slayer in residence can handle, she thought, and chuckled. Then she frowned. Only a real dope would heckle herself and laugh about it.

She had walked another fifty yards, skirting the edge of school property, when she caught the hint of something foul on the air. And not foul evil, but truly foul. She sniffed and wrinkled her nose. It smelled like a very warm low-tide beach she'd visited once with her mom. They'd built sandcastles for about twenty minutes before they caught sight of a dead seal bobbing in the waves. She was about to turn around and head back when her slaydar emitted a very soft ping. So she followed the smell instead, walking faster and then running when she heard the cries, and the thrashing of leaves.

"Hey! Is someone there?"

"Help! Somebody help me!"

Frankie leapt ahead, arms pumping, jumping over whole shrubs and swinging off low branches. "Hold on!" she shouted. But the only reply she received was an earsplitting scream. When she crashed onto the scene, she didn't see anything right away—just a pool of rain runoff from the large metal culvert that drained into the woods. She still smelled the smell, stronger now and distinctly fishy. And then she turned and saw the boy.

The boy was dead. There were deep, bloody gashes visible through tears in his hooded Razorbacks sweatshirt, and his neck was clearly broken.

The demon, her slaydar beeped. *Get the demon!*

Frankie ducked into the culvert, the demon's most likely path of escape. Shadows closed over her head as she splashed through grimy water to her ankles. She thought she heard something for a moment—more splashing and some kind of hiss—but then there was nothing, and the fishy, salty smell faded in her nose. She stopped to listen, and lowered her arms from a fighting position.

"Come on," she whispered. "Come back and attack me. I'm just a helpless, delicious, not-at-all-superpowered person. . . ." But the demon didn't take the bait. It was scared. Or it was smart. Or it was gone already and had no idea she was standing there.

Frankie turned and made her way out of the culvert. She looked down at the body of the boy. He was a senior, she thought. But she didn't know his name.

"I'm sorry," she said. "When I went looking for evil, this is not what I meant."

The Scoobies assembled in the library as soon as it cleared for the day, and Frankie recounted her tragic discovery along the edges of the school grounds.

"You didn't see what did it?" Hailey asked, leaning against a bookshelf, eyes downcast.

Frankie shook her head. "There was a smell, though, like rotten fish? And a sound . . . like wheezing or hissing."

Sigmund nodded and started pulling books, leafing through them with fast fingers. He wouldn't find it, not off that thin a description. But Frankie knew he just needed something to do.

"Do you know who the boy was?" Hailey asked.

"No. I think he was a senior."

"A senior," said Jake. "Dang. He was this close. This close to making it out."

"Jake," Hailey chided. "Don't make jokes. He was a person."

"Well, yeah. But he was a Sunnydale person. When we meet our demise, it is not exactly what you would call 'unexpected.' We know the score." He looked down. "Somehow we all know the score."

"We should figure out a way to get someone out there to discover him," Frankie said. "Though I don't enjoy the thought of someone else having to see what I saw. . . ."

"Wait, you just left him out there?" Jake asked. "You didn't tell anybody?"

Frankie shrugged helplessly.

"Frankie's right," said Spike. "Just because she's the one always finding the corpses doesn't mean she can always be the one finding the corpses. Even with the elevated Sunnydale body count, it would start to look suspicious."

"And not to be insensitive," Sigmund added, "but at least now we can go have a look at the victim. Search it for clues. I mean *him*. Search him for clues." He looked at Hailey. "Sorry."

They trudged out to the sports field, and Frankie led the way back to the culvert. Spike had to stop at the edge of the trees—"Any farther and I'll combust"—so they went on alone. The sun had started to dip lower and there was no breeze, but even so, Frankie's nose caught the scent of the demon right away. Somehow it was even stronger than when she'd left.

"Ugh." Hailey waved a hand in front of her face. "If dicing up the Countess hadn't already put me off poke, then the smell of this sure would have."

"It is quite pungent," Sigmund agreed.

"Any pungent demons springing to mind?" Jake asked. His sensitive werewolf nose was working, but unlike the others, he didn't seem to mind the reek. Sigmund shook his head and plugged his nose between his index finger and thumb.

"There he is," Frankie said, and pointed.

They fanned out around the body, grimacing at the deep red cuts in his chest and the knob of vertebrae that shouldn't have been visible in his neck from that angle. He lay on his back, his arms fallen peacefully to his sides. One knee was bent, and his eyes were fixed and open.

"I do know him," said Jake, kneeling. "It's Gustavo Fuentes. He was on the swim team. He was a good guy." He reached out and closed Gustavo's eyes. "Smart. I heard he'd gotten into some school in Maryland." Frankie's jaw clenched. Jake might've been being insensitive earlier, but he'd been right: Gustavo had been so close. So close to getting out of Sunnydale alive.

"All right." Sigmund steeled himself and knelt beside Jake.

"Let's have a look." He lifted the tears in the boy's T-shirt to peer underneath. "Four slashes, like from a hand of claws. Deep, too. Perhaps . . . a half an inch at the widest point."

"And it's obviously strong," Hailey noted. "Gustavo wasn't a small guy, and fit from swimming. Not to mention how hard it must've been to twist his neck around so far." She winced and swallowed, waving away more of the smell that was thankfully fading.

"Wait." Frankie looked around. "He's just wearing a T-shirt. When I left him, he had a sweatshirt on, too. A hoodie. One of the school ones."

"Why would a demon come back and take a sweatshirt but leave the body?" Hailey asked. "Especially when, judging by those claw marks, it was totally ruined."

"Perhaps it was after something in the pocket," Sigmund suggested. "Something he was carrying?"

"Time to question Gustavo's friends," Jake said, and sighed. "I guess I can do that tomorrow after practice. Some of the guys on the lacrosse team knew him."

"And I'll continue to search for possible culprits," said Sigmund, dabbing at a bead of sweat on his forehead.

"First we'd better get him found," said Hailey. "And get him out of here."

Frankie stared down at Gustavo grimly. "Just another beautiful day in Sunnydale," she murmured.

The slayer tugged her hood up and set her pack down by the side of the highway, not far from the old WELCOME TO SUNNYDALE sign (that someone had spray-painted WELCOME TO SUNNYHOLE). From her bag she removed several dull white stones the size of her fist and arranged them in a circle in the dirt. Then she took up a tightly wrapped bundle of herbs soaked in cow's blood, and a flint. Not a lighter—an actual, honest-to-frontier-times flint.

She dropped to a crouch and scowled as she struck it. Not that it was harder to use the flint than to flick a Zippo; with her slayer strength, she got a shower of sparks on the first try. It was just the principle of the thing. An actual flint. Move into this century, demons. Live in the now.

A second shower of sparks fell across the bundle of blood-marinated herbs and caught. Not enough to start a fire. Just enough to generate smoke. Very bad, decayed-blood-smelling smoke that made her recoil. She hated demon magic. But it was all they had. Slayers were not witches, at least not until recently. And demon magic tended to work for even the least talented practitioners. Case in point: Andrew.

She stood and let the smoke thicken. As she spoke the incantation in a demon language she could never nail the accent for, the smoke rose into the air and slowed. It ceased to behave like normal smoke and instead swirled together to create a wall. And then the wall split to form a window, in which the face of another slayer appeared, cast in shadow.

"Why do we have to do this this way?" The hooded woman gestured to the still-smelly smoke. "We do have phones, you know."

"Phones that anyone can look through. And that the red witch can hack. She won't notice these little blips of portals opening, and if she does, she won't be able to trace them. Besides, ditching burner phones is a hassle."

"Okay." The first slayer adjusted her hood. "But why do you have to be all whispery and shrouded? I feel like I'm talking to Dr. Claw."

"The longer you bust my chops the longer you have to breathe in smoke," the other slayer said. "Are you in contact with the daughter of the red witch?"

"Frankie. Her name is Frankie, apparently." Frankie Rosenberg. Born of the same magic that had been forced upon them. They didn't know precisely how. Maybe the red witch had sensed the explosion at the slayer meeting and used the Scythe to create one more last-ditch savior. Most of them thought that's what happened. The red witch, once again wielding power that was never hers to wield, and wielding it for her own benefit.

"Not yet," the hooded slayer said.

"Well, what are you waiting for?"

"I thought we needed time to find the amulet?"

"The amulet is almost found. At this very moment, she's gone to retrieve it. So you'd better get a move on."

"And what am I supposed to do, then? Make slayer small talk? Hey, I like your knife. Nice job on the decapitation."

"The beacon you planted on the Hellmouth will help you. Once it lures the demons, she'll be more than ready to accept an extra pair of slaying hands. And it's better anyway if she's kept busy."

The slayer pushed her hood back. She kicked pebbles across the hard, dry dirt. "I hate this place. You know, we could probably just ask the new slayer to help us. She's just a kid. And she seems sweet."

"We can't trust anyone but each other. So do as you're told. The red witch must know the location of the Scythe. We will find the amulet, but to find the Scythe, we need her. And when we have them both, it'll be over." The other slayer smiled, and her voice filled with hope. "We'll be free."

CHAPTER FOUR

THE BIG BAD POETRY CLUB

Spike walked through the streets of New Sunnydale, carrying a box of cinnamon shortbread. Thursday night. Poetry club meeting. His turn to bring the cookies. He didn't exactly feel much like discussing "L'Albatros," not after that poor lad had just been sliced up on school grounds, and also because he hated that bloody depressing poem, but the ladies had voted for French and he didn't want to be a poor sport about it. Not to mention that since the boy had been killed, and his body had not yet been found, alibis for school librarians with black fingernails and unorthodox manners were a good idea.

He paused at a crosswalk and sniffed the air, scenting for innocent blood before remembering that he had a soul and he didn't do that anymore. Demons. Demons and vampires and mischief afoot—that was what he was looking for these days. *Not as much fun*, whispered the demon that still resided inside him. *And much more dangerous.* Demons had teeth and claws and, on occasion, acidic spit. He'd never had half so much trouble chasing down a pretty girl.

But that wasn't who he was anymore.

"And I don't miss it," he said to the stars, and rather unconvincingly. After all, he was still the Big Bad, still able to beat down the worst of whatever the Hellmouth threw at him. And to prove it, that night he'd traded the tweed for a pair of jeans and a black sweater. Let these poetry ladies get a taste of who they were really dealing with. Someone dangerous. Someone damaged. Someone who had killed, and would kill still more, and would never get the blood off his hands.

But then again, maybe he would, if he put in enough hours teaching the kiddies how to use reference databases and the importance of proper shelving.

Spike touched his face. The glamour that Willow had cast on him, to make him believably old enough to be a high school librarian, had stuck fast and seemed to work itself deeper into his skin every day. He could feel the unimaginable lines, right there in his forehead, and there was a bit of softness across his chiseled jaw. She'd been out of practice; that's what she'd said when she cast it. Out of practice, with magic as wobbly as a baby deer. But Willow's magic was never like a baby deer. From the start, it had jumped fully formed right out of her, like the goddess Athena born leaping in armor from the head of Zeus.

Maybe the glamour would never come off. Maybe he ought to start wearing different clothes during his time away from the library. Not tweed, obviously, only wankers like Rupert Giles wore tweed during their off hours, but something more mature. Something with a collar. Polo shirts. Things that Sigmund would wear.

"Bugger that."

He sniffed the air again and closed his eyes, and the memory of Buffy's perfume flared in his senses, like it had more and more since the explosion. Old memories rising to the surface. Making sure he didn't forget.

It was stronger tonight, almost cloying, as if he could open his eyes and find her right there, standing in front of him with that look she had: amused, or disappointed. Maybe amused *and* disappointed. Maybe ready with a right hook. He would deserve it, for not being there when she needed him. For letting them all get killed.

"Now you sound as broody as Angel." Spike took a deep breath and was shocked to find the scent of the perfume still there. For a moment, he thought he really was being haunted, before he realized that Buffy didn't wear Obsession for Men, and the scent was real. Spike glanced around. Some bloke, probably, out for a nighttime stroll. Only he had a strange feeling in his gut, like he was being shadowed, or like something was hunting. He wasn't far from the cemetery. And vampires loved to cover over the smell of grave dirt with cologne. He glanced down at the store-bought tin of shortbread. He could afford one little detour. It wasn't like the cookies were going to get cold.

He followed the scent into the cemetery and kept his head on a swivel, ducking low between the rows of graves. He didn't know how Frankie managed to patrol the place. It was so open, with hardly any crypts to hide behind or to jump up on to get a better view. And no self-respecting demon would crouch behind hedges that had been trimmed into fancy rising spirals. But one was crouching somewhere. He was growing more and more certain of that. It just wasn't *there*. The scent trail led him to the edge of the cemetery, where it met the border of the old eastern woods.

Spike plunged into the trees, stepping through overgrowth and trying to hold on to the smell. He broke into a run and grinned. He was eager. Ready. He'd been letting Frankie do all of the fighting; he hadn't had a decent scrap since the Countess, and that could hardly be called one—she'd slapped him around and then tossed

40

him across a football field—and his fists itched for some evil thing to collide with. He stopped short when the cologne trail veered left, and listened for the telltale sound of moving leaves and snapping twigs. When he heard it, he darted ahead—and at the same moment heard the same sound from the other direction. Behind him.

It was a small sound. Had he not had vampiric ears, he wouldn't have heard it at all. And he let it go as he pursued the first noise—louder now, practically a herd of water buffalo crashing through the trees—after several strides of listening for footsteps on his trail, he figured it had been nothing. A raccoon maybe. Or one of those wobbly baby deer. The action, and the cologne, were ahead, amid scrambling strides and snarls. Spike caught sight of a furred, demonic haunch and leapt, knocking the demon off course and sending them both rolling into a small clearing. Spike flipped onto his feet and grabbed the beast by the shoulders to kick it in the chest, and the sight of it sailing into a tree trunk was so good for his soul that he threw his head back and howled.

So did the demon. And the howl sounded familiar.

Spike watched as the shaggy gray fur disappeared and black claws receded into human hands. Oz stood, and pulled a low branch full of leaves across him to conceal his complete nakedness.

"Spike," he said. "Patrolling?"

"No, I just thought I . . ." The vampire pursed his lips in apology and scratched the back of his head. "Never mind. Thought you were something else. What are you doing out here anyway? It's not the full moon."

"I don't hunt during the full moon. The wolf gets too wild. And I was going for that rabbit." Oz pointed, and Spike turned to see a large brown bunny crouched in the underbrush, nose twitching.

"Do you . . . still want it?" Spike stepped out of the way, and the rabbit gave them one last look before hopping into the shadows.

"Nah. The chase was enough."

"*That* chase?" the vampire asked doubtfully.

Oz pointed to the grass, where the tin of shortbread lay, tossed aside in the tumble. "You dropped your cookies."

Spike picked them up. "Want one? I did spoil your supper."

"Sure, but I left my clothes in the cemetery, so . . ." Oz was still nude behind the branch of leaves.

"Right. Well, let's get out of here. I'll go first."

They walked awkwardly through the woods, an old-faced vampire and a naked werewolf.

"You hunt out here a lot?"

"Some," Oz replied. "More since Frankie became a slayer. Like I need to stay in shape, just in—"

"Just in case," Spike finished in agreement. Though Frankie had done okay so far. She and her Scoobies had taken out the Countess's nest, and then she and Vi had taken out the Countess, all while he sat there dazed and slightly sizzled. It was one test passed. But Frankie was a slayer now, and there would be more tests ahead. Many more. A long string of tests and quests, stretched out across the rest of her life. Until one finally came along that she failed.

I won't outlive another slayer, he thought. *I won't outlive Mini Red.*

Except he would. He and his old face, and his damaged soul, they would go on, after Buffy, and even after Frankie. He clenched his teeth and felt his fangs poke through. Those thoughts, that was the soul talking. When he'd been a demon, he'd never had thoughts like that. When he was evil, it was all biting and torture and Happy Meals with legs.

They reached the edge of the cemetery, and Oz slipped through the shadows to the grave where he left his clothes. A few minutes later, he returned in the moonlight in jeans, a T-shirt, and a corduroy jacket.

"Can I ask you something?" Oz asked. "When you've been out the last few days, have you gotten the feeling that you're being watched?"

"What have you seen?"

"I haven't seen anything." Oz's nostrils flared, scenting the air. "I just get a feeling sometimes. Right between my shoulder blades. Like I'm being sighted down by a tranq gun. Only . . . not."

"Couldn't just be a werewolf thing? Tranq gun paranoia?" Oz shrugged, and Spike remembered the sound he'd heard when he entered the forest. What had that been? Nothing, probably. An animal. Except it had been perfectly behind him, and curiously timed. "Maybe I did hear something. Tonight, when I was mistakenly hunting you."

"What was it?"

"Thought it was just a raccoon."

"Should we tell Frankie?"

Spike turned back toward the trees. Nothing in there moved. No sounds. No smells. But he hadn't been lying when he told Frankie that he felt like something was coming. Something was coming, or something was already here, and he'd lived through enough bad things in Sunnydale to know that was a feeling he shouldn't ignore. "Let's keep it between us for now. I'll come out on a few patrols; you keep hunting."

"Let the old guys be the bait for a change," said Oz.

"Right," said Spike. Then he frowned. "What do you mean 'old guys'?"

"Nothing. Not what I meant."

"You know this is just a glamour! And by the way, since when do you wear Obsession for Men?"

43

"I like it." The werewolf shrugged. "It's musky. What should we tell Willow?"

"We tell Willow everything, because if we don't, she'll have us by the short hairs."

"You can bring her some cookies." Oz pointed to the tin.

Spike looked down at the slightly dented shortbread. No poetry club for him, then. He supposed the ladies would forgive him.

Sufficiently distracted, neither noticed the eyes tracking them through the moonlight, nor did they see the figure passing from headstone to headstone on silent, lithe legs, following them until they got into Oz's van, and then receding back to the shadows.

CHAPTER FIVE

FUN WITH ORACLES

When Willow heard the rumble of Oz's van in the driveway, she wasn't surprised. Nor was she surprised to peek through the curtains and see a platinum-haired vampire hop out of the passenger side.

"Frankie already texted me about the dead boy," she said when she opened the door. She looked down at Spike's hands. "You brought cookies. Come in and help me make some sandwiches, and put the blood on the stove."

"Jake texted me, too," said Oz as they moved into the kitchen. "You know our kids are very responsible and communicative, compared to what I've heard from other parents."

"That's because our kids are locked in a life-and-death battle with demons most nights of the week." Willow reached into the refrigerator and tossed Oz the mayonnaise. "Do you want carved chicken or vegan slices?"

"Let's go half and half, for Frankie. And, uh, triple load of meat—"

"Little bit of lettuce. I know."

Oz smiled. He got out the bread, unscrewed the mayonnaise cap, and started slathering.

"So, what kind of demon do you think it is?" Willow asked. "It didn't sound like a vampire."

"This close to the Hellmouth it could be anything," said Spike at the stove, tending his blood gently over a double boiler. "That's the fun. But that's not why we're here. Where's Frankie?"

"Patrolling." Willow squinted at him. "And as her Watcher, shouldn't you know that?"

"Of course; I was just testing you."

"Will," said Oz, "have you sensed anything weird, say over the last two days or so? Has anything strange pinged your radar?"

"No," she replied. "Why?"

"I've just had the sense I've been being tailed. Might be nothing."

"Might be something," amended Spike. "I can feel it, too, in my bones. Something brewing." He turned off the stove and poured his warmed blood into a mug, then grabbed the first of the finished sandwiches and dipped the corner in. If he did the same thing with his shortbread, Willow thought she might actually vomit.

"I thought Drusilla was the one with the sight."

"Yeah, well, maybe some of her gift rubbed off. We did a lot of rubbing, her and me."

"Ew," Willow said. Oz chuckled, and she gave him a look.

"I mean, yeah," he said. "Gross. But I feel it, too. Something's setting my fur on edge."

Willow frowned. "Then why don't I feel anything?" She cast out a quick net of consciousness, fast and quiet, her mind spreading into the night like a blast of ink before drawing back into herself just as quickly. Nothing. And then on the counter, her phone began to buzz.

"It's Xander." She answered. "Xander?"

"Hey, Willow."

"Is everything okay?"

"Not exactly," he said. "I'm sending you a photo; let me know when you get it." She waited while he did things with his phone. "Is everything okay with you? Frankie okay?"

"Sort of . . ." she replied. "Oz and Spike are here. We were just talking about . . ." A whole lot of nothing, in her opinion, but it was a strange stroke of fate, that Xander would call right then.

"You might want to put me on speaker."

She hit the button and set the phone down between the three of them on the counter. It gave a soft beep and vibrated when Xander's photo arrived. She opened it up.

"What are we looking at?" she asked. The photo was an aerial view of the blast site in Halifax where the slayer meeting had been held. She'd never seen it from that distance before, and it looked even more horrific. An empty, demolished circle in a sea of trees. A crater of wreckage. Oz reached out and gave her arm a soft squeeze.

"Well, you know we've been chasing down leads on the surviving slayers since Vi turned up in Sunnydale. But there hasn't been much to go on. The network that kept an eye on the mystical world—well, that network was us, and half of us have gone into hiding. So Dawn and I contacted an order in the south of France, goat herders who developed their magical gifts during a centuries-long feud with a witch coven—sorry, Will—and they said that when the slayers were attacked in Halifax there was a ripple."

"A ripple?" Oz asked.

"Sure," said Willow. "Any time that much mystical energy is ripped from the world, an order like that would feel it. I should have felt it, if I'd been paying closer attention."

"That's what I thought they meant, too," said Xander. "But they said it was different. They said the only other time they'd detected a ripple like that was May 22. *2001.*"

Willow looked at Spike.

"What?" Oz asked. "What happened that day?"

"That was the day Buffy died," Spike said gravely. "When she fought Glory. And sacrificed herself to save the world."

"Oh," said Oz. "That day."

"Yeah," said Xander. "That day. And more importantly—or rather, not more importantly but more importantly to our current conversation—the day that Buffy sacrificed herself because Glory and her scabby minions had torn a hole. Between dimensions."

Between dimensions. Did that mean a portal? Maybe Vi's portal. Except it hadn't moved through dimensions, plural. It had only moved through one, their plain old normal dimension, from Halifax to New Sunnydale.

"Does that mean there was another portal that opened that day, big enough to cross through dimensions?"

"That's why I sent you the photo. We need your portal expert to take a look. Check the area around the main building in the center of the blast site."

Spike looked at them across the counter. "But if it does mean that, then Buffy and the others are alive."

"Maybe. Depending on what dimension they were sucked into."

Spike scoffed. "They're slayers. They can handle any hell beast a world throws at them."

Willow leaned over the image and used her fingers to zoom close. Around the wreckage of the main building was a secondary circle. Much larger than the char mark left by Vi's portal to New Sunnydale. It was hard to see, faded, and not so much a burn as a whisper in the dirt. But there was a definite circle, and she thought

48

she could make out texture along the edges. Sigmund would be able to tell them more.

"We didn't even notice at first," said Xander. "Not until we zoomed out. Dawn was searching for traces of anything or anyone who might have entered the compound. She was Google Earthing and that's when she spotted the circle. From the satellite view."

"Clever Niblet," said Spike.

"Looks like we've got another portal mystery to solve," said Oz. "And . . . dimensions to search? That can't be easy."

"Definitely not easy," said Xander. "I figured it was even beyond your scope, Willow."

"You got that right. Unless you have a room full of black-magic books I can suck dry. Then we're talking."

"Probably not a good idea," he replied, and she heard the grin in his voice. "I'm half a world away and wouldn't be there to hug the evil out of you. But we have another plan. I'm sending you a demon oracle."

There was a knock at the door, and the three of them startled upright.

"What, like right now?"

"Pretty much."

"I'll go . . . let them in." Oz rounded the counter and went to the door.

"Xander, who is this person Oz is about to let into my house?"

"Not a person, Will. A demon."

"What kind of demon? This isn't like Beljoxa's Eye. . . ."

Willow looked at Oz, and he paused with his hand on the doorknob. "Xander, if I open this door to find a big bunch of eyes, I won't be happy."

"It's not Beljoxa's Eye. I don't even know how to find that thing."

Oz opened the door. The demon standing on the doorstep

looked extremely human beneath her white silk blouse and tan slacks. Except that her skin was blue and covered in silver starbursts.

She moved past Oz as if he wasn't there, and completely ignored Spike. She was fixated on Willow, and the intensity of her eye contact was a little uncomfortable.

"Willow Rosenberg," the demon said. "I felt you once." She cocked her head. "You're less now." She righted and smiled. "But you still crackle."

"She still crackles AND pops," said Xander. Willow raised a brow at the phone, and he coughed and said, "Sorry."

"Um . . ." Willow edged away from the demon. "Why did you send her to *us*?"

"She said that to track the slayers through dimensions, she needed to be close to the slayer power."

"And that is you," the demon said.

Oz returned to the counter. "Don't you mean 'that is her daughter'?" he asked.

"Yeah," said Spike. "It's Frankie's the slayer, not this one."

"I mean that is you," the demon replied, continuing to speak only to Willow. "You are the gate through which the slayer's power flows." She gestured with her hands, like a water through a river, power flowing from one blue palm to the other and back again. "From you to her and back again."

"Back again?" Willow asked.

"Back again, if you so choose."

"What does that mean?"

The demon shrugged.

"Gotta love oracles," said Spike.

The demon stared at Willow. She reached up and touched a small, swirling silver star just below her own left eye. "On the date of the attack on the slayers, the dimensions opened and a great deal of power was sucked out. They have opened again since. Many times. Small tears only, but even those are not without risk. Not without consequence. It is as if someone has forgotten what a grave thing it is to slice interdimensional holes in the first place."

Willow leaned back. On the phone, Xander was silent. That was a lot of dimensional info to get in one paragraph.

"One big hole," Willow repeated. "And a great deal of power sucked through."

"Sounds like a bunch of slayers sucked through," said Oz.

"What about the small rips? Does that mean they're alive? Could they be trying to find their way home?" Xander asked.

The oracle was silent. She stared. Her eyes grew wider. And wider. Larger and larger until they had stretched to take up half her face, the pupils and irises gone and replaced with whorls of spinning silver.

"Xander," said Spike. "Something's happening here."

"You're gonna have to be more specific, dumbass. I'm on the phone."

"The oracle's eyes . . . they're—"

The oracle's eyes shot out on long stalks and attached themselves to Willow's temples. Willow jerked, her whole body stiffening as the oracle's current ran through her.

"The oracle's attached to Will." Willow heard Oz bound across the kitchen, and then the sound of a blade being drawn from the carving block. "What do I do, Xander?"

"Just wait, let it go," Xander cried.

"For. How. Long?" Willow asked through clenched teeth. It wasn't necessarily bad, the sensation. But it was powerful, strong enough to hold her frozen. And then the demon released her, eyes reeling back into her head and shrinking down to normal size. The demon blinked, and the silver in them disappeared, flowing onto her cheeks like tears, if tears could move under the skin.

Oz set the chef's knife down on the counter. "You know, a warning would have been nice," he said to Xander.

"Why did you do that?" Willow asked the oracle. She felt up and down her arms and flexed her fingers. She felt fine. A little weird maybe. And she kind of wanted to teleport the oracle's blue-and-silver ass right into the upper atmosphere.

"The darkness is coming," the oracle said simply. She looked at Willow. "For you."

They paused, and the oracle took a light breath and turned to leave.

"The darkness is coming," said Xander. "This isn't like 'from beneath you, it devours,' is it? Because that started with a big worm and ended with a Spikesplosion."

"I thought the Spikesplosion was your favorite part," said Oz, and raised an eyebrow at the vampire.

"Guys, not now." Willow hurried after the oracle. "Wait! What is the darkness? Why is it coming for me?"

The oracle, still headed for the door, apparently decided to forego human appearances and simply disappeared. The air she left in her wake briefly sparkled, and she left a smell like burnt sugar.

"Great." Willow turned back to Oz and Spike, and Xander on the phone. "So I guess let's round up the Scoobies."

PART TWO

THE DARKNESS IS COMING

CHAPTER SIX

HOPE, FEAR, AND RE-HOPE

"'The darkness is coming'?" Hailey asked. "What does that mean?"

"We don't know," said Spike. "It was an oracle. They're always annoyingly vague."

"But she did say there was a portal. And that means that Buffy's alive, right? Doesn't it?" Frankie sat on the arm of their sofa, her knees pulled up to her chest. She was trying very hard not to get too excited, and not to panic, and not to overwhelm them with questions to which they obviously didn't have answers to yet. But that didn't stop her from wondering.

Who had sucked them through the portal? Had they done it themselves, to escape the attack? Were they stranded? Were they captives? Was Andrew with them? Because if so, he had to be driving Buffy up a wall.

Around her, the other Scoobies sat quietly, gathered in the Rosenberg living room, where Frankie's mom filled them in on the news while standing before the coffee table. Sigmund was the epitome of good posture in the armchair even with Hailey half draped over his shoulders, and Jake sat on the couch with Spike, both of them models of deep thought, leaning forward with their elbows on their knees.

"Christ," Spike said. "She's been alive this whole time."

"We hope so," said Willow. "We don't know for sure."

"Alive," Spike said again, apparently having made up his mind. "Alive and trapped in god-knows-what and facing god-knows-where."

Jake squinted slightly when Spike misspoke, but Frankie subtly shook her head. Spike was upset. And he wasn't exactly an orator under the best of circumstances. Sigmund took his laptop out and set it on the coffee table. Within moments, he was studying the satellite image of the blast site, enhancing it and blowing it up and staring at it with a very Sigmund-like intensity.

"I'm ashamed of myself," he said finally. "I was there. I portaled in—I walked right through it! And I didn't see . . ." He shook his head.

"Everybody missed it, Sig," said Hailey quietly.

"But I'm the expert."

"There's no blame here, Sigmund," said Oz.

"Of course not." Willow reached out as if to touch Sigmund's shoulder, but she was too far away. "That's not why we asked you to take a look. We just needed you to confirm it."

"We needed your expertise," Frankie agreed. "Which you have absolutely provided. But, Mom, what about the darkness? 'The darkness is coming.' What does that mean?"

"I don't know, sweetie. The oracle wasn't terribly forthcoming. And she was kind of handsy."

"Don't you mean 'eyesy'?" said Oz.

"Huh?" asked Jake.

"Could this darkness be what killed Gustavo at school?" Hailey asked.

"I don't know," Willow replied. "Maybe the start of it."

Frankie got up from the arm of the sofa and went to put on her jacket, which was hanging in the entryway. "Well, if it is, then I need to be out there."

"Is that safe? We don't know much of anything. . . ." Willow looked to Spike for agreement, but the Watcher was once again not watching.

"That's the idea," Frankie said. "If it's coming for us, or if it's here, I'd rather not wait. Maybe if we get to it sooner, we can stop it when it's weak."

"Like a little baby darkness?" Jake stood up and stretched. Then he yawned. "Sounds good to me. I'm up for a late-night prowl." Except he clearly wasn't. He was exhausted and would only slow her down.

"You're up for a late-night burrito and then a face into your pillow," Frankie ordered. "I'm going alone. Everyone else just . . . be glad about what the oracle said. Be glad about Buffy, and the others."

"But we don't *know*," Jake said. "Not for sure."

Frankie looked at her mom. "Does it feel like they're alive? Did what the oracle said about the power that was sucked through the portal—did it make sense?"

"It does," said Willow. "And it feels like they are. But I don't know if that's a Wicca feeling or an I-hope-my-friend's-not-dead feeling."

"It doesn't matter," said Frankie. "We're going to operate like they are alive until we're proven wrong. We're going to try to save them. Aren't we?"

Spike snorted and heaved himself up from the couch. He swept past them straight into the kitchen and straight into the liquor cabinet to grab the biggest bottle he could find.

"Spike?" Hailey asked.

"I need a drink," he snapped, and headed for the backyard.

"I don't have the heart to tell him he grabbed the schnapps," said Oz.

"Mom," Frankie said, and gestured after Spike. "Go after him."

"Me? Why?"

"Because you're friends. You've been friends since you were practically my age."

"I *knew* him when I was practically your age," Willow corrected. "We weren't 'friends.' He was literally trying to kill us." But Frankie gave her the sternest eye she had, and Willow groaned. "Fine. Fine, I'll go."

"I'll walk Sigmund home," said Hailey, but Oz grabbed his keys.

"We'll drive you. Stop for burritos on the way."

$$☽ ☽ ○ ☾ ☾$$

Willow found Spike standing at the edge of her patio, staring up at the stars, his shoulders slumped in a black sweater that was a little too large for him. "Hey," she said. "You okay?" When he didn't respond, she asked again, this time inside his head.

If you don't feel like talking, we can always converse telepathically.

Spike snorted. "It would be a one-sided conversation." He gestured to his temple. "Vampiric thoughts, remember? They cast no reflection."

"Okay, then. Use your words." She went to stand beside him and crossed her arms, looking up at those same stars. It didn't take a genius to know what he was thinking: that he'd like to punch a hole through them all the way to Buffy. She knew that because part of her was thinking the same thing.

"Strange how even after all these years the first thing I want to do is run off and save her," he said. "Especially considering that she never wanted me to and never needed saving. I know it's pathetic. But she's . . ."

"I know what she is," Willow said. "She's that to me, too." Spike looked at her. "Well, she's not THAT to me, but . . . Buffy's my best friend. She's my person."

He looked back up at the stars. "She's a lot of people's person, I suppose."

"Yeah, but you and I are different. If you charged across dimensions to bring her back, you don't think she'd be happy to see you? You can't . . . charge across dimensions, just to be clear—"

"I know, Red. I just wish—" He sighed. "But then, you know what they say about wishes."

Willow nodded. "Poop in one hand and see what fills up faster."

"No. I meant the one about the horses."

"Oh. Right." She leaned in and nudged him with her shoulder. "The important thing is, there's hope now. We have hope again. We have re-hope."

"Feels wrong to hope," he said. "Feels like we're gluttons for punishment. Which I always was when it came to her."

"You really were," Willow teased. "Don't you think it's time you moved on? Find some nice, terrible woman who would stoop to dating you?"

"Hey." He gave her a look. A slightly too observant look, in her opinion. "I'm not the only one stuck in the love land time forgot. When are you going to find yourself a proper lady? Stop holding yourself back?"

Willow crossed her arms.

"I'm a little bit busy, if you haven't noticed."

"Doing what?"

"Working full-time . . . raising the next savior of the world!"

"Please. I know what's holding you back, and it's Oz."

Willow opened her mouth. Then she quickly closed it again for fear that what came out would be some kind of wicked witchy hex. "Why are you like this? You know I'm gay, and I shouldn't have to keep on telling you!"

Spike made a face. "I know that. I'm not that thick. But also, there's a spectrum, right? And the way I see it, seems that first loves might always be somewhere on it." He leaned against the wooden beam that supported the rear awning, and she almost magicked him onto his back. She narrowed her eyes.

"How do you know about the spectrum?"

"You're the one who planted me in a library with books and computers for eight bloody hours a day." He adjusted his sweater like a bird ruffling its feathers. "I also have a Discord server.

"But look, Red, spectrum aside, there's feelings there that you haven't bothered to work out. Even if they're not romantic feelings. And you're tiptoeing around them. So is he, for that matter—he hasn't been with anyone since he's been back in town, has he?"

"No, but he's been with people before, and so have I. *Lots of them.*"

"But not when you were in the same town. Right in each other's faces. You and Oz need to have the talk that you should have had the moment he moved in with Jake."

"We don't need to have that! We're friends. We're just friends."

"You're not just friends," Spike said, and snorted. "You're not romantic, but you're not just friends. And until you figure out what it is that you really are, you're not going to be settled. Neither of you

60

is going to be able to relax and be the things that you are. Which is not 'just friends.'"

She let her arms fall to her sides. It was a conversation she dreaded having—something she'd hoped they could keep forever at arm's length. She didn't want to lose Oz. But to keep him, she had to make sure they were okay. In the same place. Spike was right. Spike, of all people. Willow's face scrunched, and she made a sound she had never made before, like a wounded muskrat or a puppy that just really didn't want to do anything.

"You're a right mess," Spike said happily. "Makes me feel all warm and better about myself."

"Shut up, or we'll go back to mooning over Buffy." She put her face into her hands. "What if he does have feelings? Or . . . tiny secret hopes of feelings? When I can't return those, he might— I don't want to hurt Oz. And I don't want him to go away."

"You really think he would do that?" Spike asked quietly. "Just stop being a baby about it and go get your house in order."

"Okay, okay." She gave the vampire a shove. "Stop being insightful. Your old face is making you seem wise. It's misleading."

"That's not funny." He opened the bottle and took a long pull before coughing and spitting most of it all over the patio. "Peach schnapps?" Then he shrugged and took another drink and passed her the bottle.

"Why not?" Willow sighed. The schnapps was cloyingly sweet and weak. Not a drink for courage. Not a drink to fortify her against what was to come: demons and dead students, and darkness sweeping across New Sunnydale like a black blanket.

CHAPTER SEVEN
SCHOOL'S OUT FOR MURDER

The next day at school, Frankie arrived to find that there was . . . no school. Students were pooled in the quad and in the parking lots, milling around and whispering. A few were weeping, but most seemed curiously wary. Sunnydale High didn't just close. Not for demon attacks that caused people to wash off their hands and faces, and not for one dead body that hadn't even been found on school grounds.

"Jake!" Frankie jumped up and waved over the crowd, and Jake pushed toward her along with Sam Han, the goalie of the lacrosse team.

"Hey, Frankie," said Sam, and Frankie forced a smile. It wasn't that she was unhappy to see Sam; it was practically impossible to be unhappy to see Sam—the boy was a sweetheart and almost as easy on the eyes as Sigmund, but she'd rather they be a Scooby-only zone. So they could talk.

"What's going on?"

"They found another body," said Jake, and when he realized that sounded like he knew too much, coughed and added, "I mean, like, two bodies. One out past the field and another one in the locker room."

Another one, Frankie thought. "Do they know . . . ?" She glanced at Sam. "What do they know?"

"Almost nothing," Sam said. "The information is not flowing freely." He looked over his shoulder, where school security had set up a barrier. Already the New Sunnydale police had started to arrive. Frankie didn't have much time.

"Do they know who it was?" she asked.

"Charlie Baylor."

Frankie cast Jake and Sam a blank look. Charlie Baylor. Why didn't she know anyone? "Wait," she said, remembering. "Wasn't Charlie Baylor on the swim team?" She flashed back to Gustavo's body in the woods, and his sweatshirt: It had been a New Sunnydale Razorbacks Swimming sweatshirt. "They were both on the swim team."

"And both seniors," said Jake, and shook his head.

"Wait, how do you guys know that?" Sam asked. But there was no need to answer, since Hailey, Sigmund, and Spike arrived at just the right moment, shouldering through students.

"Sorry we're late," said Spike. "Got trapped in the library. They said I had to take some students in there and 'keep them calm' until they decided whether or not to release them or resume classes." He noticed Sam. "Hey, you're not—"

"Normally in the library," Frankie interjected. "But you remember Sam, don't you? He's the goalie on Jake's team."

"Hi, Mr. Pratt." Sam put a hand up in greeting. "I was the one you wouldn't let join your D&D campaign last semester."

Spike narrowed his eyes. "Whatever you say. But don't we have some Dungeoning and Dragoning to do right about now?" He looked at Frankie and Hailey, eyebrow raised.

"We do," Hailey agreed. "My mage is totally stranded."

"You mean 'wizard,' right?" Sam cocked his head. "Or are you playing some rogue version with mages?"

"I totally meant wizard," said Hailey. "Mage is . . . just her nickname. Marjoretta Delphine Marjoram." She glanced at Frankie and bugged her eyes. "Mage."

"You guys are really into D&D," said Sam. "I wish you'd let me join sometime. But, Jake"—he nudged Jake with his shoulder—"are you in on this? Or do you want to go grab breakfast burritos from El Balcón?" He smiled charmingly. "I don't think we're going in that school today."

"Yeah." Jake clapped Sam on the shoulder and nodded to Frankie. "I'm starving."

"You just had a burrito last night," Sigmund observed.

"Breakfast burrito. Totally different thing." As Jake and Sam steered each other away, Sam gave Frankie a happy look over Jake's shoulder. Hailey stepped closer and watched them go with a puzzled expression.

"Was Sam just flirting with Jake?" she asked.

"Probably," said Frankie. "Sam flirts with everyone. Well. Except me," she added, and Sigmund smiled at her kindly.

"Wait, is Sam bi?"

"I think he's pan, actually," Spike supplied. "But he's only out at school, so if you see his parents hanging about, *be cool.*"

Frankie, Hailey, and Sigmund turned to the vampire and blinked.

"What?" he asked.

"How do you know what pan is?" Hailey asked suspiciously. "And how do you know anything about Sam?"

Spike pursed his lips. "Well—you bloody stuck me in a library! And the boy just bloody said so to someone two days ago right in bloody front of me—" He threw his hand up in Sam's direction. "It was like I wasn't even there. Does tweed make you invisible?"

"To students, apparently," said Sigmund, apologetic.

"All right," Frankie said as her Watcher quietly fumed. "We can talk about Spike's eavesdropping etiquette later. Right now: How do I get in there and get a look at that body?"

Hailey craned her neck back to watch the progress of the very casually paced New Sunnydale police force. "Whatever we do, we have to do it before the SPD gets set up. They might not be fazed by the sight of sliced-up teenagers, but they're still not going to let us go poking around behind the yellow tape."

Frankie stood on her toes and looked at the school. "Then let's go now. It's probably only Kenny the security guy back there, and I can get by him. But I'll still need a diversion."

"I got you," said Hailey.

Spike studied the gathered students. They were dispersing already, figuring like Sam did that school would indeed not be back in session. "The other boy was found near a culvert, so I'm going to check the sewers and see if I can track our beastie. Sigmund, you check around the building and see if you can find anywhere it might have gotten in if it didn't use the sewers."

"Is that safe?" Sigmund asked.

"He's right," said Frankie. "You two stick together. Nobody goes alone anywhere until I get this thing."

Spike frowned but nodded in agreement. "Don't slow me down," he said to Sigmund. "And prepare to need a new pair of shoes. Everyone reconvene at the Rosenberg house later."

They took off in separate directions, and Frankie and Hailey made their way inside the school. It wasn't hard to avoid the barriers—they'd been lazily set up and there wasn't enough security and faculty to man them—so they were able to use the hallway that ran between the chemistry labs and the cafeteria to bypass most of the traffic. But the hallway in front of the locker room was jammed. Not just Kenny the security guy, but also the principal, Ms. Jacobs, and Mrs. Rawson, Frankie's very sensible ninth-grade math teacher.

"Crap. What are we going to do?"

"Don't worry," said Hailey. "I got this." She took a deep breath, and then another, and another, like she was trying to hyperventilate. Then she let out a devastating cry and charged out from around the corner.

"Stop! You can't go in there!"

The principal put up her hands, and Kenny for some reason put his hand on his belt, like he was about to deploy pepper spray. But Hailey ran toward them undeterred.

"Charlie!" she moaned. "It's not true! Charlie!" They caught her, but she kicked up such a fuss that it took all three of them to hold her back, and Frankie slipped past on quiet feet, straight into the locker room. Though she could have gone by stomping or doing jumping jacks the way Hailey was carrying on. "We were going to go to PROOOMMM . . ." she heard Hailey wail.

Inside the locker room was quiet—warm and humid, like swimming locker rooms often were. She crept slowly past the rows of lockers, the soles of her sneakers getting wet and threatening to squeak. Her slayer senses were on high alert, muscles taut as bowstrings. But her stomach was full of wobbles. She'd seen death now, and plenty of it. But it was never easy knowing she was going to find someone she was too late for.

Charlie Baylor had died in a worse way than Gustavo Fuentes. There was no broken neck for him. He'd been slashed so many times and by so many claws it looked like he'd been run over by a lawn mower. Frankie frowned and resisted the urge to shut her eyes. She resisted the urge to shut his, too: sightless and staring at the bland white ceiling. She knelt to look at the cuts but knew they would be the same as the ones raked across Gustavo's chest. Deep and wide in sets of four. There was the occasional fifth slash, but it was lighter and from a slightly different angle. Like from a thumb? That didn't help much. Lots of demons had thumbs. Still, she would take pictures of everything for Sigmund and see what he could find.

Frankie sighed. It smelled like chlorine in there, thankfully not like blood, or death, but underneath she detected that faint, salty fishiness. It was impossible to tell how long after Gustavo was killed that Charlie had been attacked; his hair was dry now, but she guessed it was wet when he died. He was probably doing a few laps after school when the pool was free. She looked up. All the locker doors lay open, or torn off and hanging, damaged in the struggle.

"All of them open? That's odd." Frankie stood and walked from locker to locker.

They hadn't been damaged in the struggle. They'd been looted. Searched through, the contents messed with and slashed. She had no way of telling what was missing, but after checking every locker she was unable to find a single piece of New Sunnydale swim gear or sweatshirts. She put her hands on her hips.

"What the hell does a demon want with Razorback merchandise?"

CHAPTER EIGHT

NO ONE LIKES SURPRISE HOUSEGUESTS

"So now everyone thinks you wanted to go to the prom with Charlie Baylor." Sigmund and Hailey walked together arm in arm through the streets of downtown Sunnydale, heading toward the bookshop and the apartment Sigmund lived in right above it. After the principal and the math teacher had let her go, feeling she was sufficiently calm, Hailey had texted Sigmund and saved him from the rigors and shoe hazards of sewer patrol.

"So what? It was a good diversion, and I really sold it. I was so distraught that Kenny almost pepper-sprayed me."

Sigmund chuckled. "Perhaps we should start a petition to get him some supplementary training."

"And besides," Hailey said, "you can't be jealous of Charlie Baylor. He died. And if going to prom with him would bring him back, we would ALL go to prom with him."

"We would. I wonder what Frankie found. And I hope she remembered to take photos."

Hailey winced. It was part of the gig, she knew. The slayer gig.

Vi had played CSI plenty of times in her career, too. But Hailey had never known any of those people. She'd never gone to school with them—well, except that one time—and she hadn't glimpsed them in the halls, flashing charming smiles and laughing with their friends. Gustavo and Charlie. She hadn't known their names before, and now she'd like to say she'd never forget them. But in Sunnydale, who knew? Names of victims stacked up and shuffled together like cards in a deck.

"Frankie and Spike will be patrolling for a while," she said. "So, what do you want to do?"

Sigmund smiled, and she felt her pulse jump. All of a sudden, the feel of his skin touching the soft part of her arm took on another meaning. He never used his charm mojo on her—he never needed to—but sometimes she wondered what would happen if he did. She liked him so much anyway, she literally shivered every time he walked into a room. If he added the charm on top of that, her head might just pop right off.

As it was, the minute they were behind the bookstore and up the stairs, they were all over each other.

"This isn't too wrong, is it?" she whispered between kisses. "Making out after two people just died?"

"I've heard a lot of people do this after funerals," Sigmund replied. "It's a reaffirmation of life, or something." He kissed her lips again, and her neck, and her ear. "Besides, if no one made out in Sunnydale after someone died, then no one would ever make out."

Hailey smiled. "Open the door."

"I'm trying." Sigmund smiled back. "We're pressed against the keyhole."

They giggled and kissed some more, and Hailey made a game

of blocking the lock, challenging Sigmund to take his hands off her long enough to open the door. Things were nice enough anyway, right there on the landing. Maybe they didn't need to go in at all.

But they did, when the door opened from inside and they fell into Sigmund's apartment.

"It wasn't even locked?" Hailey asked from on top of him. Then she looked up and saw a very intense pair of legs, in a very intense pair of dark red heels.

"Mom?" Sigmund squeaked.

"Mom?" Hailey echoed. She sat up and looked at the woman standing in front of them, her arms crossed and her head cocked, with a very unamused expression on her face. "Oh my god." Hailey scrambled up and off Sigmund and smoothed her clothes. She was wearing black pants, a tight black suit vest, and a long-sleeved black shirt underneath, capped with a lot of silver lockets. She'd never been so glad it was February, so she wasn't in a crop top or a short skirt and knee boots.

"Mom," Sigmund said again as he got up off the floor. "What are you doing here?"

The woman in front of her—the *demon* in front of her—continued to fix Hailey with an icy stare. She had Sigmund's same deep brown skin and his same intelligent eyes. But she was distinctly more frightening. Even if Hailey hadn't known she was a demon, she still would have considered running away. Which was what she considered doing now. The door was open behind her. She could just spin and go.

"I came to see my son," the demon said. Sigmund went to her, and she presented her cheek to be kissed. "I told you I was coming."

"Yes, but you didn't say you were coming today." Sigmund kissed her and turned to Hailey apologetically. "Hailey, this is my mother, Sarafina DeWitt." Sarafina cast him a sharp look, and he cleared his throat and mumbled, "The Great."

"Mrs. DeWitt," Hailey said when she found her voice. "It's . . . it's really nice to meet you!"

"It's *Ms.* DeWitt," she replied. "But you may call me Sarafina."

"Not, the Great?" Hailey asked, and received the same sharp look that Sigmund had gotten. First impressions. They were important, right? She flashed a quick smile as the room began to spin.

"You should have called," Sigmund said. "I would have picked you up from the airport."

"The opportunity arose for a flight," Sarafina said. "I didn't think my son would object to my arrival. Of course I didn't expect to come to his apartment and find him . . . with a young woman." She looked at Hailey. "You must be the Hailey I've heard so much about."

Sigmund cleared his throat. "Apologies, Mother. This is Hailey Larsson."

Hailey noticed that he didn't say, this is Hailey Larsson, my girlfriend. Just her name. No fancy or impressive embellishments, like *Hailey Larsson, demonologist*, or *Hailey Larsson, ally of the slayer*. And those things were true, weren't they? Or almost. She might not be Hailey "the Great," but she was more than just Hailey.

"It's nice to make your acquaintance," said Sarafina. She glanced at the floor, where they'd just been lying, and Hailey's stomach dropped thinking about what she must have heard through the door. "Even if it is . . . a surprise."

An unwelcome surprise, by the sound of it. But there was nothing to do about that now. Hailey looked at Sigmund quickly, making sure there was no hint of lip gloss on his lips or neck, and did a mental check of the apartment, wondering what terrible things she had left there for his mother to disapprove of. She had never met any of her boyfriends' families before. There simply hadn't been time, and also she hadn't cared. But she did care about Sigmund, and her usually calm and cool exterior was melting by the minute. She had to do something to turn this meeting around.

Sarafina walked into the living room just off the kitchen and stood in the center, looking at the walls, at the shelves of Sigmund's books, and the embarrassing posters of vampire movies that Hailey had gotten him as a joke. *The Lost Boys. Fright Night. Underworld: Blood Wars*—that one was particularly funny. Now they stared back at her, mocking her with their fangs.

"So you just got here," Hailey said, and went into the kitchen.

"I did. I arrived at Sigmund's apartment less than an hour ago."

Hailey pulled a knife out of a drawer and pointed it at her lazily, ignoring Sigmund's horrified eyes. "So, you're sure you didn't stop by the school first and filet a couple of seniors from the swim team, then?" She sighed. "Dammit. We could've really used a lead."

Sarafina DeWitt stared past the knife to look directly into Hailey's eyes. Then she threw her head back and laughed. "I like this one," she said, and turned to Sigmund, so she didn't see Hailey's knees nearly buckle from relief.

☽ ☽ ○ ☾ ☾

Following her investigation of the locker room, Frankie returned to her house to find her mom and Spike were already there. Spike was seated at their kitchen counter, smelling a little like a sewer and nursing a mug of blood while Willow made a nervous brunch to keep herself busy, flipping pancakes and stacking them in the oven to keep warm, whipping up a fast hollandaise, and frying bacon to mask the aroma drifting up from Spike's boots.

"Mom? You're home already?"

"I took the day off when I heard about the second body," Willow replied. "It's okay; I had some things I could do remotely."

Frankie went into the kitchen and took the chair beside her Watcher; after a quick sniff, she changed her mind and switched to the chair on the end. "The 'body' was Charlie Baylor. A senior on the swim team."

"I'm sorry, sweetie. Did you know him?"

Frankie shook her head. She hadn't known either of them. She should be glad about that, she supposed, because it made their loss less personal. It sucked, but it didn't hurt. Yet she wished she had known them, because now she would never have the chance, and it felt like she'd missed out on something. "I got pictures for Sigmund." She took out her phone and set it on the counter as her mom slid across a plate piled high with eggs, a short stack, and hollandaise on the side.

"Could I get another pancake?" Spike asked. "With the little chocolate chips?"

"Sure." Willow went to the baking cupboard and came back with a bag. She poured batter and sprinkled chips in, then tossed the bag onto the counter so Spike could pick out pieces of chocolate, arranging them into tiny rows beside his blood mug.

"Did you find anything in the sewers?" Frankie asked.

"I found not a thing anywhere. And I followed those pipes almost all the way to the ocean. What about you, Mini Red?"

Frankie shrugged. Her stomach rumbled, and she forked some eggs into her mouth without really tasting them. "It was like with Gustavo but worse. More cuts. A harder beating." She unlocked her phone and opened the camera roll so Spike and Willow could look.

"That's a lot of slashes," the vampire noted. "Maybe this lad was attacked by more than one demon."

"Great, there's more than one," Willow said sarcastically, and set down Spike's chocolate-chip pancake.

"The place was ransacked, too. Like they were looking for something. Or stealing something. Just like that one came back for Gustavo's swimming sweatshirt. But what could they want with it?"

"There has to be a connection," Willow said. She set down her own plate but mostly pushed the food around on it. "Two boys on the same team—it can't be a coincidence. Maybe someone was jealous? Maybe they were getting too good and one of their rivals conjured something? Can Jake ask around and find out if anyone had a problem with them?"

"And hopefully Sigmund will be able to narrow our search based on these claw marks," said Spike. "Speaking of Sigmund, where is he? He's missing most of the meeting."

"He and Hailey probably stopped off to . . . you know." Frankie shrugged, and her mom's brow knit.

"I have to monitor that," Willow said. "I'm not her legal guardian, but I am the adult in this house. There should be boundaries. Right?" She looked at the vampire.

"Hailey does what she wants." Spike shrugged. "Just like her sister did. Besides, how important is it really? We live in a town with its very own hellmouth, and we're supposed to be worried that she's spending too much time with her boyfriend?" He shook his finger and mimed a scolding. "Hailey, I know you may die at any point, but you'd better not be having the sex!" He scoffed and picked up his mug of blood. "Bollocks. And if you're concerned about safety, don't. She's with Sigmund. That lad practically *is* a condom."

Frankie nearly choked on her pancakes. "Okay, okay, please stop talking," she said. "I'll text her." She picked up her phone and fired off a quick text: *Where are you? The witch and the Watcher are about to ground you.* Then she set it down and went back to her pancakes, waiting patiently for it to buzz. She didn't start to worry until a few minutes had gone by. And then a few minutes more. She picked her phone back up and refreshed the text thread.

And just then, Hailey and Sigmund walked through the door.

"Sorry." Hailey held up her phone. "I got your texts, but we were almost here, so . . ." She looked at Frankie, then at Spike and Willow. Then she looked at Sigmund, and they both stepped aside to reveal one of the most attractive women Frankie had ever seen. She was tall and broad-shouldered, dressed casually in beige slacks and a dark green blouse. The curls of her dark brown hair were loose and hung just past her shoulders. And she looked a lot like Sigmund.

"Sarafina!" Willow exclaimed.

"Sarafina?" Frankie looked from the woman to her mom and back again. This was Sarafina DeWitt? Sigmund's mom and her own mom's old flame? She was so gorgeous Frankie had to resist the urge to give her mom a high five. Not that Willow would have accepted it. That was highly inappropriate, and Willow seemed to have forgotten Frankie even existed. She just kept touching her hair (which looked just fine) and tugging at her soft blue sweater like tugging could suddenly make it less blue and fuzzy.

"Willow Rosenberg." Sarafina swept into the kitchen; Frankie stood up straighter when she passed, and Spike wobbled halfway off his chair, mouth slightly agape. "The great witch." She and Willow embraced, and Frankie noticed the way their fingers lingered around each other's waists. "Did you receive my gift?"

"The volume on herbaries," Willow said. "It was so thoughtful of you."

Sarafina turned. "Sigmund?"

"Yes, sorry." He stepped toward Spike. "Mother, this is Spike, the legendary vampire once known as William the Bloody. And now Watcher to the new slayer."

Spike's chest puffed slightly. "Legendary is right. I cut a swath of terror through Europe. But . . . I have a soul now."

"And this"—Sigmund gestured to Frankie—"is Frankie Rosenberg. Daughter of the great witch Willow, and the first ever slayer-witch."

"Hi," Frankie said.

"Everyone, I would like to introduce you to my mother, the great Sarafina DeWitt."

Hailey leaned close to Frankie and whispered through the side of her mouth, "That's how he has to introduce her *every time*."

"It's lovely to meet you all," said Sarafina. "I'm sorry for dropping in on you unexpected. I hope we're not interrupting."

"Of course you're not!" Willow waved them into the living room. "Let's all have a seat—Hailey, can you pull the sitting room curtains so Spike doesn't start on fire?—and Frankie and I will get us some refreshments." She steered Frankie back toward the kitchen and grabbed down a bamboo serving tray, then dove into the refrigerator for all of their cheeses, fruit, and the meat they kept on hand for the Osbourne werewolves. "Sorry about all the non-vegetarian items," she said, "but if I remember correctly, Sarafina likes meat to sink her teeth into. Can you . . . assemble?" Frankie went to the counter to arrange meat slices and to cut the apples and pears. Her mom was back in the refrigerator again, rooting around for a bottle of white wine. "All we have is sparkling!" She gripped it between her knees and popped the cork, making Frankie jump. Then she took her hair out of its low bun and shook it out down her back.

"Easy, Mom. She just got here."

"I'm not . . . doing anything. It's only . . . no one likes to look dowdy in front of an ex."

Frankie hid a smile. "Hey, I'm not trying to discourage you. She is definitely"—she stole a peek back into the living room—"impressive."

Hailey clomped into the kitchen and leaned into Frankie's shoulder. Then she put her head down on the counter and groaned.

"What?" Frankie asked. "Not making a good impression on Sigmund's mom?"

"I think it's fine." Hailey reached out to snake a piece of cheese. "It's just going to take a while to overcome the *first* impression, which was me fully on top of her son." Frankie snorted, and Hailey looked down at her black vest and silver jewelry. "Do you think I should change? Can I borrow some of your clothes?"

"Some of my clothes?"

"Yeah. All the moms and teachers love you."

"Please. You could never pull off my organic-cotton slaying pants," Frankie teased. She shoved the improvised charcuterie tray into Hailey's arms.

"Your daughter looks much like you," Sarafina said to Willow as she poured the wine and Frankie perched in one of their comfy chairs. "A little more balanced. And with the air of a fighter. Is she also a gifted witch?"

"I don't know about 'gifted,'" Frankie said.

"She's very gifted," Willow said proudly.

"But not gifted like you."

"Well. Who's gifted like me?"

Frankie blinked, surprised. Her mom was usually so self-deprecating when someone asked about her magic. But Sarafina smiled, and that seemed to be what Willow was after.

"She is beautiful, too," said Sarafina. "Like you are. And like all the slayers are. Beautiful, in their ways."

"I don't know about 'beautiful,'" Frankie said. But she sat up a little straighter.

"I would like to fight her." Sarafina drained her wineglass in one pull and stood.

"Say what now?" Frankie asked.

"Mom." Sigmund stood, as did Hailey and Frankie, rising cautiously from her chair.

"Only a sparring match, of course," said Sarafina. "It would be a great honor, to spar with a slayer." She turned to her son.

"Mother, please don't."

"Up," Sarafina said.

Sigmund sighed and stood. He turned to Frankie.

"Frankie the Vampire Slayer," he said formally. "Would you do us the honor of accepting the challenge extended to you?"

"You want me to fight your mom? Is this a Sage demon thing?"

"It is a very Sage demon thing," Sarafina answered for him. "Please. It is the warmest welcome you could give."

Frankie looked at her mom, but Willow was at a loss, so she turned to Spike, sending him a message telepathically to forbid it. After a moment, he sucked his cheeks in, shrugged, and said, "It's fine with me. You could use the extra practice. How about we do it in the cemetery, just after sundown?"

"Wonderful!" Sarafina declared.

"Wait—" Frankie turned to Hailey for help, but Hailey's eyes widened and she quickly shook her head. "Well . . ." She shrugged. "I guess let's text Jake and Oz, then. They won't want to miss this."

CHAPTER NINE

NICE TO MEET YOU, LET ME PUNCH YOU IN THE FACE

Frankie, Jake, Hailey, and Sigmund walked awkwardly through the cemetery, headed for the Rimbauer mausoleum, where Frankie would then engage in a sparring session with Sigmund's mom. With punching. And kicking. And possibly choke holds. And none of the adults seemed to think this was the least bit strange. Oz and Jake had met them at the entrance just after sundown, and Oz had happily joined in on the Sarafina welcome party, talking and laughing more animatedly than Frankie had seen him in . . . well, ever. He and her mom and even Spike walked companionably on ahead, chatting and pointing out items of interest.

"She's not using her charm mojo on them, is she?" Frankie asked Sigmund.

"Not at all," he replied. "She has far better control of her charm powers than I do. And she likes to say that all her charm is natural." He smiled at her, a little sheepishly.

"So, this is odd, right?" Frankie asked. "Or is it not? Does your mom always challenge your new friends to a round of fisticuffs?"

"Only the ones who are legendary fighters," he said.

"So she'll be challenging me next, right, bud?" Jake teased, and slapped him on the back.

"Yes." Sigmund grinned. "Any day now."

"Hey, um, your mom's a full demon, right?" Hailey asked. "So, didn't you say full Sage demons had horns?"

"She does. Not too large, and curved, but very sharp. They're glamoured into her hair." He bumped Hailey gently with his shoulder; in deference to his mother, they had cooled it with the PDA, which must have been hard for them. They were always touching, always with the entwined pinkies—once Frankie'd even caught them making out behind a headstone while she was fighting for her life against a feral Malicat demon with poison fins. "Hailey, are you all right? I know my mother can be a bit much."

Hailey shrugged. "She's great, actually. I just wish we'd met differently. And I wish I looked nicer. But Frankie wouldn't let me borrow any of her clothes!"

"You have to be yourself," Frankie reasoned. "What's the point in costumes?"

"And you don't have to look like Frankie to look nice," added Sigmund.

They reached the Rimbauer mausoleum, large and made of white granite, with two columns on the front face and a nice set of bronze doors. Someone had planted a creeping clematis vine on the eastern side, and it had grown most of the way up the left column. The whole thing was grand, and overly expensive, considering it housed only two sets of actual remains. Bronze plaques represented four others whose coffins had been lost in the Spikesplosion and subsequent Sunnydale collapse of 2003. Apparently, whatever Rimbauers still remained aboveground were quite wealthy, as they had purchased the surrounding plots to ensure their mausoleum stood alone. The open space would make a perfect little arena for Frankie to fight Sigmund's mom in.

Sarafina called to Sigmund, and he jogged ahead, probably to rub her shoulders and give her water that she would spit into an aluminum pail.

"I'm not really supposed to, like . . . pound on his mom, right?" Frankie whispered to Hailey. "I'm not supposed to use my full strength?"

"I think she'll be insulted if you don't," Hailey whispered back.

"But I'm not supposed to hurt her, you don't think?" She studied Sarafina's carefully done makeup and manicured nails. She looked like—well, she looked like Sigmund's mom, and the thought of trying to kick her in the face made Frankie's stomach go all wobbly.

"I don't even know if you can," Jake said as they watched Sarafina warm up. Even though she was only shadowboxing, Frankie could sense the force behind her movements. And the speed—at one point, her fists actually blurred they were moving so fast.

Frankie swallowed.

"Frankie the Vampire Slayer," Sigmund called. "Are you ready?"

"Sure, totally!" she called back. She shrugged out of her cardigan and handed it to Hailey, who had apparently taken the role as her second. Frankie gave her one last pleading, bewildered look, but Hailey only punched her lightly on the arm and said, "Go get her!"

"Great," Frankie muttered. She stepped into their makeshift arena and circled backward as Sarafina advanced, kicking off her high heels and toeing them to the side, where Willow retrieved them. *Whose side are you on?* Frankie wanted to ask as Willow said, "Be careful, sweetie!"

"Which one of us are you talking to, Mom?" Frankie said under her breath. She flexed her fists, and Sarafina crouched.

"Wait!" Frankie backed off and held up her hands. "Wait—I can't, I'm sorry. You're not only Sigmund's mom, but you're also my mom's ex-girlfriend. This is too weird."

"I understand that this is strange," Sarafina said. "I'm Sigmund's mother, and we have only just met. But do you not spar and train with many of your friends? Have you not struck your Watcher during your sessions? Have you not struck Hailey or Jake?"

"Definitely Jake. But this is . . . not the same."

Sarafina inhaled deeply through her nose. "Perhaps I can help you." She drew her fists into her chest and lowered her head. An intense, whispered chant passed through her lips. Frankie took a half step back as Sarafina threw her hands out with a fierce cry . . . and threw a double of herself into the night air.

Two Sarafinas. Identical to each other. And both began to circle her in the grass. Frankie spun around, and around again.

"How does this make it easier?"

"You will fight me," said the double. "And not me," said the original. "Though we are one and the same," both said together.

"Huh?" Frankie asked.

"It is the mirroring spell," the original Sarafina replied. "We use it to spar with ourselves. To face our own weaknesses."

Frankie stopped and looked from one of Sigmund's moms to the other.

"That is so cool!" Frankie turned to Sigmund. "Can you do it, too? Can you teach it to me?"

Both Sarafinas smiled. "Sage demon magic," said one. "Is not witch magic," said the other.

But Frankie could learn. Andrew had learned demon magics, even if he wasn't exactly great at them. She was deep in thought, considering the possibilities of multiple Frankies as Sarafina's double circled her.

"Oof!" Frankie landed facedown in the grass after a kick from the second Sarafina caught her in the back. "So, I guess we're doing this."

"Give me your best," the first Sarafina said. "Injuries inflicted on my second will not transfer to me when the spell ends. You may make me bleed. If you can." Frankie got to her feet just in time to see the grin on the second Sarafina's face, a second before she lunged with a series of punches almost too fast for Frankie to dodge.

Almost.

She dodged another flurry, and a reversal from an elbow. Sarafina was an excellent fighter. But she fought like many demons did, all might and no feint. There had already been many opportunities for Frankie to counterpunch, but she couldn't bring herself to do it. And as for making Sigmund's mom bleed? It was unthinkable.

Frankie leapt back and spun, ducked and rolled, emitting a few characteristic yips. But Sarafina didn't become frustrated. Instead, she learned, and when Frankie moved to slip what she thought was a punch, Sarafina grabbed her by the back of the neck and threw her almost to the steps of the Rimbauer mausoleum.

"Frankie!" Hailey shouted.

"Mom!" shouted Sigmund. He looked at the original Sarafina, exasperated.

"She is a slayer, my son. She can take it."

"But should she have to? She's my friend!"

"And this is how we honor our friends. By holding nothing back." Sarafina's double leapt, as if to land upon Frankie with both feet.

Frankie shouted, "Yipes!" and rolled out of the way, but not quite fast enough. The impact of Sarafina's heel on her hip did not feel good.

"All right, Ms. DeWitt," she said as she got up. "If that's the way you want it."

Frankie kicked high into Sarafina's chin and sent her flipping backward. Quickly, she turned toward the original, afraid she would wince. But the original Sarafina was grinning. "Huh. That really is the way you want it." Frankie advanced and ducked, punched and spun. She caught a kick from Sarafina in midair and knocked her down. It was actually kind of fun. Sarafina DeWitt was the best sparring partner she'd ever had. Spike pulled his punches, and with everyone else, Frankie had to pull hers. As for the vampires she'd been facing lately . . . they'd been third string at best. It was nice to really flex her muscles, to really push herself. Before long Frankie found herself smiling, too.

"Okay, but check this out." She readied her magic, preparing to use her telekinesis to knock the Sage demon right off her feet. It felt a little like cheating, but . . .

Before she got the chance to try, Frankie and Sarafina were suddenly shoved apart by a shape flying through the air to land on the grass. A distinctly six-foot-two shape, in a gray suit jacket and wild dark hair that framed his perfectly chiseled jaw.

"Grim?"

"Francesca Rosenberg," he said, and his eyes flashed bright blue. "I'm glad you're here."

"Whoa, no, this isn't what it looks like; we're not really fighting—"

But that wasn't what he'd meant. He wasn't intervening to save her from a Sage demon. He was already fighting something else. Something that filled the cemetery air with the salty smell of rotten sea. Frankie and Sarafina jumped back again as the monster hurled itself past them and onto Grim, its hulking, muscular shape covered in shiny black skin, and its webbed fingers tipped in claws that slashed and slashed. Along the top of its head were rows of sharp fins, and despite being clearly nautical, it looked perfectly comfortable on land, beating on the Hunter of Thrace.

"Grim!" Frankie dragged the demon off him and threw it into the side of the mausoleum. It bounced and regained its feet to leer at her with lidless eyes.

"No." Grimloch stood and placed a hand on Frankie's arm. "I began this hunt. And I would finish it."

"Well, if you're sure . . ." Frankie stood back and Grimloch advanced. She winced when the demon raked its claws across his chest, tearing his shirt in four shredded lines, just like the ones that had marked Gustavo.

"What is it?" Hailey shouted. She pulled on Sigmund's arm as Grimloch kicked the beast in the chest. "Come on, demonpedia! How do we kill it?"

"I don't know," Sigmund said. "I've never seen it before. It's like a demon Michael Phelps!"

Willow's eyes widened. "Hey, I know what it is! Wait!"

But if Grimloch heard, he didn't obey. He was an ancient demon, a hunter god, and he snapped the fish monster's neck in one brutal twist.

"Oh, good, Grimloch's back in town," Jake said semi-sarcastically.

Frankie and the others moved closer for a better look. She knelt and flipped the fish demon onto its back.

"Grimloch," Sarafina remarked. "The Hunter of Thrace. Sunnydale is full of fascinating residents." Frankie turned and watched as Sarafina stepped back into her own double, reabsorbing it as they made contact. Cool.

Willow knelt down on Frankie's other side and studied the demon's face. "It *is* one of them."

"One of what?" Spike asked.

"Not what. Who. One of the 1998 Sunnydale swim team."

"Huh?" asked Frankie.

"Back when Buffy and I were in high school, the swim coach turned evil and dosed the team with demonic, fish-DNA-laced steroids so they'd be better swimmers and win the state championship. Unfortunately the side effect was"—she gestured to the dead demon with the shiny black fins—"turning into an enormous fish monster."

"All to win a championship?" Hailey asked. "There needs to be a larger conversation about the pressures placed on our athletic divisions."

Willow looked up at Frankie. "This almost happened to your uncle Xander. He went undercover to find out what was happening. Also there were disturbing Speedos involved. But we never caught the monsters; the boys who turned into them escaped into the ocean."

Oz crouched down; his werewolf claws had come out in the excitement of the fray, and they skated dangerously over the surface of the dead demon's skin. "But what is he doing back here now?"

"I don't know. I always hoped they were happy and eating krill and maybe rescuing dolphins from fishing nets." Willow stood. "But they must have been what's responsible for killing those boys, and stealing their team sweatshirts. . . ."

"Memorabilia," said Jake. "I get that."

"They," Frankie said. "You said 'they.' How many ex-swimming champs are we talking about here?"

"I don't remember." Willow turned to Oz. "How many guys disappeared off the team in '98?"

"A few more than usual I guess. Four?"

"Then we can assume there are at least three more of these things." Frankie looked at the others, and then at Sarafina. "I'm sorry, Ms. DeWitt, but our spar is going to have to wait. I'm going back to the high school to stake out the swimming pool. I have a feeling our fish monsters are headed back there."

"I'll go with you," said Jake. "That way if you get caught by school security, you'll have an excuse for being somewhere sporty."

"Okay." She looked at Grimloch, maybe a few beats longer than she needed to. She couldn't really believe he was there. And what she really wanted to do was fling herself at him with a flurry of questions. But the mission called.

"Hailey, Spike, Sigmund, I need you to keep an eye on the rest of the swim team, just in case."

"You got it," said Hailey.

"Mom?"

"Yeah, sweetie?"

"Can you take care of this? Use that demon-composting spell we've been working on?"

Willow nodded. Sigmund turned to Sarafina to ask her permission, but before he could finish, she said, "Go, son. You are needed, and I can keep myself busy for tonight. I think I would very much like to see this demon-composting spell."

Frankie saw Willow smile to herself until she added, "And I would like to know more about this werewolf, and how he keeps such control of his claws."

"Hey, this couldn't be the darkness the oracle was referring to, could it?" Oz asked.

"I don't think so," Frankie replied. "This feels like your every-day, run-of-the-mill Sunnydale murder spree." She turned to Jake, and they headed for the exit, where he'd left his moped.

"Text us if you need backup!" Hailey shouted, and Frankie waved before breaking into a jog.

CHAPTER TEN

WELCOME TO OUR OOL. THERE'S NO P IN IT, BUT THERE MIGHT BE A DEMON.

B reaking into the school at night was not something Frankie
could have imagined herself doing even six months ago.
Now she slunk across the shadowy parking lot and kicked
through doors with hardly a second thought.

"I can't believe we don't have a better security system," Jake
whispered. "I mean, this school is practically brand-new."

"And we clearly have the budget," Frankie replied, not bothering to lower her voice. "But you know Sunnydale."

Jake nodded. Yeah. They both knew Sunnydale. They hurried
through the halls, the light of the growing moon and the overzeal-
ous streetlamps showing the way.

"Hey." Jake stopped and looked out into the almost-empty
parking lot. "Isn't that Sam's car?" They'd stashed Jake's moped in
the bushes out front, so they hadn't seen it when they came in.

"Maybe he got a ride home with someone else?" Frankie asked,
but Jake arched his brow doubtfully, which made him look a whole
lot like his uncle. "Well, even if he's here, I'm sure he's fine. What
would Sam be doing anywhere near the pool?"

"Good point." They walked on past the cafeteria and turned down the ramp past the administrative offices.

"But speaking of Sam," said Frankie, "he seemed a little more flirty than usual this morning."

"What do you mean?"

"Nothing. I'm just saying, he seemed a little into you. You don't want him to get hurt, when you inevitably start slavering after the next cheerleader who crosses your path."

"I do not slaver after cheerleaders."

"Please," said Frankie. "I've seen you wipe your mouth."

Jake laughed. "Anyway, it's not like that. Sam and I have known each other for a long time. He can't get hurt by me."

"If you say so," said Frankie, as Sam's distant screams rang out from down the hall. "But he can get hurt by something!"

"Sam!"

Jake and Frankie broke into a run, barreling down the hallways and shoving through doors, following the sound of Sam's cries straight through the boys' swim locker room, jumping over the flapping yellow tape. Chlorine and the salty smell of gill monster rose thick and warm to Frankie's nose.

"Sam!"

They burst into the swimming pool area and saw Sam in the pool, splashing desperately as he was dragged toward the deep end by not one but two of the gill monsters, with a third swimming menacingly nearby. Frankie raced to the edge and dove in, the cold, smelly water instantly bringing back her childhood dislike of swimming lessons, and heard Jake enter the pool not half a second later. They swam for Sam hard and fast and greeted the monsters with fists to their cold finned faces. The impact, or at least the surprise, was enough to make them let go, and Frankie gave Jake a shove.

"Go! Get him out of here!"

Jake put an arm around Sam and started to help him to the edge. "What about you?"

"I can—" *I can handle it* is what she'd started to say before she was dragged down and her words came out in muffled underwater bubbles. She started to fight, but fighting in water was hard. The resistance of the water made her slower and took a lot of the sting out of even her slayer strength. Also, the lighting was poor. Coupled with bubbles, splashes, and chlorine that stung her eyes, Frankie could barely see a thing. A finned appendage rose into view, and she kicked and jabbed half-blind. When she bobbed up for a gulp of air, she barely avoided being raked by a webbed hand full of black claws.

Out of the water, Jake got Sam to safety by the wall and grabbed the pool skimmer.

"Hey, hey, over here!" Jake shouted. "Come and get it, sushi boys!" He swung the skimmer hard and knocked two gill monsters in the side of the head.

"Thanks." Frankie coughed. She swam backward, for distance, and the monsters followed. They circled and dove and spun; they were made for speed in the water and moved through it as agilely as sharks.

"This is unfair, really," she said as a black finned head loomed up beside her, and she punched it. "You guys were champion swimmers even when you were human. I barely made it out of Guppies." She ducked another rake of claws and dragged the monster under, putting all her weight upon its back and driving it down with one knee.

As she held it under, she blinked.

"What am I doing? These guys don't drown!" She released him, and he erupted and struck her across the cheek with the back of his arm. Frankie sank below the surface, cheek smarting and head ringing from the impact as Jake hurled more nautically themed insults. Frankie rolled toward the surface and saw his legs through the stinging water, hurrying around the side of the pool.

Only those weren't Jake's legs. Jake wasn't wearing slim black boots. The figure beside the pool dropped something in, and Frankie watched it shine as it sank to the bottom.

A knife.

Frankie dove after it as she heard another splash, and a gill monster gave a sorry cry. Black blood clouded the water like ink as Frankie snatched the knife from the bottom of the pool and turned without surfacing to kick toward the fight.

They sensed her coming and met her underwater, them with claws and her with a knife. She slashed and turned to kick, still frustratingly slow in the water. The visibility was worse, too, as the pool began to fill with monster blood. She struck with the knife, hoping to hit something, and felt something knock into her arm. The knife slipped from her fingers—instinctively she reached out with her magic and pulled it back into her grip.

Frankie burst to the surface.

"Jake! Water doesn't slow down my telekinesis!"

"Uh, great!" Jake said, and gave her a frazzled thumbs-up.

She took a huge breath and dove. The blood in the water had whipped the monsters into a feeding frenzy. They had converged on their wounded friend, darting in and out, making slashes and trying to take bites out of each other, sometimes out of the sunken body of the gill monster who was already dead—it was gross, and Frankie was suddenly glad for the poor visibility.

She threw the knife underwater, toward the monsters, and used her magic to guide it like a missile, slicing and stabbing, so small and so fast that the gill creatures barely knew what was happening. She kept the knife moving as she swam in close and followed up with punches, keeping the monsters where she wanted them. The blood cloud was so dense that she couldn't see, but her magic knew where the knife was and kept it cutting. A few times she called the knife back a little close to her limbs as she treaded water and nearly cut herself, but it didn't take long before the monsters were dead, drifting to the bottom.

Frankie resurfaced and swam to the edge, where Jake helped her onto the red-and-white-speckled tile. "They're going to need to drain the pool," she said, a little breathless. "Also, 'sushi boys'?"

Jake grinned. "Well, I guess since they graduated with your mom, I should have said 'old sushi men.'"

"Oh my god," Sam cried. "What were those things?"

Frankie and Jake turned to him with wide eyes. They'd almost forgotten he was there. Poor Sam, terrified and soaked, pointing into the deep end at his submerged and very inhuman attackers.

"Uh . . ." Jake stammered.

"Escapees from New Sunnydale Aquarium," Frankie said. "A deep-sea species they were looking to put on exhibit." She raised her eyebrows and waited tensely. It was a terrible cover story; he was never going to buy it—

"Oh," Sam said. "Well, I guess they won't be going on exhibit now." He laughed a weak and frightened laugh. Good old Sunnydale, where people were always ready to believe any non-supernatural explanation you threw at them. Frankie wondered if that was some kind of enchantment. Maybe Mayor Wilkins had cast it when he founded the town.

Sam reached out to tug Jake close. "Good thing you found me, Cap. I was lifting late in the weight room and thought I'd come pay my respects to Charlie. But I do *not* know how to swim. I mean, beyond the doggy paddle."

"Doggy paddles are good," said Jake. "You sure you're okay?"

He put his hands on Sam's shoulders and felt them for injuries, then quickly drew back and coughed awkwardly.

"Yeah," Sam said, undeterred. He tugged Jake close again to lean on him. "I'm okay."

Jake gave another cough and kind of shuffled his feet. Frankie was about to ask him if he swallowed too much of the pool when they heard the sound of someone climbing out of it. They turned back to see the person who had given her the knife, and for the second time that night, Frankie couldn't believe her eyes.

First Grimloch appears, and now Vi.

"Vi?"

Vi Larsson smiled, her dyed-black hair slicked down by the water. She wore slim jeans and a formfitting hoodie, all dark, too, though maybe that was just because they were soaked. "Hello again," she said. "Sorry to butt in, but it looked like you could use that."

"Yeah." Frankie stared at the other slayer, whom they'd been searching for since fall. She supposed she ought to give the knife back, but for some reason, she held it tighter. "So you're back. Again."

"You know Sunnydale." Vi chuckled. "Just when you think you're out . . ."

Frankie and Jake glanced at each other.

"Have you seen Hailey?" Frankie asked.

"She's my next stop. I thought you would know where to find her."

$$) \;) \; \bigcirc \; (\; ($$

They got Sam safely into his car, and Frankie texted for the Scoobies to meet back at her place. After that, it was just a matter of fishing the old swim team out of the pool and hiding them in the bushes to be composted later. Vi rode with them to the house, and it wasn't easy getting all three of them on Jake's moped. But at least it meant no small talk. All Frankie had to do was hang on and make sure Vi didn't fall off the back. Or escape.

When they got to her house, Frankie cracked open the front door and leaned in to peer through the entrance to the kitchen. Her mom, Spike, and Oz were there, each with a mug of tea or blood. Hailey and Sigmund were sitting at the counter and turned when they heard her come in.

Frankie looked at Sigmund.

"Your mom not here?"

"In your text you said 'Scoobies,' so I asked her if she wouldn't mind going back to wait at my apartment."

"Oh. That was very thoughtful." But she wouldn't have minded if Sarafina had come. She didn't know her, but she sensed that she could trust her. You can't trade kicks to the face with a person and not feel like you got a good read on them.

"You did say Scoobies, didn't you?" Sigmund asked.

"I did," she said. "Though technically we'll be Scoobies plus one." She opened the door wide to show Vi.

"Vi?" Hailey jumped off her stool. She paused for a minute to stare and then crossed the space in a few fast strides to throw her arms around her sister.

"Whoa." Vi grinned as she braced against the impact. "Take it easy."

"Shut up," Hailey said into her hair. "You're a slayer; you could carry me around like a backpack." The hug lasted for a long time, and eventually Jake slid around them to get to the kitchen. Then Hailey shoved Vi away hard and shouted, "Where have you been?"

"I'd like to know that, too," said Spike. "You want to explain this to me?"

"Which one of your slayers are you talking to?" Vi asked.

"I'm—" He looked from Vi to Frankie and back again. "I'm talking to the good one."

"Which is me, right?" Frankie asked, pointing to herself.

"I thought you were going to stake out the pool," said Willow.

"We were. We did. And it's over, actually; the fish monsters are slayed."

"The pool is a *mess*," Jake added. "Principal Jacobs is going to flip out." He was deep in the refrigerator digging around for left-over cold cuts, and Frankie had to admire his devotion to snacks when everyone else was staring at Vi and trying not to blink.

"Vi showed up in the middle to help."

"I'm making a habit of that." Vi walked with Hailey into the kitchen. She looked at Willow, and after a moment, Willow said, "Oh my god, you're okay," and crossed the kitchen to hug her. "We thought you were all . . . But where have you been?"

"We heard that some of the slayers might have been pulled out through a portal," said Oz.

"Really? Would be news to me," said Vi.

"But," asked Frankie, "who else survived?"

Vi helped herself to an apple out of the fruit bowl and tossed it from one hand to the other. "I know you have questions," she said. "Most that I'm not willing to answer."

"Not willing to answer?" Spike asked. "Why the bloody hell not?"

"Because the ones who survived get to make their own deci-sions about who knows it," she replied, with a flash of anger. But then she smiled. "We do occasionally like to make choices for our-selves, you know, Watcher."

Spike and Willow looked at each other.

"But we're—" Willow said, puzzled. "We're Buffy's best friends. And . . . I knew you before you were even a slayer. You can trust us."

"We can't trust anyone right now," Vi replied. "And even if we could, like I said: It's not my decision to make." She rolled the apple back across the counter. "Anyway, I'm just here for my sister." She touched Hailey's elbow. "You wanna go grab something to eat? I saw an all-night diner out by the turnpike."

Hailey looked at Frankie, but Frankie looked away. It wasn't her business to give her permission to go. Vi was being odd and secretive, but she'd been through a lot. And she had helped them twice.

"Yeah, I guess," Hailey said. "I can eat."

"You can borrow the moped," Jake volunteered. "Hailey knows how to drive it, and I can ride home with Oz."

"Great." Vi put an arm around Hailey's shoulders and steered her out, but Spike jumped in the way.

"You're really going to walk out of here without telling us anything?"

"Spike," Willow said. "Just let them go. It's okay."

"Like hell it is," he grumbled, but he backed off. "What if she runs off again?"

"I'm not going to run off." Vi turned to her Watcher. It was strange to think that Spike was her Watcher, too, when she was so much older than Frankie and didn't look like she had anything left to learn, or any need of advice. Not that Spike ever gave any. And seeing them face off in the entryway didn't remind Frankie of Buffy and Mr. Giles, or even of Spike and herself—there were no mentorly, fatherly vibes. There didn't seem to be much of anything besides latent hostility.

"You're not running off," Hailey said. "But does that mean you're staying?"

"For a while. Thought I should help the new slayer get on her feet." She smiled at Frankie and then tucked a lock of hair behind Hailey's ear. "And then you and I can go . . . anywhere we want."

Hailey blinked. They all did. Frankie hadn't really thought about what it could mean if Vi came back: that Hailey would return to her old life. That Hailey would leave. But she wouldn't, would she? Not after all this, not after fighting the Countess, not after staking her own vamps. She was a Scooby, and she would never leave Sigmund. Except she was leaving now, walking right out the front door with Vi and not so much as a see-you-later wave.

"Well, that was . . . interesting," said Oz after they were gone.

"Yeah," Jake agreed. "And tame. I thought Hailey would be right in her face."

"Everyone's different with family," Sigmund said quietly.

They looked at Frankie. She should say something leaderly, something comforting, something that Buffy would say. Or at least she should try to get the scowl off her face. But it was a lot to think about. And there was nothing they could do. Hailey and Vi would have to find their own way, no matter how much she yearned to meddle. Frankie headed for the door.

"If you follow them, you'll only make things worse," Willow called out.

"I wasn't going to," said Frankie. "I'm going to go see Grimloch."

Willow's mouth dropped open. Spike's eyes narrowed, and he quickly shifted into his Watcher stance and said, "The hell you are."

"I'm just going to see if he's okay. He got cut, and he's the one who broke the case—if he hadn't killed that fish monster, we never would have known they were all mutated old swim champs!"

"I'm sure he's fine," said Willow. "Besides, it's after curfew."

Frankie squinted. "I don't have a curfew. Slayers can't have curfews!"

"Can a slayer go to school?" Willow asked, looking haughty behind the kitchen counter. "Can a slayer clean her room? Then a slayer can have a curfew."

"Ugh, Mom!" Frankie groaned.

"At least the fish monsters are taken care of." Jake tossed a cashew into the air and caught it in his mouth. "Now maybe we can focus on finding the slayers."

"With or without Vi's help," Spike grumbled. "And if we do it fast enough, we can get Buffy back here before whatever this darkness business is has a chance to put our lights out."

CHAPTER ELEVEN
HOT DEMONS ARE SLAYER CATNIP

Frankie went upstairs to her room, but she didn't go to bed. She simply lay upon it and plotted until she heard everyone leave and, eventually, heard her mom walk down the hall. Then she waited for her mom's door to close and, just to be safe, waited forty minutes more before sliding her window up and propping it open with a short sword. The diving somersault she used to escape her bedroom prison was so smooth and quiet she almost wished that Spike had been there to see it. He probably wouldn't have even ratted her out. But he would have stopped her from seeing Grim.

Frankie ran silently through the development of Sunnydale Heights, toward Marymore Park and the only place she could think of that Grimloch would go if he wanted to meet her: the old glamping tent in the woods that used to be the home of the Succoro demon.

She wasn't sure what she was going to say when she saw him. Questions raced through her head one after the other like a dog chasing a dozen tails. Had he learned anything about the explosion?

Had he seen any of the survivors? Did he find the one slayer he was looking for?

But that was a stupid question. If Grimloch had found his slayer, he wouldn't have come back here. If he had found her alive, Frankie would probably never have heard from him again.

That was an unpleasant thought. And unkind to them both. Whatever else he felt, Grimloch cared about Frankie. He wouldn't just leave and vanish without a trace. Well, without first letting her know that he was about to leave and vanish without a trace.

Frankie hopped a shrub and moved easily through the trees. She knew the way to the tent so well she could have made it there with her eyes closed. Since Grim had been gone, she had come with Hailey and Sigmund, and occasionally Jake, to keep the vines and weeds from taking it over, and making sure no raccoons had taken up residence. She didn't know why exactly, except she thought that Grimloch might need it, if he ever came back. And she suspected that Hailey and Sigmund kept it up because they occasionally used the tent as a place to make out.

Randy little scamps, she thought in Spike's voice. They already had Sigmund's whole apartment.

Frankie ducked a low branch and glanced up at the sky. The moon was nearly full; it would reach its fullness over Valentine's Day. Poor Jake, locked in a cage on the most date-heavy night of the year. Poor Jake, and all those poor cheerleaders he wouldn't take out for a movie and a sack of burgers. His idea of romance.

She was almost to the tent, still moving silently in a dark hoodie and jeans, her sneakers soft against the grass and dirt. Their frequent trips to the tent over the past months had formed a kind of game trail to it, and she made a mental note to tell Hailey and Sigmund to start taking different pathways, before their secret tent became not so secret.

She finally caught sight of it, and her heart leapt when she saw it was lit from inside. It would have been easy enough for Grimloch to avoid her if he wanted to. Coming to the tent was practically like an invitation. Like he was waiting for her. Frankie crept eagerly toward the open flap. She'd never been so happy about breaking her mother's rules.

Still, she was nervous. What would he tell her? Would he be glad to see her? Would he smile? She liked to make him smile. He was usually so serious. The more she thought, the more jittery she got, and before she reached the flap of the tent, she stepped on a fallen twig. It snapped loudly in the dark, and Grimloch's voice followed after.

"Francesca Rosenberg. You are still a terrible hunter."

Dammit. Frankie stepped inside. "I got close enough to make the kill," she said as he looked up from the book he was reading. "And that's what counts."

"I caught your movements a hundred yards ago."

"Then you should've run away."

"I'm the hunter god of Thrace," he said, and shrugged like that explained everything. He stood up from the cot, and she fought the urge to back into the tent wall. He was just so tall. And so nicely muscly. "I'm glad to see you alive."

"You thought I might be dead?" she asked. "That's insulting."

"That's the life of a slayer."

Frankie put her hands on her hips. "So much for pleasantries. No 'Hi, I missed you, too.' No souvenirs from the gift shop at the world's largest ball of string."

"You think I should have brought you a present?"

"No," Frankie said, and snorted.

"Because I did."

"Oh," she said happily. He reached into his jacket and set it into her hand, something small, and heavy, and wrapped in a bit of soft leather. A pendant maybe. Or a ring. She unfolded the leather and looked into her palm. "It's a rock." A black rock the size of a large marble and dull as a lump of coal.

"It's not a rock." Grimloch took it and held it up to the light. That did make it prettier; against the camping lantern, the center of the stone seemed to emit its own internal silver glow. "Well, it is a rock. But it's not just a rock. It's a stalker's stone. Long ago, I gifted these charms to my most favored hunters, to allow them to walk among their prey unnoticed." He pressed it back into her hand. "I thought you could use the help."

"Thank you," she said a little sarcastically, and pursed her lips as she took it back. "But I am a slayer, you know, not a hunter."

"Clearly. Your stealth is awful. I should have given you one of these stones before I left—"

"Hey, I didn't walk all the way over here at midnight just to be insulted—"

"But I was too busy being impressed," he continued, "by how far you've come. You are a very good slayer."

Frankie smiled.

"And I have known my share of slayers," he went on, and the smile fell from her face.

She lifted the stalker's stone to her eye. "So how do you use it?"

"You need only coat it in the blood of your prey and hold it in your hand. Then you may move among them and they will perceive you as one of their own."

"And it works on demons?" Frankie raised her eyebrows. It was actually a very thoughtful, useful gift. But part of her still would have preferred a ring. She looked up at Grimloch and caught him staring.

"What?" She looked down at herself. "Is there a stain on my shirt? I just changed into this."

"No." He smiled in that way he had that barely hid the tips of his fangs. "I'm just . . . looking at you."

"At me?"

The words gave her a happy shiver, until he smirked and added, "Also I'm trying to ignore the smell of salt, and rot, and chlorine."

"Hey." She arched her brow. "That's what happens when you slay all the fish monsters. Well, except for the one Vi slayed."

"Vi Larsson. So she is still in Sunnydale."

"Well, yes. No. I mean, she wasn't here the whole time, but she just got back. Actually, I kind of thought you came back together. Two mysterious allies—or sort-of allies—reappear on the same night? A bit of a coincidence. Was she with you all these months, searching?"

Grimloch shook his head. "I know Vi Larsson. But we are not close. I haven't seen her since the day when she appeared to help you fight the Countess."

Frankie sighed. She'd been hoping he was the answer to that question.

"Slayer—why have you come to see me?"

"Well." Frankie blinked. "To make sure you were okay. The fish monster cut you." Grimloch opened his jacket to show the tears that the claws had ripped through his shirt. "Are you hurt?" She slid her fingertips inside the fabric. No cuts. Only smooth, warm skin.

"They were as the scratches of a cat," he said. "And healed within the hour. Did you really think me in danger, when you have seen me survive a fist-shaped hole through my rib cage?"

Instinctively, Frankie's fingers searched higher. There was a scar there, where the Countess's hand had punched through to try and remove his heart. A patch of raised and gnarled skin. Would it mark him forever? She almost wanted it to. A mark over his heart; that would always make him remember their battle together. But forever was a long time. And he was so strong. It would probably fade after a century or two like everything else.

"What are you thinking?" he asked.

"Nothing." She withdrew her hand. "No, really. I have a hard time holding a thought in my head when I'm in a room alone with you. You probably hear that a lot."

"I don't allow many people in rooms with me," he said. "But yes, I suppose it's a high proportion."

Frankie rolled her eyes fondly.

"Thank you for the present," she said.

"You're welcome."

She returned to studying the stalker's stone. "So these are *your* charms, then. Like, the charmed stones of the Hunter of Thrace."

"Yes."

"Do you make them? Like, do you lay them like eggs?"

Grimloch growled.

"I'm just wondering. You mentioned you were hatched from one."

"I make the stones. I do not 'lay' the stones."

"And you give them to your favorite hunters?"

"Yes."

"And you gave one to me?" She turned teasingly and batted her eyelashes, and Grimloch chuckled.

"Look," she said, unable to put it off for any longer, "I'm guessing you didn't find the answers you were looking for, about your slayer. So why did you come back?"

"I—" He glanced down, measuring his words. "I didn't want to stay away."

He looked at her, and Frankie's heart thumped so loudly he had to have heard it.

"I went far," Grimloch said. "To Halifax and beyond. I spoke to witches and oracles. Many could tell me that some slayers lived. None could tell me which, for certain. None could find her, or trace her essence."

"That doesn't mean she's dead. We spoke with an oracle, too—or my mom did, or she . . . communed with her through her eyeballs—and she said the slayers were pulled through a portal into another dimension."

"Another dimension." His eyes glowed blue. "Which dimension?"

"That's what we're trying to figure out." She watched as his expression clouded, spiraling out with thoughts of his slayer, and she couldn't help feeling a little dejected. "See? You should have just stayed here with us. All the good intel comes to the Hellmouth eventually." She put the stalker's stone into her pocket. "So, what's the plan? Do you want to stay away from me, until we know more? Not that you need to stay away from me, like you can't resist me or something; I'm clearly not going to overpower you with my laser beams of hotness—"

"I already told you," he said. "I don't want to stay away."

Frankie took another deep breath. He really was far too good-looking. It was unnatural. "Okay. But don't say I didn't warn you."

Grimloch chuckled again. He seemed surprised by the sound of his own laugh. She made him laugh. She broke through his serious exterior. She was, like, a jester.

But she also made his eyes flash bright, and the way he looked at her sometimes was so intense that she felt like he had to be looking at someone else.

"I'm going to say good night now," she said, and headed for the tent flap. "Before anyone notices I'm gone."

"You snuck out?"

"Of course not. Everyone is thrilled that you're back in town. Especially Spike and my mom." She paused at the door. "Hey, did any of those oracles you talked to mention something called 'the darkness'?"

Grimloch stiffened. He thought a moment. "No. None mentioned those words."

She sighed. "Just thought I'd ask. And just so you know: My name isn't actually 'Francesca.' It's just plain Frankie. Frankie Jane Rosenberg." She shrugged. "But you can still call me Francesca, if you want."

$$) \,) \, \bigcirc \, (\, ($$

Frankie checked her phone as she ran back through Sunnydale Heights. No angry red-face emoji texts from her mom, but it was late. Like, really late. Had she and Grimloch really lingered in the tent that long? She jogged into her yard and looked up at her bedroom window, still propped open. Another good sign. Unfortunately it was propped open and facing into nothing: The development was too new to have any decent trees; the only one close enough to her window was still basically a sapling, and if she climbed that it would bend over like a bamboo pole.

"Didn't think of getting back in," she muttered, and crept up to the front door.

It would probably be all right. She knew the creaks and squeaks of her house like the back of her hand, and she was a slayer to boot.

Made for stealth, no matter what Grimloch said. She got inside and closed the door silently behind her, then crossed the entryway and went past the kitchen, past the downstairs bathroom, and up the stairs, skipping the two in the middle and keeping to the left side. Not a sound. Her mom's door was still shut, and so was Hailey's.

Frankie paused. Hailey's room. Not the guest room anymore. She didn't know when that had changed, but it had, and she wanted it to stay.

"Hailey," she whispered into the door. "Are you up?"

"Yeah."

"Can I come in?"

The door opened in reply, and Hailey stood there still dressed, even still in her boots. Only one lamp was on, and the bed was rumpled but made. There were some things strewn across it, and Hailey's bag was beside it, like she had been going through things from the past.

"You back from seeing Vi?" Frankie asked after she came in.

"Yeah," Hailey said as she closed the door softly. "Where are you coming from?" She looked at Frankie's happy, guilty face, then pointed and made a clicking sound with her tongue. "Ah. Hot demon. Got it." She went back to the bed and stuffed her things into the bag so Frankie could sit. "How is he anyway?"

"Very hot, slightly demony. So, same as usual. But how are you? Did it go okay with Vi?" Frankie chose her questions carefully. "I don't want to push. Just . . . if you want to talk about it."

"I don't know." Hailey walked to her vanity and idly put on bracelet after bracelet, leather and chains, studded and braided, like a coat of armor. For a minute, Frankie thought that Hailey would slam shut like a book again, until she grabbed the bracelets and slid them back off. "It was weird, seeing her. I mean, it was good. I'm so grateful she's okay. But she's always pissing me off."

"Yeah." Frankie nodded. "Family."

"Yeah, family. But mine's shittier than most. Mom and Dad both dead, my sister a flake who lets me think she died in an explosion just to pop up, save us, and disappear again." Hailey scowled. "She's always been this way. She's, like, a diabolical freak."

"Well, you know, weird and difficult families are a Scooby tradition. Buffy's mom died, too, when she was young, and her sister showed up one day after being transformed from a literal ball of energy. And don't forget I don't even have a second parent. My second parent isn't even human—it's an essence, which sounds like something that gets sprayed on you at a department store."

Hailey smirked. Then she shook her head. "Maybe Vi left because she wanted to stay gone. Maybe she was tired of taking care of me. I suppose she should be—I got dropped on her doorstep after my parents died, like a puppy in a cardboard box."

"You say that like surprise puppies are a bad thing. Sometimes a surprise puppy can be just what you needed."

"I guess that's true. You were kind of a surprise puppy for your mom."

"And I didn't have the courtesy to come in a cardboard box."

"Neither did I, really." Hailey cocked an eyebrow. "I showed up scared and resentful. I should've put myself in a cardboard box. It would have taken the edge off."

"Well, however you came into each other's lives, Vi loves you. She came back for you." Frankie paused and forced her voice to be high and carefree. "She wants to take you away from all of this and live together on a happy farm."

"That's what she says, but"—Hailey glanced at Frankie—"at dinner mostly it seemed like she wanted to talk about you."

"About me?"

"Yeah. How you were handling slaying and what kind of a

person you are. Don't get me wrong, I was glad to sing your praises. It's just . . . she wouldn't tell me anything about what happened at Slayerfest. She kept deflecting and saying it wasn't her business to tell. Which I get, but since Buffy and so many are missing, isn't it kind of everybody's business?"

Frankie frowned. She wanted answers as badly as anyone, but they couldn't force Vi to talk. "Give her time. She almost died. Once she realizes that we're not a team of total incompetents, I'm sure she'll tell us what happened."

"Maybe. But she was acting so weird. And there's another thing." Hailey squinted. "At one point, she referred to your mom as 'the witch that broke the world.'"

"Well, that's accurate, I guess."

"Yeah, but I thought they were kind of friends at one point? They even lived in the same house during the battle with the First." Hailey sat down heavily on the bed. "You know she actually had the nerve to be pissed that I came here? She pointed her finger in my face and actually said that. 'I told you not to come to Sunnydale.'"

"What did you say?" Frankie asked.

"I said, 'I told you not to die.'" Hailey shrugged. "So there."

Frankie snorted approvingly. "Nice." She looked around the room, at all of Hailey's things that had slowly taken it over. A closet full of black clothes. New makeup across the vanity table in shades that Frankie was physically afraid of. Hailey had stopped short of hanging anything on the walls, but that would come eventually. This was her home now. *You won't leave us, will you?* Frankie wanted to ask. *You won't go?* But those weren't fair questions to ask. Vi and Hailey were sisters. The last family they had. And it was their decision.

"But enough about my intensely cryptic sister." Hailey grabbed a pillow to hug and tossed another to Frankie. "I want to know about Grim. What did he say? Why is he back? Did he take his shirt off?"

Frankie answered carefully. "He said a lot of things; he's back because he didn't want to stay away, and . . . a little?" Hailey's eyes widened, and Frankie scrunched her nose. "Okay, he just let me touch his chest through the claw rips the fish monster made."

"He's back for one night, and you're touching his chest. Slow down, Speed Racer. What else?"

"Nothing." Frankie shrugged. "He didn't find her. His slayer. And I don't want to make assumptions, but I don't think I'm what he's into, you know?"

"No, I don't know."

"I mean, I don't think I'm like her. He said when they met they basically battled until they fell in love. It sounded really intense."

"Or intensely unhealthy," said Hailey. "But go on."

"I just don't know what he'd want . . . with me."

Hailey's shoulders slumped. "You are so like your mom sometimes. He'd want the you that is you."

"But he's so demony and . . . *intense*. I bet their relationship was constant dramatic declarations. I bet they broke lots of beds."

"Don't do this," said Hailey. "Don't compare yourself to her. Also, stop saying 'intense' so much."

"How can I not? I mean, with the comparing. She's so—"

"Stop," Hailey said. "It's not right, and she's a literal lost love. You'll drive yourself nuts. Grimloch likes you. He's drawn to you, even. And he's a nicer guy when he's around you—you make him almost human. Besides, just because he's intense doesn't mean he wants intense. Look at me and Sigmund: not an obvious couple from the outside, but we work."

"What do you mean 'not obvious'? You're both ridiculously handsome if you haven't noticed."

"I have noticed," Hailey said. "But no matter how good-looking we are, Goth orphan plus high-society academic does not a perfect equation make."

That was true. It had seemed natural to Frankie that Hailey and Sigmund would connect; they were both new in town, and both Scoobies—but besides that, they couldn't have been more different. And she'd never thought of Sigmund as high society before, but after meeting his mother, it was clear.

"Still," Hailey went on, "I adore Sigmund. He's completely unlike anyone I've ever dated. He needs me to drag him out of the library and into the real world. And I need him to hold me back from running into a bar fight."

"You need all of us for that," Frankie said, "you rogue fireball."

Hailey grinned. "Good thing I wasn't called as a slayer. I would've been dead, right out of the gate."

Frankie shrugged. "Well, without Scooby support, I would've been, too." She glanced at the bedside clock. "We'd better get some sleep."

"If we can," said Hailey. "Slayer sisters back from the void, and hot demon boyfriends returned in one night—it's like Hellmouth Christmas."

Frankie smiled and got up, opening Hailey's door to peek into the hallway before slipping out to tiptoe down the hall. When she stopped outside her bedroom to ever so gently turn the doorknob, her mom said, "Where do you think you're going?"

"Mom!" Frankie spun. Willow stood right behind her, arms crossed over a blue robe, one toe tapping in a fuzzy slipper. "I was—"

"Don't try that 'I was' crap on me. Did you think I didn't know when you left? Do you think I don't know where you've been? I'm a witch, sweetie. I know exactly where you are, exactly, all the time."

"Well, that's an exaggeration. . . ."

"Is it?" Willow asked. She stepped forward, and Frankie stepped back, into her room. "Because I know where you are right now. And that's grounded."

"Mom!"

"Grounded!" Willow declared. "So, so grounded." And to drive home the point, she snapped her fingers, and Frankie's door slammed shut on its own. "So that'll put marzipan in your pie plate, bingo!" Willow shouted from the other side.

"Mom," Frankie growled. "I still don't know what that means!"

"Neither. Did. She," Willow said mystifyingly, and Frankie heard her footsteps walk away down the hall. She leaned against the door. She wanted to pitch a fit. She felt it was within her rights. But when slayers pitched fits, things got broken, and everything in the room was, well, her stuff.

Grounded. It was unthinkable. She paced back and forth a while before giving up and getting ready for bed.

"It's a good thing I slayed those fish monsters," she muttered just before she drifted off. "So Sunnydale will be safe while I'm stuck in my room."

*After saying goodbye to Hailey at the diner, Vi walked along the lost highway to the middle of nowhere. Of course Hailey'd had questions—*Where are you going? When will I see you? How do I get in touch?*—but Vi had refused to answer. She'd let her little sister scowl, and glare, and threaten, and finally get onto the moped and peel away. She was mad, but she'd get over it. And eventually she would understand.*

Vi lit the blood-soaked herbs and spoke the incantation, holding her hand to her nose to stem the reek of smoke and rot. Demon magic was disgusting. She felt soiled every time she did it, the same way she felt every time she thought about the demon essence in her blood. It had been that way from the very beginning—when the demon power was forced upon the first slayer in those ancient days. Then it had been passed down to every slayer along the line, until Buffy had used the red witch to blow it up, to turn it loose, and to infect every last one of them so they could fight her war.

It was a calling, they said. A sacred duty. But what the Scythe spell did that day wasn't calling; it was conscription.

The smoke before her thickened and slowed, flattening and opening in a strange, murky window. Just a little hole opened, right through dimensions. And on the other side were the hiding slayers. The "survivors," as the Scoobies called them. If they only knew.

Through the window of smoke, a hooded silhouette appeared.

"Hello again, Vi."

"Hello, Sonia."

"How's Sunnydale?"

"Sunnydale is the same as it was when you all left and ditched me here," Vi replied. "The plan was never for me to stay here and be the sole 'guardian' of the Hellmouth."

"We had to go. We were too much of a target all grouped together. And you volunteered to stay when you chose to save William the Bloody and show your face to the new slayer and all her friends."

"I didn't even mean to do that," said Vi. "I just saw him flying through the air and my first thought was Grab him." She sighed. "He might be a useless moron, but he was my Watcher." She waved a hand against the smoke obscuring the other slayer's face, but she didn't really need to see her. Vi knew her by her voice. She knew all the remaining slayers' voices, even when they were speaking in hushed whispers. "You know you look ridiculous."

The other slayer paused and pushed the hood of her robe back to reveal her light brown skin and deep brown braids. "I like the hood. It's warm. This dimension is freezing."

"So why not come to Sunnydale and keep me company? It's sweater weather here even in February."

"Goes against orders."

"I'm sure Aspen wouldn't mind. Go ask." Vi peered around her as if she could see their leader, waiting in the wings. "I'll wait."

"She's not here."

"Then where is she? In this dimension?"

"I don't know. She's still seeking the amulet."

"But where, exactly?"

Through the smoke, Sonia's lips pursed and remained sealed tight.

"Right. Why tell me." Vi looked down and kicked at the sand with the toe of her boot. "You'll be pleased to know I've made contact with the new slayer."

"Finally. And how is the little witchspawn?"

"We're not going to call her that."

"Why not?"

"Because we can come up with better."

Sonia paused. "Redheaded Scythe child?"

"You're bad at this," said Vi.

"Well, whatever we decide to call her, have you seen any indications that she's not human?"

"What do you mean?" Vi asked.

"Are there any signs that she was conjured out of thin air."

"Like Dawn?"

"We don't speak that name!"

"Sorry." Vi raised her eyebrows. "I meant like that girl whose name means what happens in the morning . . . ?"

Sonia shook herself and took her hackles down, relaxing knuckle by knuckle. It was a little ridiculous, how much they hated Dawn. Not that Vi didn't hate her, too. It just wasn't personal.

"Anyway, I don't think so. There are pictures of her, memories."

"Memories and records mean nothing," Sonia said. "The unspeakable thing had memories, too. False memories, planted by the monks."

"I still don't think so. The new slayer really is the red witch's daughter. Natural born, sixteen years ago. And you know, she was just called. She's just the next in line, after us. She's not really a part of this."

"We know," Sonia said after a moment of consideration. "But that doesn't change what she is. You have to get close to her, and to the red witch. Find out if they know the location of the Scythe. It shouldn't be hard. The beacon you planted on the Hellmouth should be drawing its most-loved demons to Sunnydale by now. And nothing bonds slayers together like a few dozen demons."

Vi sighed. Sonia cocked her head sympathetically.

"It won't be for much longer. We're all impatient. Just find the Scythe, Vi. Because if Aspen makes it back with the amulet first, she won't like waiting for you to deliver on your end. Pulling off what we did in Halifax . . . it wasn't easy, and we've come too far to turn back. Don't you want it to be done?"

"Of course I do. But it's already gone further than we planned— nobody said any of us were going to die."

"We couldn't know how explosive opening the portal would be. It was an accident. . . . That part . . . really was an accident."

Vi shut her eyes. They'd only meant to imprison the senior slayer leadership. Like Buffy and Faith. Kennedy and Rona. Andrew, since he was there anyway. They hadn't meant for it to go so wrong.

"Tell Aspen I'll get the Scythe," Vi snapped, and on the other side of the window, Sonia nodded. She raised her arm and wiped away the smoke closing the interdimensional portal as easily as wiping chalk from a chalkboard. But before she could finish, Vi said, "Hang on. Just how many dozens of demons are we talking about? And what do you mean by 'most-loved'?"

"Not that many," Sonia said, and the portal shut. Stinky, blood-tinged smoke sank to Vi's ankles and disappeared.

"Not that many," Vi muttered.

She turned and walked back toward the twinkling lights of Sunnydale, keeping her eyes and ears open in the dark. No troubling sounds, no snarls, no scraping of claws. Nothing aside from the usual nocturnal animals. She couldn't see the demons moving toward them from all corners of the globe. Demons the Hellmouth had seen before.

Dozens of them, hundreds of them, lifting their heads and snapping their fangs, using their claws to drag themselves up and out of the mud, to make their way to that shining green beacon, and the Hellmouth they called home.

PART THREE

WHO PUT A QUARTER
IN THE HELLMOUTH?

CHAPTER TWELVE
HELPFUL ADULTS

Frankie's grounding didn't last long. It was true what she'd said—you couldn't really ground a slayer, but Frankie was limited to slaying-related activities only for an entire week. Willow had said it was for two, but Frankie deployed the sad Snoopy walk, and when she was free again, she made sure to text Xander to say thank you for the tip. By the time the Scoobies met in the library the day before Valentine's Day for training, she and her mom had made up and all was well. Spike even got her a getting-out-of-bedroom-jail present.

"Here," he said, and set it down on the table in front of her. It was an envelope. Black and kind of shiny.

"What's this?" Frankie asked as she and everyone else looked at it. That afternoon's training session was very full, with her mom and Oz in attendance, plus Sigmund's mom as a special guest. Frankie picked up the envelope.

"Just a little gift from a Watcher to his slayer," said Spike.

"Is it, like, tickets to the Ice Capades?" Frankie asked.

"What are 'Ice Capades'?" Hailey asked.

"I don't know," Frankie replied. "I think they're like escapades, but on ice. Ice Capades. Oh my god, I just got that right now."

"It's a figure-skating show," said Willow. "Giles used to take Buffy to them sometimes."

"We're not going to start doing that, are we?" Frankie asked Spike. "Because I don't want to."

"They're not tickets to the bloody Ice Capades," Spike snapped. He waved at the envelope. "Just open it."

Frankie tore open the envelope. "A gift card to the leather emporium."

"Well, that's not weird at all," said Hailey.

"Pipe down," said Spike. "Every slayer I've ever known has worn leather. It's like a slayer rite of passage. Even my trusty jacket once belonged to a slayer—I took it off her after I . . . killed her . . ." he mumbled, voice trailing off.

"But I don't like to wear leather," Frankie said. "I'm a vegetarian."

"I could wear it," Hailey said, and snatched the card. Then she promptly returned it when Frankie gave her a look. "But I *won't*. Maybe they have that cactus leather that vamp was talking about?"

"Maybe," said Frankie. "But why leather?" She looked at Spike. "And why now?"

He shrugged. "With Vi in town, I just think you ought to look the part. Thought you might be tired of walking around wearing whatever it is you wear"—Frankie looked down at her hoodie and jeans—"and be a little Big Bad. You could stand to look more threatening, is all."

"Plus, you might look good," Jake said, balancing a sword on the palm of his hand. He was about to flip it dangerously into the air and try to catch it when Oz took it from him and said, "No."

"Joykill," Jake said, frowning.

Spike slipped out of his tweed jacket and started unbuttoning his shirt, revealing a black T-shirt underneath. "Take it or don't, I just thought I'd mention it. Let's get to work."

He and Frankie squared off on the sparring mats, warming up with punch combinations and flip drills. "Hailey, Jake," he ordered, "on the next mat. Hailey, get a sparring stick and maintain distance. Jake, try to close the gap." He watched them get started, then nailed Frankie in the eye with a no-look punch.

"Ow," she said.

"Always be ready. Demons are happy to hit you even when they're not going to see it."

"Good tip." Frankie squinted.

She got ready to go again, but Spike stopped and said, "I've got a better idea. Since we have the adults for a day, why not use them. Oz, get in with Jake, werewolf versus werewolf. And, Ms. DeWitt, if you wouldn't mind . . ." He held his arm out toward Frankie. "Give the slayer a bit of proper demon practice."

"I have an even better idea." Willow stood before Sarafina could agree. "Why not witch versus witch? Telekinesis match."

Frankie dropped her hands in surprise. Everyone did. Even Sigmund, buried beneath books as he researched interdimensional travel, stopped scribbling down notes and raised his head.

"Mom, are you sure?"

"Sure, I'm sure." Willow nodded, and Frankie couldn't help but notice that she glanced at Sarafina. Her mom was trying to impress Ms. DeWitt. It was kind of cute. Unfortunately Sarafina didn't seem to be paying attention. Her focus was on her son, and his growing pile of reading material.

"Sigmund," she said. "Come away from there at once and pick up a weapon. Spar with your Hailey. She's a fine fighter."

"Aww, thanks, Ms. D!" Hailey smiled and winked. "I mean 'the Great Ms. D.'"

"I'm not going to throw punches at my girlfriend," Sigmund said.

Hailey spun the sparring stick deftly between her hands. "Um, pretty sure I can dodge whatever you dish, babe. But you don't have to, if you don't want to."

Sigmund looked to his mother, who gestured for him to get up with a jerk of her head. She was imperious, even in a dress of cream-colored wool and adorned with gold jewelry. Frankie wondered if she dressed like that when she hunted. Except Sage demons fed on stupidity; she'd been sitting in on Sigmund's tutoring sessions since she got to town. Did Sage demons even hunt? Maybe just for fun. Looking at the way Sarafina bared her teeth as Sigmund picked up a sparring stick and joined Hailey on the mat, Frankie definitely thought Sarafina hunted for fun.

"All right, then." Spike clapped his hands. "Fighters, to your mats. Witches, up on tables." He pointed Willow toward the table on one side of the room and Frankie toward a table on the other, then retreated to oversee all the matches.

"Okay, Mom," Frankie said, watching her mom climb gingerly onto the table. "What are we throwing?"

"Knives?" Willow suggested.

"Knives? No way, not knives! When is the last time you even used your telekinesis? Are you trying to kill me?"

"Are you forgetting I'm the greatest witch in a century?" Willow arched her eyebrow. That may be true, but still, Frankie was firm about the knives. In the end, they settled on books. There was a ready supply of them, and they were a bit ungainly, always flopping open and making distracting noises with their pages, so good for practice.

For a few minutes, they practiced floating them in a circle. They played the alphabet game and mentally summoned one book from each letter of the alphabet into their orbit. But Frankie was distracted. She was worried that Sigmund was going to put his own eye out, for one. And two, the snarls coming from the werewolf mat were turning serious.

"No fair using claws when I don't have mine!" Jake protested.

"You'll be able to control them someday," said Oz around a mouthful of fangs. "Best to get some practice being around them now."

Jake's expression darkened, and he leapt onto Oz and took him to the mat.

"Frankie, pay attention," Spike ordered, and her mom sent a large gold-bound book zipping through the air to hit Frankie in the head.

"Ow! Mom!"

"New alphabet game," said Willow. "That was a volume of *Aesop's Fables.* Your turn."

Frankie drew her lips together in a grim line and searched the floating books for her "A": an edition of *Anne of Green Gables.* Then she whisked it off toward her mother at top speed. Willow knocked it aside with a flick of her wrist. It hadn't come within ten feet of hitting her.

"Very impressive," Sarafina said, and nodded.

"Thanks." Willow blushed happily. She turned to Frankie. "First one to 'Z' wins?"

"You want me to get hit with twenty-six books? And you know X is just going to be a volume of the encyclopedia, and those have really sharp edges!"

In response, Willow let the books fly, and Frankie found herself under attack by a flock of flapping, angry editions, assaulting her senses, death by a thousand paper cuts. Through the sounds of book covers whacking against her ears she heard Spike shout, "Fight back, Mini Red."

"I can't see!"

"Doesn't matter," Spike said, sounding disappointed. "Fight back however you can!"

Frankie moved forward. She reached for a book of her own with her mind, but it was nearly impossible to focus.

"When magic fails, you're still a slayer!"

"You want me to kick my mom?" Frankie asked. She ducked low and narrowly missed being struck by a very heavy translation of the *Iliad*.

"She can take it."

Frankie flipped up high and away from the books that still circled her like seagulls after a french fry, and with two strides of a running start, leapt through the air toward her mother. But she didn't make it. The books slammed to the floor when Willow dropped them and focused her energy instead on grabbing her daughter and holding her suspended in midair.

"Gotta do better than that, sweetie."

"Mom!" Frankie gathered her magic in the pit of her stomach and pushed it out, angrily and wildly, losing focus and losing control in a flash of temper that made her sick to her stomach the moment it passed. Willow was knocked back off the table and onto the floor. Frankie dropped to the ground.

"Mom—I didn't mean—"

Willow twisted and blew her daughter backward to slide across the floor and into the base of the nearest bookshelf.

"Willow!" Oz shouted.

"What?" She watched Frankie get up, and her brow knit. "I thought we were still training! We were, weren't we? Sweetie, are you okay?" She hurried to check, and Frankie felt the way her mom's hands shook as they ran up and down her arms.

"I'm fine, Mom. Didn't even lose consciousness." She studied her closely, particularly her eyes, which were thankfully not black. "Are you okay? I didn't hurt you, did I?"

"No, of course not. You did get me, though, so . . . good job."

Behind her mom, Frankie saw a troubled look ripple over Oz's face. Then it was gone, and he was just Oz, Zen as ever.

"Well, that's probably enough for today," Frankie said. "I still have to patrol later."

Willow turned to Sigmund's mom. "Sarafina, would you like to grab dinner?"

"I'd be delighted." She smiled, then turned toward Oz like she was afraid he'd feel left out. "And perhaps the werewolf would care to join us?"

Willow moved behind Sarafina to shake her head and give Oz the kill sign, and he said. "No, thanks. Some other time. Jake, I'll see you at home; I put a roast in the Crock-Pot."

"But are you going to buy me a new shirt to replace this one you shredded?" Jake asked, and held up his tattered sleeve.

"That was weird," Jake said to Frankie after the adults left. "Your mom hates to let her magic loose. And when she does, it's to help you, not to throw you into bookshelves."

"She was just showing off," said Frankie. "She got carried away." Jake looked at Hailey, who looked at Sigmund, and Frankie stomped her foot. "Look, we're the ones who asked her to use magic again. So we can't jump all over her when she does what we asked. She's my mom. She was training me. She wasn't out of control."

"'Course she wasn't," Spike said. "Red's strong, and she knows better. She deserves our trust. Of course she also almost ended the world. So stay on top of it." The vampire rolled his shoulders back and rubbed his stomach like he was thinking of blood. "All right, you lot clean up in here and head out on patrol." Then he left them in the midst of the enormous mess.

꠵ ꠵ ◯ ꠵ ꠵

It took over an hour to clean up the library, even with all of them helping.

"I swear she pulled books from every shelf in here," Hailey said, stretching her shoulders after returning another stack to their proper places. "Frankie, can't you just wiggle your nose and whoosh them back where they belong?"

Frankie shook her head. "I don't know any cleaning spells." Though a reversion spell might work, and she knew one of those. "But even if I did, I wouldn't. Magic for convenience or frivolous purposes is a no. My mom's orders."

"Well, what's the fun in that," Hailey grumbled. She picked up another book and handed it to Sigmund, who flipped through it, tenderly unfolding any creased pages. Frankie thought she heard him whisper, "There, there, little book."

Frankie grabbed another armful and headed toward the shelves and Jake.

"You know why I can't just"—she waved her hand like it held a wand—"and take care of this mess, don't you?"

"Sure." He took a book from her and stuck it in a random open space. Frankie wondered if that's what he'd been doing the whole time. Sigmund was going to have a cow.

"Easy magic leads to a reliance on magic," Jake went on, imitating her mother's voice. "Reliance on magic leads to magic addiction. Magic addiction leads to dark magic. And dark magic leads to whisking people's skin right off their bodies." He cocked an eyebrow. "I know."

"If I worked hard enough on my magic, like, if I could just tear demons in two with my mind—would I even need the slayer powers?" Frankie swallowed. It was frightening sometimes, what magic could do. But she would never be able to do that; she was Frankie, magic proficiency level two with a flair for telekinesis. She wasn't her mom. "Even if I could, I don't think I'd want to find out."

"Why not? Why shouldn't you use every advantage you have if it means you can keep yourself and your friends safe?" Jake shoved another book into the wrong place. An edge had come into his voice, and his lips curled and twitched like he was getting ready to show teeth.

"What's with the grr?" Frankie asked. "Are you okay?"

"Yeah. No. I don't know. It's just what happened at the pool—you were in trouble, and Sam was in trouble—"

"How is Sam doing?"

Jake shrugged.

"I've been by his house, and he says he's okay. But he doesn't want to go out. He just stays in and plays video games. His mom thinks he's depressed."

"He just needs time."

"But if something had happened to him . . . He's my friend. And I think I really like him, Frankie."

"Sure, we all really like him. . . ." Frankie paused as Jake gave her the most pointed look he'd ever mustered. Then he glanced away and stared at the spines of the books. "So you . . . really like him." Her face brightened, and she smacked him across the arm. "So I was right about the extra flirting!"

"Ow." Jake rubbed his bicep. "Keep your voice down."

"But I was right?"

"Yes, okay, you were right, Miss Smartypants." He shrugged. "I guess the flirting just floated the idea and then"—he smiled a little—"I decided that I kind of liked that idea. Is it weird? It's a little weird."

"No, it's not weird."

"Well, it is considering I've never . . ." Jake said, and trailed off.

"I guess I get why it would feel weird," Frankie said, trying to imagine. "So do you think you like Sam, like, more than you like the cheerleading squad?"

Color began to creep up from the collar of Jake's shirt. "Well, maybe not more than the whole squad."

Frankie heard a giggle and stole a peek at Hailey and Sigmund, but they were still cleaning, if giggling together behind a bookcase counted as cleaning. Was Jake really telling her what she thought he was? That he had feelings for Sam? And yet also feelings for the cheerleader collective? "So . . . does he . . . ? I mean does Sam . . . ? Have you—" She stopped. She ought to be better at this, but he took her by surprise. Jake had always been about girls. She'd even thought he'd go for Hailey when she first got to town. Well, until Sigmund showed up. "Does this change . . . ?"

Jake shook his head.

"I don't know. It's too new. And anyway, that wasn't the point I was trying to make. The point was, that night at the pool all I could do was call those monsters stupid names and hit them with a net. If I had control of my wolf, if Oz had been there instead of me, or even Jordy—"

"If Jordy had been there, he would've bitten everything, and we'd be stuck dealing with werefishes," said Frankie.

"And now tonight . . ." Jake glanced up like he could see the full moon rising through the ceiling of the library, even though sundown was two hours away. "I'm locked in a cage. We can't politely ask the Big Bads to take the full moon off. One day, something big is going to go down and you're going to need me, and I'm not going to be there."

"Hey." Frankie put her hand on his shoulder. "You can't be

everywhere. I'm fine. I slay. I win the fights. I mean, eventually. Look at me, I'm out every night and I still can't protect everybody."

"Yeah, and how do you feel about the people you can't save?"

He had a point. But that was part of the deal. A hard part, but unchangeable.

"Maybe you should talk to Oz about this? Have you asked him if he'll start your werewolf apprenticeship, or whatever?"

"We don't talk much about that kind of werewolf stuff. Just maintenance and upkeep: how to check the cage locks for wear and to make sure to get enough protein and calcium."

"Well, if you're ready, don't you think it's time to start?"

"I don't know," Jake said, and Frankie didn't like it. She didn't like it when he hung his head. She didn't like seeing him torn up about stuff. Jake took so many things in stride. Even new feelings for Sam, which might have thrown other people into a tailspin. It was only his family that could really hurt him. "I guess I always thought it was a talk I would have with my mom and dad. Not Oz."

"Have you heard from them lately?"

"Not since we sent the Countess meat to Weretopia this fall," he said. "And then it was pretty much 'Yum, thanks.'"

"Look, it's their loss. Oz is here, and he's the expert on taming the beast anyway. He's the one who founded Weretopia in the first place, and he's, like, a community leader. You should talk to him, Jake."

"Maybe. Listen, I'll be fine. I just need some time to think. About . . . everything, I guess."

Frankie bit down on the retort she would usually give, which was *Since when do you think?* and nodded. Jake would be okay. After the night's patrol, she would stop over at his cage and bring him some cold cuts and one of those rotisserie chickens from the gas station. She'd tell him the story of Little Red Riding Hood and drag out the part where the wolf ate the grandma. And the woodsman. And Riding Hood. And after his wolfing was over, he'd feel better again. He'd remember how much he helped, and how much she needed him.

CHAPTER THIRTEEN
THIS SLAYER OR THAT SLAYER

Frankie and Hailey walked through New Sunnydale, making their way toward the cemetery as the sun dipped lower in the sky. They were on their own for patrol: Jake had to get himself locked up tight in the Osbourne basement, and Sigmund elected to stay behind in the library to continue looking for a solution in the search for the missing slayers. But he did put his demon-census journal into Hailey's backpack, in case they came across anything interesting.

"Hey," Hailey said. "We got time to have a slice? I'm starving." She gestured to Giovanni's on the corner, and Frankie's stomach rumbled at the thought of a nice, foldable triangle of cheese and red sauce, a little garlic and thin-sliced mushrooms. The cemetery wasn't far from there, only a few blocks over. And it wasn't even fully dark yet.

They went inside and ordered slices and sodas, then took their plates outside to eat at one of the sidewalk tables and watch people line up for an early movie at the small theater up the street.

"What's playing?" Hailey asked, and took a big bite of her pizza with Italian sausage and red peppers.

"Some art-house thing," Frankie replied. "That theater only shows indies."

"Cool."

They ate quickly as the sun went down and the streetlights came on. Frankie ate at double speed and went back in to order another.

"So, what's up with Jake?" Hailey asked. "Is he okay?"

"He's fine," Frankie replied. "Or he will be. It's just werewolf stuff." She said nothing else, though she could see Hailey suspected there was more to the story. But whatever was happening with him and Sam, that part was for Jake to tell. "What's up with Vi? You guys have been texting on the regular."

"Yeah." Hailey chewed on the end of her compostable straw. "She's still being evasive. Won't say anything useful. But I know I can get it out of her; I just need more time."

"You don't need to do that—we're not asking you to double-agent your sister."

"Yeah but . . . what else am I good for? I want to help the Scoobies as much as I can."

"What's going on with everyone?" Frankie asked. "Haven't we already proven that I can't do this without you? Without any of you?" Frankie cocked her head. "Also, you in particular are good for just about everything. Stake carving, ass kicking, research—"

"I suck at research."

"—keeping my sparring stick sharp at one end . . . making out with Sigmund . . ."

"Well, I am great at that."

Frankie grinned. "And if I recall you're pretty handy with that little ax."

"Oh yeah." Hailey grinned back. "My ax. I should've brought that." She looked down at the backpack resting against her legs. "Not that we would need it. Since we took care of those fish monsters things have really cooled off again."

"Oh my god!" someone screamed in the theater line. "What are those?"

Frankie and Hailey jumped up as more screams followed, and the line to the theater scattered in all directions, being chased by what looked to be enormous spider creatures with long green bodies.

"Why do I say anything?" Hailey asked, and Frankie said, "Let's go!"

They dashed across the street, dodging people as they fled. Hailey had a good view, being taller than many, but it was hard for Frankie to see what was happening through all the panicked theater patrons. She did, however, see one of the spider demons jump onto a man's shoulders and use its long mandibles to tear his heart out through his back and eat it.

"They eat hearts!" Frankie shouted to Hailey.

"Just like your boyfriend!" she shouted back.

"He's not my boyfriend!" Frankie kicked one of the spiders off an old woman in a pretty crocheted sweater and helped her up. "Here you go, ma'am—" But another spider attacked, and she was forced to toss the old woman into the arms of a helpful passerby who barely caught her. "Sorry, ma'am!"

Hailey pulled a knife out of her backpack and swung it hard toward the spider's legs. It sliced the foot off one but missed the other, and the demon knocked Hailey to the ground.

"Hailey!" Frankie squeaked. The spider demons were fast, and if Hailey's heart got ripped out—

"Get off my sister!" Vi grabbed the spider by the rear set of legs

135

and swung it hard into the side of the movie theater. Then she took the knife from Hailey's hand and threw it into the creature's thorax. The spider fell, and its legs curled in on itself.

"Nice!" Frankie shouted. The street had emptied, and all but two of the moviegoers had gotten away. The unlucky ones' bodies lay in the street with holes in their chests. But the remaining spiders were still hungry. Six of them, all hurrying toward Frankie, Hailey, and Vi on forty-eight fast legs.

"Lead them to the cemetery, away from people!" Vi called, and took off, with Frankie and Hailey just a beat behind.

"Call Spike!" Frankie cried, and Hailey took her phone out. "And Oz! And my mom!"

"We'll have these things beat before they get there, sport," Vi said over her shoulder.

"Sport?" Frankie said, aghast. "Who are you calling 'sport'?"

They hurtled through the gates of Silent Hills Cemetery with the spider demons hot on their tails. Frankie chanced a look back and saw one scuttle up the side of an angel statue and launch itself through the air—she jumped and sent it sprawling with a flying roundhouse kick. But that wasn't going to do; she had to get closer if she wanted to slay them.

"Vi, do you know what these things are?" Hailey shouted.

"Grimslaw demons," her sister shouted back. "Sharp claws, and watch the mouth—it extends, and its teeth can drill and chomp like a bear trap."

EW, Frankie thought. She should have brought her sparring stick. With its deadly sharpened end, it would have been perfect for slaying these things at a distance. The trouble with the sparring stick was that it was hard to bring it on patrol without looking like a wizard on a quest. Hailey took another knife out of the backpack, and Frankie used her telekinesis to tug it from her grip. She sent it flying back toward the Grimslaw demons—and watched them deflect the blade with fast movements of their many, many legs.

"Crap!"

"Well, it was worth a try," said Vi. "Guess we'll have to do this the old-fashioned way." She ran up the side of a mausoleum and flipped backward, high in the air, to land on the body of a Grimslaw demon and squish it with her boots. The long legs twitched around her for a moment, trying to stab her face, and she dodged and swatted them away. But the thing was dead. So squishing worked. Vi ducked beneath two jumping spiders and ran to catch up.

"Where's a can of Raid when you need one?" Hailey screamed.

"I thought you liked spiders," said Vi.

"Yeah," Hailey said, panting. "The cute, fuzzy ones with sweet black eyes. Not these demons with drill teeth!"

Frankie slowed as they reached the deeper part of the cemetery, where the lines of headstones were thicker and the place was less of a park and more a place with nice granite markers to throw giant bugs against. She turned just in time to catch the first Grimslaw as it screeched and vaulted through the air, then swung it round and round like they were kids on a playground before chucking it into the Murray headstone. Vi threw a knife, and the demon died, legs curling up.

Frankie used her magic to call the knife back. They didn't have enough in the backpack to just leave them lying around in demons.

"My turn," Vi said, and swung a spider through the air. Frankie took aim and threw the knife. Direct hit. Three down.

Suddenly, a snarl erupted from the other side of the cemetery. At first, Frankie thought it came from the spiders, except they had paused to listen, too.

"What is that now?" Hailey pointed. Three large humanoid

demons were running at them from the tree line, their skin a mottled green and tan. They looked faintly reptilian. Their arms were long, and as Frankie watched, mean-looking skewers extended from both wrists.

"Polgaras," Vi said. "They kill with . . . well, with those skewers they just took out."

"Do they usually hang with Grimslaws?" Hailey asked. "Are they controlling them?"

"I've never heard of that," said Vi.

"I'll handle them," Frankie said. "Larsson sisters, keep on squishing bugs." She raced ahead. She had to engage the demons far away, or the whole battle could become one big dust cloud of skewers and extra legs. She launched herself feetfirst into the nearest Polgara's chest and knocked it down, then rolled upright. "Whoa!" She ducked a sweeping skewer. "Eep!" She flipped backward to avoid a stab aimed for her intestines. One of the Polgaras got behind her, and before she knew it, she was jumping thrusting skewers like she was playing a game of double Dutch.

"Maybe I should've stayed with the spiders!"

She saw an opening and tucked tight to roll. When she popped up she jumped across the headstones, landing spinning kicks and flipping back onto the headstones to hold the high ground. She dodged another sweeping attack and leapt onto the Polgara's arm with both feet, snapping its arm skewer off at the wrist. It screeched and tried to stab her with the other, but she dropped to one knee and drove the broken end of the skewer deep into its chest.

Not bad. But there was only one more coming after her, so where was the third? She craned her neck to check on Hailey and Vi. Vi was pummeling the third Polgara, but that left Hailey on her own, still dealing with two Grimslaws.

"RAWR!" Spike roared, and landed on one of the spiders with

the full force of his weight. Good. Hailey had managed to make the phone call.

"Yipes!" Frankie shouted as her Polgara knocked her to the ground, and she rolled when it stabbed. The stab missed, but it was hard enough to drive the skewer deep into the ground. The demon tugged, stuck fast to the earth, and reared back to stab with the other arm. Frankie rolled again, and the other skewer sank deep into the ground, with the same result as the first.

"You're not too smart, are you?" Frankie said through gritted teeth. But she was in quite the predicament. The demon was stuck, but so was she, pinned underneath, her hands up to push away its head and fangs.

"This is going to suck, but I have no choice," she groaned, and broke the demon's neck. It collapsed, all its deadweight on her torso, skewers still stuck in the dirt. Farther away in the cemetery she heard the last Polgara's death cry and figured Vi must have had better luck. And sure enough, she heard their footsteps approaching on the grass.

"Frankie, are you okay?" Hailey asked.

"Yep. Demon's dead; it's just heavy. And it pinned me." She twisted under the dead Polgara and saw Spike squinting at her. He seemed a little embarrassed. "What?" she asked. "There were lots of demons!"

With a sigh, he and Vi leaned down and pulled the body off her. She stood and brushed dirt from her shoulders.

"Two kinds of demons," Vi said. "Lots for you to compost, I guess. Hailey told me about your spell. Sounds cool. Way easier than dumping them, or dismembering them and dumping them."

"Yeah, Mini Red's just full of useful tricks," said Spike. "She's still not very graceful, though. Since you're going to be hanging around, maybe you can show her some moves."

"Sure, no problem," said Vi.

"Excuse me?" Frankie asked, and pointed to the dead demons. "What's wrong with the way I fight?"

"Nothing," Spike said. "It's just a little bit Three Stooges. Vi's been a slayer a lot longer than you. She can give you some tips."

"I can," Vi said. "If you want. But you did a really good job tonight, tiger." She leaned forward and chucked Frankie on the arm.

"Hey, what about me?" Hailey asked. "I'm over here, not a slayer at all, and yet still alive. Not bad, eh?" But instead of being pleased, Vi took Hailey's bag of weapons and stuffed it into Spike's gut.

"You got the not-a-slayer part right, anyway. If the two of you had been out here alone, one of you would be dead."

"You don't know that for sure," Hailey objected.

"Well, I know that for probably," said Vi. "You should stay off patrols. Except in groups. Or with me."

"Vi," Frankie said. "I do look out for her. I know there's always risks, but—"

For a moment, the older slayer's eyes flashed bloody murder, but then she took a breath. "I know. I don't mean to say you don't. And this was"—she gestured to the cemetery full of demon corpses—"a little ridiculous, but it turned out okay. I've just seen a lot of times when it didn't."

"Hey," said Spike. "Don't scare her. She's doing her best. She's doing just what Buffy did."

Vi blinked at him slowly. "Sure. I know that. But I also know that she's going to lose someone eventually. No matter how hard she tries." She touched Frankie on the shoulder. "Like I said, it was good, tonight." She smiled. "I do like your lack of style."

Frankie took a shaky breath as the adrenaline of the fight receded and Vi and Spike walked through the cemetery to start the cleanup.

"Hey," said Hailey, and nudged her. "My sister's always like that. Doom and gloom. Don't let her freak you out."

"Yeah," said Frankie. "Let's just get to composting so we can go home."

$$\mathllap{)\ )\ \bigcirc\ (\ (}$$

Sigmund was finishing up in the library when he heard footsteps in the hallway. Quietly, he placed the last volume on demon species that used interdimensional portals into his backpack and picked up the large wooden cross that rested beside it. The figure that approached the library door had heft—he could tell by the sound of the steps. But it couldn't be Jake, coming back to hang out. It was after dark, and Jake was locked in a cage in his werewolf skin. Sigmund clenched the cross tightly. His stomach wobbled. He could use it to bludgeon with, he supposed, if whatever was coming wasn't a vampire.

The door pushed open, and the demon walked inside.

"Mother," he said, and lowered the cross.

"I thought I would find you here. Still with your books." Sarafina DeWitt raised her eyebrows at the cross drooping from his fingers. "And your vampire cross. Sigmund. You could at least have a stake."

"I do have a stake. I just didn't reach for it."

Sarafina approached his table and looked through the books he had already packed. Heavy volumes, some in languages he doubted that she could read. Other mothers might have found that impressive. The only thing his mother could have found in that backpack to please her was a severed head.

"They got into some trouble, you know," she said. "Your friends. They got into some trouble while you were lingering here, with your nose in these books."

"Frankie and Hailey? Are they okay?"

"I spoke with Willow after she left me to meet them at her home. They're fine. Apparently they were besieged by both Grimslaws and Polgara demons."

"Two new entries for the census," Sigmund said quietly. "Odd that they would be encountered together."

"The census?"

"Yes, Mother, I told you. I'm compiling a demon census to evaluate the reach of the Sunnydale Hellmouth."

She sighed. "Another research project."

"It could be very useful for the slayer," he insisted. "And perhaps I could continue to expand it. Perhaps it could be published."

"Sigmund." She took him by the shoulders, and he felt the strength always present in her hands. "The only way you can be of help to the slayer is if you pick up a blade. You are a warrior. We are warriors."

"We're warrior scholars," Sigmund corrected. "Somehow you always seem to forget that."

"And somehow I thought when you told me you were staying in Sunnydale to aid the new slayer that it meant that—"

Sigmund swallowed. That what? He would suddenly grow his horns? That his shoulders would broaden, and he would muscle out of his many sweater vests? That he would finally become less of a disappointment? He stuffed the last of his books into his bag. It wasn't easy for her, he supposed. The Great Sarafina DeWitt, the strongest fighter in the DeWitt family of Sage demons, and yet her only offspring had never even made a kill. How she must have regretted having him with his father. She must wish that he'd been spawned by any other demon. She must wish he was anything but human.

"I need to go to the Rosenbergs' house," he said tersely. "Will you be all right, waiting at my apartment?"

"Of course." She touched his cheek. "I didn't mean to upset you, my son. I only know what it is that you could be." She shrugged. "And I am very impressed by your Hailey. She follows the slayer into battle and fights without fear, even though she is so very mortal."

Hailey fights with plenty of fear, he wanted to say, but he hated to pick fights with his mother. He so rarely won them.

"Mother," he said, smiling, "thank you . . . for being so kind to Hailey. She was mortified by the way you met, and I know she wants you to like her."

Sarafina smiled back. "Of course. I like her very much. Why wouldn't I," she began to flip through one of the volumes he had left behind on the table, "when she doesn't matter?"

Sigmund paused. "What?"

"Well, of course you know that," Sarafina said. "She's just a human girl. When you find your demon bride, I will test her more thoroughly." She walked to Sigmund and kissed him on the cheek, then straightened his collar. "But there's plenty of time until then. Good night, Sigmund. Tell Willow I will call her tomorrow."

CHAPTER FOURTEEN
AT LEAST WE DON'T NEED A MAGIC BONE

Frankie stood over the stove in their kitchen, piling a plate high and deep with spaghetti noodles. High and deep, and right to the edge, that's how she liked her pasta these days. Also drenched in butter and sauce, with so much Parmesan cheese it looked like her dinner had just survived a tiny little snowstorm.

"I should buy bigger plates," Willow said. "Or maybe I should just buy a bucket and write your name on it." She peered into the steaming pot and fished out the last scoop of noodles for herself. "I remember when Jake was the only kid who'd clean out the cupboards."

Frankie spun a huge bite onto her fork. "Nothing like hot carbs to refuel after being pinned to the cemetery by a Polgara demon." She frowned. Now that the battle was over, she was tired. And what Vi said, about losing someone—she'd told Hailey she was fine before the sisters had gone off to their post-battle diner session, but she hadn't been able to shake it. Losing someone. She was going to lose someone. Maybe not today, maybe not for ten years, but someday. That is, if she managed to live long enough herself.

"You okay, sweetie?" Willow asked.

"Yeah. Yeah, I'm just wiped out. Can we eat on the sofa with our plates on our laps?"

Willow grabbed some napkins and picked up her plate and fork. "As long as you can keep that mountain of noodles from falling off onto the cushions."

Frankie nodded and followed her mom into the living room. She couldn't think about losing one of the Scoobies. She couldn't be a slayer without them. Vi could. Some slayers could go it alone. But Buffy didn't, and Frankie didn't want to either.

"Mom, did Buffy ever try to get you to stay out of the fight?"

"You mean the fight against the demons and the forces of darkness?" Willow said. "Not really."

"She didn't worry you'd get hurt?"

"Sure. Just like we worried that she'd get hurt. She ran away once, but that wasn't about keeping us safe. We were never going to be safe in Sunnydale anyway."

"That's true." Frankie brightened a little. "So it's not, like, reckless for me to have Hailey and Jake and Sigmund around?"

"No. Well. No. Besides, do you really think you could stop them? Buffy could never have stopped us. I'm a witch. I do what I want." Willow moved her shoulders in a faux swagger, and Frankie smiled. "Now eat up."

Frankie dove into her pasta. Her mom was right; there was no ditching the Scoobies. They were stuck to her like glue. And what that could eventually mean for them, well . . . who needed to think about that when she could bury it under two pounds of spaghetti?

"I am so ready for bed," said Willow when she finished.

"Me too," said Frankie. "I might not even make it there. You might find me in the morning facedown in the hallway."

Willow chuckled and set their plates on the coffee table. She had her hair twisted over her shoulder and wore a long, flowy tunic over a pair of cropped jeans.

"You're looking very Zen," Frankie said, "Considering your only daughter was almost just eaten by spiders. Must've had a good time with Sarafina?"

Willow blushed, and a sly smile crept onto her lips. "It's too early to talk about. But it is really nice to see her. Like . . . really nice."

"No arguments here. She is one hot Sigmund's mama."

"Frankie." Willow swatted her knee lightly. "But there is one thing I noticed."

"What?"

She shook her head. "No, it's probably nothing."

Frankie swatted her mom's knee.

"Well, it's just that Sarafina seems very curious about Oz."

Frankie's brow furrowed. "She probably just hasn't seen a werewolf with Oz's level of control. That would be impressive to someone who doesn't know him."

"That might be all it is."

"Of course that's all it is."

"So you haven't noticed her flirting with him or anything?"

"I've noticed her flirting with everyone. I think that's just her way. Maybe even the Sage demon way, with all the charm mojo and whatnot," Frankie said. But her mom didn't seem convinced. Her right eye had started twitching and narrowing, like she was thinking about ways to turn Oz into a wereskin rug. "Mom. It's probably all in your head."

Willow shrugged and nodded. "Sure. I know."

"Or maybe it's in Sarafina's head. She knows you and Oz have history; maybe she's scoping out the competition. She'll figure it out eventually."

"Probably sooner than we will," Willow muttered.

"Huh?"

"Nothing. Let's turn in. I'm losing consciousness." They stood, and Frankie stretched and reached to grab their plates. As they walked through the entryway toward the kitchen, both of them jumped at a series of loud knocks on the front door.

"Who is that?"

Frankie didn't know. Jake was a werewolf and Hailey would have come right in. She set the plates down and went to the door, half expecting to see Grimloch, or Vi, but instead found a frazzled Sigmund.

"Sig?" Frankie asked. "Are you all right? You look . . . rattled. Come on in."

He tried to smile at her and walked into the living room, where he removed his glasses and rubbed his eyes; they were a little red and watery. Stressed, and very un-Sigmund-like.

"Sig?"

"Yes, um, please excuse the lateness of the hour. And I know I look rather miserable, but the reason I'm here isn't." He put his glasses back on and looked from Frankie to her mom. "I have good news. Or what could be good news. I think I've found a way to trace the missing slayers across dimensions."

"Oh my god," said Frankie. She and Willow looked at each other, suddenly very much awake. "How?"

"Well," Sigmund said, beginning to pace, "I was spending so much time focusing on the dimensional tear, and whether the traces of that could be reverse-engineered, scouring spellbooks and texts on interdimensional travel—I read about so many different demon dimensions that I think I briefly went blind—"

"I know how that feels," said Frankie.

"And then I realized: Why focus on the portal when we can focus on what went through it?"

"You mean the slayers?" Willow asked.

"Precisely."

"Can we do that? How do we do that?"

"With the power of the slayers." Sigmund looked at Frankie and then at Willow. "The slayer power is unique. And plenty strong enough to be traceable. Especially if a lot of it is grouped together."

"Strong enough to trace across dimensions?" Frankie asked.

"I think so. As long as we have something that would call to it." Again he looked at Willow, and again at Frankie, like he was hinting at something but didn't want to come out and ask.

"Are we supposed to guess?" Willow asked. "Because as brainy as we Rosenbergs are, it's late."

Sigmund glanced down boyishly. Frankie had the brief urge to squeeze him like a body pillow and knew he was nervous and accidentally sending out vibes of charm. "It's just that I feel strange about asking," he said. "But I was thinking that we could use the Scythe."

The Scythe. The weapon of the slayer, forged in secret for the original slayer to use to defeat the last of the Old Ones. Before the battle with the First, Buffy had found it and pulled it from a stone, and then Willow had used it to cast the spell that activated all of the Potentials. And created Frankie.

"But we don't have that," Frankie said. Or she had certainly never seen it. "Don't the Watchers have that for safekeeping?" She looked at her mom.

"No, I have it," said Willow. "It's in the garage."

Willow led the way as Frankie and Sigmund followed through the house and out the side door that led to the garage. Frankie watched, open-mouthed, as Willow flipped on the light and walked past the Prius to a green metal trunk that held some of their old clothes and photo albums.

"It's not in there," Frankie said as Willow knelt and undid the latch. That trunk wasn't even locked. And Frankie had rifled through it lots of times, searching for hidden Hanukkah presents, or heck, just searching for the Scythe when she and Jake used to play Find the Scythe. All that was in that trunk were newspaper clippings of Jake's early lacrosse games and an article about Frankie placing second in the district spelling bee. There were some of her baby clothes and an old, very padded mobile that used to hang above her crib. A lamb costume from her third or fourth Halloween. She'd been through it top to bottom, and there was no . . .

Willow reached into the trunk and pulled out the Scythe, shimmering sharply red under the fluorescent lights.

"Mom! How did you— Where did you—" Frankie and Sigmund hurried to her. Frankie gaped at the Scythe in awe, then peered into the trunk, the contents of which looked no different from the many times she'd searched through it. "When did you put that in there?"

"It's been in there the whole time."

"But—I looked—"

Willow tugged the Scythe closer to her body. "Well, I wasn't going to store an ancient mythical weapon in our garage without putting an enchantment on it first," she said. "I'm no dummy." She used the sleeve of her tunic to wipe a bit of dust from the blade and carried it happily into the house.

She brought it into the living room and brandished it slowly back and forth. Frankie's eyes and head followed it like she was one of those charmed snakes in a basket. The Scythe. The for-real Scythe, right there, right in front of her. The original slayer had wielded that. Buffy had wielded that. And just looking at it, she could sense its power, calling to her, like to like. It was old, and it was hers. It was a slayer-family heirloom, and it had been in their garage trunk the whole time.

"Mom, I can't believe you never told me."

"If I'd told you where it was hidden, it wouldn't have been much of a hiding," said Willow. "This spell, Sigmund. Do you know where to start?"

"I have some ideas," said Sigmund. He pushed up his glasses. "It will be delicate, and I'll need a few days to gather ingredients. But now that we have the Scythe"—he looked at Frankie, his eyes bright—"this could really work."

Frankie reached up to touch the handle with her fingertips, but pulled her hand back before she could. If she touched it, she would want to hold it. And if she held it, she would want to slay with it, and it was way too late and she was way too tired.

"This is strictly Scooby business," Frankie said. "Scoobies only. No one else should know. At least until we know if it will work." She turned to her mom. "We could really get them back. She could really come home. I just hope they're not trapped in some hell dimension where one month is, like, a hundred years or something."

"If that's the case, sweetie," her mom said, "then we are already very too late."

CHAPTER FIFTEEN
SCOOBY DOOBY DON'T

Patrol on Valentine's Day. It was an affront to romance everywhere. Not that Frankie had anywhere else to be, though she did wonder what Grimloch was up to, and if he even knew what Valentine's Day was. And she felt bad that everyone else had been dragged out, too, when she was certain they'd rather be somewhere else and doing . . . other things. Well, except Vi.

"Stop moping, Mini Red," Spike ordered. "Valentine's isn't like Halloween. Demons do not take the night off. Actually it's one of their favorite nights. All the youthful energy in the air, all the body heat and pheromones"—he lifted his nose like he could catch a whiff—"it's practically like egging them on."

"This isn't much of a Valentine's," Frankie heard her mom whisper to Sarafina as they trailed behind. "Following our kids around on slay patrol."

"I welcome the chance to face a vampire," Sarafina replied. "And as for Valentine's, the night is young."

Frankie glanced back as the witch and the Sage demon leaned their heads together. Willow put her arm out to share the warmth of her wrap, and Sarafina caught the end and pulled it tight. She looked less formal than usual but still like herself: dressed for a fight and yet also for a four-star restaurant in attractive black slacks and flats, her jewelry light and close to her body—unlikely to get torn off.

"Our moms are pretty cute," Frankie said, and nudged Sigmund.

"What?" He looked over his shoulder. "Oh. Yes, they certainly are."

"You okay, Sig?" Hailey asked. She slipped her hand up his arm.

"Of course. My mother's visit has just been a bit longer than I planned on." He flashed a very Sigmund smile and stepped out of Hailey's embrace to walk beside Oz and Vi.

"What's going on?" Frankie asked Hailey.

"Must be just what he said. Fight with his mom." But as they turned up the street that led to Silent Hills, her eyes remained trained on Sigmund's back.

When they got to the cemetery, they immediately saw that Spike was right. There was no need to go looking: a group of five vampires was right there for the picking, lingering near the entrance, fangs and yellow eyes on full display. Three guys and two girls: one of the girls had a sweet punk-rock hairdo; the other was a pretty blond trying to check her makeup in a mirror she could no longer see herself in. The guys looked like recruits from the skate park. One had a wicked Mohawk. Another had a hacky sack. They all looked a little bored and seemed genuinely surprised when the Scoobies rolled in.

"Must be new in town," Frankie commented as the vampires fanned out. "Haven't heard of me and my patrol routes."

For a moment, the two sides stood, team to team, as Frankie tried to pick out the leader. The group didn't look like too much trouble; even with Jake still in his cage and Sigmund not fighting, the Scoobies still outnumbered them.

"This isn't going to devolve into an embarrassing dance-off, is it?" Hailey asked, and took out her ax.

The vampires looked at the ax. They looked at Sigmund's cross and Oz's claws. They didn't look at Frankie, which she thought was rude, before taking off in different directions through the headstones. Punk Girl, Mohawk Boy, and the hacky-sack vamp ran to the left, and the blond girl and the other vamp ran to the right.

"Runners," Spike said. "Should be good practice. Frankie, you're with me. We'll take the left three."

"I've got Blondie," Hailey said, and hefted her ax. She didn't wait for clearance before racing after the vampire into the night.

"She's going to sever her damned leg with that thing." Vi started running. "I can't believe you just let her go!"

"Go after her, then!" Spike yelled as Vi shouted, "Hailey! You are not a slayer! Give me that ax!"

"I'll back them up," said Oz, and jogged into the dark, claws out.

Spike looked over his shoulder. "Sigmund, lad, stay here and keep an eye on the gate with the mums. If they double back, give a shout."

"The mums?" Willow curled her lip. Sarafina also seemed to disapprove, less about being called a mum than by her son being left behind. But there was no time to argue; the vampires weren't slowing, and even as Spike and Frankie took shortcuts, using the best routes over and around the headstones, they almost didn't catch up before the tree line.

"Ready, Mini Red?" Spike asked, and threw himself into the fray.

Frankie pulled up short as Spike unleashed his inner badness.

He jammed the Mohawk Guy's nose with a palm thrust before splitting his lip with a reverse elbow. While Mohawk Guy was holding his nose and mouth, Spike kicked the legs out from underneath Punk Girl and left her sprawling.

"All right, slayer. Your turn."

Frankie stepped in, resisting the urge to hold her hand out and say, *Tag me!* as Punk Girl flipped back onto her feet.

"We heard you were here," said the vamp holding his nose. "William the Bloody."

"Look who's talking," said Spike, gesturing to the redness dripping down the vampire's chin.

"Fang traitor." Punk Girl sneered. "With a *soul*."

"Jealous?" Spike asked, and spin-kicked the guy with the broken nose so hard that he bounced off the side of a crypt.

"Okay, *now* is it my turn?" Frankie asked. Punk Girl kicked her hard from behind, and Frankie wheeled forward. "Guess so." She turned and kicked, and their kicks met in midair, their feet locking at the ankle. The vampire twisted and pulled Frankie off-balance, then somehow managed to flip her own supporting foot up to corkscrew with her other foot and break loose. Frankie wavered and ducked as the vampire with the broken nose came back to throw wild punch after wild punch, blood from his nose flying off his fists.

"Yeesh." Frankie backed off, bobbing and weaving.

"No, no, no!" Spike shouted. "Be the aggressor! Like this." He reached into the fight and jerked the Mohawked vampire's legs out from under him, then threw him backward into the air. The vamp flipped once and landed squarely on the tines of a wrought-iron fence, dusting instantly. "See?"

"You want me to backflip them to death?" Frankie asked, and punched Punk Girl in the face. Not much of a punch, just enough to give her some breathing room so she could confer with her Watcher.

"I want you to get it done," Spike snapped. He grabbed the hacky-sack kid by the neck and twisted his arm up behind him, holding one opponent back to make it easier for his slayer. "And watch that kick!"

Frankie flew backward from a kick to the gut. But she had seen it coming—half the backward flight was her own doing. Rolling with kicks and punches instead of absorbing them had kind of become her specialty. But it didn't look flashy enough for Spike. She drew her stake and tried to zero in on the vampire's feet. She could grab her ankles and give her a good toss—the girl couldn't weigh more than a hundred and twenty. But before she could, the vampire kicked at her wrist, and the stake went flying out of her hand.

"Ow," Frankie said. She blocked a flurry of punches, backing up and backing up, ignoring Spike's groans and his repeated admonishments of "No, no, no." She led the vampire toward a low-hanging branch, and then, when the punk wound up for a devastating punch, Frankie ducked and scurried through her legs.

"What?" the vampire asked as Frankie popped up behind her and gave her a shove, right onto the branch, impaling her through the heart.

"Boom! Dusted." Frankie grinned and turned toward Spike, who was still holding Mr. Hacky Sack.

"That was," Spike said with a sigh, "truly pathetic."

"What do you mean 'pathetic'?" Frankie gestured to the open air. "They're dust, and we're alive! That is triumph."

"I can't argue with the result. But do you have to 'eep' and 'yeesh' all the time? And stop taking so many hits when you don't have to. It's dangerous, and it's bloody embarrassing."

Frankie sucked offended air inward in a gasp. "My slaying is embarrassing? How dare you." They might've gotten into a proper argument with only a vampire there to referee, had Hailey and Vi not shown up very clearly already in the middle of one.

"Just leave me alone, Vi!" Hailey yelled. "You don't get to show up and start telling me I can't do things!"

"That's all I used to do before you came to this stupid place," Vi snapped.

"What is your problem?"

"Well, what have your grades been like since you've been here?" Vi put her hands on her hips, and Hailey mirrored her stance. Frankie'd never thought they looked much like sisters—Hailey was taller and thicker, with tan skin and naturally black hair, where Vi was pale and small and looked more like a long-lost Rosenberg. But those angry expressions on their faces . . . they both must've inherited their angry face from their dad.

"My grades have been fine. The same as always." Hailey glanced at Frankie and gave her a bit of an eye. Just like Frankie's grades, hers had gotten a bit worse. "And what does it matter anyway? I'm a Scooby now, and the Watchers Council is fully funded. I won't need a real job—"

"So you're just going to give up on everything else in your life?"

In the corner of her eye, Frankie saw Sigmund and their moms walking tentatively closer, drawn by the noise of the argument.

"Everything else?" Hailey asked. "What was I even doing before? Hanging out in The Dalles with Mollie? It wasn't like I was on track for a scholarship, Vi; it wasn't like I had any big dreams!"

"You were going to go to art school."

"And I can still do that! But even if I can't, doesn't fighting evil seem, I don't know . . . more important? I thought you of all people would understand that!"

"And I thought you of all people would understand the opposite!" Vi screamed. "After seeing me do this every night of every
day of my life!" She stopped to breathe, but she wasn't done. "Every
day and every night having nothing and no one! Do you even know
what I wanted to be before I had to be a slayer? Well, I don't either!
Because I can't even goddamn remember!"

"Vi," Hailey said, quieting. "I—"

Perhaps her next words would have soothed Vi and ended the
argument. Unfortunately they would never know. Because before
she could say them, something snarled, and Spike and Frankie
turned to see another vamp, standing right behind Sigmund.

"You're new," said Spike. And the vampire truly was. Newly
turned and newly risen, still in the gray suit he'd been buried in,
and his fingers all filthy with dirt from digging out.

"I'm sorry to intrude," he said. He looked disoriented. He
blinked yellow eyes and seemed confused by the fangs in his mouth.
"I just heard shouting. Is everything okay?"

"Well—" Willow looked at him regretfully. "Not exactly."

"Oh. I should leave you alone, then. I'm just . . ." His gaze shifted
to Sigmund's neck. "I'm just . . . hungry." He grabbed Sigmund by
the shoulder and dragged him close, lifting him onto his toes.

"Sigmund!" Hailey shouted.

"Fight him!" Sarafina growled. But Sigmund was clearly not
fighting. He struggled in the vampire's grasp, one hand fending
off fangs and the other searching his bag for a cross to replace the
one he'd just dropped. Sarafina roared and went to her son in one
leap. She wrapped her hands around the sides of the vampire's head
and twisted it cleanly off, and the vampire collapsed into bones
and then into dust, and Sigmund landed back on his own feet.
"Sigmund! Are you all right?"

"Don't celebrate yet," Vi said. She glanced around the cemetery, and Frankie followed her gaze: There were other figures in the cemetery now, making their way toward them through the dark on disoriented legs, all wearing suits and dresses that had been cut up by an undertaker and pinned together at the back.

"Hey." Spike shook the hacky-sack enthusiast, whose arm he still had pinned behind him. "What the bloody hell is this? How many fledglings did you lot make?"

"So many," the vampire admitted, with wide eyes. "Like, I was starting to feel woozy."

"Well, why did you make so many?" Frankie squeaked.

"It was like"—the vampire gestured with an open palm, searching for the right words—"we were *compelled* to." Then he twisted hard and broke free of Spike's grip to run away toward the cemetery gate.

"Never mind that," Spike said when Frankie moved to chase him. "Worry about Bill and Ted Esquire later. We've got bigger problems."

And they did. Frankie and Vi went to work, with support from Spike and Hailey, Oz, and Sarafina, who had seemingly discovered a new hobby of twisting off vampiric heads. But even with the six of them, it was overwhelming. Each fledgling took time; they were young and hungry and inexplicably good at fighting. As Frankie dusted the last one, she heard the sound of another, emerging from the dirt.

"This is ridiculous!" she shouted. "They just keep on coming!"

"I think I can help," her mom called.

Frankie felt something shift as her mom marshaled her magic. And she marshaled a lot of it, so much that Frankie felt a little of her own magic push at her edges, like it wanted to join in the fun.

Willow closed her eyes. When she opened them, they were black, and Frankie stiffened.

"*Lutum induresco.*"

The spell swept out across the cemetery, and Frankie felt the earth tighten—for a moment, she even felt her legs tighten, like they were turning to stone.

"There," her mom said, and when she looked, Willow's eyes were back to normal.

"What'd you do?" Spike asked, and absently touched the old glamour on his face, like he was making sure it was still there.

"I trapped them in the dirt," said Willow. "Now we can deal with them one at a time."

Frankie walked through the graves until she found one: a fledgling stuck half in and half out, pushing against the ground that gripped his waist.

"Hey, uh, I don't know how this happened," he said. "But could you maybe give me a hand?"

"Sure," said Frankie, and quickly staked him. It was easy, but it didn't feel . . . sporting. Like plucking a flower from a flowerpot.

"You continue to impress me," Sarafina said, and Willow smiled.

Frankie looked at Oz, and Oz looked back. It was a lot of magic, and Willow had done it to help. But she had also clearly done it to impress the Sage demon.

"Well, that's one crisis averted," said Spike. "This was odd, though. *Compelled*, he said. What could compel five normal, not-so-bright vampires to do all this?"

"Plus all the Grimslaw demons and that herd of Polgaras," said Oz. "It's like someone put a quarter in the Hellmouth."

Vi shifted her weight uncomfortably, and even though she didn't know her, Frankie recognized the stance of someone about to cut and run. But Hailey wasn't letting her off the hook so easy.

"Hey, where do you think you're going?"

"Back to my hovel. You don't need me for anything, apparently," Vi said.

"Don't you think you owe them an apology?" Hailey asked, nodding toward the group.

Vi glanced at Frankie. "For what?"

"Or maybe you even owe them a thank-you." Hailey put her hands on her hips. "They've been looking out for me since you disappeared. They've become my friends. Made me a Scooby. And all you do is treat them like they're Emperor Palpatine."

"I'm not—" Vi sighed, and rubbed her temples. "It's just that since you were a kid, what have I told you? Stay away from this. If anything happens to me, just go. Live a normal life. And the first thing you do is run here and become—*a Scooby*."

Hailey shrugged. "Being a Scooby seems pretty normal to me. Doesn't even seem that dangerous when you think about it. At least we know what's in the dark; at least we can fight it."

Frankie winced. Somehow those were not the right words. Vi looked like her head was about to explode.

"Not that dangerous?" she said. She pointed at Oz. "That one got turned into a werewolf. Their precious Xander lost an eye. Anya got sliced in half in the battle with the First, and I think there was a prom queen who followed Angelus to LA and died in a supernaturally induced coma. How safe does that sound? And let's not forget the red witch, who nearly ended all life on this planet."

"Mind your words," said Sarafina. "The red witch deserves respect."

"And what about me?" Spike asked. "I'm fine."

"You got blown up, you moron." She pointed at her sister. "And you're not staying here."

"Yes, I am," said Hailey.

"Then you're doing it without me," Vi said, and walked away.

"Vi! Dammit, Vi!" Hailey went after her, and turned to Frankie and Sigmund. "I'll be right back. I just have to calm her down."

"It's okay." Oz moved to stand beside a fledgling half stuck in its grave, and Sigmund handed him a stake. "We'll clean up here."

"And I'll go after Mr. Hacky Sack," said Frankie. "Can't let him just keep on running around, making himself woozy."

$$\text{))} \bigcirc \text{((}$$

It didn't take long for Frankie to find the escaped vampire.

"She can't just take Hailey and go," Frankie said as she mercilessly pummeled the poor creature who still clutched his hacky sack in one of his hands. "Who does she think she is?" she asked as her fists rapid-fire connected with his ribs like she was aiming to use his lungs as speed bags. "As if she's not old enough to make her own decisions?" She hit one more time, hard, and the vampire flew back and struck a dumpster, then fell to the ground clutching his ribs.

"Are you having a bad night or something?" he asked breathlessly as Frankie advanced. But Frankie barely heard. She just punched, and punched, and punched again.

"And that crack about my mom! My mom!"

"She insulted your mom?" the vampire asked innocently. "Whoa."

"I'm sorry," Frankie said, drawing her stake. "This really isn't personal. I'm just working through some things." She darted forward, and her stake sank into the vampire's chest. He barely had time to shrug and say "It's okay" before he turned to dust.

Frankie stared down at the pile and, with a mental heave, used her magic to dash it to the wind—vampire dust scattering in all directions. This wasn't fair. Vi couldn't just come and take Hailey away. And what about Sigmund? What if his mom said he had to go back with her to DC? What if Jake decided to go to Weretopia to train with Jordy?

Frankie turned around searching the alley for something else to dust.

"I need something to dust!" she shouted.

"I'm afraid I don't turn to dust," Grimloch replied. Frankie spun, and her shoulders slumped with relief. He had a real way of stepping right out of the shadows. "Bad night?"

"Well, it wasn't great," she said. "Is it about to get better?"

Grimloch smiled. He held out his arm and she stepped into it, and it was easy to lean her head on his chest and walk with him. She was glad he was a demon and not a vampire, so his hand on the small of her back was pleasantly warm. And somehow, despite his pervasive hotness, his presence took all the tension out of her limbs. Grimloch was solid and comforting. He was someone she could lean on. Because who else could you count on if not a two-thousand-year-old demon? It's not like he was going anywhere.

"Have you noticed increased demon activity over the last several days?" he asked as they walked.

"Oh, good," she said, and lifted her head from his chest. "Shop talk. But yes, I have, since you asked. After months of quiet, it's like suddenly our hellmouth is the most popular hellmouth at the party. Have you seen this before? Do hellmouths ebb and flow?"

Grimloch cocked his head, his long strides slowing to match her shorter ones. "I am admittedly not an expert on hellmouths."

"Just thought I'd ask. Maybe this is what the oracle meant when she said the darkness was headed our way. Maybe the darkness is a huge wave of demons, so many demons that they blot out the sun."

Frankie sighed. "It's a good thing Vi's back in town. And Sarafina, Sigmund's mom. If not for their help tonight . . ."

"Your words say it's a good thing, but your voice . . ."

"No," Frankie said, intentionally brightening. "It is a good thing. I'm glad my mom has someone she's interested in, and I'm glad Vi's not dead . . . but now I'd like them to leave."

"Why do you want them to leave?" Grimloch asked.

"It's just . . . having so much family in town is messing with my Scooby family."

"There's that word again," Grimloch said. "Scooby. When I was away, I watched a film to better understand you, and the redheaded girl in the purple dress is very pretty. The dog, however, is terrifyingly rendered."

"So you're into redheads," Frankie teased, and Grimloch flashed his fangs. She wondered if she would feel those if he kissed her. She wondered if he was a nipper, and felt a flush rising up her throat. He looked good. Button-down black shirt, dark hair tucked behind his ear. And his eyes, softly glowing, like little blue methane torches.

"I worried about you, you know. When you were gone."

"There was no need," he said. "I've been alive for a few thousand years. And I have yet to lose . . . anything that won't grow back."

Frankie made a mental note to ask him what indeed would grow back. And then made a second mental note to be careful to phrase it in a way that didn't sound pervy. "So, how's the tent holding up? Hailey and Sigmund and Jake and I came by every now and then to tidy it. I think we were hoping that one day you'd be back."

"You wanted me to live in a tent? You know you could have tidied a nice loft space downtown, in the restaurant district." She opened her mouth to tell him to do his own real estate shopping, and the corner of his mouth crooked in a smile.

"You're teasing."

"Is that allowed?"

"Sure. I just—I didn't even know you could be unserious."

"You bring it out in me," he said, and chuckled.

She felt the chuckle though his ribs, pressed against her side. They were so close. If she wanted to touch his stomach, she needed only to extend her hand.

"Frankie," Grimloch said, and stopped walking.

"Yes?" She pulled her hands back tight to her sides. All he would need to do was bend toward her. He touched her face, and she froze.

"Perhaps it would be a good idea if I joined you on patrol," he said. "As an extra pair of hands until Sunnydale grows calm again."

"I think that would be a very good idea."

His fingertips traced a line along her jaw and down the side of her neck.

"Huh," she said.

"What?"

"I just never realized I had all those nerve endings."

Grimloch smiled, and Frankie reached up and threaded her fingers into his. As he leaned closer, her mind raced ahead to patrols with just the two of them, moonlit strolls on the trail of evil, elevated pulses and fast breath. Suddenly, all the extra patrolling didn't seem so bad.

"Bring on the demons," Frankie whispered as Grimloch dipped his head and their lips met.

☽ ☽ ○ ☾ ☾

A kiss from Grim. And on Valentine's Day, no less. Frankie touched her lips, the memory still singing across every inch of her skin.

Who could have thought that only a few weeks after Spike had told her to get out there and cavort, that she would wind up with not just anyone, but the one she most wanted. The one she'd tried to talk herself out of, and who'd seemed impossibly out of reach. She was so lost in the replay of their kiss and their walk home that when Hailey slammed through the front door she didn't even startle.

"It's fine," Hailey declared. "I've talked her down, just like I always do." She stripped out of her black cardigan and tossed it onto the secretary desk where they kept their mail to pace in a white tank and black suspenders. *Goth nerd*, Frankie thought of that look. And it was cute when she and Sigmund both wore suspenders on the same day.

"Huh?" Frankie asked.

"Vi," Hailey said, puzzled. "She's A-OK now. Back on the slay board. I did have to promise to use a less dangerous weapon than my ax, but I can work her up to that. The important thing is, she's not leaving, and she's not forbidding me from being a Scooby. Are you okay, Frankie? Are you even listening?"

"I am," Frankie said. "And that's great. I'm really glad things are good with you and your sister."

"Honestly. Because we really do need her help around here. This place is jumpin'." Calmer now, Hailey peeked into the kitchen and back toward the stairs. "Your mom not here?"

"We have the house to ourselves. She and Sarafina went for a late dinner."

"Fantastic," Hailey groaned gratefully, and walked into the living room to fling herself onto the sofa. "What should we do? Movie? Plow our way through one of those boxes of chocolate your mom has stashed in the junk drawer?"

Frankie walked dreamily into the living room. Any of the above was fine with her, as long as they could talk about Grim. But before she could say one happy word, Hailey began to punch through channels on the TV. Like, hard.

"Are you sure you're okay?" Frankie sat down next to her.

"Sure, I'm sure. Vi's cool, like I said."

"Yeah but . . ." Frankie gently took away the remote control. "It's Valentine's night. Shouldn't you be off somewhere with Sig?"

"We're not joined at the hip, Frankie," Hailey said, and made a grab for the remote. She missed and tried again.

"Don't try to outgrab the slayer reflexes. Now what's going on? You guys actually are joined at the hip. But tonight he seemed . . . distant."

"He did seem distant, didn't he?" Hailey shook her head. "He wouldn't tell me why, or what's going on with his mom. He doesn't really talk to me about family stuff. And it feels kind of . . . bad."

"Maybe he just needs time? I mean, he's obviously crazy about you."

"Yeah. That's what I thought, too." Hailey's expression wobbled, and Frankie froze. She didn't know what to do if Hailey crumbled. But she didn't need to figure it out, because a moment later, Hailey quickly wiped at her eyes and heaved off the couch.

"Hailey?"

"It's going to be fine, Frankie," she called as she ran up the stairs. "I'm just tired, okay?"

Frankie slumped as the door to Hailey's room slammed shut. What was happening to them? To all of them? Jake was angry and full of doubts; Hailey was pulled in two directions, between the Scoobies and Vi; and Sigmund was just pulling away.

"Please, Scoobies," Frankie whispered. "Please don't fall apart."

CHAPTER SIXTEEN
TWO SLAYERS, NO WAITING

Frankie and Vi raced through the wooded hills northwest of New Sunnydale, leading a pack of hellhounds on a merry chase. There were six of them, each a spindle-legged, long-fanged mass of wiry gray fur and rage, and each with an appetite big enough to eat at least half a slayer apiece. So no matter what happened . . . two would go hungry. The hounds had been headed for the north-end restaurant district when Frankie and Vi had found them, and with some quick thinking, Frankie had tied a string of sausages around her waist. She'd had to break the butcher shop window to do it, and as a vegetarian, she didn't like being draped in so much meat, but it got the hellhounds' attention.

"You do have a plan, right?" Vi asked.

"Why is everyone so obsessed with plans?" Frankie asked back. "Can't you just be impressed by my sausage belt?"

"That is stylish," Vi admitted. "But I don't think it's going to be much of a diversion once they catch us."

Frankie pulled out her phone. She did have a plan, actually.

They were headed in the direction of the Countess's old mansion. More importantly, they were headed to the winding road that led to the mansion, where Frankie distinctly recalled there was a very steep drop-off down a big stone wall. They would drop down and cling to the side, and the dumb, bloodthirsty puppies would fall right over the edge. After that, it would just be a question of picking them off. And all she needed for that was her trusty crossbow. She tried to text Jake, who had taken it on patrol with Hailey, but texting while running? Even with slayer coordination, that was a real challenge.

She called Jake and put the phone to her ear. Out of breath as she was, all she could manage when he answered was "Jake! Crossbow! Old road to the Countess's place! Drop-off to the big wall!" Then she had to hang up and veer sharply as one of the hellhounds made a sprinting dash for the sausages.

"I hope Jake got that," said Vi as she leveled a spinning kick at a hound that got too close. "Because I didn't. Where's Grim? Shouldn't the Hunter of Thrace be all over these?"

"He's hunting in the eastern woods, and he doesn't have a phone!" Frankie scowled. Demon activity had continued to rise—so much that Sigmund's census had to be expanded from a notebook to an Excel spreadsheet. Just in the last week they'd fought vampires (of course), a demon with long, sharply tipped fingers that stripped off a bit of Jake's skin and left him briefly paralyzed, and now these hellhounds. They'd been so busy that she and Grim had barely had a chance to talk, let alone kiss again.

Frankie and Vi reached the road with the hellhounds close behind. She hoped the drop-off wasn't much farther; the sound of hellhound claws scrambling after them on asphalt was monstrously unsettling.

"It's around a curve," Frankie said. "Be ready to drop down and cling to the wall when I say!"

"You got it, junior," said Vi.

"Don't call me junior!"

"What? You would prefer Slayer Baby?"

"I would *not*," Frankie said, and raced ahead, around the curve where the drop-off loomed. "There it is! Get ready! I'm going to get another blast of speed out of them!"

Vi gritted her teeth and ran faster as Frankie grabbed the rope of sausages hanging from her belt and shook it enticingly from side to side. The hellhounds snarled and snapped and sped up toward the wall.

"Okay!" Frankie shouted. "Drop and hang!" They went over the edge, like they were rappelling except they weren't attached to a rope. The pain in Frankie's fingers when she grabbed on to the wall was quickly dulled by the pain of her face smacking into it as she pulled herself in tight. Over the tops of their heads, the hellhounds leapt off the edge and fell like cartoon coyotes, twisting in midair and snapping their jaws until they landed on the grass below. One or two of them yipped, but none were really hurt, and before long, they were jumping halfway up the wall to snap at the soles of Vi's and Frankie's shoes.

Vi climbed back up the wall and helped Frankie over the edge. For a moment when she grabbed her arm, Frankie's slaydar pinged: There was something in Vi's eyes—like she was deciding whether to help Frankie or give her a shove. And then it was gone.

Frankie dusted herself off. She must have imagined that. No matter how mad Vi was about Hailey being a Scooby, she was a slayer. Slayers didn't hurt other slayers. Unless you counted Buffy and Faith.

"So," Frankie said, "think this recent wave of baddies could be the darkness the oracle was talking about?"

Vi glanced at her, and there it was again. That flash of hostility, and the ping in her slaydar.

Vi peered over the edge at the snarling hounds. "They don't look that dark. They look . . . ashy gray. And they kind of smell."

"Well, they are hellhounds. I guess we can't expect them to smell like roses." Frankie tried to smile. Vi's hostility could be her fault. She'd been a little terse with Vi ever since she'd blown up at Hailey in the cemetery and insulted every Scooby in history. Things were cool now, they were totally cool, but what Vi had said was hard to forget.

"Here comes the cavalry." Vi nodded, and Frankie turned toward the unmistakable sound that was Oz's van hurtling up the road. Jake leaned out the driver's-side window and shouted her name, hanging the crossbow out like he might have to throw it to her as he drove by. When she made a *What are you doing?* gesture, he stopped shouting and pulled over so he and Hailey could get out.

"What is it?" Jake asked as they jogged over. "Frankie, are you okay?"

"She's clearly okay; she's standing there not bleeding," said Hailey. "But seriously, are you okay? What's that noise?"

"That noise is angry hellhounds," Vi answered.

Jake and Hailey leaned over the edge and were greeted by a cacophony of yips and snaps—hellhounds excited to see the appearance of more food. So excited that one of them intrepidly dug its claws into the rock and began to scrabble up the wall.

"He's making good progress." Vi held out her hand. "Crossbow." Jake handed it over, and Vi shot, striking the hellhound clean through the head. "Want to try one?" She passed the crossbow to Frankie.

Frankie adjusted her grip. She knew they were hellhounds—demons, essentially—but they were demon dogs. And as she looked down at them circling angrily, trying to figure out a way to rip her to pieces, she couldn't help but imagine what they might look like as puppies. Probably just like they did now, but smaller. But still. Puppies!

"Do we have to? Can't we . . . relocate them? Does Oz still keep his tranq gun in the van?"

"Of course he does," Jake replied in a strangely disapproving tone.

"Relocate them to where?" Vi asked. "Anywhere you put them they're just going to kill everything they come across. And I do mean everything."

"Yeah." Hailey looked down at the hounds. She and Vi still hadn't completely settled their argument, but the extra demon activity had served as a buffer to keep the peace. "I know they're kind of animals, and even cute in a disgusting, not-at-all-cute kind of way, but this isn't a catch-and-release situation."

"Wish I could fight one," said Jake, and stepped to the edge. "I've always wondered who would come out on top. Hellhound or werewolf."

Hailey tugged him backward. "I think you'd better save that for the full moon," she said, and Frankie winced inwardly as Jake shrugged her off.

Frankie sighed and raised the crossbow to aim. She took a deep breath. The hellhounds had to be slayed, but there were five left, and she knew she didn't have the heart to shoot five times. She closed her eyes and focused her magic on the crossbow bolts, floating them off the weapon to hover in midair, taking aim upon the hounds below. She knew it was working when she heard Jake say, "Whoa," and opened her eyes to pull the trigger, simultaneously firing with her telekinesis. Five crossbow bolts found their mark and five hellhounds fell soundlessly dead, ready for composting.

$$) \;) \; \bigcirc \; (\!(\; (\!($$

"That was not bad, back there." Vi punched Frankie's arm lightly as they walked up her driveway after getting out of the van. "I mean with the floating and the whoosh! And the—*pew! pew!*—dead hellhounds." Vi wiggled her fingers in the air as if commanding invisible crossbow bolts. "Using magic for slaying; what a concept."

"It's not easy to do," Frankie said. "The slayer gift and my witch magic are not into mingling." She shrugged. "I could only do it because it was calm, and I could focus. It was very shooting hellhounds in a barrel."

"Yeah, but it was still cool," said Vi, and Frankie smiled a little.

"Thanks for the help," Frankie said. She traded a look with Hailey as the taller girl shouldered past them to go up the walk with Jake. "Are you and Hailey okay now?"

"We're sisters. It's a real ebb and flow between hugs and middle fingers." Vi smirked. "I'm just kidding. There are no hugs. And hey, I'm sorry about what I said in the cemetery. I didn't mean to"—she gestured indistinctly toward Frankie's house and friends and everyone inside—"malign the Scoobies."

"So you're not going to make Hailey leave?"

"I didn't say that."

Frankie stopped. "We do care about her, you know. You're not the only one who can protect her."

"That's just it. None of us can protect her. Not you. Not me. I don't want my sister to be a part of this, do you understand? Not if she doesn't have to be."

"But it is her choice," Frankie said. "Isn't it?"

"We'll talk about it," said Vi. "But she's sixteen. I know she seems older, but that's just because she had to grow up fast. But I am her guardian and I make the rules. At least for a few more years. Okay?" She cuffed Frankie on the shoulder. "I'm not just going to rip her away from you. It's not like you'd never see her again."

"But we want her here. Even Spike. And he's your Watcher, too—you could both stay!"

Vi put her hands into her pockets. There was no telling what the older slayer had seen. What she'd had to do. Frankie's mom had said that before she was a slayer, Vi was timid and a little quiet, and liked to wear a lot of knit things in bright colors. Looking at her now, Frankie couldn't imagine it.

"You're a sweet kid," Vi said. "I'm going to hate watching you grow up."

"Frankie."

She turned at the sound of her name. Sigmund had appeared in the doorway of their house.

"Oh, Sig's here. I thought he was hanging with his mom tonight."

As Frankie watched, Sigmund discreetly pulled the corner of a volume on interdimensional portals out of his bag and tapped it with his index finger.

"Let me guess," said Vi. "Secret Scooby business."

"Seems like."

"Well, don't let me keep you. But eventually you're going to have to trust me. Slayers shouldn't keep secrets from other slayers." She turned around. "Night, night, tiger. Hailey!"

"Yeah?"

"Text me tomorrow if you want to grab dinner." Vi walked away up the street, and Frankie watched her go a while before following the Scoobies up to the front door. When she looked back, Vi had disappeared. Such a slayery exit. Frankie was going to have to learn that, if she could ever stop being ambushed in playgrounds and staking herself in the leg.

Frankie and the rest of the Scoobies: Junior Edition walked into the house and headed for the kitchen, where Sigmund began to unload items from his backpack: another bound journal, a few small texts in fibrous brown buckram with titles embossed in gold, and some jars of herbs.

"Demon magic?" Jake asked, and sniffed a jar. "What's this one do?"

"Well, for a start, if you inhale it, you'll go blind." Sigmund grinned and snatched it back. "Only kidding, Thriller."

"I ought to sprinkle some of these herbs on you, Sage demon," said Jake, mock-angry. "But it seems you're already spicy enough."

"Okay, okay," said Hailey, turning to Sigmund. "I want to know what the big news is. The Scooby-only news that not even my sister or your mom could hear." She snaked her arms around Sigmund's neck and he smiled a little, and seeing his smile, Frankie relaxed.

"Or Grimloch," said Jake.

"Why not Grimloch?" Frankie asked. "He's just as invested in finding the missing slayers as we are!"

"Scooby only means Scooby only. And your broody demon boyfriend is not"—Jake pointed his finger—"one of us."

"He's practically one of us," Frankie muttered.

"And shouldn't you want him to become one?" Hailey teased. "He also has fangs—he can take over the role of Scooby Doo from you."

"I'm not Scooby Doo," Jake declared, incensed. "I'm Fred!"

"Apologies, Jake," said Sigmund. "But I am clearly Fred. But Hailey's right—we should get started." He looked around the kitchen just as Willow came in, staring at her phone.

"Oh, good," she said. "You're home. And safe! I've just been texting Xander and Dawn. They're eager for updates on what we can do with the Scythe. Spike and Oz should be back from patrol any time now. Jake? Help me with some Scooby snacks?"

Frankie, Hailey, and Sigmund sat down at the table to wait while Willow and Jake assembled the food: boxes of crackers and a pitcher of apple cider, some wedges of cheese and pears, and some smoked salmon for the wolfies. They would wait to warm up Spike's blood until he got there; if it cooled more than two degrees, he'd only turn up his nose. It wasn't long after Jake set down the trays that the door opened and Oz and Spike came in, smelling like beer.

"So much for patrol," said Frankie.

"No, there was much patrol," said Oz. "Four vamps and some pink-skinned biker demons who were trying to take over the road-house out on Nine."

"So we tossed them," said Spike. "And then stayed for celebra-tory keg stands. I mean cocktails," he amended, and burped.

Hailey sighed and disentangled herself from Sigmund. "I'll start some coffee."

"Well, thank you very much, Hailey. That's very kind of you." Spike threw an arm around Oz's shoulders. "This guy. I never knew he was such an animal. Throwing demons left and right. And the big bloke—" Spike broke off with laughter. "He messed his leather trousers when you tore out his nose ring."

"I know." Oz grinned. "I was there."

"And now you're here," said Sigmund, in a very adult voice. "All original Scoobies present, so I may as well say it: I think I've found a way to use the Scythe to open a window between us and the miss-ing slayers."

Spike sobered instantly. "You mean . . ." He looked at Willow and back at Sigmund. "When?"

"As soon as we gather the materials. See here—" Sigmund

opened a spellbook, and everyone leaned over the table as he explained his idea in overly mystical, technical language that didn't skimp on the methodology of the sorcerers who had come before him or the history of the spell materials involved.

"You sure know how to make exciting things boring, babe," Hailey said.

"Yeah," said Spike. "You ever thought about becoming a Watcher?"

"How soon can we get what we need?" Sigmund asked, and Oz leaned closer to look at the list of ingredients again.

"I can get all that from the new magic shop tomorrow."

"Tomorrow," said Spike, and he and Willow looked at each other. "Just what kind of a window are we talking about? Big enough that we can pull Buffy back through it?"

Frankie's heart jumped in her chest, beating as hard as she was sure Spike's would have, if it did any beating at all.

"Let's not get ahead of ourselves." Sigmund pushed his glasses farther up his nose. "What we're opening is a window, not a door. We may be able to push it, to allow a few to come through, but that will depend on the Scythe. And on you, Ms. Rosenberg."

"Me?" Willow asked.

"I think the spell you performed to activate all the Potential Slayers turned you into a sort of gate. That the energy of the slayer line moved through you, like the oracle said. You'll be the one fueling this spell. I'll just be the one guiding it."

"Will?" Oz asked. "Are you okay to do that?"

"Sure," she said, but Frankie thought she sounded not sure at all. "Absolutely."

"It's a big spell," Sigmund cautioned. "It deals in dimensions and trades in ancient magics. It could be dangerous."

Frankie looked at her mom. She wanted to tell her it was okay, that she didn't have to do it. But she did have to, didn't she? If it meant it could lead to Buffy and the others? If it meant they could bring them home? But Willow didn't seem afraid.

"Just get me the stuff, and meet here tomorrow."

CHAPTER SEVENTEEN

IT'S LIKE A SWISS ARMY SCYTHE

T he next day, the Scoobies took their lunch hour in the library, not eating. Just staring at each other, and at the clock. Frankie couldn't stop tapping her foot, and Hailey wore her black hair up in two space buns secured by long red ribbons and stuck the ends of both ribbons in her mouth until they were all wet and frayed.

"When can we go to the house?" Spike asked. He stood at the head of the table with his arms crossed.

"Well, we do have half a day of school left," said Frankie.

"Can't we ditch it?" the librarian moaned. "It's not like any of you are going to be able to pay attention to Biology 101 or the War of the Roses."

"They don't really teach the War of the Roses here," Hailey said. "Do you even know what classes we take?"

"No. Why should I?"

Hailey rolled her eyes and turned to Sigmund, who was, as usual, poring over a book. "Sig . . ." She walked her fingers up his arm flirtatiously. "Do you *still* have more reading to do?"

Sigmund looked up and smiled at her distractedly. "I'm sorry. But this spell . . . kind of demands all of my attention." He patted Hailey's hand and went back to reading. Hailey shrugged and went back to chewing on her ribbon ends, but Frankie's eyes narrowed.

Spike stepped away from the table.

"That's it. You lot can waste your time in school if that's what you want. But I'm leaving." He tugged at his tweed lapels. "I'm going to jump down a manhole and get out of this rubbish."

"Don't want Buffy seeing you in tweed, huh?" Jake said. "I get it. That might be jarring. But what about your old face?"

Spike's hands flew to his cheeks.

"I'm sure it'll be fine!" Frankie interjected. She reached over to whack Jake. "You look great. Good, even. Besides, I bet she'll like it."

"Yeah," Hailey added. "You're, you know . . . age-appropriate."

Spike relaxed and fixed them all with a glare. "Good day, Scoobies. I'll see you at the Rosenbergs'."

They watched him walk out, ignoring students who needed library help as he went. When one of the freshmen asked him where the printed periodicals were, he simply extended a palm and said, "No."

"You know," Hailey mused. "I never really thought about the fact that Willow's glamour was only on his face. Like, he has a forty-year-old face on a hot, toned vampire bod. That is too weird."

Jake snorted and Frankie smiled, but Sigmund seemed to not have heard. He should have been the one to arch an eyebrow and grin. *Hailey, my darling,* he should have said, *please don't make us all imagine what Spike looks like naked.* But instead he didn't say anything. He didn't even look at her.

"Well." Hailey got up and found a pair of scissors, then cut off the ruined ends of her red ribbons. "I have to admit I don't feel like staying anymore either. You guys wanna ditch for coffee and pastries?"

"We're going to get caught," Jake cautioned. "Ever since she found the fish-monster leftovers in the pool drain, Principal Jacobs has been watching this place like a hawk."

"And I did hear her talking the other day about how she was the longest-surviving principal in Sunnydale history," said Frankie. "She's being proactive about keeping that title. More security. Fresh pepper spray for Kenny . . ." She shrugged. "But so what? If we get caught, my mom will write us a note."

"If we can stop for smoothies and subs, I'm in," said Jake. "Sig?"

"I'll meet you later," he said, and went straight back to reading. But he wasn't going to get away with that. Frankie was about to wave the others on without her, when the library doors swung open and in walked Sam Han.

Lacrosse goalie Sam Han. Fish-monster-survivor Sam Han. Sweet, charming, attractive-enough-to-be-in-a-K-pop-group Sam Han. And lest she forget, the Sam Han that Jake was starting to have bonus feelings for.

"Sam!" Jake said, and stood. They did their bro-hug thing, and Frankie watched without blinking to try and catch any telltale flirtatious body language. There seemed to be a little bit: Sam's and Jake's hands slid against each other's a tiny bit longer than usual during the parting handshake. "What brings you to the library?"

"Figured I might find you guys here," said Sam. "You spend a lot more time in here than anyone else at school. Like, a lot more time."

"We love the books," said Hailey, and nodded. "And there's that great manga section."

"Yeah." Sam cleared his throat awkwardly. Frankie straightened and tried to appear friendly; she didn't want them to give Sam an outsider vibe. "Anyway, uh, Frankie, I know I should have said this sooner, but I wanted to say thank you, for pulling me out of that pool. I couldn't remember if I did, in the confusion." He looked at Hailey and Sigmund. "This girl is seriously good at wrangling escaped zoo animals." He turned to Frankie. "Have you thought about becoming a zookeeper? Or, like, I bet you could have one of those extreme nature shows."

"Certainly something to consider," Frankie said. She paused to really consider it. She liked animals. And it seemed like the schedule might be flexible, so it wouldn't interfere much with slaying. "I think I'd like that better than being a cop."

"Huh?" asked Sam.

"Nothing. Just that usually people say law enforcement is my only viable option."

"Oh. Well, you'd be great at that, too!" He grinned at her and turned to Jake. "So, when I was coming in here, did I hear something about ditching?"

"Coffee, pastries, subs, and smoothies," said Jake. "Wanna come?"

"I'm in."

Jake and Hailey gathered their things and looked at Frankie, but she waved them on ahead. "I'll catch up. I'm going to stay and bug Sigmund a little more." Hailey shrugged and walked off without a second look, but Jake gave her a nod. She gave him one back. Then she discreetly motioned at Sam and waggled her eyebrows, making Jake snort a snort that was dangerously close to a giggle.

"You're not bugging me, Frankie," Sigmund said after the others had gone. "It's very important that you especially understand what's going to happen." He opened his notebook and turned it toward her for her to read. "You see, the Scythe is the sacred slayer weapon and intrinsically linked to the slayer power. So our aim is to use it as a slayer tracker."

"We can do that?" Frankie asked. "First it was used to slice and dice, then it was used to channel the power to activate the Potentials, and now we're using it like a bloodhound? What is it, a Swiss Army Scythe? Ha." She laughed. But it was kind of true: It had lots of nice, sharp blade edges, and a pointy handle end for stabbing. . . . So many options, and Frankie wanted to try them all.

"Very funny, and exactly," said Sigmund. "But more importantly, I believe that the Scythe will want us to use it this way."

"Huh?"

"Are you familiar with *The Lord of the Rings*?" Sigmund asked.

"Sure. Sometimes Jake makes me watch the extended editions, and there goes a whole day."

"Well, think of the Scythe like the One Ring. The One Ring wants to get back to the Dark Lord Sauron, and I think the Scythe wants to be wielded by a slayer."

Frankie nodded. She'd felt that the moment her mom pulled it out of their old trunk in the garage.

"So I hope it will want us to find them," Sigmund said. "See here." He opened another book, and Frankie remembered why she'd stayed behind.

"Hang on a sec, Sig. I notice you're a lot more chatty now that Hailey's gone," she said, and Sigmund closed his mouth. "Is something going on? Did you guys have a fight?"

"No, of course not."

"Then . . . do you not like her so much anymore?" Frankie asked.

"I think I love her," Sigmund replied. "It's just—" He adjusted his glasses. "I'm sorry, Frankie, but I'm afraid it's Sage demon business."

"Oh," Frankie said. "I didn't mean to pry."

"You haven't! It's just . . . something I have to figure out on my own." He sighed and returned his attention to the texts and notes before him. "Right now, however, I have to focus on this spell. I'll see you after school at your house, all right?"

Frankie grabbed her things and slung her backpack straps over her shoulders. "But you know, you can always talk to me if you need to. I don't even have to weigh in; I can just listen. And I wouldn't even tell Hailey. As long as you expressly said, 'Don't tell Hailey.' Otherwise I'd have to tell her. You know."

Sigmund smiled. "You're a good friend, Frankie."

Frankie smiled back and left the library to catch up with the others.

"Then why doesn't it seem like I'm helping anyone?" she muttered.

$$\text{)} \text{)} \bigcirc \text{(} \text{(}$$

Oz arrived at the Rosenberg house to find Sigmund's hybrid parked in the driveway. He checked his phone. School wasn't out yet, but maybe Sigmund decided to skip and come over early. Oz parked the van on the street and grabbed the tote full of supplies he'd purchased from the new magic shop. He let himself in the front door after only a brief knock and immediately regretted it; his werewolf ears detected a very flirty brand of giggling coming from the living room. It was Sarafina, and not Sigmund, who had decided to arrive early.

At the sight of Oz, Willow stood quickly from where she and Sarafina had been sitting on the sofa, but not so fast that he didn't see the way their legs were entwined and how close they had been leaning.

Canoodling, Oz thought. *I walked in on a canoodle.*

"Sorry." Oz cocked an eyebrow and turned to check the wall clock. "I thought we were meeting here to prep at two."

"We are." Willow glanced regretfully at Sarafina, who stood. "Let's go into the kitchen and have a look."

Oz set the tote down on the counter, but when Willow went to peek inside, he grabbed on and held it closed. "Ah, I think Frankie wanted this to be Scoobies only." He gave Sarafina a closed-lipped, apologetic smile.

"Well, that's not—" Willow started.

"Of course." Sarafina slipped a hand onto the small of Willow's back and kissed her cheek.

"But, Sarafina—"

"It's fine. Scooby business is Scooby business. I understand. There will be plenty of time for me to see your big magic." The Sage demon nodded to Oz and left. A moment later, they heard the hybrid back out of the driveway.

"That was rude," Willow said.

"I was just respecting Frankie's wishes."

"Well, you didn't have to run her off—"

"Willow." Oz softened his expression. "You can see her later. She didn't need to be here." He reached into the bag and began to pull out spell ingredients. Bundles of herbs, a couple of bat wings. He hadn't been able to find everything on the list at the new magic shop, but he'd done his best. And the new shop had some nice vegan alternatives, so he'd picked up a few things for Frankie. He kept on unloading even though the kitchen had turned tense and silent—it wasn't often that Oz used that tone of voice with Willow. It wasn't often that he used that tone with anyone. And he didn't like doing it. But he didn't like how much magic Willow was doing lately either, all to impress Sarafina DeWitt.

"This isn't eye of newt," Willow said, peering at a jar.

"They were out of eye of newt, but they had eye of gecko."

Willow's face scrunched. "A gecko is not a newt. The spells you cast with gecko eyes feel dry and crunchy. Not to mention jerky and a little sarcastic. You should have gotten eye of frog. At least that's another amphibian."

"I figured it would be okay, since eye of newt was under the 'optional' heading of the list," said Oz. "I also got some mustard seed in case the list was written in old witch code rather than in literal lizard body parts. Are you going to be mad at me the whole time we're doing this?"

"I don't know." Willow set down the jar. "What's your problem with Sarafina?"

"I don't have a problem with Sarafina."

"Really? Because it sure seems like you do. Are you not 'over me' or something? Because I thought we were in a good place."

Oz stopped, and Willow stopped too, and she looked at him when she realized what she'd said.

"I'm sorry. I didn't— That was mean. And dumb." She picked up the gecko eyes again and then set them down again, harder. "But don't you think it's weird, Oz? You being around all the time, and us being like a pair of parents?"

"I kind of thought of us more as a co-op. Me, you, and Spike."

"Spike? A parent? Spike's still a child."

"He is sometimes. He floats." Oz stifled a smile, his eyes mischievous, but Willow was in no mood to joke. "Willow, do you want me to go?"

"No! And see, this is why I didn't want to say anything! Because I don't want you to go. But we're not ever . . ." She gestured between the two of them and shook her head.

"I think that's pretty clear. And it has been for a while."

"Then why doesn't it feel clear?"

Oz paused. "Does it not feel clear to you?"

"It usually does," she said. "I mean, it does. But you're always going to be you, Oz, and I'm always going to be me."

His brow knit. "That does seem likely."

"And there's always going to be all that stuff from our past between us."

"I don't think it's between us, Will. I think it's part of us." She looked at him, and he took a breath, about to use more words than normal. He reached across the counter and took her hand.

"Listen," he said gently. "Sometimes I think about it."

"You do?"

"Sure. Like when I'm at the center, staring out the window. Or messing around on the guitar and the tune slips into an old Dingoes riff. And I wonder: Even though we're different people now, and even though things have changed, I wonder what would have happened if I had never left." He squeezed her fingers, and let them go. "But that's all it is. Wondering."

"And that's okay? It doesn't hurt?"

Oz shrugged. "The past is full of hurts. But not all of them are bad."

"Then why don't you like Sarafina?" Willow asked.

"I do like Sarafina," said Oz. "What I don't like is how much magic you're doing to impress her."

Willow made a dismissive expression and coupled it with lots of dismissive sounds. "I'm not doing too much magic. And it's all to help Frankie, which is what everyone said I'm supposed to be doing."

"I just want you to be careful. I know I wasn't around when it went bad, and I don't know what that looks like. But I have to think . . ." He stopped to consider whether he had the right to say what he was going to say. But he had more than a right; he had an obligation. "I have to think that if Tara was here, she would be saying the same thing."

Willow put down the herbs and jars. "I won't do that again," she said.

"Hey, Willow . . ."

"I won't," she said.

"I'm not trying to scare you."

"You don't need to; I scare myself."

"Then I guess I didn't need to say anything."

"No." Willow nodded. "You did. Because I've noticed, too. Sometimes magic feels like a toy. Sometimes it feels too easy." The haunted look on her face stung him. He knew how that felt. He had seen the same face in the mirror when the wolf was out of control and he'd wake up with no memory of what he'd done.

"It's not always easy. Remember when you had to try so hard to float a pencil you thought you would break a blood vessel?" he asked. "It's going to be okay, Will." Oz frowned. The air in the kitchen had gotten way too heavy. He dove back into the bag and pulled out the vegan chicken feet. They looked like two pieces of dried fruit twisted into the shape of talons. "I got Frankie some imitation-chicken chicken feet."

Willow glanced up dismally. "Those aren't going to work for anything."

Oz set down the feet. Maybe he shouldn't have said anything, or maybe he just shouldn't have said anything now. But it was done.

He kept on unloading supplies and categorizing them by type; he sniffed the herbs for mold and checked the leaves for wilt. He scraped a fingernail along the edge of the angelica root to check the inner flesh for redness. And after a little while, Willow started to help again.

"This bat wing looks suspect," she grumbled, and extended it to inspect the snap when it pulled back.

"Are we okay?" she asked quietly.

"We're okay, Willow. And just for the record, there's nothing you could ever do that would make us not okay. Except maybe ending the world."

She gave him a look and then swatted his shoulder playfully. But in the next moment, the crinkle in her forehead started to come back.

"Oh no," he said. "Don't do that."

"But don't we need to define—"

"We defy definition," said Oz.

"But shouldn't we label—"

"We defy labels," said Oz.

Willow narrowed her eyes. "Well," she said, "I guess we're just a couple of rebels."

Oz snorted.

"Hug now?" he asked.

"Hug now," she said, and they put their arms around each other.

Oz touched his pocket. "Oh, I almost forgot."

"What?" Willow asked, jumping back a little.

"The final ingredient." He took it out and held it up: a fresh yellow crayon. "I don't know what it means, but Xander said it was important."

By the time Frankie, Jake, and Hailey got to the house, Willow and Oz had prepared the spell space in the living room. The furniture had been moved into one corner, and so had the potted and hanging plants, so that one section of the house looked like a tiny, densely furnished jungle. Unlit candles were set at the four directional corners. Spike was also there already, so they'd draped a big, dark blanket across the curtains to make extra sure that he wouldn't accidentally combust.

"Wow," Frankie said. The moment she walked through the door, her witch senses began to tingle, all the magic in her blood perking up its ears. And not just because the house was stocked to the brim with magical ingredients, but because her mom, one of the world's greatest witches, was nervous and sending energy vibrating through the air like a tuning fork. "You guys have been busy."

"Busy and prepared," said Sigmund, who stepped out of the kitchen with his arms full. "We even made snack trays." He set down a platter piled high with pretzels, cubed cheeses, cut vegetables, and a variety of dips. A second platter held a deli's worth of rolled meat slices, and Jake rubbed his palms together.

"Jake," said Hailey. "We just came from the sub shop."

"When I'm nervous, I eat," Jake replied, and shrugged.

"When you're sleeping, you eat," said Frankie. She grabbed a few carrot sticks and dunked them in hummus. "Mom, you want me to make you a little plate?"

"No thanks, sweetie. My stomach is not . . . where it normally is." Willow rubbed her fingers and cracked her knuckles. She stole a glance at the Scythe, where it rested on the kitchen table. Not that Frankie could blame her. The Scythe was a thing of beauty, so sharp and preternaturally shiny. She moved to stand beside her mom.

"Are you okay?" Frankie asked.

"Sure. Are you okay?"

"Sure. Only sometimes I swear I can feel that thing looking at me. But I suppose that's a slayer thing."

Willow swallowed. "I suppose so. Though ever since I did the spell to activate the Potentials, sometimes I swear I can feel it, too." She looked at the Scythe. "Like right now, I can hear it chanting: 'Wil-low. Wil-low.'"

"At least it's being encouraging." Frankie shifted her weight and felt the shape of the stalker's stone in her pocket. She had taken to carrying it as a good-luck charm, and maybe to feel closer to Grim when he wasn't allowed to be around. *Which is stupid*, she thought. There must be a reason he hadn't been by to see her. *Probably because that kiss was a mistake. He loves someone else. He's waiting for someone else.*

Spike clapped his hands and stretched his arms in his black duster, and Frankie jumped. "You all right, Mini Red? You seem distracted."

"I'm good." She pushed all thoughts of Grimloch from her mind. "All good." She nodded at her Watcher, who, she noticed, was looking particularly Big Baddy. He'd also painted a new layer of black onto his fingernails.

"What about you, Red?" he asked. "Are you sure you're up for this?"

"Do I have a choice?" Willow replied. "And why does everyone keep asking me that?"

Spike pointed at her. "Because your forehead is doing that scrunchy thing. And I can feel your magic tugging at the edges of my glamoured face."

"Let's just do it," Willow said, and walked into the living room.

"Fine by me," Spike said. "I'm not getting any younger."

"Or any older, technically," said Jake.

They gathered in the living room, and Sigmund went to the kitchen to retrieve the Scythe. He handed it to Willow, who held it far from her body like she wasn't sure where she should put it.

"So that's it, huh?" Hailey leaned as close to the Scythe as she dared, studying the silver razor edge.

"The weapon of the slayer," said Frankie.

"What do you feel when you look at it?" Hailey asked.

"Only the urge to rip it out of my mom's hands and run away with it into the mountains, where I would name it Scythey McScytheface and we would live together forever." She cocked her head and smiled. "Not that I'm really going to do it."

Sigmund and Oz went back into the kitchen and returned holding bowls of fragrant, herb-infused oil. They moved to the center of the room with Frankie and Willow, while Jake, Hailey, and Spike instinctively stepped back.

"No, no, we should all kneel," said Sigmund. "Willow, if you would set the Scythe on the floor, just there." He pointed to her feet, and she knelt to lay the weapon down. Frankie knelt across from her, and the Scoobies filled in the circle. "Oz, if you would anoint her cheeks."

"Anointing Willow Rosenberg," Oz said. He dipped his finger into the bowl of herbal oil and dragged a line down each of her cheeks. Frankie leaned close to watch so he also booped a little on the end of her nose.

"Sig," Frankie asked, "is this really going to work? If the Scythe wants to get back to the slayers, then why hasn't it done anything about it already?"

"Do you remember what I said about the Scythe being like the One Ring?"

"Yeah."

"Well, even the One Ring needed a bunch of hobbits to carry it."

"Just two hobbits," Jake protested. "Bilbo, and then Frodo."

"Three if you count Samwise Gamgee," said Sigmund. "Which I do."

"Three still isn't a bunch," Jake said, sulking. "And they weren't carrying it where it wanted to go. . . ."

"Can we just do the magic?" Willow asked. She took a shaky breath and looked at Frankie.

"You can do this, Mom."

"Yellow crayon," Willow said. "And for Buffy."

"For Buffy," echoed Frankie and Spike together.

Her mom began to focus her energy on the Scythe. It was weird for Frankie, to be so near it and not have it in her hands. To see it just lying there, with no slayer attached. She could almost feel it pulling at her wrists and fingers. It was like Sigmund said: It wanted her to have it.

Sigmund leaned down and used his index finger to slick the edge of the Scythe with oil. In the four directional corners, the candles flared like torches, and he began to chant an incantation.

"What is that language?" Jake asked from the side of his mouth.

"Mok'tagar," said Spike. "I think. The accent's a bit off."

"Shush!" Willow's breath came fast. She was starting to tremble. The current of magic running through their living room made Frankie's hair lift as if from static. It was changing the air, turning it into air from someplace else. Behind her mom, Frankie saw the crimson ribbons in Hailey's space buns start to float.

"Frankie, lay your hand upon the Scythe."

"Me?"

"I just want it to know you're here, that you're not the slayer it should be looking for."

"What about Vi?"

"I'm hoping it will go for the bigger bait," Sigmund replied. "Several slayers, lumped together."

Frankie swallowed. This was a big spell, and Frankie glanced away, noting the sliver of orange daylight creeping through the sides of the blanket-covered curtains. They would have to patrol soon. . . . She blinked hard and forced herself to focus. No self-sabotage this time. This was important. This was Aunt Buffy. It was the slayers.

Frankie laid her hand upon the blade of the Scythe. She expected to feel a jolt, like a magnetic field or a snap of electricity. Instead the weapon felt warm and soft. The curve of the blade seemed to mold itself to fit perfectly against her palm. It was like patting a very old and well-loved pet.

"And, Willow, now you."

Her mom's hand rose shakily and hovered over the Scythe. Frankie wanted to tell her that there was nothing to fear, that it was nice—comfortable even. But the spell had her solidly in its grip, and Frankie couldn't say a word. All she felt was her own energy flowing into the Scythe, and the Scythe strengthening it and sending it back clearer. Willow made a brief fist, released it, and placed her palm against the blade.

At once, Sigmund resumed the chant, so loudly that everyone in the circle winced. Frankie felt air sucked out through her ears, and her whole head pulled toward the ceiling. She looked up.

Their ceiling was gone. A swirling vortex had appeared in its place. It pulled at her weight, and Frankie saw Hailey grab helplessly at one of her red ribbons as it was yanked away and sucked into the void.

"Don't lose your focus!" Sigmund shouted over the noise of the portal. "Direct the search. Tell the Scythe what to seek! Think of the slayers! Think of Buffy!"

Frankie squinted through the wind; it was like being caught in a cyclone in the middle of their living room. "Mom?" But Willow didn't seem to hear. Her eyes black, she grabbed for the bowl of anointing oil and dashed it against the blade, shattering it and coating the Scythe completely. She bared her teeth and shouted, "Buffy Summers!"

"Mom!" Frankie tried to grab her, but her hands were stuck fast to the Scythe. The potted plants that had been stacked in the corner fell, spilling dirt that was quickly sucked toward the ceiling. Hailey screamed, so did Jake, and Spike and Oz tried to cover them both.

And then a voice cut through the din.

"Willow?"

"Buffy!" Willow's eyes shifted back toward normal, and her grip on the spell wobbled. "Buffy, we're here!"

"Will? Is that you?"

"Aunt Buffy!" Frankie cried. "We're here!"

"Can you get to us?" Spike shouted. "Can you see your way through?"

"I can't see anything. There's just a wind . . . pulling. . . ."

"Let it pull!" Spike yelled. He looked at Sigmund. "Should she let it pull? Should she go into it?"

"I don't know," Sigmund called back. "It might be dangerous! It might not even really be her—demon dimensions are . . . Well, they're jerks sometimes!"

"It's her," Frankie said. "That's her voice!" A large potted fern flew toward Jake's head, and Frankie dove to catch it—and broke her connection with the Scythe. "Oh shoot! Is that okay?"

"It should be," Sigmund said. "It's all right. Just—"

The Scythe leapt out of Willow's hands.

"No," Willow shouted. "Buffy!"

"Willow!" Buffy cried.

Willow started to chant, not in the demon language that

Sigmund had but in something else. Her eyes were black as pitch again, and her fingers hooked into claws. But despite her push, the spell began to fail. The wind flagged, and the vortex faded. It pulled into itself so quickly that watching it diminish was like watching a light go out. There was a small pop, and something silver fell back from the ceiling and hit the floor. The portal was closed.

"Buffy!" Willow shouted.

"Mom, it's okay—"

"No! I'll do it again!" She searched for the Scythe with black eyes and called for it, holding out her hand.

The Scythe jumped five inches in the opposite direction.

Willow's brow knit. She tried again, and the Scythe hopped away, sliding farther out of reach. The more times she failed, the more Willow's magic receded, until her eyes were her eyes, and her breath came in ragged gasps.

"Sweetie," she asked Frankie. "Are you doing that?"

Frankie shook her head.

Willow walked to where the Scythe lay and flexed her fingers. She tried one more time, grabbing fast for the handle.

The Scythe erupted off the ground. It flew through the air, spinning like a thrown hatchet, vertically and sideways. Hailey covered her head and ducked as it flew perilously close, and Jake darted over to pull her clear. It whizzed over Oz's shoulder, and the werewolf moved his head smoothly out of the way, seemingly unaffected, as if he hadn't been mere centimeters from total decapitation.

"Sigmund!" Spike yelled, tracking the path of the weapon through the air like he was trying to decide whether to make a grab for it or dive behind the sofa. "What's happening?"

"I don't know!" Sigmund looked helplessly from the Scythe to the oil dripping from his fingers. He thought a moment and stood. He held out his hand. "Weapon of the slayer! Return!"

The Scythe changed direction and returned toward them, the blade arcing wickedly as it sliced through the air.

"Sigmund, down!" Frankie grabbed his ankles and pulled him off his feet. The Scythe whipped past them and buried itself deep into their wall, between one of their impressionist paintings and Frankie's third-grade portrait, which was the year of unfortunate pigtails.

Willow again approached the Scythe.

"Careful, Red," Spike cautioned.

"I just want to try once more." Her eyes went black again and she whispered under her breath. Also she was not actually walking. She was floating, with her toes dragging across the floor.

"Mom?"

Willow reached up to pull the Scythe from the wall. But before she could touch it, it freed itself and flew. Hailey and Jake screamed, but Frankie leapt. She vaulted through the air, corkscrewing toward the Scythe, and caught it in one twisting motion. The next thing she knew, she was standing there holding it, though she had no idea how she'd managed to land on her feet.

"Wow," she breathed. The feeling of the Scythe in her grip was intense. She could feel the power of it, and that it was a power they shared. Holding it wasn't like holding a weapon. The Scythe was an extension of herself.

After they were certain it was back under control, the others crept closer.

"What the heck was that?" Jake asked. "What happened?" He looked toward the ceiling, and Spike stepped across the rug and picked up the thing that had fallen. He held it up by its chain: a small silver cross.

"The back of it says 'Joyce,'" he whispered.

"Buffy wore a cross for Joyce," Willow said sadly. Joyce. She had been Buffy's mom, a pretty lady with soft brown '70s hair who Frankie knew only from stories and pictures. Willow looked at the cross one more time and passed it quietly to Spike.

After the discovery of Buffy's cross, they didn't bother cleaning up the living room. They just gathered in the kitchen over mugs of cocoa. Spike was so upset he didn't even bother adding blood to his.

"It's hers all right," he said, holding the cross gently by its chain and sniffing it.

"Do you have to do your weird smell test?" Willow asked. "We know it's hers. We know it was her. She was there."

"She's alive," said Oz, and snorted softly. "I kind of knew it."

Frankie and Jake smiled, but only a little. The casting of the spell, and its implosion, had exhausted them all, as did the outcome. Buffy was alive. They'd spoken to her. But they hadn't been able to bring her back.

At least, not yet.

"How soon can we do the spell again?" Frankie asked. She looked at Sigmund, who looked at the Scythe where it lay safely against the wall across the kitchen.

"I'm not sure," he said, and turned to Willow. "It was like it didn't want to be near you. Or like you didn't want to be near it."

"You think I was doing that on purpose?" she asked.

"Maybe not consciously," said Spike. "But you have been able to cast spells without knowing it. Remember that time you made Buffy and me almost get hitched. And made Giles go blind. And . . . I don't remember what you made happen to Xander." He shrugged and sipped his cocoa.

"So, what do we do?" Hailey asked. "Can you do the spell if Willow can't touch it?"

"No." Sigmund leaned back. Frankie pushed her chair away and went to retrieve the Scythe.

"Mom, try to hold it now." She held it out. Willow took a breath and grabbed it with no trouble, unless you counted the extra tug she had to give so Frankie would let go.

"It seems fine," said Oz.

"Fine?" Spike pointed at Willow. "Look how she's holding it. Like it's a bomb about to go off."

"I am not," Willow said, and moved the Scythe marginally closer to her body.

"No, he's right." Sigmund adjusted his eyeglasses. He'd had to take them off to clean a bit of oil off the lenses. "You're clearly not comfortable with the Scythe. Or it is clearly not comfortable with you. It's one of the most powerful magical talismans in the world, and you changed it, fundamentally. You need to get back into its good graces."

"How am I supposed to do that?" Willow asked.

"I suggest that you keep it with you at all times. On your person. Day and night."

"You want me to sleep with this thing?" She brandished the silver edge, and it shimmered under their living room lights. "I'm going to cut off my arm!"

"I don't want you to cuddle it," Sigmund said. "Just keep it near. Glamour it when you have to be seen in public."

Willow adjusted it in her grip. "It's kind of awkward to just have on me. And this is never going to work."

"We have to try. If we want to get Buffy and whatever slayers are with her out of there, we have to try."

"Please, Mom?" Frankie begged.

"I can make you a kind of sling for it to make it easier to carry," said Oz. He looked at the Scythe-shaped hole in their wall. "And I can . . . spackle that."

Willow sighed. "Okay. I guess it's worth a shot."

CHAPTER EIGHTEEN
RANDY DEMONS (NOT DEMONS NAMED RANDY) AND HORNY DEMONS (OF THE HORNED VARIETY)

"So the Scythe and your mother are at odds," Grimloch said as he and Frankie walked through the woods on the eastern hill. "And now she must keep it on her person to renew their bond."

"Exactly," Frankie said.

"But Buffy Summers is alive, and you spoke to her." Grimloch smiled. "Good."

"It is good. It's amazing. I just wish we'd gotten her back. And the others. Maybe someone who you miss . . ."

"Frankie—"

"You know, I really shouldn't be telling you this." But she couldn't help it. The Scoobies had paired off for patrol, and it was the first chance she'd had to be alone with Grim in weeks. Jake and Oz had taken the cemetery, while Hailey and Vi watched the north end of town. Sigmund and Sarafina were walking the streets near the library and the high school. Frankie didn't know what her mom and the Scythe were doing. Maybe sitting together on the couch, reading a book. Maybe they were out on the backyard swing. As for Spike, he was probably holed up at his place with a bottle of whiskey and Buffy's cross.

"Then why are you telling me?" Grimloch asked. "I understand what 'strictly Scooby business' means."

"I'm telling you because—it felt wrong not to say when we might be on the verge of finding your slayer. Especially with how guilty I felt after . . ."

"You feel guilty about what happened between us?"

"Don't you?" Frankie rounded on him. "Your slayer could be alive. We could be weeks—days—from getting her back. She could be in another dimension right now, maybe a dimension full of windows into this one, just watching our every move!"

"I've never heard of a dimension like that."

"Well, I haven't either." She sighed and went on, stalking higher up the hill through crunchy winter leaves. "But I still feel guilty. How can you not feel guilty?"

"I'm a demon." Grimloch shrugged, his strides long and sure even on the dark, uneven ground. "If I feel guilty . . . then I like it."

"I don't know what to do with that." Frankie raised her head to look at the sky. With the moon on the serious wane, there wasn't a lot of light to go on in the woods away from the city. But at least the air was crisp and quiet, and . . . smelled like gasoline? "Do you smell that?" She sniffed. "Where the heck even are we?"

"Francesca Rosenberg." She turned. Standing uphill from Grim they were almost the same height, and when he looked at her, his eyes flashed brightly. "I don't know what I feel," he said, and drew her close. "But I don't wish for you to feel guilty. This is my choice."

"Our choice," she whispered, and slid her arms around his neck. She felt his hand tighten around her waist, and she moaned.

Except she hadn't moaned. Frankie drew back. "That wasn't me."

"It wasn't me either," he said. Yet there it was again: a moan, and a decidedly pleased one. Followed by laughter, and a happy little squeal. Frankie and Grimloch let go of each other and climbed to the top of the hill.

"What is this?" Grimloch asked, squinting against the headlights as another car pulled in to park.

"I think it's a movie from the 1950s," Frankie replied. What they had stumbled upon were rows of cars. Almost a dozen of them, parked a few feet apart. With people inside. Most in the front seat, but a few were in the back, and some of the cars were distinctly rocking. They had stumbled on New Sunnydale's secret make-out point. As far as Frankie knew, Sunnydale had no secret make-out point. Her mom had certainly never mentioned it. But then, when her mom was in high school, Sunnydale didn't have all these nice, sloping hills around it, forming convenient scenic overlooks.

Grimloch walked curiously between the cars, leaning close to see into the fogged-up windows, and came up blinking. "Doesn't this bother them?" He looked from one car to the next. "They are parked so closely together. And I'm standing right outside the window."

"Apparently not." Frankie shrugged. She scanned the cars. Nothing seemed amiss, except that it was weird and she didn't know why anyone would ever go parking, or ever had. Still, with demon activity being what it was, it didn't feel safe to leave them, even in cars. "We should stick around, I guess. Aunt Buffy always said that when the kids get randy, the demons get—"

"Horny," Grimloch said, and nodded.

"No." Frankie made a face. "*Hungry.*"

"That's what I said. Their horns and claws come out to hunt."

"Oh. We need to talk about your lingo." She gestured for him to come with her to the edge of the gravel lot. Once there, they settled in, leaning against a particularly thick tree, one of the old-growth ones that had been spared from the Spikesplosion. Frankie took a stake out of her pocket and idly twirled it while they listened for the sounds of demons mingling with the mixed music and happy giggles. She stole a glance at Grimloch's tense profile—it hardly seemed fair that they were stuck there not touching when everyone else was having a great time with roaming hands.

"It's not that I don't care for her," Grimloch said suddenly. "It's not that I'm heartless. I just didn't expect to grow so fond of you." He glanced at her, not at her face, but at the rest of her, and she tingled everywhere that his gaze touched. "I think I expected that you would be like her: daring and fearless. Violently passionate."

"But I'm none of those things, obviously." She frowned. She wouldn't have minded being some of those things. Daring and fearless. Maybe passionate, without the violence. "So what am I?"

"You're—" He paused, and chuckled. He looked incredibly charming when he chuckled, showing the bare tips of his fangs.

"I get it," she grumbled. "I'm amusing."

"You are amusing. But don't misunderstand me. There's something about you—"

"Demon!"

Grimloch drew back and touched his chest. "Yes, I am."

"Not you." Frankie rolled her eyes and pointed as the first of several demons fell from the trees to land on the hoods of cars. They were thick and dark skinned, their bodies flat and longer than they were wide. They each had what looked to be two muscular, bowed forearms, and a swinging, tapering tail that ended in a wicked barb. "It's like an alligator had a baby with a scorpion!" Frankie and Grimloch rushed to the center, watching them fall from the sky like rain. "And this is, like, the worst biblical plague ever!"

Inside the cars, people began to notice what was happening, and the screaming began. Frankie turned at the sound of shattering glass and grabbed a demon that had smashed in the windshield of a Ford; she swung it around hard by its tail and flung it into a tree. Then she promptly backflipped out of the path of a car. Drivers were peeling out of the gravel lot; the car that almost hit her fish-tailed and threw rocks into Grimloch's face. She heard a hissing and spun out of the way as a barbed tail struck the ground where she'd just been standing.

"Watch the tail!" Grimloch shouted.

"Is it poisonous?"

"It's a northern Semnar demon." Grimloch grabbed another demon and tore it off the trunk of a Pontiac as it zoomed past. He deftly dodged the barb strikes and then threw the creature into another tree, where Frankie heard its bones snap. "The bite is non-venomous, but the poison in the barb is paralytic."

"You know a lot about them."

"I've hunted them before. They don't come this far south. And they never travel in packs."

Frankie turned toward a scream—one of the Semnars had reached its jaws into an open window and was pulling a boy out by the head. "Let. Him. Go!" Frankie said, beating against the Semnar while blocking strikes from its dangling tail.

"Frankie? Is that you?" Frankie looked across the front seat and saw Jasmine Finnegan, her brown braids held up in a very pretty date-night bun.

"Jasmine?" Frankie wrenched the Semnar's jaws open, and Chad Noble fell out from between its teeth back into the driver's seat. "Chad? I didn't know you guys were dating!"

"We just got together over Valentine's," Jasmine said. "What are these things?"

"Uh . . ." Frankie drop-kicked the Semnar toward Grim, who stomped it into oblivion with one muscular motion. "You know, the zoo is really having problems with the locks on their enclosures."

"I heard that," Jasmine said. "Just a few weeks ago, Sam Han was attacked by some kind of deep-sea fish in the pool."

"You guys better get out of here," Frankie said. "Chad, drive carefully."

He didn't need any more convincing and spun the car around in reverse to career out of the lot.

"Grim, watch the car!" she shouted, but she was too late. It hit him, and he rolled up the windshield and over the back to land on the ground. But at least it hadn't run over him. And at least it had only been a Camry. She hurried to help him up, coughing against the dust kicked up by the tires. The lot was empty now, and all the couples were safe. Except for Grimloch and Frankie, who were circled by two more Semnars with snapping jaws and lashing tail barbs.

"So what are they doing here? Mating season? Are they migrating?"

"They don't mate or migrate. A brood of them is born from a hellmouth, and when they die out, another brood comes forth. They are never supposed to return to the hellmouth that birthed them. This behavior is strange. They should be solitary. And this time of year, they should be hibernating."

"Well, these don't look the least bit sleepy," said Frankie. If her mom were there, they could have teleported them back into hibernation. But there was no time for that. The Semnars gathered their muscles to charge.

Frankie didn't like fighting non-humanoid demons all that much—they seemed more innocent. Like animals. But when one collided with her chest and drove her onto her back, she didn't have much choice.

"Time to go full-on Dundee." She grabbed the end of the barbed tail with one hand and kept it from stinging her face (which took some effort), and with her other, she drew a knife from her belt and drove it down through the Semnar demon's head. The Semnar shivered a moment, and she rolled out from under it just in time to see Grimloch break the neck of the last one.

"A good kill," he said.

"Do you . . . want to eat the heart?" She offered up her knife.

Grimloch looked at her quietly. "I don't think you would enjoy watching me feed."

He was probably right about that, but just then, Frankie couldn't imagine ever being turned off by him. With her pulse racing from the fight and her adrenaline singing, he looked like nothing else than a snack. A delicious Grim snack with wild dark hair and piercing blue eyes and just-the-right-size fangs to do the right amount of nibbling. Without a word, they closed the distance between each other, and Frankie jumped into his arms, their second kiss nothing so sweet as their first. This time it was fueled by combat and desire and maybe even the leftover make-out vibes in the air. Frankie gave a little yip as her back met the trunk of a tree and then they were kissing again, and her hands slipped inside his jacket to clutch the muscle of his back.

I should say something, Frankie thought as he touched her cheek. But no, she shouldn't. She should shut right up and see where this went. Never mind missing loves of his life, never mind the fact that he was two thousand years old and her mom was going to have a bird—all of those thoughts just melted away.

Until her Watcher showed up and grabbed her demon boyfriend to throw him across the empty parking lot.

"Spike!" Frankie sputtered. "Stop!"

"No!" Spike pointed a finger at her. "No, no, no, no, no! You stop! And you—" He turned to Grim and ran at him to deck him hard across the face. Grimloch growled, but to his credit, he didn't try to hit Spike back. He simply took it and licked the blood from his split bottom lip.

"Spike! Knock it off! We were—" Frankie gestured to the bodies of the Semnars. "Do you see all the dead demons?"

"Yeah, and I see the live one." He pointed at Grimloch. "The very, very live one. Get going, Frankie."

"You can't tell me what to do."

"You want the demonic underwear model to see your Watcher drag you off this hill by the back of your shirt?"

Frankie blanched.

"Then get moving. We're going home."

$$\supset \; \supset \; \bigcirc \; \subset \; \subset$$

Spike didn't talk to Frankie all the way home. Which was kind of a relief. Unfortunately the moment he burst through their front door he bellowed for her mom.

"What's wrong?" Willow came to the entryway and grabbed Frankie by the shoulders, looking for wounds. "Are you okay, sweetie?"

"I'm okay, Mom."

"Yeah, I'll say," said Spike. "I found her up at inspiration point, wrapped around the Hunter of Thrace. Making out with a two-thousand-year-old, when she's supposed to be slaying!"

Willow let go of Frankie as she processed the information. She fell back heavily against the closed front door.

"I can't believe you just told her like that!" Frankie shouted. "Mom? Are you alive?"

"I'm having flashbacks to Joyce," she whispered with wide eyes. "And all the terrifying things we must have put her through . . . All those late nights . . . and sneaking around . . . and secret smoochies with Angel . . ." Spike interjected a snort. "And I encouraged it!" Willow looked at her daughter in horror. "I was her alibi."

"But see, this is good," Frankie said, sensing the conversation was about to turn against her. "You already know I'm a slayer; I don't need an alibi."

"Well," said Willow thoughtfully, "I don't want you to feel like you have to keep secrets from me."

"Willow!" Spike said. "Are you bloody serious?" He stuck his arm out and pointed at Frankie. "She kissed a demon!"

"We've all kissed a demon," Willow said reasonably.

"Yeah," said Frankie. "Hailey kisses a demon every day."

"That's not the same thing, and you know it. This isn't Sigmund. This is the Hunter of Thrace. He eats organs!"

"You drink blood!"

"Frankie, go upstairs."

"But, Mom!"

"I said go. Your Watcher and I are going to discuss what to do about this."

Frankie looked from one to the other, but there was nothing to be done. No more arguments to make. They were going to discuss her, without her, which was totally unfair. She clenched her hands into fists and yelled at Spike. "Sometimes I wish you weren't my Watcher!"

His mouth dropped open, and she regretted it the moment she said it, but she couldn't take it back.

"Oh yeah?" Spike said. "One day I'll tell you what happened between Giles and Joyce on a police car!"

"Spike!" Willow cuffed him. "No, you won't."

"It could be worse is all I'm saying."

Frankie trudged upstairs, grumbling to herself about unfairness and hypocrisy and the inability to ground a slayer, when she saw that Hailey's door was open a crack and the light was on inside. She stopped and knocked.

"Come on in."

"I didn't think you'd be home. Thought you'd be catching a late dinner with your sister."

"Vi said she had something she needed to do. Though I had no idea what that could be . . ." Hailey rolled her eyes. She sat up and marked her page in the manga she was reading, then used the book to gesture downstairs. "So, what was that about? You grounded again?"

Frankie closed the door and fell against it, much like her mom had done. "Probably. Except I don't think they can, with New Sunnydale gone demon wild. I'm the slayer. I have to help these people; I'm their only hope."

"That's Obi-Wan Kenobi." Hailey smirked. "Maybe they'll do like, a deferred grounding. Like you'll be grounded after the demon crisis abates."

"Jeez, I hope they don't think of that. But when is it going to abate anyway? We've been running ourselves ragged for weeks now, and the demons keep coming. And they aren't behaving like normal demons. Grim says this is weird even for the Hellmouth." She sighed. "This has to be the darkness that oracle was referring to."

"It sure seems like something," Hailey agreed. Her face turned sly. "I notice you mentioned Grim. So I take it you've seen him? And I take it your grounding has something to do with that?"

Frankie blushed. She tried to maintain an air of frustration about her guardians, but she couldn't keep the smile from creeping up. "Spike . . . he kind of caught Grim and me . . . making out."

"*What?*"

Hailey fell backward onto her bed and held one of her pillows over her face to scream into while she kicked her feet. Then she removed it and threw it at Frankie's chest. "Hey, I thought I told you to stay away from him!"

"You did."

"Good. Then I've done my due diligence." She patted the end of the bed, and Frankie sat down. "Tell me everything. I bet it was, like *intense*. Ooh, I bet he bit a little. Did he bite a little?"

"He did, actually," Frankie said, and Hailey squealed into another pillow.

"How did he do it? Who started it? Weren't you guys supposed to be on patrol?"

"We were. We actually just slayed a bunch of these northern Semnar demons, which were like alligators but with scorpion tails?"

"Terrifying," Hailey said. "Go on."

"And then it kind of just . . . happened. Also, did you know there was a make-out overlook up on the south hill? I saw Jasmine Finnegan there with Chad Noble. He's going to need some stitches."

"Jasmine and Chad?" Hailey made a face, then waved it away. "Later. More details now."

"There aren't more details. We were just . . . getting started, and Spike showed up and punched him in the face."

Hailey winced. "Mortifying."

"Exactly."

"So you and Grimloch got all sweaty and stakey and then just started making out?" she laughed. "You guys are so twisted."

Frankie laughed, too, and picked up a pillow and threw it at her. Hailey sighed happily.

"I'm going to miss this."

"What? Listening to my mom and Watcher downstairs deciding my punishment?"

"No, just . . ." She gestured between them. "This after-slay talk. Vi doesn't do this. She never wanted to talk about it. She mostly wanted to pretend it didn't exist."

"But it won't be like that now. You're not a civilian anymore, Hailey—you're in it. And you're pretty darned good at it if you haven't noticed. Like seriously, you are way more of a natural fighter than—"

"Than you are?" Hailey finished.

"Well, yeah. If not for the superpowers, you would kick my ass."

"I could. But I wouldn't." Hailey winked. "I have been wondering about that, though. Like about . . . my heritage? Like I've been wondering lately if the Saulteaux have any traditional magic or anything. Like maybe they had their own version of a slayer. Maybe I came from that."

"Maybe? Or maybe your parents were just athletic?"

Hailey shrugged. "Plus, I'm also naturally good at ice-skating and math, so according to my logic the Saulteaux should be doing killer choreography at those Ice Capades you're so fond of."

"Do you know anything about that side of your family?" Frankie asked.

"Virtually nothing. I never really thought about it, to be honest. My mom grew up in Ottawa and met my dad when she moved from Canada to Philadelphia. Only my grandmother was still with the tribe, and I never knew her. And Vi and I don't share that side of my family, so . . ." Hailey shrugged again. "She says that after we leave Sunnydale we'll go up there and find them. Maybe get to know some cousins we don't know we have. It could be cool."

Frankie's face fell.

"So . . . you're leaving?"

"I don't know," Hailey said. "Vi seems set on it. She keeps saying there won't be any choice and 'you'll understand when it's over.' Whatever that means."

"What does that mean? 'When it's over.' What's *it*?"

"No idea." Hailey rolled her eyes. "She loves to be cryptic like that." Frankie frowned but didn't press. Vi was her sister; Hailey couldn't just stay in Sunnydale and let Vi go off on her own. Not when Vi was the only family Hailey had left.

But we're your family, too, now, aren't we? Frankie thought. Except it wouldn't have been fair to say so. "What about Sigmund?" she asked.

"I don't even know about Sigmund these days," Hailey said, and sighed. "But cheer up." She smacked Frankie's knee. "Nothing's decided yet, and we have plenty of time. We're not leaving until we get those other slayers back, and once that happens, Vi might change her mind about everything."

CHAPTER NINETEEN
THE PAST RETURNS

As Frankie predicted, her new grounding never materialized. The Scoobies simply had too much on their hands. By the following weekend, the demon problem had only increased, as demons both new and familiar continued to march into New Sunnydale.

"You'd better figure out what's causing this pretty soon," Vi said to Frankie when they met in the cemetery. She was bent over and slightly breathless from tackling their second M'Fashnik demon of the evening. "Or come up with a better way to slay. More magic, maybe? Or a better weapon? Buffy used to have a Scythe, but no one's seen it for years. Don't suppose you know where it is?"

It's strapped to my mom and glamoured invisible, Frankie almost said. But instead she shook her head. "No one knows where the Scythe is."

"Well, it would come in handy. Maybe your mom knows?"

"Maybe," Frankie said as the others circled up. They were meeting in the cemetery: Jake, Hailey and Sigmund, Spike and Oz, even her mom and Sarafina, and all but Willow and Sigmund looked exhausted. Frankie didn't know what kind of demon Sarafina had come up against, but she was wearing its black blood across most of the front of her silk blouse, and there were dark bits of it stuck to her extremely deadly-looking mace.

"We have to do something about this," said Willow. "Maybe a spell on the Hellmouth? To calm it down?"

"I'll start researching," said Sigmund. He looked at Willow meaningfully. "How are things going with your . . . special project?"

Willow shifted the weight of the invisible Scythe. "Good, I think."

"Good enough to try again soon?"

"A few more slayer hands on deck would be nice," Spike panted.

Out of the corner of her eye, Frankie watched Vi as her eyes moved from Sigmund to Frankie's mom, trying to puzzle out their secret.

"There ought to be a curfew," said Sarafina. "There have been so many attacks you are running out of zoo animals to blame them on."

"And it's not fair to blame it on them anyway," said Jake. "They're going to shut down the zoo."

"At least the Sunnydale sixth sense is doing its job," Spike commented. And it was true. Stores were closing earlier without needing to be told. Restaurants ran specials on takeout and delivery. And the school had advised parents not to let their kids walk home for the rest of the month, even in daylight.

"But there should still be more," said Frankie. "Sigmund's mom is right." She looked at Jake regretfully. "Do you think the school would suspend outdoor sports for a while?"

"Outdoor sports?" His face scrunched. "That means lacrosse. No lacrosse?" He gaped at her a moment, then turned to fellow fan Sigmund, and gaped some more until, finally, his shoulders slumped.

"I'll bring it up to the team after our game next week," he said.

"That is all well and good for next week, but as for this one—" Sarafina tossed her mace through the air to Sigmund, who almost took off his own kneecap trying to catch it.

"Uh-uh, no way." Hailey yanked the mace out of Sigmund's hands and threw it back to his mother with surprising ease. "He's not carrying that. He's going to hurt himself."

"My son is a Sage demon. He is a warrior." Sarafina threw the mace back again, and again Sigmund bobbled it and nearly impaled his foot.

"Well, he's not a mace-carrying warrior," Hailey said, and sent it sailing through the air. "At least, not yet. That thing might even be a challenge for Frankie. Better to keep it with you."

"Or perhaps with you," Sarafina said, and nodded at Hailey, impressed. "But he must carry something."

"Why? Why does he have to?"

"Hailey." Sigmund cleared his throat. "Stay out of this, please."

Hailey blinked. So did everyone. Sigmund never used that tone with her; he never told her to "stay out" of things.

"Sig?" she asked.

"May I just have something smaller," he asked. "Like a stake?"

Hailey handed one to him and watched with a troubled expression while he adjusted and readjusted his grip. "Just be careful not to stake yourself," she cautioned. "We all know it's possible."

"I'll be fine."

Across from them, Sarafina nodded. "It's a start," she said. "To carry a weapon is the duty of a Sage demon. Even a tiny one like that."

215

The muscles in Sigmund's jaw twitched. "It seems that a Sage demon has many duties that I wasn't fully aware of," he muttered.

"All right, now that that's settled." Spike stretched his back, and Frankie winced as she heard far too many joints crack and pop. "Let's do one more sweep and then call it a night. I'm bloody exhausted."

They split into groups and fanned out across the cemetery. Spike and Willow headed toward the Rimbauer mausoleum. Oz and Jake went east to skirt the woods. Sarafina and Sigmund headed north, toward the gazebo and the fountain. Frankie, Hailey, and Vi walked the graves to the west.

"That was pretty brave," Frankie said to Hailey. "Standing up to Sarafina when she's all pelted in gore like that."

"She is pretty terrifying," Hailey agreed. "But I don't think I have to worry about her. She seems to be very Team Hailey. It's Sig that I'm not so sure about."

"What do you mean?" Frankie asked, even though she knew. She'd felt it brewing: the trouble, the distance, and the mere mention of it made her want to grab Sigmund and Hailey and forcibly twine their PDA pinkies together. *Don't break up*, she thought fearfully. *Don't pull away from the Scoobies.*

"He barely wants to be around me lately. And he won't talk. . . . I don't know. I'm just getting the sense that he's got one foot on either side of a line. And he's getting pulled further over to the side I'm not on."

"The warrior stuff versus the scholar stuff," said Frankie, and Hailey nodded.

"But . . . Sigmund is a scholar. Sigmund is a nerd. We saw him staring way too long through the window of that store that sells historical miniatures!" Frankie didn't understand it. That was the Sigmund she knew. The only face he'd ever shown them.

"But maybe that's not what he's going to be," said Hailey. "Maybe it's time for a break from books. And for some reason, that also means a break from me."

"And you're just going to let him?" Frankie asked.

"I don't have the right to not let him. If that's what he's meant to be."

"What about what he wants?" Vi interjected a little tersely. "Does he just have to let the demon side have its way? He's half human, too. It should be his decision."

"I guess." Hailey frowned. "Either way, if he does embrace the demon side, it's going to be a long journey. He's never even staked a vamp, and I don't like to think of him fighting up close. Frankie, maybe he could borrow your sparring stick."

"You want me to lend him Mr. Stabby?" Frankie asked.

"Mr. Stabby," Hailey remarked, and looked at her sister. "Hey, Vi, you never told me what your favorite stake was called."

"That's because I never named one."

Frankie and Hailey exchanged a look.

"Okay, okay," Vi said. "Its name is Spot. I never got to have a dog."

Hailey snorted and rubbed her shoulder. She looked kind of terrible. Layers of concealer hid dark circles beneath her eyes, and Frankie had begun to detect the distinct waft of Bengay from beneath her bedroom door at night. The extra battles had worn on Frankie, too, but at least she had a slayer's constitution; fully human Hailey must have felt like a bag of loose garbage that someone had taken a broomstick to.

They had to figure out what was happening. They couldn't keep this up much longer.

Vi knows, Frankie's slaydar whispered. *Or at least she knows more than she's saying.*

"So," Vi said to Frankie, eyes on every shadow to see if it would move, "is this what you expected when you became a slayer? Long hours and thankless wounds?"

"I didn't expect anything," said Frankie. "I was just trying not to mess it up."

Vi nodded.

"And I wanted to be the kind of slayer that the other slayers would be proud of," Frankie said.

Vi looked at her, surprised, but the expression quickly faded into bitterness. "Don't worry about what we think. It doesn't matter what we think. All that matters is staying alive."

"I thought all that mattered was saving people. And looking out for your friends." Frankie stopped walking.

"Yeah," Vi said, and stopped, too. "And that."

"Guys," Hailey said, and tugged on Vi's sleeve. "Hey, slayers—did you hear that?"

Frankie listened. For a minute, there was nothing. And then she heard the snarl. It set Frankie's teeth on edge the moment she heard it, and she didn't know why. She'd never heard it before. But just the same, she knew in her bones that they should run, and from the look of it, so did Vi. The other slayer was frozen, staring in the opposite direction as if she was too terrified to turn around and see what was coming.

"No," Vi whispered, and started to shake.

"Vi?" Hailey's hand strayed to the whistle around her neck, the one that each team carried in case they needed to call for backup. "Vi? What's wrong?"

"It can't be," Vi said.

The vampire crept out of the shadows, and Frankie took a half step back.

It wasn't a normal vampire. It was enormous and gray-skinned, with deep, darkened eye sockets, the pupils of its eyes slitted like a reptile's. Its hands were tipped in long, thick claws, and it wore the tanned leather clothing of an ancient warrior. This vampire had never been human. This was a vampire born.

"Uber . . ." Frankie stammered.

"Uber? To where?" Hailey asked, misunderstanding.

"No. Uber!" Frankie shouted. "Ubervamp! It's a Turok-Han! Whistle, Hailey! Whistle!"

Hailey put the silver whistle to her lips and blew, and the sound signaled the Turok-Han like a starter's pistol. It leapt at them, and Frankie jumped ahead to meet it, throwing everything she had into a punch.

The punch barely turned its head. It twisted back and opened its mouth. The sound that came out was a hiss, but to Frankie, it sounded like laughter.

Frankie hit again, and it hit back harder. She blocked, and it felt like it might break her arm.

Focus, she thought, and went back in, using every ounce of speed she could muster. It worked for a few moments. She dodged its blows and landed her own, but they didn't seem to have much effect. The Turok-Han absorbed her punches. Her kicks barely moved it a foot. Eventually she forgot to jump back when it swung, and felt herself sail through the air to bounce off a headstone. In comparison to the Turok-Han's fists, the granite felt soft.

"Frankie, what do we do?" Hailey cried. "Vi won't move!"

A little panicked, Frankie hugged her ribs and rolled to her feet. She needed a moment. She needed to think. She raised her arm and heaved her magic out. It sent the monster sprawling—but her feeling of triumph was short-lived, as another Ubervamp slunk out of the shadows.

"We've got to move. Move!" she shouted at Hailey, and Hailey shouted at Vi, trying to snap her out of her fear. Hailey tried to drag Vi, then moved behind her to push. It was a bad move. She never saw the second Ubervamp coming.

"Hailey!" Frankie screamed as the Turok-Han lifted Hailey by the neck.

Frankie's perception shifted into slow motion as Hailey's feet kicked in midair. One clench of the Turok-Han's fist and it would be over. Her throat would be torn out, her neck broken. Frankie could almost see it happening: the shock in Hailey's eyes, how her body would fold to the grass. She heard Vi's warning in her ears like a prophecy: One day, no matter how hard she fought, she would lose a Scooby.

But today was not that day. Frankie charged and collided with the trunk of the Turok-Han at full force. It flew back, and Hailey was tossed aside.

The vampire righted itself, and Frankie raised her fists. A Turok-Han could kill a slayer without much trouble. *Just punch*, she thought. *And don't stop.* She unloaded combinations on it and used her telekinesis not to attack, but to vault out of harm's away. She landed a hit; it landed one back. But she couldn't afford a stalemate: The other Turok-Han was circling, and Vi was still paralyzed.

"We killed you!" Vi cried. "We beat you!"

"And we will again!" Frankie promised. "We just have to run a little first!" Frankie flipped both feet into the Ubervamp's chin and ran to Vi and Hailey, making them flee with her through sheer force of will. She sent her magic out in bursts to roll the Turok-Han and give them some breathing room, but the vampires were too fast and gaining ground. "Hailey, keep on that whistle!"

She did, and Frankie heard a familiar howl: Jake and Oz, coming to the rescue. But she wasn't after the Osbourne werewolves.

She wasn't after Sarafina, or even Spike. Frankie needed her mom. "There! Mom!"

Willow and Spike emerged from around the bend in the path, racing toward them at full speed. Or half speed for Spike, who then charged ahead and left the witch in his dust to leap upon an Ubervamp and flip it over his shoulders. Frankie glanced back. She had to hurry. Against a Turok-Han, not even Spike was safe.

"Mom!" she called, and held her hands out. Willow stopped running. She knew exactly what Frankie wanted.

She reached down and grabbed the Scythe, tearing it through the concealment of the glamour, and heaved it through the air. The red and silver of the blade gleamed even under the thin light of the slivered moon, as the Scythe spun into Frankie's hands like she'd pulled it on a string.

She gripped the weapon and felt its power race through her body.

"Hey!" Frankie shouted as one of the Ubervamps threw Spike against a headstone. "Don't. Hurt. My. Watcher."

Frankie charged, and the Turok-Han charged in kind, the two of them like trains or angry rams about to collide. At the last moment, Frankie slid and ducked under the Ubervamp's arms as it swiped, its fangs closing on empty air. She popped back up and knocked the Scythe's only blunt edge against the back of its head. It growled and turned around, surprised. But the game had changed now. She was actually a little insulted to note that the Turok-Han seemed to be growling mostly at the Scythe and not at her.

Newly cautious, the ancient vampire circled and snapped its fangs. Frankie knew from the stories Buffy told that the Ubervamps were extremely hard to kill. That Buffy's stake had failed to pierce the armor of bone that protected its heart. But cutting its head off? That had worked nicely.

Frankie leapt forward and swung the weapon in a smooth arc. The Turok-Han jumped back to dodge—a nice change—but it couldn't dodge forever. Eventually it tried an unlucky punch, and the Scythe was there, sharp and hungry, to cut its arm off. The creature barely had time to hiss its displeasure before Frankie swung again, and the Turok-Han's head bounced across the grass and exploded into dust. Like all the rest.

No time for victory poses, though, as the second Turok-Han attacked, and Frankie engaged it with a spinning flip, cutting and kicking, enjoying the feel of the Scythe in her hands. It was, she admitted, a little bit showboaty, but she couldn't seem to help herself. To hold the Scythe was to be invincible. To wield the Scythe was to have the strength of the whole line of slayers standing at her back.

Frankie spun the weapon in her hands as the dust of the last Turok-Han settled into the grass. "Damn," she said. "Where have you been all my life?"

She looked at Vi. Vi looked like she was thinking the exact same thing.

"Vi!" Hailey shook her sister by the shoulders, and Vi tore her gaze away from the Scythe.

"I'm okay. I'm okay, kid."

"Don't call me 'kid,'" Hailey snapped. "What just happened? Why did you freeze up like that?"

Vi looked at Willow, and Willow's face scrunched in sympathy. "It's okay, Vi."

"It was because it was an Ubervamp," Frankie said. "Because those were the things that the First used to terrorize and kill the Potentials, back when they were still just Potentials." Buffy and Frankie's mom had told them the stories. No other demon was more of a bogeyman to the slayers than the Turok-Han.

Spike picked himself up from where he'd landed against the headstone and went to his other slayer. "You all right, Larsson?"

"I'm fine." Vi looked at Frankie, and more specifically, at the Scythe. "Looks like someone's been keeping secrets after all."

"Like you said"—Frankie shrugged—"after what happened in Halifax, you can't be too careful. Who knows who you can trust?"

"Smart." Vi smiled. She touched Hailey's neck. "Listen, I'm going to get out of here."

"I'll go with you—"

"No. You should go home with Willow and Frankie. Get some ice on those bruises." She looked at the marks on her sister's neck and turned to Frankie. "You saved her. You saved both of us." She gave a small, haunted smile. "Nice work," she said, and for once she didn't call Frankie "junior" or "tiger" or "sport." "Thank you."

Vi waited only until she was inside a deserted warehouse before she lit the blood-soaked herbs and opened the communication portal to the Darkness.

"Aspen!" she shouted into the smoke. But it wasn't Aspen she saw. It was Sonia again, taken by surprise, adjusting the hood of her ridiculous black robe.

"Vi? What's wrong?"

"I have to talk to Aspen."

"She's busy."

"She's not too busy for this. Get her. Now."

Sonia hesitated; the hood of the robe bobbed with indecision. But in the end she went scurrying off to find their fearless leader. Vi paced while she waited, back and forth over the concrete, her limbs still tight and buzzing with adrenaline. She'd sold her "I'm fine" routine quite well to the Scoobies. But Vi was not fine. She could barely catch her breath. And every time she stopped moving or closed her eyes, she heard the snarl of the Turok-Han emerging from the shadows.

It had been almost twenty years since she'd seen one. Since she and the other Potentials had dropped into the Hellmouth and fought an army of them. But twenty years was not long enough. There was no measure of time sufficient to erase that terror. The terror of seeing Buffy nearly lose. The terror of being hunted underground after Faith led them into a trap. When she'd looked at that Turok-Han, she wasn't even Vi anymore— she was Violet, just a kid, just a Potential, helpless and afraid.

"Aspen!" she shouted.

"What?" The leader of the Darkness stepped before the window of smoke. A flash of annoyance crossed her features. Then it smoothed away into concern. "Vi, what's wrong? Are you all right?"

"No. I'm not all right. No one told me that the beacon I planted on the Hellmouth could call forth a Turok-Han," Vi snapped. Aspen looked at her blankly, and Vi remembered: Aspen hadn't been there for the fight with the First. She'd joined them later, like most of them had, those unknown slayers activated all over the world. Turok-Han was just a name to her. A demon like any other. But that didn't matter to Vi just then. "You didn't tell me! You should have known!"

"Vi, I'm sorry," Aspen said. "I didn't realize."

"It almost killed my sister. It had its hand around her neck—" When the Turok-Han grabbed Hailey, Vi had screamed and screamed inside her mind. But only inside her mind. Outside it, she hadn't been able to make a sound. She hadn't been able to move. Frankie had had to save her. Frankie had saved them all.

"We have to stop this, now," said Vi. "We have to destroy the beacon. And find another way to get the—" She stopped. In her anger about Hailey and her fear of the Ubervamp, she'd actually forgotten: the Scythe. The Scythe was found.

"Tell me," Vi said. "Tell me exactly what the beacon is. Everything you know about it."

"The beacon draws familiar demons to the Hellmouth," said Aspen. "Eventually they will reach it, and it will welcome them home." She shrugged.

"What does that mean?"

"It means the demons aren't being drawn to Sunnydale for the farmers markets. They'll try to reopen the Hellmouth. They're going to jump into it. And when they do—" Aspen paused. "The mage wasn't exactly clear on that part. It's supposed to summon demons

225

that the Hellmouth knows—that have been there before—and once the Hellmouth eats enough of them . . . something equally known, and equally bad, is supposed to come out. The demon-mage used a lot of grand hand gestures. I'm sure it was mostly for show."

"For show?"

"Yeah, you know. Big demon-mage talk."

"And what if it wasn't?" Vi asked. "I can't believe you would do this. My sister is here! And no matter how we felt about Buffy Summers, our plans were never supposed to involve reopening a hellmouth!"

"Our plans weren't supposed to involve a lot of things," Aspen said, her voice low. "But plans change. We've come too far now, Vi. We're too close. Besides, if you want to destroy the beacon, you have to find the Scythe."

"I already found the Scythe."

Aspen stopped. "Where is it?"

"The new slayer has it. You were right; it seems like the red witch was hiding it the whole time."

"And she brought it out to slay the Turok-Han," Aspen said, lips curling slightly.

"Does that just make your night?" Vi asked. "Are you just so pleased how your plans are coming together?"

"Vi—"

"Forget it. You were right, I said. Frankie has the Scythe, and I'm going to take it and then this will all be over with."

"Wait." Aspen stopped her when Vi moved to stomp out the blood-soaked herbs. "If you make a move for the Scythe and fail, you'll lose their trust. The witch will hide it again. Maybe someplace we'll never find it. I'm sorry about what happened tonight, but we can't be rushed."

"If you're asking me to wait, you're asking too much." Vi shifted

226

her weight. She was still shaking. She knew what she looked like: a
slayer pushed to the edge. Off her game.

Aspen pursed her lips.

"We're coming now," she said. She called for the others over her
shoulder and then spoke demonic words in an accent far more pro-
ficient than Vi could ever manage. The window of smoke expanded
and stretched until it was large enough to step through. Aspen moved
aside to allow Sonia to pass, still hooded. Gabby came next. Then
Neha. Then a tall and scruffy slayer with perpetually bad hair-
cuts called Kate. One by one they stepped through the smoke and
appeared in the warehouse on the other side. Aspen was the last, her
brown boots stepping agilely into their home dimension.

"I shouldn't have left you here on your own for so long." Aspen put
her hands on Vi's shoulders, and Vi exhaled as the fearful, springy
energy leaked out of her body. "But we were always here. And now
we're really here. To help."

"Thank you," Vi said. She put her hand on Aspen's and squeezed.

Aspen turned and surveyed the warehouse like she was determin-
ing how to make use of it while the other slayers waited for orders.
She smiled her dazzling smile and stretched out her arms.

"Say hello, Sunnydale, because the Darkness has arrived!"

$$) \;) \; \bigcirc \; (\; ($$

In the happy reunion of slayers that followed, no one noticed
Frankie's face pressed to the bottom corner of one of the warehouse's
fly-specked windows. And no one heard her when she whispered,
"Dammit, Vi," and quietly crept away.

PART FOUR

THE DARKNESS, LIKE
SOYLENT GREEN, IS PEOPLE

CHAPTER TWENTY

JUST ONE OF THE SLAYERS

Frankie met the Scoobies in the school library the next morning. She was the first to arrive, having gotten up so early for school that she had been out the door before her mom had even come down to make the coffee. She had also been the last one home, returning long after the house lights were off and everyone had fallen exhaustedly into bed. But that was for the best. If she had seen Hailey right after being at the warehouse— seeing what she'd seen, hearing what she'd heard—she didn't know what she would have done.

Frankie sat quietly at the table as Hailey, Jake, and Sigmund arrived. Sigmund had a tray of coffees and set one down in front of her.

"Mocha frappe no whip for Frankie," he said. "Cinnamon latte with oat milk and several sugars." He handed it to Hailey. "And a Puppuccino for Jake."

Jake grabbed for his berry smoothie. "Ha-ha, very funny."

"I got a mocha frappe with extra whip for Spike, too." Sigmund looked down through the clear dome of the plastic cap. "Had them throw in some of those little marshmallows. Is he here yet?"

"I'm right behind you."

Sigmund turned as the vampire came through the swinging doors. He looked rough. Still in tweed, but his shirt was misbuttoned and his tie was loose. As for his face—well, his face looked like it had been pummeled the night before by a Turok-Han.

"Geez," said Jake. "I guess I didn't realize how much of a beating you took."

"Neither did I until I woke up to blood on my pillow and felt all these scabs." Spike gestured to his head. "I'll be fine, though it probably won't do to have the school librarian looking like he just came from a barroom brawl. Can you patch me up, Mini Red?"

"Willow probably could," Hailey said when Frankie didn't answer. "I think she has recipes for mystical ointments and stuff."

"Well, that's very helpful, Hailey, considering Willow's not here." Spike frowned. "For now, can you just glamour it? You know, blend it away?" He wiggled his fingers in the air as if that's how spells were done.

"I don't think I should," said Frankie glumly. "Your face is already glamoured old. A glamour on a glamour . . . that's like putting a hat on a hat."

"I'll handle it." Hailey reached for her bag and dug around for her makeup and brushes. She came up with a bottle of foundation and some pressed powder. "I've started carrying some very pale shades around for Frankie."

Spike shrugged and sat down to straddle a chair so Hailey could fix his face. The end result wasn't terrible: no visible bruises or scabs. He did look a little overdone, like he'd just gotten offstage from a lead role in *Cabaret*.

"Fancy," said Jake, and whistled. "You should be able to wipe most of it off by lunch—aren't you vampires all about the speed healing?" He took a long sip of his smoothie and stretched. "So what's with the ultra-early Scooby-ing?" he asked. "You'd think we could have a break after all the extra patrols."

"That's just it," Frankie said. "I know why we've been needing all the extra patrols. Someone planted a beacon on the Hellmouth."

The Scoobies paused mid-drink.

"Excuse me?" said Spike.

"It's meant to summon demons, which explains why we've been seeing so many different varieties, and from so far away. And it's also meant to summon demons that are familiar to this particular hellmouth."

"Which explains why the 1998 Sunnydale swim champs suddenly swam back upstream," Jake said, with his straw in the corner of his lips.

"But why would someone do that?" Sigmund asked.

"I don't know," Frankie said. "I think to keep me busy. Distracted. And to make it so I needed help." She watched their confusion travel around the table and land on Spike.

"But who would do it?" Spike asked.

Frankie looked down. She didn't know how to say this part. Or at least she didn't know how to say it to Hailey.

"It was my sister, wasn't it?" Hailey said quietly. She made a disgusted expression and pushed away from the table. "Goddammit, Vi. I knew there was something going on; I knew she was acting dodgy—"

"It wasn't just her. It was her and a group of other slayers." Frankie looked at Spike. "I think they've been hiding in some other dimension, but they're here now. In New Sunnydale. I watched them step into a warehouse through a nifty portal last night after I tailed Vi." She glanced at Hailey guiltily. "I just had a vibe. And I wanted to make sure she was okay, after the Ubervamp shook her up so bad."

"That was nice of you." Hailey's jaw clenched. "I'm glad you were there to check on her and uncover her treachery!"

"Another dimension," Spike said. "Was Buffy with them?"

"If Buffy was with them, we wouldn't be having this conversation," said Frankie. "These slayers . . . I think they planned the attack in Halifax."

"Slayers?" Jake blinked. "Other slayers? Why would you think that?"

"We shouldn't jump to conclusions," said Sigmund. "One portal and one demon beacon don't necessarily make them evil. Maybe there's an explanation."

"If they have one, I didn't hear it," Frankie said. Though maybe she'd missed it. It had taken some time to creep up to her hiding place outside the warehouse, and even though Vi was shouting, the other slayer's voice—the leader, Aspen—was annoyingly hard to make out. "All I know is that they're after the Scythe."

"Well, that's fine, then," said Jake. "Your mom's not letting it out of her sight—"

"But who is watching my mom?" Frankie asked. "We should tell my mom to hide it again, to use that spell like she did in the trunk. I don't want the Scythe used, or seen, until we know what they want it for."

"Right." Spike took one more sip of his mocha frappe with tiny marshmallows. "Then let's go ask them. They're slayers, I'm a Watcher—they have to tell me."

"I don't think so," Frankie said.

"Let me go and talk to Vi," said Hailey. "I'll lay on the guilt, and she'll be wrapped around my tiny pinkie finger. They're probably just scared—"

"No." Frankie stood up to pace. "Everything about the explosion in Halifax, about them being survivors, and being scared . . . That was just a line that Vi was feeding us. There was something that they said last night, about Buffy and the way they felt about her." Frankie stopped and crossed her arms. "And then, of course, there's their name: the Darkness."

"The Darkness," said Jake. "As in, the darkness that's coming?"

"And now it's here," Frankie said. "When they came through the portal, they convenie████████████emselves."

It took a moment for everyone to swallow that bit of information, and Frankie watched them wrestle with it, trying to find some way around. She'd done the same thing herself, lying awake in her bed last night. Spike stood and tore off his jacket and threw it across his chair.

"How many?" he asked.

"What?"

"How many were there?" he half shouted.

"At least eight," Frankie replied. "But I didn't hang around long. I can't be sure of a final count."

"Eight rogue slayers," he said. Then he laughed, and his laugh chilled Frankie to the bone. He sounded scared.

For a moment, all of the Scoobies were silent, and then the fears and doubts erupted.

"What's Frankie supposed to do against eight rogue slayers?" Jake asked. "Even one would be enough to keep her busy."

"What are any of us supposed to do?" asked Hailey. "You don't think they want the Scythe bad enough to hurt us, do you?"

"What we need are answers," said Spike. "And a slayer army of our own. What we need is Buffy."

"I have an idea," said Frankie.

"But we don't have Buffy," Hailey went on, talking over her. "And I just don't believe that these Darkness slayers were the ones who— Vi might be messed up, but she wouldn't kill Buffy and the others on purpose!"

"But would she trap Buffy and the others on purpose?" said Sigmund. "After all, we can assume that they are the ones who've been casting the portals, and that might include the large inter-dimensional portal that Buffy and the others were pulled through."

"Hey. Guys." Frankie crossed her arms.

"We've got to get them back," said Spike. "If we strike first, the Darkness won't be ready for it. We have to use the Scythe and open that portal now."

"Who knows if it will work," said Jake. "After last time—"

"Guys!" Frankie shouted. The Scooby panic stopped, and they looked at her. "I said, I have an idea." She reached into her pocket and tossed the stalker's stone onto the table.

"It's a stalker's stone. I got it from Grim. And I'm going to use it to infiltrate the Darkness."

The Scoobies stared down at the small stone, dark and barely larger than a quarter, sitting in the middle of the table. Jake slid down to get an eye-level view, moving slowly, like the stone might jump up and smack him in the forehead.

"So Grimloch gave this to you as a present?" he asked. "What's it called again?"

"A stalker's stone."

"So he's just coming right out and admitting it," Jake said, and Frankie smacked him lightly.

"Not that kind of stalker, Jake. It's used for hunting. Stalking. You smear a little of your prey's blood on it, and you're supposed to be able to move among them undetected. Or they'll perceive you as one of their own. Something like that."

"What does that mean?" Hailey asked. She reached out curiously to prod the stone with a finger. "Like if you smear it in deer's blood, other deer will think you're a deer?"

"Or maybe they don't see you at all?" asked Spike.

"Or they just don't perceive you as a threat," said Sigmund.

"I don't know, you guys," said Frankie. "I've never actually used it."

They looked at it again. Just a little stone, shiny and black, that oddly seemed to catch the light deep down at its center.

"Well, how are you going to use it now?" asked Jake. "Does it even work on people? And don't you need some of the rogue slayers' blood?"

"Want me to go stab Vi?" Hailey asked jokingly.

"Don't need to," said Frankie. "Grimloch said we only needed the blood of our prey, and as luck would have it, the blood of our prey is running right through my veins."

"Slayer's blood," said Sigmund.

"Exactly. I'm going to use the stalker's stone to blend in with the Darkness and eavesdrop on their plans in plain sight."

"The bloody hell you are," Spike exclaimed. "You're not going into that nest of vipers all alone with an untested spell."

"Yes, I am."

"What if it doesn't work? What if you get caught?"

"Then I'm the one of us most likely to be able to get away." She looked at Jake, Hailey, and Sigmund. "I'm not sending anybody else in to do this. It's too dangerous."

Hailey stared at the stone. "Are you sure? You could probably send me. Even if they caught me, I'm Vi's sister. They wouldn't kill me."

"That's brave of you," said Sigmund. "But you only know that Vi wouldn't kill you. What the others might do, none can say."

"It has to be me," Frankie said. "I'll be safe. I'll be careful."

CHAPTER TWENTY-ONE

STALKING WITH THE STALKER'S STONE

"**W**here have you been?" Willow demanded when Frankie came through the front door. "You think you can just walk around out there after you text me about rogue slayers?" But before she could answer, Willow wrapped her in a tight hug. "You're grounded."

"Mom. You can't ground me. I have work to do."

"Not when you're grounded," Willow said into her hair. But Frankie could tell by the tone of her voice—it was a wishful grounding. Her mom was really bad at this.

They'd had Spike write them notes to get them out of classes (though they weren't quite sure why that should work and neither was Principal Jacobs) and gathered at the Rosenberg house to regroup. Sigmund called his mom, who met them in the driveway.

"Where's Oz?" Jake asked, craning his neck to look down the street for the van and nearly incinerating Spike with a shaft of sunlight.

"Hey! Watch it, Fido."

"Sorry," Jake said.

"He said he has a long shift at the youth center," Willow replied. "But he'll be here soon. He doesn't want you to go anywhere on your own, Jake."

"But it's perfectly fine for him to," Jake grumbled.

"He's very protective of his pack," said Sarafina. "And he will be safe. He has his teeth and claws, always at his disposal." She blinked innocently when Willow gave her a look. "What? It is very impressive."

"Speaking of impressive," said Frankie. "Since we have the Great Sarafina DeWitt with us, I was wondering if you would be willing to guard my mom. Not, like, stand outside her bedroom door every night, but just, stay close? Make it seem like you two are reconnecting and joined at the hip."

Sarafina looked at Willow and put a hand on the witch's waist to toy with her belt loops. "That would be my pleasure."

"M'kay," said Frankie. She and Sigmund quickly turned away, eyebrows raised. He went to the table and began to unload book after book from his backpack. "What're those for?" Frankie asked.

"Well, we thought we would start researching ways to destroy the demon beacon." He glanced at Willow, then back at Frankie and smiled. "Something to keep our minds occupied so we don't spend the whole time worrying."

"Yeah," Jake said, and sat down heavily. "Since there's nothing we can do to actually help you."

Frankie touched the werewolf's shoulder. "This is actual help. Listen, I'll be right back. I just need to grab something from my room."

Upstairs, she pulled Buffy's old leather jacket out of her closet, where she'd hidden it with her scant pieces of formal wear, and her mom's old homecoming gown, now stained with blood from the battle of the Promise Dance. She put the jacket on, sliding her arms into the cool sleeves and feeling the weight settle on her shoulders. Of course, if the stalker's stone worked, none of the other slayers would even see it, but it still felt right. And it felt like luck, like a blanket, and like Buffy's own arms around her.

"I really wish you didn't have to do this," said Willow.

She spun around to see her mom and Spike standing in her room.

"Guys," she said. "Knock." She reached into her jewelry box for Buffy's old cross and fastened it around her neck.

Spike awkwardly took out a cigarette and flicked open his lighter; Willow deftly snatched it out of his hand.

"What are you guys so worried for?" Frankie asked. "The stone will work. And even if it doesn't, I do have a chance, you know. Buffy wasn't that much older than me when she fought Faith."

"Well, yeah"—her mom cocked her head—"but we always knew Buffy would win."

"Buffy was Buffy," said Spike with the unlit smoke between his teeth. "Faith was just an angry kid who was afraid to face her mistakes. These slayers aren't the same. If they were responsible for the attack on Slayerfest, then they're tactical. Organized. And apparently psychotic."

"Not psychotic," Frankie said. "We don't know for sure that they did what we think they did, and if they did, we don't know why. There might be an explanation."

"I'm sure there is. And as long as Buffy and the others aren't hurt, an argument can be made that they get to live." He looked at her, and Frankie knew what he saw: Mini Red, playing dress-up in Buffy's clothes. He probably thought she looked ridiculous. That it didn't suit her at all.

"See?" she said, and tugged on the jacket. "Sometimes I wear a big slayer's clothes."

"And sometimes you're just as bullheaded," he said. "I ought to be going with you."

"I need you here. To look after her." She smiled at her mom. "And I need to be alone, and stealthy."

When Frankie went downstairs, clutching the stalker's stone tight in her fist, she said no goodbyes, only walked out the front door. Spike and Willow walked out after her and watched her stride down the driveway and into the dark.

"How do we do this?" Spike asked, and crossed his arms over his chest. "How do we let her walk out there all alone? Just one girl against the bloody world?"

Willow crossed her arms, too. "How did Joyce?" she asked. "How did Giles?"

Spike raised his eyebrows. "I think they drank."

"Yeah," said Willow, and they turned back inside. "That's a good idea."

☽ ☽ ○ ☾ ☾

Frankie clutched the stalker's stone tightly as she neared the warehouse, unsure of when she should activate it. Soon, or she could be spotted on her way inside. Or not so soon, if the stone's powers only had a short duration. If only the demon who had given it to her had a phone, she could text and ask.

"Stupid Luddite hunter god," Frankie mumbled as she dragged her knife across her palm.

Bright red blood pooled in the cut and coated the surface of the charm, and instinctively, Frankie rolled it in her hand so her blood would coat every surface. It kind of hurt, and it took a while, like trying to glaze a very disgusting doughnut hole. When she was finished, she closed her fist and waited. But she didn't need to ask if the stone was working. As soon as her fingers wrapped around it, the stalker's stone grew warm, almost to the point of being hot.

She held her fist up before her face and caught a soft glow emanating from between her fingers. And not the stone's usual ethereal internal glow, but a red one. Red as blood or as a beating heart. Frankie held it carefully, letting the cut bleed and keeping the stone against the cut in case the blood needed to be wet or in constant supply.

She hurried toward the warehouse, slipping from one shadow to the next, and pressed herself against the building, behind a pile of stacked pallets. Of course, if the stone was working, she probably didn't need to do any of that.

She raised her face to the dirty glass and looked inside. The warehouse was deserted. Empty. The Darkness had already moved, already found a safe house somewhere. She would have to return home and get help from the Scoobies, possibly get Sigmund to attempt another spell with the Swiss Army Scythe to track them. At the thought of the Scythe, she reached down to her hip, where she wished she were carrying it. The weapon of the slayers would certainly have been a nice thing to have when facing down a roomful of them. But after what she'd overheard, she had to keep the Scythe far away from the Darkness, no matter how much help it would have been.

Frankie was about to put the stalker's stone away and slink back through the parking lot when she heard a toilet flush. She looked back through the window and saw a tall girl with a decidedly uneven haircut coming out of a ground-floor bathroom. Frankie crouched and watched as she disappeared down a staircase near the rear.

"These warehouses have basements?" she asked out loud, and when the other slayer was out of sight, she quietly opened the side door and slipped inside.

Once she was in, and padding silently across the dusty floor, she could hear them: several voices coming from the basement, talking and laughing over each other like a weird, industrial slumber party. Frankie reached the top of the stairs and looked at her glowing fist. *Now or never*, she thought.

The part of the basement she saw when she walked down the stairs looked like it had once been a break room. It had a sink and a very nonworking refrigerator. There were a few old tables and chairs, and a small counter with cabinets. The slayers had hastily converted it into living quarters, with dingy mattresses thrown on the cement, and sleeping bags rolled up on top. The whole place smelled like a mixture of dust, motor oil, and french fries, and most of it was littered with fast-food bags. Lots of fast-food bags to feed lots of slayer metabolisms. The slayers were spread out and grouped in twos and threes, a few seated on metal chairs but most cross-legged on mattresses. Frankie counted eight, but Vi wasn't there. Nor was the leader, Aspen. More of them must have come through the portal after she'd slunk away.

Frankie licked her lips nervously. Standing on the stairs, she was in plain sight, but none of the slayers seemed to notice. Nor did they seem to notice when she stepped onto the basement floor, not even when one of them got up to grab another hamburger and accidentally bumped into her.

"Oops, sorry," the young woman said, a Middle Eastern girl with a short black bob. She reached out and steadied Frankie with two hands.

"It's okay," Frankie murmured, and the slayer took a pile of three paper-wrapped burgers and returned to her seat. It was just like Grimloch had said—Frankie was there, and they could see her; some of them even made eye contact as she passed by. They simply didn't detect her. She could move within them without notice.

She could probably even do jumping jacks and sing, but she wasn't going to push it.

"Is anybody else irritated that we moved from a warehouse in one dimension to a warehouse in another?" asked a Black girl with long brown braids. She was wearing some kind of dark robe with a hood.

"At least it's a warehouse in *our* dimension this time," another slayer replied. "I have so missed Doublemeat Palace."

"Doublemeat," the Middle Eastern girl sang. "It's double sweet." She laughed and threw a fry into the first slayer's mouth.

Another dimension, Frankie thought. So that was where they'd been hiding. But was it the same dimension where Buffy and the others were?

Frankie looked around. The slayers in the basement of the warehouse didn't seem like dangerous, tactical rogues. They were just young women. Friends behaving like friends. It was strange to think how much power they had, and how they would change if they knew that she was there. It was frightening to think of what they would do to her.

"Hey, save a few of those burgers for me, okay?"

Frankie froze at the sound of Vi's voice. Would the magic of the stalker's stone work on people who knew her? She squeezed more blood from her palm and held her breath when it dripped down onto the floor. But no one seemed to notice that either. And as for Vi, she stepped deftly around Frankie and walked toward the rear of the basement, her boot heel dragging right through the drops of Frankie's blood.

Vi walked quickly through the gathered slayers and out of the break room, which was separated from the rest of the basement by most of a wall and a thick brick pillar. Frankie picked her way through the Doublemeat Palace wrappers and followed, peering around the bricks to watch as Vi made her way past high stacks of pallets piled with boxes of goods and wrapped in plastic. Someone had used the pallets to form another room of sorts, and Vi walked through the winding path of boxes like a kid going to a secret fort.

For a deserted warehouse, there sure were a lot of abandoned goods, and Frankie frowned at all the waste. Maybe after she'd dealt with these rogues she'd come back and figure out how to donate or recycle . . . whatever all this stuff was.

"We have everything we need. All we're missing is the Scythe."

Frankie's ears perked up. There was a meeting happening behind those boxes. She crept forward, still not completely trusting the magic of the stalker's stone. And even if she did, it felt too brazen to stride into a secret meeting that even other members of the Darkness were not invited to. She stepped carefully between the pallets and stretched her neck to peer over the top. Vi was there, her dyed-black hair poking out of a knit cap. She looked like she didn't really want to be there—her boot heel clicked against the floor like an impatient horse. To Vi's right and left were two slayers she didn't recognize and the one with the bad haircut, which brought the count up to a dozen not counting the leader. All seemed younger than Vi, some by several years. Twentysomethings, Frankie guessed. Which meant they'd been children when they'd been activated.

Just kids. And what had their parents done when they'd woken up one morning able to rip doors off their hinges?

It couldn't have been easy.

"But how do we get it?" asked the tall slayer with the terribly uneven haircut. "I mean we're here now, so why don't we just take it? There are all of us, and she's just a little baby abomination."

A baby abomination? Frankie wondered. Did they mean her?

"If it was just her we were stealing it from, that would be fine. But it isn't. According to Vi, the red witch has the Scythe, and we can't chance attacking her."

"Because she's too dangerous?"

"No," said a new voice. "Because if we spook her, she might hide it again, and I'm tired of looking."

Frankie knew that voice. That was the leader, who had come through the portal last. Frankie edged left to see around the bad haircut.

The leader of the Darkness was beautiful. Her brown hair hung long and loose to her elbows, and her eyes were a warm shade of hazel. She pressed her fingers to a gold medallion that hung around her neck, and the way she touched it gave Frankie a funny feeling in her gut.

"Just give me time," said Vi. "Frankie is starting to trust me. In a few weeks, she'll probably just let me borrow it."

"A few weeks?" said the haircut angrily.

"We've been waiting this long, Kate. What's another few weeks?"

"Kate's right." The leader touched the amulet around her neck again, rubbing at the green stone of the charm. "I'm tired of waiting. I want to get back to my life. Don't you?"

"Yeah, but," Vi objected, "if we do this wrong, my sister will never forgive me."

"You think she'll forgive you now?" Kate snorted. "After the ones who died?"

"We didn't mean for that to happen," said Vi. "But no, I guess maybe she won't. I know I don't."

The dead slayers. The explosion. The Darkness was responsible for it. Frankie clenched her teeth and dug the stalker's stone into her cut fist.

At a noise from the other room, Frankie ducked low behind

the crates. Someone else had come into the warehouse. Someone who put an instant stop to the slayer-slumber-party shenanigans. Cautiously, Frankie poked her head up over the edge to look and nearly gasped.

Grimloch was standing beside the brick pillar.

"And speaking of my old life . . ." The leader smiled and ran toward him. Frankie's eyes widened as she jumped into his arms and wrapped her legs around his waist to kiss him like she hadn't seen him in months and had been presumed dead.

Frankie went so cold that she nearly dropped the stone. She couldn't believe what was happening right before her eyes. And her ears. Grimloch was making small growls deep in his throat, and the sound of their lips smacking . . . she might never forget that, the smacking.

"Aspen," he said when she finally released him. "I thought—" Grimloch touched her hair. His eyes moved over her face like Frankie had seen them move over hers. He was drinking her in. Searching for wounds and injuries.

"I'm sorry," she whispered. "I should have told you, but I couldn't chance it."

Frankie backed up. She had to get out of there. It felt like she couldn't breathe. She took a wrong step and stumbled into the side of a stack of boxes, which promptly and loudly crashed to the floor.

"Oh, dammit." She froze. Every head in the room had turned her way, and the rest of the slayers hurried in from the break room. They blinked at the boxes, and at her, but no one moved. The stalker's stone, she realized, and squeezed more of her blood onto it. It was a hell of a spell.

"Frankie?" Grimloch asked.

"Frankie?" Vi echoed, and looked at Frankie for real. All the slayers looked at her then as the magic faded from their eyes.

"Get her!"

"Well, that did it," Frankie said, and shoved crates into the slayers' path. She fumbled past the makeshift walls before changing her mind and bulldozing right through them. But it was futile. She hadn't even reached the break room before they had her by the arms, and by the legs, their grips as strong as vises.

The leader, and apparently Grimloch's long, and not-at-all-lost-or-dead love, glared at Vi as Frankie was hauled before her. "You must have been followed." She motioned to the rest of the warehouse. "Sonia, Kate, sweep the rest of the building. Make sure none of her little Scooby friends came along for the ride."

"I came alone," Frankie growled, and narrowed her eyes at Grimloch. "Which I see now was stupid."

"Frankie, I—"

"Why did you follow me?" Vi asked.

"You seemed like you were upset. I wanted to make sure you were okay."

"That's sweet," Aspen said coldly. But then her expression changed. "It is really. Actually sweet." She blinked at Frankie, and the look on her face was at once contrite and beguiling. It was easy to see why she was the leader, with those eyes and that smile, the kind of smile that made you light up inside. The kind of eyes that made you feel seen. But underneath, she was mean. Some people might have missed that, but Frankie didn't.

"Don't hurt her," Aspen said to the slayers who held her. "She's one of us."

"One of you?" Frankie struggled in their looser grip. "I don't think so."

"We just want the Scythe!" Frankie turned to look into the face of a young slayer, beautiful like many of the slayers were, despite a deep scar that ran from her forehead to her chin, and an eye that had been blinded. "We don't want to hurt anyone!"

"Really?" Frankie continued to tug. She didn't like being held. She didn't like that her slayer strength was matched. "What about Sadie? What about the slayers they recovered from the explosion in Halifax?"

"That was an accident," Aspen said. "We didn't know . . . There was—"

"Not terribly interested in your explanations just now," Frankie snapped. "What do you want with the Scythe?"

She waited while the slayers looked to Aspen, afraid to speak.

"We want to give our powers back."

Frankie stopped struggling. "Huh?"

"I found a ritual," Aspen said. "It will allow us to use the Scythe to reverse the flow of the spell that your mother did all those years ago. It will allow those of us who don't want to be slayers anymore to return the gift." She smirked a little, around those words. "It'll give us our choice back."

"You . . ." Frankie looked from one young woman to the next. "None of you want to be slayers anymore?"

"Why would we?" the scarred girl asked, and let Frankie go. "You might think it's fun now, being chased around by demons and the forces of darkness, but after a decade? It gets old." The others let go of her, too, and Frankie rubbed her wrists.

"If that's all you want, why didn't you just ask? My mom would have helped you. Buffy would have—"

"No, they wouldn't," Aspen snapped. "They wouldn't listen. They never listen. And we all know how the council deals with slayers who don't stay in line."

"What are you talking about?" Frankie asked. "Are you talking about Faith? That was, like, twenty years ago and an isolated incident by an entirely different Watchers Council. Which you could have asked her about," Frankie added, "if you hadn't blown her up!" Frankie balled a fist and punched Aspen across the face, almost without meaning to. Aspen righted herself and touched her jaw as a murmur ran through the others. "Where are Buffy and the others?" Frankie demanded.

"They're fine," Vi answered. "They're safe. They're just in a holding dimension with Andrew and—" She stopped talking when Aspen's head snapped toward her.

"A holding dimension," said Frankie. "What are you going to do with them?"

"We'll let them go," said Vi. "After the ritual is complete, they won't have any business with us anymore." She smiled an awkward, cockeyed smile. "We'll be out of their jurisdiction." Frankie looked into the faces of the other slayers, who waited and watched with a mix of cautious hope and gritty readiness. They would do what Aspen told them to do. And though Vi said they would let Buffy and the others go, Frankie noticed that Aspen had said nothing of the kind.

"Just give us the Scythe," said the slayer with the uneven hair, called Kate, when she returned from her pointless sweep of the warehouse. "Just let us be people again."

"Sorry," Frankie said sarcastically. "I don't have it on me."

Aspen snorted. "Tie her up. We can use her to trade with the red witch."

"Funny you should mention that red witch," Frankie said, and the tone of her voice made Aspen's eyes narrow to slits. "But you seem to have totally forgotten about this one." She drew her magic up hard and set it loose, her telekinesis sweeping through them like an invisible club and knocking those nearest to the floor.

"Get her!" Aspen screamed as she got to her feet. "Don't let her out of this warehouse!"

The slayers began to give chase, and Grimloch grabbed two of them, lifting them high by the backs of their belts and letting them kick in the air before tossing them aside.

"Frankie, run!"

Frankie did, but back at Grim to drag him out alongside her. "You're running, too, you stupid jerk!" she shouted, and spin-kicked her way through another slayer who was barring the stairs. She and Grim raced through the empty warehouse, their feet slamming against the cement. They broke through the doors and into the sunlight and didn't stop running until they'd left the warehouse district far behind.

CHAPTER TWENTY-TWO

HIS GIRLFRIEND'S BACK, AND YOU'RE GONNA BE IN TROUBLE

"Frankie, stop! We can stop!" Frankie and Grimloch's pace slowed once they were away from the warehouses. None of the Darkness had given chase. "Frankie!"

She heard him, but she kept on running. She would stop when she damn well felt like it; she would run all the way back to her house. . . . He grabbed her by the elbow and pulled her into the shadows behind a rickety, leaning wooden gate.

Frankie bared her teeth. She took Grim by the wrist and spun, flinging him hard. The sound of his impact against the wood was loud and satisfying.

"You'd better be careful who you go grabbing and pulling into alleys," Frankie hissed.

"I'm sorry," he said. "I didn't mean to . . . tug you. And I didn't mean to end the magic of the stalker's stone. I didn't realize you were using it. What were you doing there? What were you thinking?"

"What were YOU doing there? What were YOU thinking?"

"Francesca Rosenberg." He reached for the hand that still held the stalker's stone and raised it between their faces. "The magic of the stalker's stone is short in duration. You would have been revealed in a matter of minutes."

Frankie looked at the stone in her palm. It had gone cold and dark again, the only glow that strange, unearthly one from deep in its center. Grimloch opened her fingers and plucked it from her grasp.

"Hey, that's mine!"

"It was my gift to give and mine to reclaim, when it is not used properly."

"You need to look up the definition of 'gift,'" Frankie snapped. "And I did use it properly. It's not my fault you showed up and broke the spell!"

Grimloch stepped closer. He looked her over from head to toe, like she might be hurt, just like he had done to Aspen. "Did I hurt you? When I grabbed your arm?"

"No," Frankie said, but she rubbed her elbow anyway. "You hurt me when you made out with your evil ex-girlfriend!"

"She surprised me," he said. He looked down. But what did he have to feel bad about, really? He'd never said Aspen was his ex. And when he kissed her, he hadn't known that she was evil.

"Did you know?" Frankie asked. "That those slayers were the Darkness? That Aspen was responsible for the explosion in Halifax?"

"You know I didn't."

"I don't know anything anymore."

Grimloch frowned. "Give me your hand." She lifted it and let him bandage and bind the cut in her palm. "You didn't need this much blood, you know. A few drops are more than sufficient."

"That would have been nice to know. Maybe next time you give one of these you should include a stalker's stone instruction manual!"

He ran his fingers over the trails of blood that had bled down her wrist.

"I suppose this means we're enemies now," Frankie said, and Grimloch looked at her. "Because you love her. Because you're a demon and don't have a firm rule against evil?"

"I don't know, Frankie."

"I saw the way you kissed her. You never kissed me like that."

"Not yet," he said, and Frankie's stomach fluttered. "But I have never been reunited with you after thinking you were dead." He touched her face, and his eyes moved to her mouth.

"Do not even think about kissing me when you still have rogue, evil slayer on your lips." He let go. "Look," Frankie said. "I don't want to ask you to take sides. But that's what's happening. Aspen and the Darkness are on one side, and I'm on the other. And if you can't see which side is right, then at least stay out of the way."

$$☽ ☽ ○ ☾ ☾$$

Jake pulled the curtains back and peered out the window for what felt like the hundredth time. He'd done it so repeatedly that Spike had finally gotten fed up with being scorched and headed to the basement.

"I'm telling you, this is taking too long."

"She's only been gone an hour," said Hailey. "Give her a chance." But she had to admit that time was positively inching by. She'd paged through almost an entire book on portal magic without reading a word.

"I just . . . hate that she's on her own," Jake said, and raked the fabric of the curtains like his fingers were claws. And it nearly seemed they were; even when he wasn't in his wolf form, Jake was strong, and the drapes tore partially off the curtain rod.

"Hey," Oz called from the kitchen. "Keep your cool or that'll come out of your allowance." It was a joke—Jake didn't get an allowance—and Hailey smiled, but Jake didn't seem to find it funny.

"I'd have an easier time keeping it if you would teach me," he snapped, and Oz raised his eyebrows. He got up from the table where he was researching with Sigmund and came into the living room.

"You haven't asked me to teach you."

"Well, I'm asking."

"Are you sure you're ready for that?"

Jake nodded. "I've been thinking about it for a while."

Oz looked at him quietly, and Hailey turned back to her book, pretending to pay no attention to the wolves. It was none of her business, true, but they were right there, and she found it so fascinating to watch Oz and Jake when they were together. Oz was so much smaller, but it was clear by their posture that he was the pack leader, and Hailey sensed that it was taking a lot of Jake's nerve to ask Oz what he was asking.

"I think I know for about how long," Oz said. "Right around the time Frankie got called to be a slayer. You want to master the wolf so you can be more help in a fight."

"What's so wrong with that?" Jake asked.

"There's nothing wrong with that," Oz replied. "I want you to help Frankie, too. But there's a big difference between owning and understanding the wolf, and controlling the wolf to use it whenever you want. One of those things takes a long time."

Jake's jaw clenched. "Well, I don't have a long time. Frankie's out there now."

"You can't go at this the wrong way. Especially with how strong your wolf is. You were born, Jake, not bitten. I don't even know all the ways you might be different."

"Don't tell me to wait."

Oz put a hand on his shoulder as Hailey finally crept out of the living room. It really was Osbourne-only business.

"I'm not saying that," Oz said. "Just . . . let me think about this a while. What you're asking for, there is no rushing it."

"Poor Jake," Hailey whispered as she slid into the chair beside Sigmund. "Werewolf stuff is really complicated." Sigmund didn't reply. He didn't even notice she'd sat down and spoken. She poked him in the shoulder.

"Hmm? Oh, yes." He looked up at Jake and Oz. "I imagine it is."

"And what about us?"

"What about us?" Sigmund asked. His eyes had already returned to his book and notes.

Hailey almost didn't go on. She hadn't intended to come over and hash out what was wrong with them. But it was too late now, and to be honest, she was getting tired of wondering.

"I mean, if it's over, you should just say so." She looked him straight in his too-handsome face. *Say it isn't*, she thought. *Say you've been distracted. Say you're mad at your mom. Say anything else.*

"I don't know if it's over," Sigmund said. "I don't want it to be." He set down his pen. "But it feels like it is."

Hailey's heart jumped into her throat. He didn't just say that. Boys didn't break up with her; she broke up with them. So Sigmund couldn't, not when he was the only one she didn't want to lose.

"Why? Do you just not like me anymore?"

"Hailey, I—" he started. His voice dropped lower. "There is just a whole other world of things that we don't fit into. Having my mother here, I suppose I just . . . came to realize that."

"But is it what you want?" she asked.

"No." He pinched the bridge of his nose and squeezed his eyes shut. "Hailey—" He wanted to reach for her hand. She could feel it. "We shouldn't be talking about this now. I'm sorry. I shouldn't have . . . when Frankie's out there facing who knows what. And I'm not myself; with all the extra research, I haven't had time to tutor and I'm starving—" He gathered his books and prepared to get up, like he could find someone to feed on in the very next room.

"Sigmund?" she asked, and hated the sound of her voice. She sounded sad. She sounded desperate. She even sounded weak.

"I'm sorry," he said, and left the table and the kitchen without looking back.

☽ ☽ ○ ☾ ☾

When Frankie got home, she walked through her front door and was immediately swarmed by Jake, her mom, and Spike.

"You didn't get caught," Jake said, circling her in that unconsciously canine way he had.

"Unless she did get caught," said Oz from the kitchen, his eyebrow raised, "and now she's under some kind of evil-slayer mind control."

"I didn't get caught," Frankie said.

"So what did you hear?" asked Hailey. She was seated at the table and looked a little pale as Frankie made her way into the kitchen. She'd probably been staring at spellbooks since the moment Frankie left.

"I heard . . . some stuff. And then the evil slayers and I had a bit of a chitchat when Grimloch showed up and wrecked the enchantment from the stalker's stone."

"Grimloch showed up?" asked Spike. "What the bloody hell was the Hunter of Hotpants doing there? You didn't tell him about the mission, did you?"

"No." Frankie squinted one eye at her Watcher. Then she sighed. "As it turns out, the leader of the Darkness is his long-lost girlfriend, Aspen."

For a moment, the Scoobies just blinked. Even Sarafina, who was seated beside their kitchen window with a cup of tea and a very large knife, pursed her lips in sympathy and clucked her tongue. Then Jake said, "Aspen. That's a terrible name."

Frankie smiled a little. Good old loyal Jake.

"Here," said Oz, and set a cup of coffee down at the kitchen table. "Let your mom take a look at that hand." Frankie sat, and Hailey obligingly spooned extra sugar into the coffee cup and stirred in some oat milk while Willow undid the makeshift bandages that Grim had ripped off his shirt. Frankie wondered where he was now. At the Succoro's old glamping tent maybe. Or maybe he had turned around the moment she'd left him and gone back to Aspen. Maybe they were . . .

She didn't want to think any more about Grim.

Frankie sniffed the air as the Scoobies gathered around her. A smell lingered in the kitchen: like herbs and ozone and scorched sugar. A distinctly magical smell, the smell of a big spell lingering. "Magic?" she asked her mom.

"Sigmund helped me put an extra cloak around the Scythe."

"The Scythe." Frankie half jumped out of her chair. "They were going to take me hostage and try and trade for it—"

"It's okay." Willow pressed her back into the seat. Hailey scooted the coffee mug closer. "The Scythe is safe. It's right here, tucked behind a glamour, and an itty-bitty parallel-dimensional purse."

"A what?"

"Don't make them explain it again," said Jake. "My head still hurts from the first time."

Frankie reached out curiously with her magic and prodded the air around her mother. Before, when the Scythe had simply been hidden by a glamour, Frankie had been able to feel it. Now when she searched, there was nothing. Not even a whisper. Not even a hole. Frankie breathed out in relief.

"Why don't you just tell us what you heard, Mini Red."

Slowly, and with many intelligent questions interjected from Sigmund, and a few not-so-intelligent ones from Jake, Frankie told them what she knew, about where Buffy and the others were being held, about what the rogue slayers wanted to do with the Scythe.

"How can they do this?" Sarafina asked, and picked up the large knife to stab the point of it deep into the wood of their kitchen table. "How can they recast a spell that was once a challenge even for your mother?"

"You don't necessarily have to have big magic to work a ritual," said Willow. "Especially with magical talismans involved. Xander summoned the song-and-dance demon using only its pendant, and mostly by accident."

"The necklace!" Frankie stood. "Aspen was wearing some kind of a necklace, like an amulet. She kept on touching it, and it was definitely pinging my slaydar." She gestured for a pen and paper and tried to draw it, but she was no artist. Eventually she had to describe it to Hailey, who worked feverishly with pencil and eraser as Frankie said, "Narrower at the bottom. More facets."

"Is that it?" Hailey asked, and held it up. The sketch was good. Hailey had captured the proportions and even the shading of the dark stone embedded in an engraved setting of thick, heavy gold.

"Pretty bauble," said Spike. "I don't recognize it."

"I don't either," said Willow.

Sigmund shook his head.

"Is the necklace pinging your slaydar," Jake asked, "or your jealous-girlfriend-dar?"

"I don't have that kind of dar, Jake," Frankie snapped. "And you weren't there. You didn't see her. She's evil. I know it." The Scoobies looked at each other doubtfully, and Frankie knew how it sounded. But she didn't want to hate Aspen. Okay, she did, but only a little bit. And anyway, that wasn't what this was. The necklace wasn't just a necklace.

"Well," said Sigmund, "clearly this Aspen is of questionable morality. She's the leader of the group that was responsible for an attack that caused the deaths of several slayers, purposely or not. And she did send Vi to us with less-than-honorable intentions."

"Plus they were going to hold Frankie for ransom," said Jake.

"I still can't believe they put a demon magnet on the Hellmouth." Spike shook his head. "I mean, it's a bloody good idea and I wish I'd thought of it back in the day. But they're slayers. It's not right."

"Did you find anything that could help us stop it?" Frankie asked.

"A few possibilities," said Sigmund, but Frankie got the impression that he was lying to make her feel better. "It would be easier if we could identify the beacon. But so far, no luck."

"Then let's focus on the necklace for now," Frankie pressed. "I'm telling you, there's something going on with it. Can we try? Please?"

"I'll hit the books right away," said Sigmund.

"And Jake and I can help during our free period," said Hailey.

"Research mode," said Jake, and looked like he wanted to nap.

"Thank you," Frankie said gratefully. "And until we figure this out, New Sunnydale just got a lot more dangerous. If you want to patrol, it has to be in threes and fours. And my mom has to be guarded at all times. Sarafina? Can you help? And Oz?"

"No problem," said Oz.

"It would be my honor." Sarafina pulled the enormous blade

out of the table. "I will just need to return briefly to my suitcase, to retrieve a bigger knife."

"I don't see how that's possible," said Oz. "Any bigger and it's a sword."

"Hang on." Hailey crossed her arms. "I don't mean to play devil-slayer's advocate, but if they want to give their power back, shouldn't we . . . let them? Wouldn't they be far less dangerous as normal people? And isn't that their choice?"

"Maybe," said Willow. "But they're messing with huge mystical forces. If they don't know what they're doing"—she looked at Frankie and Spike—"they could reverse the flow not only for themselves but for all the slayers. They could lose not only their powers but their lives. And Buffy's. And Frankie's."

"And on top of that, I don't believe them," Frankie said. "The whole time I was in that warehouse, my slaydar was going off like a car alarm. I don't think that Aspen wants to be a normal person. I think there's more."

Hailey sighed. "What do I do in the meantime, if I see my sister?" she asked.

"Stay away from her," Frankie replied. "I'm sorry, but we just can't trust her."

"I know. And that's her fault. But you know if you really want to find out the Darkness's plans, let me double-agent Vi. I'll crack her like an egg."

"I have no doubt," said Frankie. "But it isn't just Vi, and this is too dangerous."

After a few somber exchanged looks, the meeting disbanded; the werewolves went home, and Sigmund and his mom went to his apartment—in the morning Sarafina would return with that bigger knife. Spike would stay and camp out in their basement. For tonight at least, they were safe.

"Hey, Frankie." Hailey caught her as she went up the stairs to her bedroom. "Are you okay? You didn't say much about seeing Grimloch with his old girlfriend. Do you need to talk about your stupid hot demon?"

Frankie shook her head. "Not right now. Right now there are more important things to think about. But when this is all over, yes. There will be chocolate, and there will be much wallowing."

"Like two pigs in mud," said Hailey. She smiled wanly. "Just say the word."

CHAPTER TWENTY-THREE

NOT EVERYONE CAN PULL OFF LEATHER PANTS

rankie flew backward through the cemetery and hit the ground to roll with a vampire on top of her; they were gripping each other's arms and summersaulting head over feet like a disturbing, slayer-vampire hamster ball. She felt ridiculous, but it was also kind of fun, and when her back rolled on solid soil, she kicked up hard with both feet. It sent the vampire into orbit, and she roll-flipped upright and prepared to stake.

"No. No, no, no. Don't stake him yet. Do it again, Mini Red. And this time, do it without all the rolling about."

Spike stood atop the Rimbauer mausoleum in his black duster and paced, keeping one eye on her and one on the horizon for any members of the Darkness. So far there had been silence. Well, aside from the steady stream of demons being drawn by the Hellmouth magnet. Vi hadn't even reached out to Hailey. Not even by text.

"Again?" Frankie groaned.

"Yes, again. And use that reversal I showed you."

Frankie squared off against the vampire again and tried,

drawing his strikes in one direction and letting one land to immediately spin and counter to the back of his head.

"Good. Now takedowns."

She moved to sweep the legs, but the vampire anticipated it—probably because Spike was audibly telegraphing her every next move—and leapt over her instead. He grabbed her from behind in a bear hug and dragged her backward, and Frankie kicked and yipped. Atop the mausoleum, Spike rolled his eyes.

"Break out of it."

"This is your fault!" Frankie seethed, talking through clenched teeth. She used her magic to blast through the vampire's grip, only to hear Spike say, "No magic tonight; that's cheating," and faced the vampire's very sudden punches.

"Whoa!" She dodged to the left. "Whoa!" She dodged to the right. Then she popped up in the center, made a V with her fingers, and jabbed them into the vampire's eyes.

"Ow!" he cried, and grabbed his face. Frankie shrugged and jump-kicked him in the chin.

"Takedowns, I said!" shouted Spike. But of course the vampire heard and evaded her every attempt. Finally, Frankie grabbed him in a diving leap, and the two of them went rolling past the headstones together.

"Again with the rolling." Spike put his hands on his hips and shook his head. "Are you even trying? I want punch combinations, I want roundhouse kicks for distance, I want *better quips than 'whoa.'*"

Frankie threw up her hands, and the vampire got to his feet.

"Excuse me," he said. "I did not become a member of the blood-drinking undead to be a slayer's crash-test dummy." He bared his chest. "Do you mind?"

"Sorry," said Frankie, and obligingly staked him.

"Thank y—" he said as he crumbled to dust.

Spike sighed and scanned the cemetery. "Don't worry. Another will be along. It's actually a good thing that the demon magnet's still magnetized—with rogue slayers afoot, you need the bloody practice."

"I don't need this kind of practice," Frankie said. "I could've staked that vamp twenty minutes ago. My technique was flawless!"

"Your technique was falling and doing backflips until he stumbled trying to chase you down."

"Yeah. And I executed it flawlessly."

Spike shook his head, his cheeks sucked in so far it was like the only features he had were cheekbones. "That's not going to cut it, Mini Red. Someday all your clowning around is going to get you killed, and I'm not letting it happen. To be a slayer is to be a warrior. A deliberate warrior. It's vampires and demons like me who are the blunt instruments, bashing through things without thinking, bent on destruction."

"Hey. I'm not a blunt instrument!"

"No, you're a floppy instrument." Frankie and Spike looked at each other a moment. "That didn't sound right," he said. "But if you think you can fight like you do and beat other slayers, like the Darkness . . . you wouldn't last five minutes."

"Oh yeah? I've already escaped from their clutches once."

"You did, and no doubt to the tune of 'Yakety Sax.'"

Standing below him in the grass, Frankie's eyes began to sting. Spike didn't think anything of her slaying abilities. He thought she was a joke. And the way he trained her, nothing but *no*s, nothing was good enough. He shook his head every time she made a move; he was a constant source of sighs and groans. But she'd fought the Countess, hadn't she? She'd taken out vampire nests. She'd fought so many demons this year that they filled a spreadsheet, and her most serious injury had come from herself, when she stabbed her own stake into her leg.

"I'm doing my best," she whispered.

"But you're not, Mini Red. There's so much more in you. You're going to change in ways that you can't imagine, do things that you never thought possible—"

"No, I won't," Frankie snapped, and Spike looked down, brow knit. "You're not even talking about me. You're talking about Buffy. But I'm not Buffy, Uncle Spike!"

"Frankie." He jumped down and landed in the grass beside her. "That's not what I'm saying. No one wants you to be Buffy."

"Everyone wants me to be Buffy! And who can blame them? But I'm not, okay? I don't save the world every Tuesday, and I don't use bazookas, and I don't die and keep on coming back all the time! And I don't wear leather because it's mean to cows!" Spike glanced at his black jacket. "And if you don't like the way I fight . . . then don't watch, Watcher."

Frankie turned on her heel and stalked out of the cemetery.

CHAPTER TWENTY-FOUR

GRIM REALLY DOESN'T HAVE A TYPE

Grimloch wasn't surprised when Aspen appeared at the flap of the Succoro's old tent. She had always been good at tracking him. Which had made it all the more hurtful, that she'd gone for so many months without doing it.

"I was wondering when you'd show up," he said. He stood at his hot plate, stirring his stew, then tapped the wooden spoon twice on the rim before setting it onto his camping plate.

"Never afraid nor surprised to see me," Aspen said, crossing her arms.

"Why should I be afraid?"

"Most demons are, when a slayer shows up."

"Is that what still you are, then?" he asked. "A slayer? I thought you said you had become the Darkness?" He faced her. Tore a loaf of bread in two and offered her a half.

She took it. "Got any butter?"

He pointed to the table beside the cot and watched her from the corner of his eye. She looked so like he remembered, and he had wanted to see her for so long.

She glanced at him, too, as she buttered her bread. "I seem to recall you were more of a raw, internal-organ kind of demon."

"There are chicken hearts in the stew."

"And since when do you cook?" she asked, and licked the tip of her finger flirtatiously.

"Since I ate the foodie demon who used to live in this tent," he replied. "Now answer my question."

Aspen sat down on the cot with a sigh, her long, denim-clad legs bent for her long, sweater-clad arms to rest against. She was built like a ballerina, and the way she fought reminded him of the bow of a violin—lean and taut. Precise and elegant. Not like Frankie, who fought like a madcap cartoon character: tripping and falling down, lucking into weaponry, her determined face giving way to fear with every demon swipe she dodged. A very sensible amount of fear, Frankie would say. Grimloch smiled.

"What are you smiling about?" Aspen asked.

"Nothing. And I'm the one who gets to ask the questions."

"You don't make the rules. And don't you think I should get to ask a few, when you helped that little baby slayer escape and raced after her like a knight in shining armor?"

"She's not a baby," he said, which was not the response she wanted. She'd been mostly teasing; she didn't take Frankie seriously, not for a second. But should she? With Aspen returned, Grimloch was faced with a choice he never really thought to make. And he was surprised by how in doubt he was. Just as surprised as Aspen that Frankie had gotten under his skin.

Aspen leaned back on the cot and shook off her doubts like she shook off most things. She stretched her neck and let her hair fall in that way she knew he liked. He couldn't deny that she was beautiful. More beautiful than Frankie. And not worried in the slightest about who he would choose in the end.

"Come over here," she said. When he didn't, she got up from the cot and grabbed his forearm. "Or should we fight first? Like old times." She cast her eyes to the side and grabbed for a knife beside the hot plate. He caught her by the wrist and twisted until she gasped and dropped it. "That's better," she whispered, and kissed him.

He was angry, but not kissing her back felt impossible. He clutched her to him and ground his lips against hers, part passion and part punishment. He devoured her until his flaring nostrils caught a hint of char as his chicken-heart stew began to burn.

"Enough," he said, and turned away to shut off the hot plate.

"Enough? Since when?"

"Since you were dead. And since you decided to hunt your own kind."

"It wasn't that much of a hunt." Aspen's lip curled meanly. She had only gotten sharper since she'd done what she did. Since she became the Darkness. And he would be lying if he said that part of him didn't like it. "Grim." She snaked her arms around his neck. "I'm sorry about that. But I'm here, and I'm alive." She drew him toward her again. "So be happy. Reunite with me."

"Reunite?"

"The Darkness will rise," Aspen said, turning to kiss his jaw, and his throat. "And the light of the slayers will set upon the world."

He grasped her by the shoulders and shoved her roughly away. "What does that mean?"

Aspen laughed. "Maybe I did leave you on your own for too long."

"You killed slayers, Aspen. You left their bodies broken in the rubble."

"We didn't know that opening the portal would be so explosive.

We weren't trying to kill anyone. Not even the ones we got rid of. We just . . . moved them to another dimension."

"A hell dimension?"

Aspen shrugged. "Hell is relative. And theirs was earned. Train up an army full of forced soldiers and then mistreat them. See what happens."

Grimloch scoffed and turned his back on her. "You sound like a spoiled child."

"Spoiled?"

He heard the sharp metallic draw of a knife. But the leader of the Darkness was no fool. She would never attack him on her own. Not for real. She knew it would not go well.

"We had nothing," she said, voice shaking. "No life, no choice— all we knew was danger and fear. We were dying. And don't go clutching your pearls about dead slayers. Are you mad because we killed them? Or because we didn't save their hearts for you?"

Grimloch shifted to face her, this angry young woman he loved. "You are lying to yourself. Your skin is thinner than you pretend. Did you never think to ask Buffy Summers if she would just let you go?"

Aspen snorted. "That would have been a waste. She gave us no choice, then, so why start now? All she wanted us for was to fight, and fear, and die."

"All slayers fight, and fear, and die. Frankie Rosenberg will someday die, and far before her time. Perhaps if she lives to fight for as long as you have, she, too, will be this resentful." He looked at Aspen. "But somehow I don't think so."

She clenched her teeth. She wanted to attack, wanted to fight. The strain of it was evident in every line of her body, and he felt the response waiting in every line of his. If she tried it, he wouldn't be able to resist her.

"You still love me," she said. "You're still mine."

"As you are still mine. And always will be."

A shadow crossed her face. That didn't sound like an invitation. It sounded more like a goodbye, and she wasn't ready to accept that.

"Stay out of our way, Grim. The Darkness is coming. We took out an army of slayers. Do you really think we'll have trouble with one hunter god of Thrace?" She dipped a finger into the stew and tasted it. "This is burnt," she said. Then she ducked out of the tent and was gone.

CHAPTER TWENTY-FIVE
THE AMULET OF JUMANJI

In the library, Frankie sat balanced on the back of a chair while she waited for the Scoobies, her feet on the seat, and her eyes burning holes in the few remaining students who had ignored the final bell and kept on studying. They were a pair of industrious freshmen, but not even they could withstand Frankie's glower, and eventually they gathered their things and walked toward the doors, tossing their paper snack bags into the trash along with two half-empty cans of soda.

"Recycle!" Frankie growl-shouted, and the freshmen cried out and dove through the doors. With a sigh, she stood and jumped down from her chair to fish their cans out of the trash.

"Scaring the freshmen again?" Jake asked, coming through the door as Frankie dug, half in and half out of the garbage. "You're going to get a reputation."

"I *have* a reputation," Frankie said, and righted herself to show him two shining cans.

"Failure to recycle." Jake raised his eyebrows. "The younglings must learn. Seriously, though, what's bothering you?"

"You mean besides the looming threat of rogue slayers, Buffy being trapped in another dimension, and the constant flow of good old demons returning to their hellmouth?" Frankie shrugged. "Nothing."

"It's the underwear model's ex-girlfriend, isn't it?" Jake said knowingly.

And it was. But it also wasn't. She'd actually been thinking about Spike. She hadn't really spoken to him since their argument in the cemetery, and fighting with her Watcher gave her a queasy feeling in the pit of her stomach.

"Cheer me up." Frankie sat down with Jake. "Tell me how Sam is."

"I've hardly had time to see him, with everything that's going on," said Jake, but a big, slow smile spread across his face. "But he's good."

"Have you told him?" she asked. "That you're starting to like him, too?"

Jake blushed, and it took every bit of her restraint not to tease him about it. "Yeah. He's into it. He's . . . helping me figure things out. Very nicely, I might add." As he leaned back with satisfaction, Frankie scrunched her nose.

"Don't add too much," she said. "It's still me you're talking to." She leaned closer, and chose her next words carefully, trying not to pry. "So you . . . you never . . ." She followed that up with a lot of head shakes and eyebrow movements.

"What. Are. You. Trying. To. Say?"

But she didn't know. She hadn't thought she'd be so awkward—she'd grown up with a gay mom after all, and she and Willow never shied away from talking about it—but this was Jake, and he had his own story. Everyone was different. "Like . . . guys. Of the male . . . persuasion. You've never said . . ."

"Because I never did. This is definitely new. Definitely weird." Jake grinned. "So far, definitely good."

"But does this mean no more cheerleaders? I mean are you bi now or what?" Frankie blurted.

Jake laughed. He tipped his head back and forth, like he was weighing the options in his mind. Cheerleaders and Sam. Sam and cheerleaders. If he mentioned trying to make a Jake sandwich, he was going to get a whack.

"I don't know," he said. "I do like those cheerleaders."

Frankie smiled. "Well, that's cool, too."

"Yeah. Maybe if I made a sandwich—"

"Hey, Jake. Hey, Frankie." Sigmund walked in carrying coffees in two cup holders.

"Hey, Sig." Frankie looked around. "Where's—"

"I'm right here." Hailey walked in a moment later.

"Oh." Frankie smiled. But Hailey didn't look at Sigmund, and when Sigmund looked at Hailey, he seemed . . . sad. Frankie turned to Jake, figuring he was oblivious, but the werewolf's eyebrow was raised. Something had happened. Something was wrong.

But there was no time to figure it out as Willow, Oz, and Sarafina walked through the double doors ahead of Spike, who pointedly ignored Frankie and grabbed a beverage off the tray.

"Watcher is here," he said, and sat down to put his feet up on the table. "Meeting shall commence." Frankie pursed her lips uncomfortably. There was enough tension in the room already without him adding to it—she'd been ready to talk it out and forgive him, but now? For once why couldn't Spike be an adult and pretend that everything was fine?

Oh yeah, she remembered. *Because he's Spike.*

"Okay," said Sigmund. "Well, the reason I asked you all here is because it seems that Frankie was right." He pulled a book out of his backpack and flipped it open to a page he'd marked. "This is the Amulet of Junjari."

Frankie grabbed the book. The amulet was drawn in dark brown ink, a pear-shaped, multifaceted gem in a thick setting, with engravings along the outer edges of the metal square. Frankie remembered it clearly, shining against Aspen's long, pretty neck.

"The chain's different," she said, "but that's it all right. In real life, the gem is dark green and the setting is gold. What does the book say about it?"

Sigmund took the book back and spun it around to read.

"It was crafted by a very gifted sorcerer in the Far East, but the gem at the center seems to have been around before that. There isn't a clear accounting of what the sorcerer was making it for, but there is a reference to harnessing the power of an army. Or draining the power of an army." He paused to reread the section. "It's not terribly detailed."

"Well, is it harnessing or draining?" Oz asked. "That seems like an important distinction."

"That part is unclear," Sigmund replied. "But it seems that the one wearing the amulet is the wielder, or the recipient, of the power."

"I knew it," Frankie declared triumphantly. "She's going to use the Scythe to reverse the flow of their slayer powers and then use the Amulet of Junjari to suck it right into herself."

"What would that do?" Willow looked at Spike. "Is more slayer power, like, more slayer power? Would it turn her into some kind of a super slayer?"

"Why are you looking at me?" he asked, and Frankie rolled her eyes.

"I thought you were the super slayer," Hailey said to Frankie kindly. "You know, slayer-witch, first of your name, born of the original slayer essence . . ."

"You are so sweet," Frankie said. "But I don't feel particularly super. And this doesn't sound particularly good. Any one slayer in the Darkness is trouble, let alone all of them rolled into one."

Jake sipped his smoothie and thought. "So how do we stop her, then? Do we rip it off her neck and scream the name of the amulet?"

"It's 'Junjari,' Jake, not 'Jumanji.'" Frankie turned to Hailey. "What if we told Vi? This can't be what she really wants."

"Maybe it is," Hailey said. "And even if it's not, I don't think she'd believe us."

"Well, this is bloody lovely," said Spike. "There's a deranged slayer leading a troop of other deranged slayers by the nose, looking to fashion herself into a slayer-god, and we have no idea how to stop her."

Frankie sank in her chair. She knew he didn't mean that the way she'd heard it, but she'd heard it all the same: If Buffy were here, Aspen wouldn't have a chance. If Buffy were here, it never would have gotten this far.

"I know how to stop her," Frankie said suddenly.

Spike looked over.

"How, sweetie?" Willow asked.

"By destroying the Scythe. With it gone, the Darkness has nowhere else to turn."

There was a long pause, and lots of eyes boring into her to see if she was serious.

"Absolutely not." Spike kicked away from the table. "If we destroy the Scythe, how are we supposed to rescue Buffy and the others? I'm not going to let them stay stranded in another dimension; I don't care how dangerous this bitch is."

"Spike." Willow frowned. "Language. But he's right—we can't let Buffy and the other slayers stay lost, no matter how big of an asshole Aspen is."

"How come you can say that, but he can't say the other thing?" asked Jake.

"Because it's not a gendered slur, Jakey."

"Oh." He looked at Frankie and shrugged.

"Guys." Frankie leaned forward. "I'm not suggesting that we don't rescue Aunt Buffy. I'm saying we don't need the Scythe to do it." She looked at Willow. "Because we have my mom."

The eyes around the table shifted from Frankie to Willow.

"Huh?" Willow asked. "Stop looking at me."

"It's true, Mom. It's like the oracle said: The power flows through you and back again. I think when you did the spell to activate the Potentials, you made yourself into something you didn't intend to. A gate. A permanent link to the slayer line."

"Even if that's true," said Willow, "and who knows if it is . . . that's a bigger spell than I've done in . . . well, since the one you just mentioned. With the Scythe to guide me, maybe, but—"

"You can find them, Mom. I know you can."

Willow looked at Oz, who raised his brows. She looked at Spike.

"I've seen you do some incredible things," said the vampire. "But I can't— If I have to tear holes through ten dimensions, I'm getting our slayer back."

"Don't you mean slayers, plural?" Sarafina asked.

"Right, that's . . . what I meant."

"Hang on," said Hailey. "Is it even possible to destroy the Scythe? I mean, it looks pretty . . . non-destroyable."

"Yeah," said Jake. "Just how much like the One Ring is it? We don't have to walk it into Mordor and throw it into a volcano, do we?"

"Wow, you guys are nerds," said Oz.

"I know a spell that might work," said Willow. "It'll just need some modifications. And I don't know if I should be the one—even now I can feel the Scythe in the liminal space, trying to get away from me."

"You shouldn't," said Frankie. "I'll do it. Believe me, I don't want to." She looked around at them. "I want to keep it. I might even want to marry it. It's old, and it's ours, and it was made for us. But that's why I can't let it be used against us."

No one seemed particularly eager, but one by one, they nodded.

"I'll need some time to gather the ingredients," said Willow.

"I'll help you," Sigmund offered. "When do you want to do it?"

"How about after my lacrosse game Friday?" Jake suggested. "You'll all be there watching anyway, right? Right?" He reached across the table and whacked Sigmund. "It's our last game before we suspend the season!" He frowned. "And besides, after that I'll be out of commission for the full moon."

"Okay," Frankie said. "We'll go to the lacrosse game and then head back to our place for celebratory root beer floats and the destruction of an ancient, mystical weapon."

"Wait," said Hailey. "Celebratory floats makes it sound like Jake's team is going to win."

"Ha-ha, very funny." Jake crossed his arms. "But no, we're not going to."

Spike cursed under his breath and grabbed his jacket. He strode toward the library doors without a look back.

"Spike?" Oz asked. "You okay?"

"No," the vampire snapped, and shoved through the exit.

"I'm not going after him this time," said Willow.

"That's fine." Frankie stared after her Watcher sadly. "He wants to be alone anyway."

CHAPTER TWENTY-SIX

BUSINESS AS (UN)USUAL

With all the new demons in Sunnydale, not even downtown was safe, and that night, Frankie patrolled the streets of the restaurant district. So far it had been quiet, but the demons were growing bold. Just last week, some rampaging thing with claws had ransacked the lovely little crepe truck that parked on the corner, smashing the windshield and getting batter everywhere, finally rocking it so hard that it tipped over on its side and needed a crew to come and lift it with a winch. Luckily, the creperie workers got away unharmed, and Oz was able to follow the smell of buttery goodness to the woods, where he found the demon covered in thin pancakes and chocolate-hazelnut spread. Oz had declared it his most delicious slay yet.

Frankie's slayer belly rumbled as she walked past the Italian place with the red canopy. The outdoor patio was strung with small yellow lights. It was the kind of place couples went to order wine and be alone in shadowy, candlelit corners. So, not the kind of place for her. She scuffed the toe of her boot against the pavement and kept on walking. Past the coffee shop that was already closed. Past the charming British pub that Spike decried as "not authentic." He would be pissed that she was out there by herself; he'd ordered no solo patrols. But that didn't apply to her. She was a slayer. Of course, so was the Darkness. And they were not only "a" slayer, but a baker's dozen. Frankie was just wondering why it was that bakers got a bigger dozen than everyone else, when she heard a subtle shifting in the alley to her right. Between the butcher shop—the window she'd broken a few weeks ago to steal ropes of sausages freshly replaced and shining—and the store that sold fancy houseplants and old-ladies' clothes. She stopped walking and sighed.

"Stop following me."

Grimloch stepped out from behind a dumpster. He was dressed casually in a dark gray jacket over a button-down shirt and jeans, his dark hair blowing back from his temples. All she was missing was an internal voice-over to announce that a mysterious and handsome man had emerged from the shadows.

"I wasn't following you." He held up a take-out bag. "I was waiting for my order from Forkable." He lowered it as Frankie approached, unable to stop herself from peering inside. "Roasted chicken with tarragon gravy."

"Mmm." Frankie leaned down and inhaled deeply.

"Aren't you a vegetarian?"

"I'm only smelling the tarragon," she said, and he snorted, the tips of his fangs visible for just a second. Frankie let go of the bag. "Forkable isn't even on this street. You were following me. This counts as following."

"I didn't know how else to see you. And I wanted to make sure you weren't being hunted by the Darkness. Should you really be on your own?"

"I'm a slayer, just like they are." Frankie shrugged. "Besides, they wouldn't try something here. In downtown, right out in the open.

Though you have just lured me into a darkened alley, so thanks for that." She turned around and walked back onto the street.

"Are you really so much safer," Grimloch asked, following her again, "with the early closures and quiet streets?"

Frankie looked around. It was eerily empty for that time of night. The bigger restaurants, like the Italian place, were still crowded, but they seemed to be filled with large parties, tables pushed together to seat four or more. Those who were out on dates strangely seemed to leave in pairs of two or three couples at a time and walked so fast that they were nearly jogging to their cars.

"The Hellmouth has been closed for nearly twenty years. So how do they know?" Grimloch asked, watching the diners. "Is it herd instinct, perhaps? Or an extra sense? Do humans have it everywhere, or does it run through Sunnydale alone?"

"Also probably through Cleveland," Frankie said. "But it's true: New Sunnydale has started to look after itself. Just not well enough." Frankie crossed her arms. "Last week an arm and part of a gnawed-on torso washed up on the beach. And last Tuesday, I had to stake my first-grade teacher when he rose from his grave. He was wearing the same little polka-dot tie he wore to teach me verbs. So that was fairly traumatizing. People are dying, Grim. Sunnydale is under siege, and that is all the Darkness's fault. My aunt is stuck in a prison dimension, and that is all the Darkness's fault. Are you absolutely sure you had no idea what Aspen was planning?"

Grimloch shook his head. "She kept it from me. She let me believe she had perished."

"Then how did you know to go to the warehouse? That day when I was using the stalker's stone, how did you know they were there?"

"I received a message with an address. I didn't know what I would find."

Frankie uncrossed her arms. "I really want to believe you." And she wanted to trust him. He'd never done anything to make her doubt or give her cause, but Aspen's arrival had changed all that. He'd been in love with her. He probably still was. Those feelings didn't just dry up overnight, even if you discovered that the person you loved was a soul-sucking, slayer-killing leader of an evil organization. Frankie would have to be an idiot to think that his loyalties weren't split.

"Francesca Rosenberg, I—"

"Wait. Something's happening."

Frankie turned up the street. Screams rang out from the direction of the Italian restaurant, and guests began to pour out the front doors in the kind of panicked running that was every-man-for-himself, leave-your-belongings-behind-and-come-back-if-you-live. People stormed through the outdoor patio, overturning tables. And as Frankie and Grim watched, a man was thrown into the strings of yellow lights, tearing them down with him as he fell to the pavement.

"Are you helping?" Frankie asked as she broke into a run. Grim was fast beside her, and she frowned as inside the restaurant, something bellowed. "What do you think it is?" she asked.

"Whatever it is," he growled, "I will kill it quickly. And I will kill it extra, for the interruption!"

Frankie didn't know what "killing it extra" entailed, but figured it couldn't hurt. The man who'd been thrown into the lights was lying on the pavement in an expanding pool of blood.

She and Grim dodged the last fleeing customers and burst inside. The cozy, firelit interior was in shambles: spilled food and broken plates were everywhere, and the crisp white tablecloths were streaked with red that was too deep to be marinara sauce but too bright to be wine.

"Do you see anyone injured or trapped?" Frankie quickly scanned the dining room, but the only person still inside was the owner, terrified and cowering against the far wall. Well, him and the person who was on the ground, being fed upon.

The demon was a humanoid type. It wore a black leather jacket and had bright yellow skin, and its skull was spiked in sharp spines. On closer inspection, so was its back: bony white spines had pierced through the leather, giving the coat a studded look. It raised its head to look at them and slurped down a length of ragged, bloody skin.

"A skin eater," Grimloch said with a snarl, and Frankie gagged.

"That is so gross."

Frankie ran through the restaurant and slid across a table to drive a heel into the demon's face. A fresh strip of skin went flying from its mouth, and it turned back to bare grisly red teeth.

"You need to floss." Frankie kicked again and punched twice, then ducked to avoid the demon's claws. She gave it a roundhouse, and it flew toward Grim, crashing through what little remained of the restaurant's decor.

"Please," the owner cried as Grimloch collided with the demon and fell with it across a set table, sending up a cascade of breaking plates and glassware. "My restaurant!"

"Sorry, sir!" Frankie turned and shouted to Grim, "Grim! Out the back!"

He nodded and charged into the demon's midsection to drive it through the double doors of the kitchen.

"Not the kitchen!" The owner gestured wildly to the right. "The alley! The alley!"

"Got it," Frankie said, and ran. "We'll do our best!" She burst through the doors of the kitchen as Grimloch struggled with the demon near the grill. A quick look and a peek underneath the counters told her the place was empty; the staff had already fled, leaving half-assembled plates of food on the line and pots burning on the stove. There were knives, too, the blades dotted with bits of herbs, and a good-looking cleaver stuck into a raw roast of beef.

"Convenient," she said. Of course it was also convenient for the demon, as it knocked Grim to one side, and turned toward her with a chef's knife.

Frankie grabbed a pan to block with and rolled over the metal counter to the other side. The demon leaned across to slash, and she knocked the knife out of its hand with her pan and then raised it high to slam it down onto the demon's head. The demon's face bounced against a little bell on the counter and it chimed twice; Frankie shouted, "Order up!" and swung her frying pan against the demon's temple. The skin eater slid across the counter to Grim, who caught it around the waist.

"Through the side door to the alley!" Frankie called, and Grim jerked the demon down the hallway. They knocked the door to the alley clean off its hinges when they went through, but that had to be better than doing more damage to the kitchen.

Frankie ran into the alley and ducked to avoid Grimloch as he sailed over her head to land against a dumpster.

She turned.

"Geez." In the open air of the alley, she could get a better look at the demon, and it was big. Taller than Grim, and more muscular, and now that it was outside it seemed to be . . . swelling.

"No fair getting bigger," she said, then watched in awe as it ran up the side of the restaurant. "And no fair . . . defying gravity! Oof!" She doubled over as the demon flipped off the roof to land a punch that drove her to one knee. "You're very agile despite your size." She counterpunched, bursting up with a haymaker uppercut, but her fist found only air. The damned demon was already gone, racing up the other side of the building and flipping back down to hit her in the face again.

"All right, I'll give you those two," she said, cheeks burning from the hits. She lurched forward as the demon punched her in the back. "Okay," she said, wincing, "maybe one more. Whoa!" The world spun as the demon threw her across the alley to bounce off the dumpster and land beside Grim.

"Hey . . . are you unconscious?" Frankie asked as she struggled up.

"Mm," Grimloch moaned, still on his back like a flipped turtle.

"Great."

The enormous, fast demon stood, happily flexing its hands and grinning a grin full of skin bits. She raced to it and jumped high to land a brutal punch, then heard herself give a yip as she dodged the demon's counter swing, and another yelp as she dropped to slide between its legs.

She popped upright behind it and sent it stumbling, then spun around to kick. In a moment of wicked brilliance, she reached up and cracked off one of the demon's own spines and stabbed it through the neck.

"Ha!" Frankie jumped away as it clutched its wound and wobbled. Except it kept on wobbling. And eventually stopped and pulled the spine out to clatter against the pavement. With a grimace, Frankie squared her shoulders and prepared to break off another one of its back spikes. But before she could, Grimloch put his hand on her arm.

"Allow me," he said.

"Go ahead," she said, happy to see him on his feet. "You did say you wanted to kill it extra."

As it turned out, "killing it extra" meant twisting its head off amid a rushing deluge of red gore. And then dropping the head, and body, into the open dumpster.

"You should have let me do it." Frankie picked up the demon spine and used it to point to Grimloch's shirt, wet and stained with demon blood. "Then again, maybe not." She looked at the spine. "I can't decide if killing it with its own spine would have been poetic justice or just mean." Grimloch walked to her, and she touched his chest. "Are you hurt?"

"None of the blood is mine." He touched her face and moved her hair behind her ear, just as Spike's clapping rang out from the entrance of the alley.

"Spike?" Frankie asked.

"Not bad, Mini Red."

"Oh, really. It wasn't too much yelping and rolling for you?"

"No," he said. "I mean it. I was watching—saw you when you ran in." He gestured back toward the street and the trashed patio with lights lying on the ground.

"And you decided not to help and see how big a mess I could get myself into?"

Spike took a deep breath. He made that face where his cheekbones came out. "I decided to stay out of it. Because I knew you had it under control."

Frankie blinked in surprise. "You did?"

"I'm trying to say good job. Maybe even apologize. But I'm not doing it in front of that bloody looming underwear model!"

"I was not looming," Grimloch said. "I do not 'loom.'"

"Oh yeah, what's this, then?" Spike asked, and mimed looming around in a big billowy coat. Grimloch showed his fangs.

"I fought beside her. I didn't just stand back and *watch*."

"All right, that's it—"

"No!" Frankie stepped in between them and pointed the demon spine in both directions. She turned to Grim. "Grim, I know we have things that we need to hash out. But I need to talk to my Watcher right now."

"Of course." He straightened his jacket, which was torn at the shoulder, and walked past, a simmering growl low in his throat and directed at Spike.

"That's right," the vampire taunted. "She's my slayer, mind your own business."

"She would be better served by training with me," said Grimloch as he left the alley.

"In your dreams, loomer."

Frankie groaned. Then she waited. And waited. And waited some more.

"What?" Spike asked.

"My apology?" she prodded.

"Oh. Yeah. I'm sorry," he said, and shrugged.

"That's it?"

He made a face. "No. I had a whole speech planned, but I don't want to do it now. The Hunter of Banana Hammocks put me off it."

"Fine." Frankie turned on her heel and started to leave, but he hurried alongside.

"Wait a minute." He sighed. "I am sorry, Mini Red. I shouldn't have pushed you like I did. And I don't want you to be anything more than what you are." He pointed toward the rear of the restaurant. "Your method might look ridiculous, but it works. That is one dead demon in the dumpster."

"Well, actually Grimloch tore its head off."

"You would've gotten it eventually."

She looked at her Watcher. "I'm sorry I got so mad at you. I suppose Buffy never behaved like that with Mr. Giles."

"Then you suppose wrong. Buffy could stomp her feet and whine with the best of them. She was your age, too, when she started this. I ought to try to remember that." He smiled at her and she laughed. "What?"

"Nothing. It's just still a little weird seeing you with your face all old. Like with you being my Watcher and with that face it feels like . . . well, kind of like . . . you're my dad?" The way he recoiled made her stop laughing and smack him on the arm. "Hey! Buffy and Mr. Giles had a slayer-and-dad thing, and it was no big deal. It feels almost natural."

Spike turned sideways to shove his hands deep into the pockets of his black duster. "Well, it's all kinds of unnatural. Me, a dad. I never had a child. Never wanted one." He turned back to her. "Don't particularly want one now."

"I'm so glad I said this," Frankie said sarcastically, and crossed her arms. But as she stood there, Spike awkwardly sidled closer, until he reached out and squeezed her in a brief one-armed hug.

"I'm glad you said it, too, Mini Red." Then he shoved her. "But don't get all weird about it!"

They walked home together and heard the sound of approaching sirens in the distance.

"Sunnydale PD," said Spike. "Timely as ever."

"We should be glad about that. They'd only get themselves hurt. And they respond to other things okay."

"It must be an open secret," Spike suggested. "Some calls that they know you give ten minutes before heading out."

"Like all the recent escaped zoo animals," said Frankie. She thought of the man in the restaurant, lying dead and missing skin. She thought of the man outside, lying in a puddle of blood. Thanks to the Darkness and their Hellmouth magnet, it couldn't have been the only attack that night. And it was only going to get worse, until the Scoobies figured out a way to shut it down. "The other slayers," she said suddenly. "Can I beat them?"

"What do you mean?"

"I mean you've been a Watcher a long time. You've trained Vi, you've seen her fight—"

"I've trained them all, at one point or another," he said.

"Even Aspen?"

Spike studied her warily and nodded.

"And now you've trained me. So I want to know: Can I beat them? Am I good enough, to beat any of them?"

He stopped walking.

"I guess your silence is answer enough," said Frankie.

"No, it isn't. That's not what I mean."

"Then what do you mean?"

"Can you kill them?" he asked, and looked at her seriously. "Could you kill them, if it came down to it?"

Frankie swallowed. She didn't even need to think about it. She just shook her head.

"Then that's what I mean," said Spike. "Because not one of them would hesitate to kill you."

Vi stared through the window of the dusty, deserted warehouse and saw nothing, just like she always did during the new patrols that Aspen had ordered of the grounds. There were three of them doing sweeps at any given time, two on the ground level and one stationed outside and up high on the roof of a nearby building. But there were no threats. No Scoobies peeling into the parking lot in a beat-up old van, no steely-eyed Frankie embarking on a suicide mission. No red witch, floating through the sky with black veins and black eyes, ready to tear the skin from their bodies with a look.

There weren't even any noisy crows to eat their leftovers from Doublemeat Palace.

"Vape?"

Vi turned, as Sonia came to relieve her, and held out her green vape pen.

"No thanks. That's not good for you, you know."

Sonia shrugged. "Slayer constitution. You should take advantage of the health benefits while you still can." Her light brown braids were loose today and framed her face prettily. She was from upstate New York somewhere, as Vi recalled. Maybe Buffalo. She had family back there, a bunch of brothers and a mom and dad, even both sets of grandparents. And for all they knew, their Sonia had died, killed in the explosion in Halifax.

"It's nice to see you out of your ridiculous Sith Lord cloak," Vi said.

"Nice not to smell you coming through blood-soaked herb smoke," said Sonia. The mood in the warehouse was tense and growing tenser. Aspen said they had nothing to fear, that they were the threat and not the other way around. But the endless patrols of the warehouse didn't inspire much confidence. And Aspen's mood had shifted since she'd come back from seeing Grimloch.

"Suppose I don't need to ask if you've seen anything suspicious." Sonia inhaled from her pen and exhaled vapor that smelled like sickly fake strawberries.

"That's disgusting. Almost worse than the smoke from the bloody herbs." Vi waved the vapor away and went to return to the basement. "And you know," she said over her shoulder, "we don't really know if a slayer constitution protects us from terminal diseases. None of us really live long enough to find out."

Vi found Aspen alone, sitting in an old leather easy chair that someone had dragged into the middle of the ruined fort of boxes. She didn't look up when Vi approached, just kept on toying with the jewel of the amulet around her neck.

"Thinking about nuclear fission?" Vi asked, and went to stand beside her.

The leader of the Darkness regarded Vi with a smile. She was younger than Vi by some ten years—only a little girl when the Scythe spell was cast. But she still wasn't the youngest slayer alive. That honor, Vi supposed . . . went to Frankie now.

"Actually I was thinking about what they're doing over there. Buffy Summers and the others." Aspen hadn't been back to the dimension where the slayers' former leadership was being held captive. Since Frankie and the red witch knew what they'd done, it was too dangerous. They couldn't risk being tracked, or outright followed.

"How . . . were they when you left them last time?" Vi asked awkwardly. It seemed hypocritical to be concerned. But the goal had never been for Buffy and the rest to die. Those girls who died in the *explosion, those young women—* Vi took a breath. *It was unfair to be sentimental now. She'd known there was a risk. They all had.*

"When I left them, they were spitting mad and plotting," Aspen said, and smirked. "And Kennedy was actually spitting."

"They're still that upset?"

Aspen shrugged. She tapped her index finger against the leather, long brown hair falling to her elbows. She looked a little mean sometimes. Vi had always thought that. Just mean enough to curb dissent.

But she does care, Vi reminded herself. That's why she did all this. *To stop any more of us from dying without a choice.*

Buffy Summers and Willow Rosenberg had made them slayers without giving them a choice. They'd tried to make it seem like one, but who could really make a choice with their backs against a wall from being hunted by the First? So the Darkness would take it back. They would take the Scythe, and for the first time, the power that should have been theirs to begin with would be theirs to control. Every one of them would have the choice to keep fighting or to give it up.

Vi knew what she would choose. No more knives, no more bruises. No more monsters in the dark. Vi would choose a normal life. With Hailey, somewhere far away from demons and danger. Somewhere far enough away that they could forget. Somewhere in Kansas sounded nice.

"Time in the prison dimension flows differently," Aspen said. "A few months to us is only a few days to them. So yeah, they're still that mad."

"They'll get over it," said Vi. "After we let them go. After we have the Scythe."

Aspen nodded curtly. "So, about that Scythe?"

Vi looked away.

"I thought they would move on us," Aspen said. "I thought the red witch would do something. Or that idiot girl of hers would charge in, stakes blazing."

"Frankie's not an idiot. She's . . . different. But she's not stupid. And she's surrounded by good advisers."

"Including my Grimloch, it seems."

"So it didn't go well when you went to see him?"

Aspen sighed. Her grip on the leather armchair loosened. "It went very well, actually. Or as well as I had any right to expect after I let him believe I was dead for months." She arched her brow. "He and I just need some time together, alone. Then it will be just like it was before. I could feel that when he kissed me."

"He still loves you," Vi said, not quite a question, but a little.

"And he always will."

Vi watched Aspen quietly. It had been a long time since Vi had seen her vulnerable. Not since the day that the slayer Geraldine, Aspen's best friend, had been killed during a raid. After that, Aspen lost her girlish ease. She'd lost her innocence. And she'd become the leader of a movement.

Every slayer had a day like that. A day where they were no longer innocent. Vi knew she must have had one. Hers had just happened so fast that it was like a blur. She was one thing, and then she wasn't. She was Violet, full of fight and possibilities. And then she was Vi, the slayer, and all that remained was the fight.

Until Hailey came around, and she found something to fight for again.

"I want you to go get my Scythe, Vi."

"I will," she said. "Only I don't know how, now that our cover is well and verily blown."

"Verily," Aspen repeated, and narrowed her eyes. "Are you a closet LARPer or something? Never mind. Just go and get it. They'll still let you close. Use your sister if you have to."

"I'm not using my sister for anything. That was never the agreement."

Aspen stood. "We're your sisters, too, you know. And we're losing

293

hope." She turned soft eyes back toward the break room, where the slayer slumber party had become the slayer somber chamber. They were sad, and scared, and frustrated. Vi knew that as well as anyone. And it was her job to take care of them. They'd come so far, and she was the only senior slayer that had joined the Darkness. By rights she should have been the leader. But harsh as she could sometimes be, Vi was no leader.

"I know where to find them."

Aspen's eyes sharpened into focus. "The witchspawn? And her Scoobies?"

"All of them. The junior werewolf has a lacrosse game tomorrow night—the last of his all-important season."

"Perfect. Right on top of the Hellmouth, and the beacon." Aspen touched the amulet again and began to pace.

"But I still don't understand how I'm supposed to get the Scythe."

"The Scythe is the only thing that can destroy the beacon."

"What?"

"She'll have no choice. That beacon has some real surprises in store. If she doesn't let you use it in time, we may all live to regret it."

"What does that mean?" Vi asked. But Aspen didn't reply. "So you want me to get her down to the basement, tell her I know how to destroy the beacon, then take the Scythe from her and destroy it?"

"Of course. We don't need the trouble of a wide-open Hellmouth on top of everything else," Aspen said, but when she said it, she shrugged, like she didn't really care one way or the other.

"And then what? I just fight my way back here, through a wall of Scoobies?"

"With the Scythe in your hands, none of them can stand against you. Not even the red witch, if you cut her down with it fast enough. Can you do that?"

Vi swallowed. She'd known Willow a long time. But it felt like she'd hated her for longer.

PART FIVE

THE WEAPON OF THE SLAYER

CHAPTER TWENTY-SEVEN

A DEMON FOR ALL SEASONS

Frankie stood with her mother in the kitchen as they worked together, crafting the spell that would allow Frankie to destroy the Scythe. The weapon of the slayer. Nearly as ancient as the slayer line itself. And now she, Frankie, the slayer-by-accident who had been created in part by the Scythe in question, would be the one to destroy it. It felt wrong. It felt like a betrayal. It felt like a slayer party foul.

"Should we really be doing this while the Scythe is right there?" Frankie stared dismally at her mother's side, where the Scythe remained cloaked behind magic. "Whipping up the spell we're going to use to kill it, right under its very nose? It seems rude."

Willow added ground quartz to her mortar and pestle and whispered to it until it sparkled like gold. "We're not trying to kill it," she said. "And no matter how you feel about it, try to remember that the Scythe isn't actually alive. Besides, we aren't going to completely destroy it. I don't think something this powerful can ever really be destroyed. How's the white rose coming?"

Frankie had harvested the dried petals and crushed them in a clay bowl, blowing on them softly and thinking of destruction. "Here you go."

Willow poured them into her palm and sprinkled them into the mixture. "This is basically a souped-up banishing powder. It'll be more of a . . . dismantling into particles than a true obliteration. Okay, time to prick your finger."

Frankie frowned and picked up the stem she'd taken the petals from. With a small wince, she pressed a thorn to her finger and held out her hand so Willow could squeeze her blood into the powder. Drop after drop, squeezing hard enough to juice a lemon. "Mom. Ow."

"You're a slayer; you can take it," Willow said.

"You know, you get a little sharp when you're doing magic."

Willow let go, and the grinding of the powder stopped.

"Hey, it's okay," said Frankie. "I was only kidding. See?" She wiggled her fingers, the drops of blood gone, the thorn prick already closed.

"I'm sorry, sweetie. Sometimes I forget that I shouldn't enjoy it."

"Of course you should enjoy it," Frankie said. "You're good at it. You're . . . the best at it, arguably."

Willow smiled a little. Then she shook her head. "No. I should never enjoy it. Ever again." She set aside her pestle and looked down into the bowl of the mortar.

Frankie leaned in to look too. Despite the addition of her blood, the powder wasn't red, or even rust colored. It was white, crystalline and sparkling. She took a sniff and detected sugar and flowers, and . . . She wrinkled her nose. Oh. There was the blood. "Don't worry so much. You're doing really great. Look what we made." She held up the bowl. "And you froze those vamps in their graves and pummeled me with book titles in all letters of the alphabet. . . ."

"And I threw my daughter across a room," she said. "Oz thought I was doing it all to impress Sarafina. Which I was." Her mom looked at her guiltily. "But it wasn't only that. It's still so easy. I could feel it being so easy, and there was this voice in my head saying it was okay, that it was all for you, and that everything would be fine."

"Voices? Mom, you were hearing voices?"

Willow shrugged. "It might've been my voice."

"I wish it wasn't this way for you," Frankie said. "I hate that you can't be your whole self."

"I can! I am! Just because I'm not balls to the wall, black eyes, and ending the world doesn't mean I'm not my whole self."

Frankie studied her mom's eyes. "I find your words disturbing. Do you still have Uncle Xander's yellow crayon? What's the deal with that thing, anyway?"

Her mom smiled and took it out from where she'd hidden it, tucked behind her multicolored woven belt. "It's a long story," she said. "But all it really is, is kindergarten magic. Like you and Jake have."

Frankie nodded. She certainly understood that. She looked back into the mortar.

"Is it finished?" she asked.

"Ready to annihilate," said Willow.

"Good," Frankie said. Jake's final lacrosse game of the season was that night. They would go to the game and cheer him on, and then band together to destroy the greatest weapon the slayers had ever been gifted.

"What do you think the Darkness will do after they realize there's no more Scythe?" Willow asked. "I mean, if what you say is true, and I have become a gateway, couldn't the Darkness just use me in the same way they were going to use the Scythe?"

Frankie winced. She had thought of that. She just hoped it wasn't immediately obvious.

"Let's hope that they don't figure that part out," she said. "Or at least that we can get Buffy and the other slayers home before they do."

$$\text{☽ ☽ ○ ☾ ☾}$$

Watching the New Sunnydale Razorbacks take the field for their last lacrosse game of the soon-to-be suspended season was kind of sad. And not just because they were terrible. But because of the stoic expression on Jake's face. The way he rallied each of his teammates with a brief hug and a clash of helmets. He was a good captain. A good leader. Someday she could see him taking over from Oz and becoming the head of the Osbourne clan of werewolves.

Frankie shivered in her jacket. Not from cold—the day had been sunny and the temp had touched seventy—but from nerves. Tonight they would destroy the Scythe. The beautiful, wonderful Scythe that she'd just gotten to use for the first time.

Hailey stood with Frankie in the stands, and Sigmund, too, though not like he should have been, behind Hailey with his arms around her waist. Instead he stood on Frankie's opposite side. And no matter how she tried to shift out of the way, they refused to be next to each other. But they did cheer, loud in the darkening air, especially amid the weak claps and hoots of the large but decidedly unenthusiastic crowd. Frankie wondered why they'd even come—it was kind of like a farewell game, but the lacrosse team never pulled this kind of a crowd. Maybe it was more of that Sunnydale sixth sense: No one wanted to pass up the opportunity to gather together en masse, at night, in relative safety.

Closer to the field, in the seats nearest the home-team bench, Oz, Willow, Sarafina, and Spike sat watching. Oz had brought a few thermoses of soup and passed around softly steaming mugs. Except for Spike, their cheeks were ruddy, and their smiles were warm. It would have felt like the start of a great, memory-making evening, if not for the warning in Frankie's gut.

"You okay?" Hailey asked, and nudged her. "I can sense your tension. And I can see it—you keep biting your lip."

"I'm fine. I just can't shake this bad feeling."

"Me neither," said Hailey. "But if we get through tonight, then tomorrow, everything changes. The Darkness's plans go poof, right along with the Scythe."

"You make it sound so easy," said Frankie.

"It will be easy," Sigmund said. "We'll be with you."

"Whoa, whoa, check it out." Hailey tensed. In the stands below was Vi, looking directly up at them. "My wayward sister makes the scene."

Down on the bench, Vi's presence hadn't gone unnoticed. Spike and Oz stood, along with Sarafina, who held Willow by the arm, ready to defend her. Spike looked at Frankie, and she subtly shook her head.

"She's alone," said Frankie. "So go ahead and give her a nice, warm wave."

A nice, warm wave was too much for Hailey, but she did manage a tight-lipped scowl and a gruff jerk of her head that said, *Come on up.*

Vi looked around awkwardly and picked her way up the crowded bleachers. She looked a little ashamed, Frankie thought, which was appropriate. She also looked afraid, like a deer making her way through an unfamiliar wood.

"What are you doing here?" Hailey asked when Vi reached them.

"I don't know. I'm not here to fight." She looked at Frankie.

"Then don't start one," Frankie said.

Vi looked down. Then for a moment, she gazed at the field, like she would actually try to hang out and watch the game.

"Well?" Hailey demanded. "Aren't you going to beg for forgiveness? Aren't you going to explain?"

"I don't know if I can explain."

Frankie saw Vi glance guiltily at the last of the yellow bruises the Turok-Han had left on Hailey's throat. Vi loved Hailey. Frankie was sure of that. And seeing the fear on Vi's face when the Turok-Han had appeared—she knew that Vi had been hurt by traumas that had never healed. Frankie understood why the Darkness might have seemed like the only option. But that didn't mean she forgave it.

On the field, Sam blocked a hard shot, and his teammates immediately launched into a chant. "Sam Han! Obi-Wan!" They chanted so loud that the crowd woke up and joined in, and Sam bowed and brandished his stick like it was a lightsaber.

"What does that mean?" Vi asked.

"Because he's so good it's like he's using the Force." Sigmund shrugged. "Or something."

Vi stuffed her hands into her pockets. "I know I shouldn't have come here, okay?" She looked at Hailey. "I just can't have you thinking— I don't want you thinking that—" She exhaled hard and shook her head. "Can we go somewhere and talk?"

Hailey frowned and turned to Frankie. "Is that cool?"

"Just stay where we can see you," said Frankie, and the sisters started down from the stands.

"Hailey," Sigmund said quietly. "If she tries something—if she tries to take you somewhere against your will—"

"What do you care, Sigmund?" Hailey asked, and the Sage demon swallowed. After she was gone, Frankie heard him whisper, "I care very much."

"Okay," Frankie said. "What is going on with you two? You were perfect, and now you're hardly speaking. Did you have a fight?"

"Sometimes there is no fight to be had," Sigmund replied, his eyes still tracking his girl. "Sometimes things just aren't meant to be."

"Says who?" Frankie asked. But before he could respond, she felt a distinct ping from her slaydar. It was coming from beneath the bleachers. "Hang on a second; I'll be right back."

Frankie walked the bleachers to a less crowded area. When another cheer rose from the crowd, she slipped down between the gaps in the metal seats and dropped to the ground. Right behind the Hunter of Thrace.

"You saw me," he said.

"No, I sensed you. I'm getting better at this. Pretty soon you won't be able to pull your shadow-guy shtick anymore." She put her hands on her hips. "What are you doing here?"

His blue eyes flashed in the dark. "Watching the game."

"Nobody comes to watch the game," Frankie said. "Even I'm only here for the soup." She saw his nose twitch, trying to catch a whiff of Oz's thermoses, and fought a smile. She was angry with Grim. And she couldn't trust him. She had the image of him kissing the leader of the Darkness burned into the backs of her eyelids. But he was still Grim. "Were you planning to come up? Or were you just going to stay down here being Seemore Butts all night?"

"I didn't know if I would be welcome."

"Well, that depends. Have you broken up with your evil girlfriend yet?" Frankie cocked her head. She didn't know what response she'd expected, but when he looked away, her heart sank.

"It's not that easy, Frankie."

"Sure it is. You say, 'Aspen, I can't see you anymore because you're evil.' You don't even have to do it to her face; just do it in your mind if you haven't seen her—"

"I have seen her."

Frankie stopped. She knew what that meant from the way he said it. He hadn't only seen her. There had been embraces. And kisses. And—she squeezed her eyes shut—other things she didn't want to think about.

"She found me in my tent," he said. "She's always been good at finding me."

Frankie swallowed. He could convey a lot in the tone of his voice. And what she heard in it was regret, only not the right kind. It was regret that he still loved someone he shouldn't.

"Okay, then," Frankie whispered. She hadn't been a slayer long, but she could still recognize a losing battle. Aspen had the history. She had the tragic story. And she had his heart.

"You know I'm not asking you to choose me, don't you?" she said. "I'm telling you to choose NOT HER. The things she's planning to do, the things she's already done—I know you're a demon, but I shouldn't have to tell you why that's messed up."

"She's making a mistake. A mistake I would help her not to make. I can't turn my back on her any more than I could turn my back on you. This is difficult."

"Yes, so difficult for you," she said. "So many hot chicks with superpowers—what a burden!"

Grimloch looked at her sadly and tried to smile.

"Her on one side and you on the other. Perhaps if I made a sandwich—"

"Are you serious?" Frankie's eyes narrowed. "Have you been talking to Jake?"

"Sorry." He coughed awkwardly. "I'm still learning to joke. Frankie, I—" He reached for her, and she didn't know if she would have let him touch her. Because before he could, the crowd started screaming.

Frankie turned.

New Sunnydale lacrosse crowds did not scream. Unless—

Frankie broke away from Grimloch and looked toward the field. At first, she didn't understand what she was seeing. The players were running toward the benches, and overhead the stands rumbled like thunder as spectators stomped and jumped their way to ground level.

"What's going on?" Frankie shouted to her mom, or Spike, or anyone who could hear her.

"Look!" Her mom pointed across the field, and Frankie craned her neck over fleeing people and squinted against the lights.

Demons. At the edge of the field, advancing like the lines of an army, were demons.

More demons than Frankie had ever seen at once, and never in such variety. Vampires. Demons with spiked heads and pinkish skin. Demons that slithered. Demons that crawled on all fours.

Frankie ran around the bleachers and fought her way through the first of the people escaping to their cars. Grimloch was right beside her, and they shoved their way to Spike and the others, where Hailey and Vi joined them.

"Are we really bloody seeing this?" Spike asked, gripping the fence. There were so many demons, emerging from the woods in waves and heading straight for the school.

Oz looked back toward New Sunnydale High. "Well, at least we know where they're going."

"The beacon on the Hellmouth," said Vi. "There must finally be enough of them. They're going for it."

"Going for what?" Hailey asked, and smacked her sister on the arm.

Frankie took a deep breath as a pack of five hellhounds leapt out of the trees. On the field, Jake stopped trying to help his teammates flee and turned to fight.

"Jake!" Oz snarled, and flexed his arms. His wolf ripped through his skin, and he launched himself over the fence, fangs and claws out.

"Oz!" Willow shouted.

"No," Frankie said, "He's got the right idea." Frankie turned to Sigmund in the stands. "Sig! Can you get your charm on and lure those people toward the parking lot? Get them to their cars?"

"Sure!" he shouted back, dodging people as they fell over themselves to get down from the bleachers. "Though I think they already get it!"

"No!" Sarafina bellowed as Sigmund bent to help an older man and keep him from being trampled. "Stay! Stay and fight!"

"Don't worry," Frankie said. "I think everyone's going to have a chance to do that tonight." She boosted herself over the chain-link fence. "Everybody but Sigmund with me!"

She took off at top speed with Spike to her left and Grimloch to her right. Sarafina sprinted ahead and drew an absolutely enormous knife, so enormous that Frankie briefly wondered how she'd hidden it in her dress. With a great cry, she targeted a massive demon with horns like a bull and leapt on top of it like a rodeo rider. It bucked back and forth a few times, which seemed to thrill her, and then

306

she sank her massive knife into the side of its head. Farther afield, Oz and Jake slashed and spun with claws and a lacrosse stick, dead hellhounds at their feet.

"You should have run!" she heard Oz shout.

Jake swung his stick and took out another hound. "I'm tired of running!" he shouted back.

"No fighting!" Frankie yelled. "There's more coming!"

She pushed her legs faster, drawing away from Spike and Grim to zero in on the demons ahead. She couldn't think about Jake and Oz right now. There was no time to worry about Hailey and Sigmund, or even her mom. Frankie had to trust that the Scoobies could take care of themselves.

"Eeny," she said, looking at an approaching vampire. "Meeny." A white-skinned demon with a mouth like a lamprey. "Miney." Something red and horned and dressed like a member of the Hells Angels. "Moe." She leapt over the top of a demon with black tentacles that floated above the ground and grabbed on to its head as she passed, wrenching with all her strength. The sickening series of pops and cracks she felt as its neck snapped was momentarily gratifying as she hit the grass on the other side.

Frankie spun and punched through vampires, drawing her stake and dusting as she went. This was no battle for flowery moves, just stakes and takedowns and moving on. Though Grim and Spike had apparently missed that memo and were currently trying to out badass each other, spending far too much energy on a single demon apiece. Behind her, her mom had four demons off their feet, floating, while Sarafina gleefully leapt onto each one to finish them off. The spell broke when a hellhound slipped away from Oz and Jake and tackled Willow to the ground.

"Mom!"

Frankie ran to her, but Jake got there first. He used his lacrosse stick as a decoy for the hound's snapping jaws and flung it to one side, where Frankie slayed it with a quick twist of its neck.

"Exactly what is going on here?" Jake asked, panting.

"I wish I knew." Frankie scanned the field. Vi and Hailey were fighting back-to-back, Vi striking high over the top of her sister when anything got too close. At least the stands were basically empty. "It's a good thing you guys suck so bad and don't draw very many fans."

"Whatever," Jake said. "The place was almost full."

A large, gray-skinned demon with ridges along the side of its head and no mouth grabbed for them, and Frankie quickly kicked it away. She sank a knife into its chest and squinted at the phosphorescent blood on the blade.

"Don't touch that!" Willow screeched. "I know those demons! Buffy fought them once, and the blood, it makes you telepathic and drives you insane!"

Frankie wiped the blood on the grass. "On second thought," she said, and threw the whole knife away. She had others, and that blood sounded terrible. She helped Willow to her feet.

"Mom, are you okay?"

"Sure." Willow raised her hand and blew four demons back twenty feet. "But we're not making enough headway." Frankie looked around. She was right. They were too spread out. They were going to be overrun.

"Fall back to the school!" she shouted. She ran backward, signaling, making sure everyone got the message to regroup.

"Bejesus!" Jake squeaked, and pointed. "Is that a huge freaking praying mantis?!"

Frankie followed his pointing finger and caught a glimpse of something large and green skittering beneath the bleachers. But they'd have to deal with that later. Once they got to the school, they could barricade and control the flow. They could fight them off. They could figure out just what the hell was happening.

"Oz!" Jake shouted. "Oz, dammit!"

Frankie craned her neck. Oz either hadn't heard or wasn't following the regroup order. He was still fighting, snarling and swiping madly, and with every moment the werewolf delayed, he was more and more boxed in.

"He's in trouble," Frankie said. But when she moved to help, Vi raced past her.

"I'll help him!"

"I'll come with you!" Hailey shouted.

"No. Stay with Frankie. Stay with the slayer!" Vi looked at Frankie. "Fall back into the school. Get everyone inside and bar the doors. Don't let them into the basement. Don't let them near the beacon!"

"I was already planning that!" Frankie shouted, and she and Hailey started to run. By the time they reached the parking lot, Oz and Vi had caught up, and the Scoobies and their allies raced toward the entrance of the school.

"Here!" Sigmund shouted. He was already there, holding the doors open. When they got inside, Frankie saw that the fast-thinking Sage demon had grabbed tables from nearby classrooms to use as barricades, and he, Spike, and Grimloch quickly set about placing them against the doors and windows.

"Sig, did you get the people out?" Frankie asked.

"Every last one," Sigmund said, a little proudly. "And even slightly charmed. They'll go home and laugh to each other about the lacrosse team's strange prank for publicity."

"Gotta love that Sunnydale demon denial," Hailey said. Amid all the danger, she ignored their fight and touched his face. "You okay?"

"Are you?" he asked, and she nodded.

Frankie peered over the barricades at the angry demons trying to batter through the doors. They'd left more than a dozen dead on the field, but there were still too many to face head-on.

"All right," she said. "What the hell is happening here?"

"It's my fault," Vi said.

"Well, duh," said Hailey.

"But what's happening right now?" Spike demanded. "Why are they giving us the bum's rush all of a sudden?"

"Because it's time to open the Hellmouth. They're going to jump down into it, and when enough of them do . . ."

"The Hellmouth is back open for business." Spike gave his other slayer a contemptuous look. "Do you know what I had to do to close it the last time?"

Vi looked at Hailey and Frankie. "I'm sorry."

"Save the apologies for later, and give us the helping now," Frankie said. She didn't trust Vi as far as she could throw her, but she wasn't going to look a gift slayer in the mouth. "How do we destroy it?"

"Only one thing can," said Vi. "The slayer Scythe."

Frankie groaned. "Of course." The only thing that could solve the problem was the thing the Darkness wanted. They were forcing her hand. "Then let's get to the basement and take care of it before—"

They flinched at the sound of the doors breaking. The roars of the demons rang out, once again clear in the air, pinging off the hard surfaces of the hallways. Grimloch and Sarafina threw themselves against the barricades.

"This isn't going to hold," Grimloch growled.

Sarafina pointed. "Hailey, behind you!"

Hailey turned and was promptly grabbed and dragged away by a small humanoid demon wearing what looked like a filthy, unbuckled straitjacket. Frankie and Vi dove after her to help and were pummeled away by three more. They were small but surprisingly strong and threw both slayers against the walls. Frankie picked herself up, vision swimming in the shadowy hallway, and saw two pairs of feet float by in very nice black dress shoes.

She blinked. Her eyes tracked upward. Black shoes attached to black slacks. Black slacks to finely cut black jackets. And above the well-knotted black ties were two of the ugliest demon faces she had ever seen. Their eyes were sunken and yellow, their mouths stretched wide into rictus grins. As she tried to make sense of their delicate manners and gesturing, one reached down and slashed Hailey across the arm with a scalpel.

Vi and Frankie jumped. Sigmund, too, grabbed on to one of the demonic henchmen and dragged it backward as it flailed its straitjacketed arms.

"I know them," Frankie heard her mom say as she ducked a swipe of the scalpel. "They're the Gentlemen."

"Don't seem like gentlemen to me," Vi grunted, but Frankie paused. The Gentlemen. She knew that story!

"Can't even shout, can't even cry, the Gentlemen are coming by." As she spoke their rhyme, the Gentlemen turned to her and grinned wider. The taller of the two opened a small wooden box, and Frankie felt something leave her throat. She knew even before she heard her allies' words cut sharply off, even before she saw Spike and Jake start to frantically mime. The Gentlemen had taken her voice.

Frankie frowned and grabbed the box. Before the demons could so much as gasp, she threw it to the floor and smashed it with her foot. Their voices escaped, and she and Willow screamed at the tops of their lungs. The Gentlemen's heads exploded into satisfying yellow goo.

"Whoa. Does that work on all of them?" Jake asked. "AAAHH! AAAAHH!" But of course it didn't, and the other demons surged past the breaking barricades.

"Fall back!" Frankie shouted, and braced for impact.

But luckily, or unluckily enough, the demons were far less interested in killing them than they were in reaching the basement.

"We've got to stop them!" Frankie shouted. "Less defend, more chase!"

They barreled down the halls after the demons in full slay mode. Sarafina was a sight to see, leaping and stabbing alongside Grimloch—watching the pair of them fall upon a demon was like watching lions take down a wildebeest. Oz, Hailey, and Jake left plenty of dead demons in their wake, and Vi and Frankie dusted vamps and broke necks as fast as they could grab them. But many more slipped or slithered past, and eventually Frankie and the others found themselves in the basement, bracing the door as the demons pounded on the other side, trying to reach the beacon.

"Where's the bloody demon magnet?" Spike shouted, and Vi ran to the Hellmouth. A significant crack had already formed in the surface.

"Right here!" Vi tossed aside a fire blanket to reveal the beacon: a bowling-ball-sized orb of glowing, swirling green. "Frankie! Give me the Scythe!"

"No way!" Frankie shouted. "I'll do it myself! Mom!" She held her hand out and looked around for Willow.

"Mom?" She searched frantically, but her mom wasn't in the basement. "Grimloch, Spike! Open the door! My mom's still out there!"

Grimloch looked at her like she had lost her mind as he braced against every impact against the steel.

"You want me to open this door?"

"Without the Scythe, there's no chance," said Vi.

"And she's my mom!" Frankie shouted.

"Well," Spike sputtered, also braced against the door. "Red can look after herself. . . ." Then he groaned and stepped back. "Bollocks. Open it up."

Grimloch took a breath and heaved it open. Demons flooded in as Frankie, Spike, and Oz tried to thread the current, looking for Willow. In the corner of her eye, Frankie saw the oversized mantis that Jake had spotted earlier scurry from the shadows and scramble through the crack of the Hellmouth like a cockroach.

"Hey, they're going in it!" Jake shouted happily. "Should we just . . . let them?"

"No!" Vi shouted. "They're charging it up like batteries. And once the Hellmouth eats enough of them, before it opens"—she looked at Frankie regretfully—"Aspen said it vomits up a nasty toy surprise."

"Great," Frankie said sarcastically as another slithering white demon with a lamprey mouth squirreled its way through the opening.

Beside her, Spike punched a demon hard enough to knock a few of its fangs out. "You know, a lot of these blokes look familiar."

"Yeah," Oz commented on her other side. "Is it just me, or are we fighting an army of our greatest hits?"

"Well, sure," Frankie called. "The beacon summons demons that the Hellmouth knows. You've probably seen a lot of them before." She punched another vampire and paused as, through the door opening, she saw Willow bobbing and weaving her way through demons, using her magic to blast them right and left.

"Come on, Red!" Spike reached for her as she dove, and pulled her to one side to keep her from being trampled. The demons were positively pouring in. There was no re-closing the door.

Frankie looked back. Vi and Hailey were gamely defending the Hellmouth, but as Frankie watched, one, two, three more demons squirmed down into it.

"See what I mean about Sunnydale being dangerous?" Vi shouted.

"You!" Hailey yelled. "You made it dangerous!" But Vi half smiled.

"I know, kid. Just try not to die!" She snapped a demon neck, but when she dropped it, it fell right into the Hellmouth. "Oops. Do you think that counts?"

"Maybe not!" Jake shouted as he brained a demon with his lacrosse stick. "Maybe if we stuff the opening with enough dead ones, it will form a natural plug!" Somehow Frankie doubted that, but before she could say so, she froze at the sound of the loudest roar she had ever heard.

Standing in the doorway and, having to practically squeeze through it, was an enormous demon with curved horns, red-tinged skin and odd, fur-tufted ears.

"Hey, I know that one," Spike said. "That's a Fyarl demon. Giles was turned into one of those once—we need to make sure it's not Giles!" As the Fyarl charged, Spike jumped in front of it and punched it hard. Then he grabbed it by the shoulders and shouted, "ARE YOU GILES?" very loudly into its face.

Alas, the Fyarl demon was not Giles, and it threw Spike so hard that he careened through the rolling shelves of supplies that took up one side of the basement. The Fyarl shook itself and ran for the Hellmouth. Frankie had just enough time to think, *There's no way that's fitting down there*, before it squeezed through, and the Hellmouth began to quake.

Foul-smelling white smoke rolled out of the crack in the ground as the Hellmouth yawned wider.

"Mom, the Scythe!" Frankie held out her hand, and Willow broke the barrier spell and tore the weapon free from its hiding place. But as she placed it into Frankie's hands, her eyes went wide.

"No!" she cried.

Frankie turned. The nasty toy surprise, as Vi had called it, had begun to emerge from the Hellmouth. Except it was no toy. It was her mother, black veined and black eyed, crawling up through the crack in the floor with no expression on her face.

"That's not me!" Willow shouted as the doppelgänger snaked one arm out of the earth and hooked into the ground with clawed fingers. "It's not!"

And maybe it wasn't. But even a half-decent imitation would be more than they could handle at the moment. Frankie looked at her shaking, terrified mother. She looked at the black-eyed thing wrenching its way out of the Hellmouth. And she looked at Vi, the other slayer—the only one close enough to stop it.

There was no choice.

"Vi!"

Frankie threw the Scythe through the air.

Vi spun and caught it and, after one fast look between them, turned to smash the glowing green beacon.

It exploded. Shards of stone and magic flung in all directions. Hailey was cut, and so was Sigmund. Frankie and Willow were blown back against the wall by the force of the spell. The opening of the Hellmouth slammed shut on the thing it had conjured in the image of Frankie's mother, cutting its arm off and crushing part of its head so that only one eye and part of the skull remained above-ground, staring at them.

The remaining demons fell dead to the ground as if the re-closing Hellmouth had sucked out their life force.

Vi stood over the broken beacon with the Scythe in her hand, and Frankie held her breath.

"Vi?" Hailey said.

"I'm sorry," said Vi, and turned away.

CHAPTER TWENTY-EIGHT

FLASH FORWARD: ONE NIGHT LATER

"This is it," Jake said. "Are you ready?"

Frankie looked at him. He was inside his cage with the door open, his hands lightly gripping the bars. When she didn't answer, he flexed his arms and angrily rattled them.

"I hate this damned cage! I hate that I'm going to be in here while you're out there!" He wrenched at the bars again, and she was surprised at how much they moved, the way they vibrated and shook. Jake was getting stronger. Growing into an adult werewolf. "I hate that I'm not there when you need me."

"I still need you, Jake."

He looked up hopefully. "Then you'll wait until the full moon passes?"

Frankie shook her head. It was bad timing, things coming together right before the full moon. But it was what it was. "It has to happen tonight."

"Then," he asked, "what do you need me for?"

"Well," Frankie said, and sighed, "there's a reason that I find myself here before what will be the biggest fight of my slayer life. There's a reason that I'm here and not anywhere else, in the basement of my oldest and most trusted friend."

"Is it the vegetarian jerky?" Jake held up a piece.

"It's kindergarten magic, you doofus. And courage. You give me courage."

He smiled and stepped out of the cage to pull her into a hug. His arms were warm and Jake-smelling, and nothing could hurt her there, nothing could go wrong. She needed this moment, to center herself. To make herself believe she could do what she had to do.

"I guess we've come a long way, little witch," Jake said with his chin on the top of her head.

"I guess we have." She frowned. "I'm not going to call you little wolf, if that's what you're waiting for."

Jake let go and walked back into his cage. "I just . . . I swear this is it, Frankie. I'm going to learn to control this curse. Learn to control the wolf so I can be there all the time. I mean, if my brother did it . . ." he said, and shrugged.

Frankie swung the door closed and heard the heavy *click* of the lock. "You don't have to do anything that you're not ready for. Oz says it takes time."

"Jordy says there's a shortcut. And I should have done it sooner. I should have started the minute we found out you were a slayer." He looked up the stairs, as if he could see the sun going down through the closed door. She supposed he could feel it, the moonrise coming on. "Are you sure you guys can pull this off?" he asked.

Frankie took a deep breath.

"There's only one way to find out."

☽ ☽ ◯ ☾ ☾

As the sun dipped below the horizon, Frankie looked at her friends. At her Scoobies, and at her Watcher and her mom. They were armed to the teeth with claws and fangs and witchcraft. Hailey nervously spun her ax by the handle as Sigmund clutched a baseball bat. No stakes or crosses this time, as they were no use against slayers. Not that the bat was going to be of much more help to Sigmund.

"I wish Jake was here," said Sigmund. "It doesn't feel right that he's not."

"He's going to be sorry he missed it," Oz said. "Maybe try to take pictures." He smiled at Sigmund, and the Sage demon smiled back shakily.

"This is bigger than anything we've had to pull off in a long time," said Willow.

"But I can do it," Frankie said. "And we can. The Rosenberg witches."

Willow smiled. In a pouch at Frankie's belt—not a fanny pack, she kept insisting—was the spell powder she and her mom had made to destroy the Scythe.

"All right," said Spike. "Are we ready?"

"Frankie?" Hailey asked. "You sure you don't want, like, a big sword or something?"

Frankie glanced at her empty hands resting against the kitchen table. "My weapon is in the warehouse." She looked at them all one more time. "Does everyone remember the plan?"

They nodded.

"Then let's go sell it."

☽ ☽ ○ ☾ ☾

Just past dusk, Frankie, Hailey, Sigmund, Spike, Oz, and Willow walked through the deserted loading lots of the warehouse district, toward one warehouse in particular. There was no question as to which one. The warehouse where the Darkness had taken up residence glowed with yellow through every window. The lights were on, and everyone was home.

Frankie listened to their footsteps against the pavement. To the breath in their lungs, light and fast. There was no stalker's stone this time, no cloaking. Anyone who bothered to look was going to see them coming.

And if they didn't bother to look, they would certainly notice when Frankie ripped the door off and walked inside.

"Ready?" Frankie asked, and heard the Scoobies whisper back. She called up her magic, that most familiar and reliable magic—her telekinesis, which never failed her—and used it to tear the warehouse door from its hinges. Hailey's and Sigmund's mouths hung agape as they tracked its progress across the sky, sailing like a door-shaped Frisbee to clatter to the ground a hundred feet behind.

Frankie led the way into the building, and the others fanned out like good soldiers. They were met by the surprised faces of five slayers, soon joined by more who came up from the basement. Surprised, but not afraid. Not even worried as they scanned the shapes of Frankie's allies. Well, except a few who swallowed when they looked at Willow.

"A slayer club meeting without me?" Frankie cocked her head. "No one remembers to invite the new girl."

Her glance shifted as Aspen strode up the rear stairs. The leader passed through the group of slayers, and the rest of the Darkness turned slightly, deferring to her like water rippling around a rock. She wore the Amulet of Junjari around her neck, the dark, pear-shaped stone glittering in its setting. But there was no Scythe in her hands.

"Sorry," she said. "Your invitation must have gotten lost in the mail."

"Who sends mail anymore?" Hailey asked through one side of her mouth.

Aspen looked Frankie up and down, her head tilted back by the littlest bit, in a way that reminded Frankie of Jane Montclair before Jane's face fell off after being snared by the Insta-demon. When Aspen finished her assessment, the corners of her mouth curled. *Nothing much to be threatened by there*, that smile said. *May as well be polite.*

"Frankie Rosenberg. It's nice to see you again. I didn't like the way we left it—"

"Where's the Scythe?"

Aspen's words cut off. Her mouth closed delicately, and she looked at Frankie with a flicker of annoyance. "I thought you had it." Her eyes moved to Willow. "Or you did."

"Enough games," said Spike. "We know you have it. We know Vi brought it to you after we lost her last night."

When she heard that, Aspen took a fast gulp of air, and Frankie was reminded of a snake swallowing something. How the other slayers didn't see through her facade, Frankie had no idea. Maybe their slaydar was broken. Or maybe the promises she dangled before their eyes blinded them to everything else.

"Aren't you happy to see us alive, Watcher?" Aspen smiled. "Spike. Aren't you happy to see me?"

"I'll be happy enough to punch your nose for you soon as Frankie gets her Scythe back."

"*Her* Scythe?"

"It belongs to the slayer," he replied. "And the way I see it, you lot have given up that title."

"We know who you are," said Hailey. "We know what you're about. The Darkness. Isn't that what you call yourselves?"

"Who came up with that name anyway?" Willow asked. "The Darkness. Whatever happened to a good acronym?"

"How about: Slayers Against Sanity and Sense?" suggested Sigmund.

"SASS?" Aspen sneered. "You want us to be called SASS?"

Oz shrugged. "Or you can drop the first *S*."

"Enough of this," one of the slayers beside Aspen said. Kate, the tall one with the terrible haircut. "Let's just take them down and find Vi and the Scythe later."

The two sides tensed, but no one attacked. A few of the slayers looked at Frankie and Spike. More looked at Willow.

"There are enough of us," the tall slayer said. "We don't have to be afraid of the red witch."

"Don't call her that," Frankie warned.

"Or what?" Kate asked. She walked closer and turned in a half circle before Frankie, looking down at her with menace. "Are we supposed to be intimidated because you're the first ever slayer-witch? Big deal. What use are magic spells in combat? Magic is for weaklings and Watchers like Andrew. It's like they mashed a soldier together with the support staff."

"And you're not the only one who can do it anyway," said the slayer with the scarred face. "Aspen is a better demon sorceress than Andrew ever was."

"On behalf of Andrew, I object," Spike said, his voice low. Kate looked at Frankie and curled her lip.

"You're not even a real slayer. You were made, not called. You were an accident. You know what we call you? Witchspawn. Abomination."

"Kate, enough," Aspen said, but before Kate could back off, she was blasted across the warehouse into the far wall.

Frankie turned to Willow, whose eyes quickly changed from black back to normal.

"Nobody talks about my daughter like that," Willow said. "Sweetie, you were a very happy accident."

"In any case . . ." Aspen cleared her throat and eyed Kate as she got shakily up off the ground. "We don't know where Vi is and we don't have the Scythe, so I suppose . . . the first one to find Vi wins."

"I know she's here," Frankie said. "I know you have it. And I'm not leaving without my Scythe."

Aspen looked around at the Darkness. "My god, were we all this annoying? New girl, I told you. We don't have it yet."

Hailey took a half step forward and clutched her ax. "Stop playing! Where is my sister?"

"I'm right here, kid."

Everyone turned as Vi stepped through the missing warehouse door. In the light, she looked rough, like she'd been on the run all night, and hiding for most of the day. Dirt streaked her cheeks, and there were grass stains on her jeans. She'd lost her knit cap somewhere, and her dyed-black hair hung limply around her ears. Vi raised the Scythe in her right hand, and Aspen's eyes sparkled.

"You should get out of here, Hailey." Vi walked into the warehouse. "You too, Frankie. Just stay out of our way."

"Can't do that," Frankie said, and stepped into Vi's path.

"Sure you can," said Aspen. "Or let us help you. Neha, attack."

Frankie dodged back as one of the slayers, a tan girl with a shiny black bob darted forward and aimed a high kick for her head. The kick was crisp and practiced. Backed up by slayer strength. It would have knocked Frankie around in a full circle had she not dodged and blocked. She rolled right to counter, but her punch was pushed wide. This wasn't like fighting a demon. She had no advantage of wit or training. And she had the disadvantage of far fewer fights over far fewer years.

The warehouse erupted with noise as the Scoobies and the rest of the Darkness joined the fray, and Frankie's stomach tightened. Spike could hold his own against a slayer, and he was particularly motivated against these. Oz was less assured, but he had Willow providing magical support. Sigmund was already on the run, ducking for cover. And as for Hailey, well, Hailey's only protection was that the Darkness knew she was Vi's sister. Frankie just hoped that would be enough.

Frankie held Neha by the arm and landed two hard kicks to her rib cage, but when she flung the girl aside, she rolled back up and returned for more. She flipped head over feet and faked a half kick to grab Frankie by the knees and pull her legs out from under her.

"Hey!" Spike shouted. "No using moves I taught you! Not on my slayer!"

Frankie popped back up and looked for Vi. She hadn't moved, still standing frozen.

"Don't take it to them!" Hailey shouted. "Vi! You can't!"

"You don't know what you're talking about, kid!" Vi shouted back. But even though Aspen called for the Scythe, dodging strikes from Oz's claws with no effort, Vi didn't obey.

Finally, Aspen grabbed Oz by the throat. She lifted him into the air and drew a long-bladed knife.

"Oz!" Willow shouted, and threw her hands out—the knife burned in Aspen's palm. She dropped it, and Oz, and with an angry cry she reached for a metal pole. She struck Oz hard and he flew, landing across the warehouse with a sickening crack and a yip.

"Oz!" Frankie shouted. Sigmund ran to him, but Oz wasn't

getting up. And two more slayers now stood between Frankie and Vi.

"Frankie, use your magic!" Hailey cried.

"Feels like cheating," Frankie said. It felt like she should face them fair and square. Slayer to slayer, not slayer to abomination, like they said she was.

"Who cares?" Hailey and Spike yelled together, and Frankie cocked her head and shrugged.

"Since they already think it anyway." She pushed her magic out hard, like a bubble, and the slayers went flying. And just like that, Frankie was face-to-face with Vi.

"You stole that from me," Frankie said. "I trusted you, and you stole it from me."

"Because we needed it. You don't understand."

"I understand that you attacked other slayers. I understand that you burned them. Killed them. I understand that you attacked my aunt Buffy!" Frankie dove, leveling punches at Vi's face and arms, and Vi dodged backward and defended, holding the Scythe in both hands like a shield.

"We didn't mean for that to happen! We had no choice!" She finally stopped and struck Frankie in the chest; Frankie stumbled back.

"You had a choice. There's always a choice."

"Vi," Aspen called. "Stop arguing. You don't need to justify yourself to her. Use the Scythe. Finish it!"

Vi adjusted her grip on the weapon.

"Vi, don't!" Hailey cried as Vi raised the Scythe and swung.

Frankie felt the air quiver as the blade passed inches from her face. It fell again, and again, and she backpedaled, shocked by the speed. The Scythe seemed to bring out the best in Vi and made her deadlier; it added grace to her already-graceful movements.

And Frankie was surprised by how much it stung to see the Scythe aimed in her direction. It felt like being scratched by her own cat.

Frankie spun and dashed out of the way as Vi advanced. The rest of the battle had gone on pause to watch.

"I don't want to do this," Vi said as Frankie wheeled to the right. She was flubbing up the fight as usual, stumbling and careening her way toward survival and halfway counting on dumb luck. A few of the slayers laughed. A few seemed embarrassed for her. But they didn't know: This was how she always fought.

"I'm sorry," Vi said as Frankie stood panting and backed against the west wall of the warehouse. Frankie looked beaten. She looked afraid. But of course, she often looked like that.

Vi raised the Scythe to swing.

Just like Frankie was waiting for. She threaded her magic between Vi's fingers and forced them loose. Vi spun around, unbalanced by the sudden lack of weight as the Scythe left her hands, and she, like the other members of the Darkness, stared in awe as Frankie held it suspended in midair. When Frankie reached up and plucked it from her magic, the feeling of wrapping her hand around the handle was like cupping a warm mug of cocoa after coming in from the cold.

"I told you," Frankie said as she drew it down and gripped it tightly, "the Scythe is mine."

She spun it in her hands and sliced through the air before Vi's face. Having it again, Frankie felt whole; it was another of her limbs, another arm, an extra leg. She spun and struck and whirled like a figure skater, pulling the Scythe in tight and flinging it back out to cut. Vi backed off, and so did the other slayers. Even their leader.

"Vi!" Aspen ordered. "Get it back!"

Vi took a deep breath and grabbed for it. But she missed.

Frankie sank the blade deep, deep into Vi's belly.

"VI!"

Hailey dropped her ax and ran to catch her sister as she crumpled to the ground. She pressed her hand frantically to the wound as blood spread across Vi's middle and a thin dribble escaped the corner of her mouth. "Hailey," Vi whispered, and her teeth shone red.

"No," Hailey cried. "Frankie, no!"

Frankie stared at Vi. Another slayer, bleeding. Dying on the floor. She looked at Aspen, and the look in her eyes made Aspen back up a step.

"Damn you," Frankie growled. "Don't you see? Don't you see what this does?" She held up the Scythe and shook it. It was tainted in her hands. Soiled. Blood dripped down the blade that was never meant to be there. "You turned slayer against slayer, and now look!"

Aspen glanced at Vi. But in the end, her gaze caught on the Scythe. She still wanted it.

"You can't use this against me." Frankie opened her hand. She pushed her magic to float the Scythe into the air. "And I can't use it against you. This is not what it was made for." She began the chant: slow, reluctant sounds on her tongue as she raised her arm and her magic lifted the Scythe higher and higher, out of both of their reach.

"What are you doing?" Aspen cried as the Scythe spun slowly overhead.

Frankie breathed deep, in and out. Even after all this, she didn't want to do it. Even after this, she, too, still wanted the Scythe. Still felt ownership of it. Responsibility for it. But it was the responsibility that won out.

"Absentia," she whispered.

She reached into the pouch at her belt and threw the spell powder into the air. It surrounded the Scythe like a cloud, beautiful and sparkling, gaining in brightness until everyone watching had to shield their eyes and even Frankie had to turn away. No one saw the moment when the slayer's Scythe winked out of existence. But every slayer felt that it was gone.

"What . . . what have you done?" Aspen asked.

"What you made me do," Frankie replied.

"Aspen, come on." The tall slayer, Kate, pulled at her elbow. "It's gone." Her eyes fell to Vi, dead on the floor. "Let's go."

"It's not over," Aspen said as she allowed herself to be dragged away.

"Come on!" Kate tugged harder, and the Darkness fled through the back door of the warehouse and into the night.

"You're right," Frankie said as Hailey cried loudly over the body of her sister. "It's not over."

CHAPTER TWENTY-NINE

FLASHBACK: THE NIGHT BEFORE ON THE RE-CLOSED HELLMOUTH

"I'm sorry," Vi said, and turned away.

Frankie tensed. It was all up to Vi now. She had the Scythe. If she tried to run with it, tried to fight her way out, chances were good that she would succeed. Frankie held her mom's hand, the witches ready to do what they could, if they had to try to stop her.

"I'm just . . . so sorry!" Vi threw the Scythe to the ground and buried her face in her hands. Hailey struggled out from underneath a dead demon and went to wrap an arm around her sister's shoulders.

"Hey," she said softly. "It's okay. We're all okay, and the Hellmouth is closed, and Frankie's mom's bad twin didn't make it all the way out." She glanced down at the severed arm and crushed head of the Dark Willow doppelgänger. "Which I am personally very happy about. Frankie's going to have a lot of demon composting to do, but . . . Vi, it's okay."

"Tell that to Sadie," Vi whispered. "Tell that to Becca and Rachel. To Zoe and all the others we blasted apart and blew into rubble. I did that. I helped them do that. I wish I could take it all back."

She hugged Hailey tight, and Hailey discreetly gestured for everyone else to climb out from under their dead demons. Spike disentangled himself from the pile of fallen shelving. Oz got to his feet, clothes torn and face bloody, mostly around the mouth. Grim and Sarafina were so slicked with gore it looked like they'd rolled in it. Jake helped Sigmund from under a Polgara and then quickly jogged past Hailey and Vi to grab the Scythe. He tossed it lightly to Frankie.

"You can't take it all back," Frankie said, and Vi looked up. "But you can help us beat them."

"There's no beating Aspen," Vi said. "She gets what she wants. And ultimately, I don't think that what she wants is to give up being a slayer. I think she wants to be the only slayer."

"Well, duh," Sigmund said uncharacteristically.

"Sig," Hailey hissed, but she couldn't help smiling.

"No, he's right." Vi wiped at her eyes. "I felt it the moment she put that amulet around her neck. I just told myself I didn't. I was just so tired. . . . I wanted to give my power back so much. That's what we all wanted."

"So you were knowingly going to feed your slayer strength to the most rogue, unhinged, psychopathic slayer in the world?" Spike asked, and Hailey gave him a look. "What? Somebody had to say it."

Vi looked at the Scythe sadly. "Not my best moment. None of this was my best moment."

"But what's done is done," said Frankie. "And now the Darkness is the Darkness, and we have to figure out a way to stop them."

"So, how do we stop them?" Grimloch asked, and Frankie looked up.

"You have the Scythe." Vi wiped her face. "And one more slayer. So that's a start."

"It's not enough." Frankie flipped the Scythe in her hands.

"We need more time," said Spike. "And more weapons."

"More advantages," said Willow. "It would be nice if the Darkness didn't know that Vi had changed sides."

"Like she could play double agent?" Hailey asked. "Isn't that dangerous?"

"And I couldn't do it." Vi shook her head. "Aspen would suspect it. I'm not that good an actress, and she's already seen me wavering."

"Too bad I wasn't the rogue evil slayer," said Hailey. "I'm a way better actress than you."

Frankie turned. "That's not a bad idea."

"I wasn't serious," Hailey said.

"But you think you could do it?"

"How?" asked Sigmund. "Why would the Darkness ever believe she had changed sides?"

"Because you're going to watch me kill your sister," Frankie said. She looked at each of them. She looked at Vi.

"Huh?" Jake asked finally.

"Vi is going to take the Scythe tonight. And we're going to chase her. Make a real show of it. By morning, she'll have ditched us and hid out somewhere to wait for the cover of dark. Then we're all going to close in on the warehouse. Vi will bring the Scythe. And I am going to kill her with it." Frankie turned to Sarafina, and Sarafina leaned back in understanding.

"Isn't that risky?" Hailey asked as Spike and Oz nodded in appreciation of the plan.

"There's risk in any battle," said Willow.

"And you won't have me," said Sarafina, "if I am to be outside, casting the mirroring spell."

"I say again," said Jake. "Huh?"

Hailey and Sigmund sighed, and raised their eyebrows at Jake.

"Oh," he said a moment later, and pointed between Sarafina and Vi. "I get it."

"Good," said Frankie. "Then listen up. This is exactly what we're going to do. . . ."

CHAPTER THIRTY
AND NOW WE'RE ALL CAUGHT UP

Hailey cradled Vi's body on the cold floor of the warehouse, holding it close and weeping. Tears ran down her cheeks as Frankie, Spike, and Willow looked on. Eventually Sigmund joined them, supporting most of a very injured Oz on his shoulders.

"Is she going to be okay?" Oz asked, and Willow hurried to his other side to help hold him up. The words came out a little garbled by his fangs. "I should stay in the wolf form," he explained. "It will help me heal faster."

"Then you should go full wolf," Willow said.

Oz nodded and let all his fur out. Sigmund and Willow promptly let go as the beast fell to all fours and then lay down upon the floor, still Oz, but panting.

"I think that's just about enough," Vi said as she walked into the warehouse beside Sarafina.

"We saw the other slayers flee," Sarafina said. "They are long gone by now."

"Oh good." Hailey righted herself and wiped at both eyes. "I thought I was going to hyperventilate."

"You sold that pretty well," said Spike. "Fooled the Darkness right and proper."

"Yeah," said Vi. "I've never felt so loved. Or so . . . dead." She peered down at her own corpse. "This is weird."

Sarafina held her by the arm. "Do not get too close. If you touch your mirror, you will reabsorb it."

"Is that bad?" Hailey looked from Sarafina to Sigmund. "Is that dangerous? To reabsorb your mirror-spell twin if it's dead?"

Sigmund and his mother shrugged.

"We don't often kill ourselves when sparring," Sarafina replied. "So I don't know."

"Either way," said Frankie, toeing the dead version of Vi, "we need the body. Something to bury in case the Darkness start poking around and want to dig it up."

"Is that . . . okay?" asked Vi. "If I don't reabsorb her, or me, or whatever . . . am I still me? Am I whole?"

Sigmund and his mother looked at each other.

"Of course," Sigmund said, but neither seemed entirely sure.

"Great," Vi said uncertainly.

Hailey got up from underneath her dead sister and slapped her living one across the arm. "Oh, come on. You're fine. You're alive. And you're not evil anymore, so yay." She looked down at dead Vi. Despite her words and her upbeat tone, her lips pursed. It had to be troubling to see that body and all that blood. Like her worst fears were getting a practice run. "Maybe we can just say that this half was your evil half, and now it's dead. Like an exorcism."

"If only exorcisms were that easy," Willow said knowingly.

Frankie took a deep breath. She walked to the back of the warehouse and eventually her friends followed, looking out across the loading lots where the Darkness had fled. But they weren't gone. And they weren't finished. There would be another attack, another plan, another battle coming. And Frankie had no idea which side would win.

Just another day in Sunnydale, eh? She could hear Jake say, and she smiled.

"You really pulled it off," said Vi.

"Yeah," said Hailey. "Like, I totally believed you when you said you regretted killing Vi." She punched Frankie in the shoulder. "Maybe you should be the double agent."

Frankie smiled. She looked up into the empty air of the warehouse, where perhaps, in a form beyond her perception, the Scythe still floated in tiny particles.

"So the Scythe is gone," said Sigmund. "Destroyed."

"But that doesn't mean Aspen will give up." Vi stared after the Darkness. "She's going to try to find another way to take the other slayers' powers. And if she finds out that this was a ruse, and I'm still alive . . ."

"That's why you have to go," said Frankie, and Hailey frowned regretfully as she realized it, too. "Just until this is over."

"I will go with her," said Sarafina. "Help her to hide. Perhaps help her to hunt and have some adventures of our own."

Sigmund looked surprised.

"I'll stop back home and take a leave of absence," Sarafina said. "But to be the companion of a slayer is a great honor." She touched Sigmund's chin. "My son taught me that."

"You're going?" Willow asked sadly. "But we were just starting. . . ."

"And when I return, we will finish," Sarafina said. She took Willow's face in her hands and kissed her, as the rest of them turned discreetly aside. The kiss went on for quite a while. Until Frankie and Sigmund finally clapped their hands and coughed.

Hailey pulled Vi into a tight hug. "Take care of yourself out there, okay? Don't die for real. Promise?"

"Promise." Vi let go and brushed Hailey's black hair away from her face. She looked at Frankie. "And you take care of her, all right?" Frankie nodded, and Vi looked again at her own dead body. "Managed to kill me and destroyed the Scythe," she mused. "Does this mean I have to stop calling you *junior*?"

"Yes," Frankie said quickly. "That is exactly what it means."

$$\text{☽ ☽ ◯ ☾ ☾}$$

After the battle, the Scoobies returned to the school to drag demon bodies away from the Hellmouth to be turned into compost. There was going to be so much compost. So much that it felt like a waste actually, and Frankie wondered if they had time to float a few dead demons over some Sunnydale folks' home gardens.

"This is a lot of dead demons," Willow said, tiredly wiping at her forehead. "At least vampires have the good manners to turn to dust already."

"Mom?" Frankie asked. "Are you okay?"

"Sure, sweetie," she replied, making sure not to look at the dark-veined pieces of herself that protruded from the closed crack in the Hellmouth. "Why do you ask?"

"You know that wasn't real, don't you? It was just a trick."

Willow turned to face the dead quarter of her dark self. It must have been strange, seeing parts of her own corpse, though there had been a lot of that going around lately. But instead of seeming disturbed, Willow's expression turned grim.

"It wasn't a trick," she said. "It was a reminder."

"Mom—"

"Frankie." She squeezed Frankie's arm. "I'm going to be okay."

"Are you sure?"

"Sure, I'm sure. Just . . ." Willow glanced again at her dead evil imposter. "Compost that one when I'm not looking." Then she smiled and floated a pile of dead hellhounds through the basement door.

Behind her, Frankie heard Spike grunt and turned to see him hoisting a scraggly-furred demon around his shoulders. It kind of looked like he was wearing a fancy demon stole, and she couldn't help but chuckle.

"What?" he asked.

"Nothing. You just look very fashionable."

He snorted a little and glanced into the hallway. "Speaking of fashionable . . ." He heaved the demon higher and walked out, passing Grimloch. "Nice of you to turn up again to help clean up bodies. Would have been nicer to have had your help at the warehouse. Lurker."

"Is it *lurker* or *loomer*?" Grimloch asked.

"It's both!" Spike shouted as he went on his way.

Frankie sighed and joined Grimloch in the hallway to watch Spike follow the parade of floating demon bodies through the school. She glanced into the corners, at the dark orbs of security cameras. "Sig and Spike are going to have some real work to do with the security footage."

"Yes," Grimloch agreed. "This was quite a battle. I was disappointed your Watcher allowed the Fyarl demon into the Hellmouth—I would have liked to eat its heart. Fyarls are great, brutal warriors."

"Well," she said, "if you have your eye on any choice demon pieces, let me know, and I can wait to compost them."

She must have had a slightly disgusted look on her face because he laughed and asked, "Are you beginning to wish I was the kind of demon who ate salad?"

"Are there demons who eat sal—?"

"No, I don't think there are," he interrupted.

"And this is why I slay them." Frankie looked at Grimloch from the corner of her eye. "I understand why you couldn't help against the Darkness. And it could've been worse. You could have taken their side."

He looked down.

"Will you go after her?" Frankie asked. "After them, now that they've scattered?" She steeled herself for his response, ready with a stoic smile, trying to think of a plucky quip with which to send him on his way.

"If I left," he said, "who would look after my tent?"

"Huh?"

"I can't always be relying on you and Hailey and Sigmund to do my housekeeping."

"Does that mean you're staying?" she asked. "Does that mean you're choosing?"

He looked away again, his profile troubled in the shadowed hall. "The fight isn't over. Aspen will return to Sunnydale. And I would be here when she does." His eyes flashed blue in the dark. "I know that's not the answer you were hoping for."

"Well, it was half of it," Frankie grumbled. "But if you stay, can I trust you?"

"You trusted me with your plans last night," he said, and walked away.

Frankie watched him go, her heart pulling against the confines of her chest. He was an ancient demon–hunter god whose kisses made her lose feeling in her knees and who was just as dangerous as he was protective. He was not popular with her mother, or her Watcher. He was in love with their mortal enemy.

"Frankie?" Hailey called from down in the basement. "Wanna help me with this Polgara?"

"Sure!" Frankie took one last look at Grimloch, whose jacket did seem to billow a bit when he walked. "Stupid hot demon," she muttered, and went back into the basement.

CHAPTER THIRTY-ONE

THE WORLD IS DEFINITELY DOOMED

Monday morning dawned bright and sunny, like most every day did in New Sunnydale, as if even the weather was willfully ignoring the darkness that pressed in at its corners. But that day, Frankie was glad of it. She let the sun warm her cheeks like a celebration, an assertion that the demons and the Hellmouth would never win, that it would remain forever banished to the nighttime and buried beneath the school.

"Aw, man!"

Frankie grinned as Jake literally squirmed on his back on a cement bench in the quad, while Hailey and Sigmund excitedly told him everything he had missed at the warehouse.

"I wish I could've been there."

"But you didn't need to be." Hailey looked at Frankie proudly. "Frankie handled it."

"Still," Jake said. "I could've stopped Oz from being pounded like a speedbag; he's still limping around on three legs and whining. He even tried to bite me when I was brushing him this morning."

Of course, thank you to my agent, Adriann Zurhellen, without whom I am nothing. No but seriously, Adriann is awesome and I highly recommend her for anything and everything. Agenting, bowling, developing a new breed of water-conserving tomato . . . except for agenting I don't know if she does those other things, but I bet she could.

Thank you to Crystal Patriarche and the folks at BookSparks, always amazing and fun to work with. Thank you to my coworkers in the PNW, the writers in our delightful and ever-expanding bookish community: Marissa Meyer, Lish McBride, Rori Shay, Martha Brockenbrough, Tara Goedjen, Arnée Flores, Nova McBee, and Margaret Owen. It's inspiring to be surrounded by your talent. Also it keeps me from slacking off.

Thanks to my mom and dad. Thanks to Susan Murray, who has now finally watched all of *Buffy*. Thanks to my pet children, who will never know I thanked them because they still don't know how to read dear god I have failed as a parent.

And as usual, thanks to Dylan Zoerb, for luck.

ACKNOWLEDGMENTS

Time for some joyful Buffy acknowledgments. Everything about this book has been a joy: Traipsing through New Sunnydale, following the Scoobies around, both new and OG. And getting to work with the incredible people who brought me to the project and breathe life into these beautiful books. Hey there, Jocelyn Davies, fantastic editor of story and character, ultimate Buffy champion and supplier of emergency chapter titles. Hello also to Elanna Heda, and big thanks for your help whenever I have annoying questions! Also thanks for the idea of Buffy's cross. Thank you to the cover design and art folks, Tyler Nevins and Marci Senders, who have given *One Girl* such a badass look. And the artist collective I LOVE DUST for creating the badass artwork. Thank you to Lyssa Hurvitz and Crystal McCoy, masters of publicity. Thank you to Jacqueline Hornberger, Mark Amundsen, Daniel Kaufman, and Guy Cunningham for, in addition to the usual copyediting necessities, keeping track of the lingo of the Buffyverse. And thank you to the entire team at Hyperion for bringing Buffy back with gusto.

"Really just want to know if you're ever going to let me into your D&D club."

Jake raised a brow at Frankie, and she smiled. "Well, that depends," she said to Sam. "How good are you at fighting demons?"

"Seriously?" Sam asked. "I mean, I'm the best. The best of the best." Jake grinned and jumped up to put an arm around Sam and lead him away.

"We'll work him in slow," he called over his shoulder as the bell rang for class.

"That's us." Hailey grabbed her bag. "Better not be late again. You'd think we'd get a pass, having just saved the world."

"Next time Spike should write us another note," Sigmund said. "You coming, Frankie?"

Frankie looked across the green of the quad, at the flowering vines and the growing crowd of her oblivious classmates, goofing off before class. For just a moment, she let herself imagine what it would be like if just once things could be easy. If one day she turned around and saw Buffy, walking across the quad. But even if she did, things wouldn't go back to the way they were. Sigmund and Hailey were happy enough today, but after the adrenaline of the victory wore off, they would remember the distance opening up between them. And another full moon would rise and find Jake restless in his cage again.

Frankie stared across the quad. But there was no Buffy walking toward her, and inside her chest, her slaydar gave off a soft ping.

"Maybe," Frankie whispered. "Someday."

A distinctly disturbed expression wrinkled Sigmund's face. "Just stop . . . brushing your uncle."

"He's not my uncle. He's my cousin," Jake said, like that made it any less odd.

Frankie smiled as her friends laughed and joked, as Jake made plans to reinstate the rest of the lacrosse season, as Sigmund nerded out over new volumes of demon lore he'd gotten into the library focusing on demon talismans. It was nice. It was comforting. It was their momentary reward for thwarting the Darkness's plans and once again saving the unknowing people of New Sunnydale. But it was only momentary.

"This is it." Frankie's voice was quiet, but Hailey, Sigmund, and Jake all stopped talking. "This is it for a while. To everyone watching"—she looked at Hailey—"we won't be friends. Things won't be easy between us. No more meetings. No more coffees. And Hailey's going to move out of our house."

"But just for a while, right?" asked Jake. "Just until we see if this Darkness a-hole is going to take the bait."

"Maybe she won't," Hailey said hopefully. "And we can go right back to Saturday patrols through the graveyard."

"Demon study sessions," added Sigmund.

"Maybe with the Scythe gone, they'll just give up and run scared." Hailey raised her eyebrows. "Maybe they'll just let Buffy and the others go."

"I like this new, overly optimistic you," said Jake.

Frankie smiled.

"Jake!"

Frankie looked up and saw Sam Han jogging toward them.

"Hi, Frankie. Hi, guys." He nodded to Hailey and Sigmund and stood there awkwardly. "Look, I . . ." He glanced shyly at Jake.